RE-WIRED

by
Karl Manke

Author of
Unintended Consequences
The Prodigal Father
Secrets, Lies, and Dreams
Age of Shame
The Scourge of Captain Seavey
Gone to Pot
The Adventures of Railcar Rogues
Harsens Island Revenge
Available at karlmanke.com

Dedicated to the following veterans without whose shared experience, I could not have written this book.

Tom Wetzel
Jim Toby
Bob Gould
Jon Harris
George (G.B.) Welte
Dave Freeman
Jim Pouillon
Don Smith
Jack Davis
Jim Mills
Bob Morehead

Publisher: Curwood Publishing
Cover Design: Kirsten Pappas
Editor, book design, and formatting: Jeffery Gulick
Copyright ©2019 Karl Manke/Curwood Publishing

ISBN-10: 1-7338029-0-8
ISBN-13: 978-1-7338029-0-1

The author and publisher have made every effort in the preparation of this book to ensure the accuracy of the information. However, the information in this book is sold without warranty, either express or implied. Neither the author nor Curwood Publishing will be liable for any damages caused or alleged to be caused directly, indirectly, incidentally, or consequentially by the information in this book.

The opinions expressed in this book are solely those of the author and are not necessarily those of Curwood Publishing.

Trademarks: Names of products mentioned in this book known to be or suspected of being trademarks or service marks are capitalized. The usage of a trademark or service mark in this book should not be regarded as affecting the validity of any trademark or service mark.

Curwood Publishing

All of Karl's books are available at KarlManke.com

Karl Manke was born in Frankfort, Michigan. He has spent most of his life in the small Mid-Michigan town of Owosso, home to author and conservationist James Oliver Curwood. He and his wife Carolyn have twin daughters and five grandchildren.

A graduate of Michigan State University, the author has been a self-employed entrepreneur his entire working career. After discovering his inclination for telling a good story, he now spends much of his time fine-tuning the writing craft.

Prologue

The sounds of modern warfare are the same: a mixture of male voices barking barely audible shouts and the hard eruptions from explosions ripping through the atmosphere. Men on both sides are hit indiscriminately with artillery designed to incapacitate the other side. It tosses them about like dogs shaking dolls. In spite of this unforgiving chaos, men cling fiercely to a natural desire to survive. As with all humans, there are three possible survival reactions: fight, flight, or freeze. Boot camp training is specifically designed to eliminate the latter two. After this initial shock of attack, many of these unseasoned young eighteen-year-old warriors are frantically scurrying about and struggling to remember their roles as soldiers. Their hardwired officers quickly take responsibility to coordinate a defense and an offense. Some of these men designated as infantrymen have a responsibility to inflict as much pain on their enemies along with the hope that it will be enough to incapacitate their capabilities. Others are noncombatants with the responsibility of gathering up the dead and wounded. Meanwhile, helicopters hover overhead, searching for landing sites in their role of evacuating the wounded. This is a dangerous undertaking, considering they are taking on enemy ground fire while waiting for a turn to land. Stretchers are manned by teams of four or five in an effort to get the wounded on board quickly without further incident. In desperation, blood and dirt are as inextricably mixed as coffee and cream.

One of these casualties is a young sergeant struck with multiple wounds caused by an enemy mortar. He's semi-conscious and not fully aware of his circumstances. He's aware of being jostled around by a group of shouting men jamming him and other wounded soldiers into a waiting helicopter with the realization that his fate rests wholly in the hands of this support team.

This scenario has played out hundreds and hundreds of times in similar ways in this war and promises to play out hundreds if not thousands of times more if this war is to continue along this path. It's driven by misinformed politicians with the distorted American media leading the way.

CHAPTER 1
HIGH SCHOOL GRADUATION

Michael David Murphy was born July 5, 1949. His paternal grandfather tagged him "Micky" as a toddler. The tag stuck. Presently, he's a nearly twenty-year-old private heading home. His latest assignment was as a chaplain's assistant in Vietnam. A little over a year ago, he had been a member of a small-town Michigan Christian high school graduating class of 1967. This is as good a place as any to begin his story.

Micky is an above average student with all kinds of outstanding qualities. He is the student body president and head of the debate team. When he debates, there is never a question concerning his preparation. His ability to employ the King's English when needed is unrivaled among his peers. It's heard by more than one to say, "If Micky can't dazzle you with brilliance, he'll baffle you with BS." His broad-shouldered athletic stature alone is enough to set him apart. He has competed in track, football, and baseball, where he's always drawn attention to his hitting and pitching style. In track, his long legs were enough to gain an All-State award in the high hurdles. As the team captain of each of these sports, he earned letters in all three. He pinned enough medals to his varsity jacket to add an extra ten pounds. The voices of not only his peers, but also those of the townspeople are gushing over his accomplishments. His involvement with the opposite sex is at a standstill; he's totally wrapped up in his own world of athletics and the debate team.

Today, all this effort has come to a halt. Micky, along with his class, find themselves sitting in a hot church listening to teacher after teacher pay tribute to all their hard work. His school superintendent, who is also his pastor, is giving endorsements to all the graduates. He's telling them the only true evolution is a spiritual evolution and how, as young high school graduates, they have evolved to become more and more Christ-like as they've passed through their cocoon-like childhood and are now emerging as Christian butterflies.

This compliment and the eloquence of this man of God strike Micky in a very personal way. As he listens, an unexpected cascade of thoughts overwhelms him, coming up on his blindside. It's not without the usual status-seeking attention he desires, but it is different. This one gives him the chills. It's striking him at his very essence. He knows in his heart of hearts that he can do what this man is doing and do it even better. He feels a strange kind of quickening he hasn't experienced before.

I believe I want to become a missionary, is his overpowering reflection. His escalating imagination begins to take a life of its own: *Maybe it's possible I can become another Paul of Tarsus, or at a minimum another Billy Graham.* Not certain he can pull off either of these, his imaginings tell him, *I think both these guys are outdated. I would be more modern, and I could become the Billy Graham of my generation.* This revelation is not something he wishes to share with his parents—or anyone, for that matter. It's the kind of revelation that conveys the impression that it's a private revelation.

Micky is the youngest of four older siblings. He's a late-in-life child. His mother, a stay-at-home housewife, was nearly forty-five when he was born, and his father, a pharmaceutical salesman, was fifty. His next oldest sibling is a sister who is nine years older than himself. She married young and is the mother of three herself. The other three are older brothers, with the oldest being seventeen years older than himself. All three are successful in various fields of business. With this family legacy of college graduates firmly connected to the secular sector of the culture, he's expected to follow suit. For him to suggest using his formative years to traipse off to some God-forsaken third-world country to save souls is not what his parents would expect. After all, they had not sent him to a Christian school to foster some hope that he would eventually become some kind of self-sacrificing hermit in some faraway land. They had merely hoped the Christian atmosphere would insulate their son against the devil's worldly wiles.

As alarming and grandiose as this missionary notion is, Micky is not able to release himself from its grip. His consuming fear is one of not accomplishing its demand. Totally ignorant as to how he will start, he nonetheless envisions it as an effort that will command all of him. At this point, he simply believes that if he wants something bad enough, it will somehow come to fruition.

As a high school senior, Micky has spent thirteen years inside this closed community studying how to affect himself to gain the admiration of his teachers and fellow students. He has excelled in every undertaking. Nonetheless, as a fresh high school graduate entering the world outside the world of high school, his skill set for some vague missionary undertaking is undeveloped, and despite his excellent grades in theology, his understanding of the scriptures is rudimentary at best. But let's return to what is prompting him for the moment. For Micky, it's the undulating tenors of his pastor's voice and how it has the power to hold an audience in its grip. He envisions himself possessing the same spellbinding power and doing the same with an audience of his own.

Like everything in life, it has a season. Today, for Micky, high school is over—it's finished. Now, with the end of that journey, a new passage begins.

Micky's best friend since kindergarten has been Burt Wilson. Micky has always been able to depend on Burt to be a supportive team player on the track and baseball team. Burt is twenty pounds lighter and several inches shorter than Micky. In spite of a seeming difference in their physical development, Burt's mental development has Micky's stamp on it. Burt is more of a follower and more inclined to fall into intellectual lethargy, allowing Micky's stronger personality to take the lead—that is, until lately. Burt has been letting his hair grow longer in a Beatles style and has begun to wear bell-bottom jeans. This change has not escaped Micky's attention.

"What are you trying to prove, Burt? You're starting to look like one of those hippies," criticizes Micky.

Looking a bit sheepish, Burt is hardly equipped to defend himself against Micky's censure. He's struggling to put a defensive spin on Micky's disapproval.

"Nah, I just ain't had the money to get a haircut, and my sister gave me these bell-bottom pants for my birthday," Burt says.

The truth is, the allure of the morally unfettered hippie lifestyle is making a strong impression on Burt. He has always reacted much more viscerally to life than his pragmatic, borderline anal friend. Besides, there is a special allure to the kind of promise held by this new and unique hippie life. It's a promise of freedom. All one has to do is throw off the fetters of an oppressive government, religion, or anything that appears to restrain one's freedom of expression—only then can one can find true happiness. It's the visceral stuff that catches Burt's attention. Burt isn't alone, as this new school of permissiveness is well on its way to capturing many of America's youthful enthusiasms. Much like their earlier immigrant ancestors who had relied on language, religion, and traditions from their old-world villages to gather into new world communities, this generation of young people are developing a language and traditions of their own apart from the so-called "staid and true" middle-class identities of their parents. The Micky types are quickly eroding into this new, radical progressive movement and all its visions.

Micky certainly doesn't view this cultural interloper as a plus; rather, he sees it as a risk. "The behavior of these degenerates is going to put them right in hell where they belong! They got the moral integrity of alley cats!" is Micky's final word when confronted with his take on this upcoming, unrestrained youth movement. Micky is of the opinion that there are times when principled persons must stand alone on their values, even if it means being marginalized by their peer group. Micky definitely believes he is doing God's bidding by making a point to rebuke anyone who challenges his views—and lately, that includes Burt.

Out of curiosity, Burt has been attending some underground meetings held in the home of a college professor claiming to be a member of a group known as "Students for a Democratic Society," or SDS.

Burt makes another appeal. "He argued against the war, claimin' that it ain't nothin' but an 'imperial war.'" Burt isn't sure he knows what an "imperial war" means, but it sounded like something he would stand against if he understood more about it.

"Micky, this guy's really cool. You gotta come an' listen to what he's sayin' about the war," begs Burt.

Burt has known his friend long enough to know this is not going to be an easy sale. Micky gives the impression he's listening, but he's already formulating a defense.

"I don't think we oughtta be listenin' to a bunch of damnable Godless commies like this guy," says Micky. "Whatever they got to say is gonna be just the opposite of what you and I been taught. You and I both know God has placed his hand on our god-fearing leaders and is blessing our country's efforts to defeat these communist heathens."

"You don't still believe all that crap, do ya?" says Burt, shaking his head with a doubtful squint—more at Micky's words than at Micky.

"Well, it's not crap, Burt—what's happing to you lately?" asks a mystified Micky. "You sound like you're buying into all this anti-war stuff!"

"I dunno about that. I been curious to find out what all them hippies been talkin' about. Some of it makes a lot of sense to me," answers Burt.

Micky is mystified; there isn't a hint of shame in Burt's voice. He's making these near treasonous statements as stoically as if he's held this mindset his entire life.

"Burt, sometimes you baffle me. It's as if I've never known you at all," declares Micky.

Burt considers Micky's concern for a moment. Regardless of his indifferent demeanor, he realizes he's stepped over a line into independent thinking. Burt isn't used to the isolation that accompanies his new experiment. The more aware he becomes of his detachment from his previous conventional understandings, the lonelier he begins to feel. Not able to persevere, he finds himself retreating into a more comfortable, obsequious, sycophantic role.

"Well, it ain't as if I was joinin' up. I just think they sound kinda cool," says Burt, hoping to redeem himself. Pausing for a moment, Burt adds, "I still feel I'm close to God, Micky. It ain't like I'm abandonin' my faith, you know."

Micky considers Burt's answer for a moment, then adds, "Remember this, Burt: the devil don't care how close you feel to God, just as long as you're not."

When Burt senses he can't win and he's on the ropes with Micky, he clams up. He's not willing to attempt to outmaneuver his old cohort. Micky takes Burt's silence as a quiet surrender; he's taking unspoken satisfaction that Burt's attitude is returning to a more restrained mode.

CHAPTER 2
MEADOW

The summer, like all Michigan summers, proves to be unpredictably hot on one day and just as unpredictably cool on the next. The relationship between Burt and Micky has also taken on a hot and cold stance. Despite Micky's disapproving eye toward Burt's new hairdo, his choice of paisley shirts and bellbottom jeans, and his insistence on using terms like "far out" for nearly everything that's said, they have managed to keep a link of sorts. They have both enrolled in the same junior college and plan to room together in the fall. What they continue to have in common is a deep sense of wanting to be involved with movements that are worthwhile. Micky's interests, on one hand, are firmly entrenched in the sober actions of conservatives—whether in religion or politics. On the other hand, Burt's focus is often on slogans that tend to provoke an immediate, visceral reaction.

Burt is an only child, and in truth, his conception was a mistake. The composition of Burt's life has been left primarily to the care of his Christian teachers. His parents are well off and lead professional lives. Satisfied they're fulfilling their parental duties, they've assured themselves they've left Burt in good hands. Consequently, they're hardly aware of the new influences that are invading their son's life. Like many parents, they assume their offspring will be no more or no less than an extension of themselves who shares the same religious and political worldview.

Struggling through a world that's seemingly out of control, Burt is a compilation of disconnected thoughts and opinions. Unaware that many of his opinions can't undergo the hard scrutiny of truth doesn't prevent him from forming them. The common thread is that he attempts to make sense of things that baffle him—at least for the moment. Burt will often see the good in an opinion by how it makes him feel and fail to see how it can be the worst enemy of the better opinion that often supplies unpopular facts. This phenomenon is not limited to Burt; it encompasses many young people in this generation.

As the summer school break wanes, it becomes apparent that neither of these young men are ready to surrender their opinions. They each have their talking points, spend hours defending them, and are convinced that they have the only viable hope for the world to prevail. Individually, each has just enough knowledge to be dangerous. As is true of many young people throughout all ages, they are passionate to begin their adult life with meaning and are mutually convinced "If you don't stand for something, you'll fall for any old thing." Neither remembers where they heard this statement, but they are willing to stand on its premise.

Lately, Micky has been accused of having nothing new to offer in his debates but the same old conservative slogans centering around God, flag, and country. To counter this charge, he's begun to study the history of the West's involvement in Asian affairs. Today, he believes he's ready to meet Burt's criticisms.

"You ever heard of the Domino Theory, Burt?" Micky asks. He doesn't wait for Burt to answer because he already assumes that if he hadn't been aware of it until today, Burt certainly wouldn't know anything about it. Seeing he has Burt's attention, Micky begins with a clear air of authority, "It says that once the communists take one country, the others will begin to fall into their hands like dominos if we don't do something to stop it."

Burt's face takes on a serious demeanor. "No, I don't know nothin' about no dominos. But I do know if I was these countries, I'd figure I was smart enough to know what kind of government I wanted. I'd be mad if I was them an' some people like you or me was tryin' to tell me what we oughtta do," says Burt. "Besides, those SDS guys I met are sayin' that those guys callin' themselves 'Viet Cong' ain't really commies but are just joinin' up with them long enough to kick us out, and then they're gonna join up with the North Vietnamese an' kick the commies out next."

Micky's face tells the whole tale. Burt's studied response was not expected. Micky's not sure he's going to get Burt back to a place where he can be his primary influence. He's growing more and more uncomfortable with Burt's avant-garde view.

Realizing, he has once again put himself out on that lonely limb apart from Micky, Burt's old fear of having to go it alone returns to haunt him. He quickly tries to heal the wound.

"But I'd be willin' to learn some more about them 'dominos' you keep talkin' about, Micky," says Burt. His tone of apology is clear.

For the first time in their relationship, Micky is experiencing the fallout of Burt's breach with their shared religious and political viewpoints. Micky finds it disconcerting. As much as he hates to admit it, in their young adult search for life's meaning, he's relied on Burt's friendship in much the same way Burt has relied on him. It's been described as a Lone Ranger/Tonto relationship. Micky recalls how after seeing a ritual of blood mixing in a movie, they removed the safety pin required to hold Burt's pants up against a worn-out elastic waistband to scratch their skin enough to mix each other's blood, making them blood brothers. In their adolescent minds, this seemed legitimate enough to be regarded as a genuine bonding ceremony. But in Micky's words, this bond is being threatened by Burt's willingness to have his "ears tickled" by "Godless liberals" spewing their "heathenish philosophy."

As is usual with this unsettling connection between these two, they go their separate ways for a few days to let things settle down. Nonetheless, in going forward, there is an uncomfortable awareness that things between them are charting in different directions.

Allowing a couple of weeks of separation, Burt is the first to make a move. Finding Micky in the back yard of his parents' home, he says, "Hey, Mick. Long time, no see."

Engrossed in a book, Micky responds with the same enthusiasm he's had since kindergarten when they first agreed to be best friends.

"Hey, Burt! What ya been up to?"

In response to Micky's greeting, Burt pauses for a moment, at the same time looking over Micky's backyard. "Well, I sure as heck ain't wastin' my time sittin' around readin'."

Flipping the book over to expose its cover, Micky responds, "Barry Goldwater doesn't think his book is boring." In big, bold letters designed to catch the attention of a reader is the title, *THE CONSCIENCE OF A CONSERVATIVE*.

If Micky had expected introducing such an enticing title to Burt would produce curiosity, he's dead wrong. Burt couldn't care less. It's not that Burt doesn't keep up with things; it's more to do with him not being a reader. He gathers most, if not all, of his information from listening to others, whereas Micky delves deep into the core of some authors' minds by reading their books. Burt will readily glean all the thoughts others have assembled by letting them do all the reading, listen to what they have to say, and verbally spew out their findings. Since we all have cracked instruments for brains, whatever gets run through them isn't likely to come out completely right. Consequently, a lot of notions get tossed about by well-meaning people, but none have the whole picture. However, this notion doesn't prevent Micky and Burt from their attempts to bring the other around to their individual persuasions. Today is going to be one of those days.

Burt has stopped by Micky's in the hopes of getting him to accompany him on a sit-in to protest American involvement in the Vietnam War. He has already given Micky his canned speech as to why he needs to listen to the counterculture's viewpoints on why we as Americans have no business involving ourselves in Asian affairs. Micky prides himself in his debating skills—after all, hadn't he been the captain of the debate team? He's nearly as given over to his debating skills as he is to the merit of his viewpoint. With thirteen years of school accomplishments, he's gained some confidence in his abilities. He's convinced he has specified all the defense he needs in insisting on the United States' moral implementation of a just war. To add to this, he believes he has most American Christians behind him.

"Burt, you're wasting your time with these people. They're shallow and spineless," Micky says. It's impossible to miss the concern in his eyes.

On his way over, Burt had rehearsed everything he was going to present to Micky, though he knew that Micky would not budge. Even so, he once again knowingly presents his neck to Micky's foot.

"Oh, come on, Micky. Just listen to what they have to say," begs Burt.

"I already know what they're gonna say. They'll start out by saying the United States is some kind of imperialistic country with its primary intention being to crush its weaker neighbors. Next, they'll harp on by saying the only reason we're at war is to fatten the purses of a military industrial complex. And for certain, they won't mention how we are fighting for our freedom and the freedom of the Vietnamese people against a bunch of godless communists."

Burt continues standing in front of a seated Micky. He's staring directly at him with unblinking eyes, wondering how he is going to respond. He's always had this problem. Since they were little boys, Micky has been able to persuade Burt that his ideas are inferior.

"What you're sayin' might be true, Micky, but politicians have always tried to line their own pockets at the expense of somebody else. I don't see this as anything different. If they got one of these military plants in their district, they're gonna do everything they can to keep these jobs—even if it means sendin' us guys to fight their damn war just to keep everybody workin'. Besides, I don't see how these people are threatenin' our freedom from thousands of miles across the ocean," replies Burt.

With the wry smirk of one who sees himself as an all-American boy and has spent his life building his confidence in his ability to control his circumstances, Micky faces Burt head on. "Do you actually believe God is on the side of these pagans, Burt? Their godless propaganda has you under their spell. You need to ask God for His forgiveness and to give you the mind to see things more clearly." Micky pronounces this with an unmistakable air of church authority.

Micky has proven to be the stronger mind between them, once again leaving Burt without a convincing response. Convinced he can't persuade his friend to join him at the sit-in, Burt formulates a clumsy exit, saying, "You don't know what you're missin', Micky. There's gonna be a bunch of far-out chicks there, too. I wish you'd change your mind."

Burt's disappointment is apparent. Nonetheless, there is nothing in the wind that is destined to daunt Burt from experiencing this anti-war sit-in. He has carefully chosen his clothing to wear as he would for any other event. There is a protocol: tie-dye T-shirts, anything leather, and bell-bottom jeans. He has sophomorically chosen a paisley shirt and bell-bottoms. He has also met a girl who shares the same mindset toward the war as himself. Her name is Meadow Larkens. Her parents are part of the left over Bohemian movement that dominated the counterculture a generation before. She's a natural blond with ironed swaths of long hair flowing to the center of her back. She's small-breasted with lengthy bird like legs and a round-shouldered slouch. When she walks, she almost seems to lope. Burt met her at a previous sit-in and was instantly struck by her entire demeanor. She is never lost for words when it comes to giving an opinion on the state of the country. She is against the war and against killing seals and whales. She's ready to support anything an obscure journalist named Gloria Steinem advocates and the feminist movement stands for, including abortions on demand, unrestricted sex between consenting adults, pot, the Age of Aquarius, and everything to do with astronomy. Burt has found her to be the female version of a guru ready to free him from the restrictive, repressive shackles of the world of his parents, ready to lead him into the waiting arms of the new nirvana. He senses it's probably a sin he's falling into, but it's a festive sin. It can't be all that bad when it sounds and feels so good.

Burt has made his way to the designated location for the sit-in. It's located in the downtown business district, in front of the draft office. There are already tents set up in the grassy boulevard that separates the east and west lanes of traffic. Various musicians are playing guitars, all featuring countless Joan Baez protest songs with numerous protesters singing along. Some of the protestors are carrying handmade signs with slogans like "HELL NO! WE WON'T GO," or "LBJ, HOW MANY KIDS DID YOU KILL TODAY?" At least for the present, these are distractions for Burt. His primary focus is on locating Meadow. With a sigh of relief, he soon spots her. She's singing along with one of the musicians. A smile quickly forms on his anxious face. Catching sight of her long blond hair and blithe demeanor, his anticipation swells at the prospect of being with her again. Coming up behind her, he playfully places his hands over her eyes with the lighthearted words, "Guess who?"

"Somebody with reefer, I hope," is Meadow's response. Turning around, she realizes it's just Burt. Her look of disappointment is hardly missed. She has taken on Burt more as an interesting project than for any committed reason. His straight-laced naiveté has been a source of amusement for Meadow. It's true that his muscular body has captured her attention and attracted an effort at revolutionizing the rest of him. But then, Burt is at a point where he is so enamored with the attention he's receiving from Meadow that he wouldn't care if she ordered him to graze on the lawn—he'd gladly do it. Rather than disappoint Meadow, he scrambles to remember a boy he knows named Chuckie who earlier had offered to sell him some weed. Before he realizes what he's saying, he blurts out, "No, I don't have any right now, but I can have some soon." He had seen Chuckie on a street further away from the sit-in, hoping the police would be too busy monitoring the demonstration to pay attention to him.

Before Meadow can answer, Burt's on his way. Smiling inwardly, she remains wholly secure in the realization that she has a good grip on his attentions.

Within minutes, Burt has made his way to Chuckie, who he finds posing innocently, listening to the radio in his 1955 Chevy convertible. With Burt making his wishes known, Chuckie carefully looks around. Satisfied they're out of sight of the prying eyes of the authorities, he pops the trunk open to display plastic baggies of weed neatly placed in rows. Examining the price of each container, Burt chooses a "nickel" bag. Handing a five-dollar bill to Chuckie, he quickly stuffs the weed into his pocket. Turning to leave, he's confronted once more by Chuckie. "You need some papers, man?"

The question gives him pause. This is all new stuff to him. Since he's never bought dope before, much less smoked it, and not wanting to appear out of the loop, Burt says, "Na man, I got papers."

Certain that this lie may come back to bite him when it comes to Meadow's final assessment, he nonetheless beats it back to where he had left Meadow minutes before.

The smile on Burt's face meeting the smile on Meadow's face tells the whole story.

"You scored some weed, didn't you, you rascal?" she exclaims.

Excited he has met with Meadow's approval, Burt pulls the long-awaited bag of pot from his pocket. Within a second, someone appears with a paper plate and some rolling papers. Meadow snatches the bag of weed from Burt's hand as well as the plate and papers, and with one deft movement of her own, she demonstrates the art of rolling a proper joint. Happy he has gotten this far without anyone detecting his inexperience, Burt quietly looks on without comment. Despite this, his mind is racing at near warp speed. This new experience has all the hall marks of both danger and excitement. It doesn't take Meadow more than a few minutes to roll the entire bag, leaving a neat row of well-rolled joints on the plate. One by one, the pure white joints are picked off the plate, lit, and passed to a waiting hand. It's only then that a single word begins to follow the inhalation of the pungent vapors: "Wow!" Meadow has taken her turn and is passing the burning roll-up to Burt. He takes it without saying a word. After watching the rest, and not sure what to expect but, determined not to look like a novice, he takes the handoff, places it to his lips, and draws in enough of its vapors to bring his entire respiratory system into a sudden revolt. The smoke intended for his lungs is abruptly forced back through his sinuses, blowing out his nose with enough force to shoot out snot, which lands several feet away. For the next several minutes, Burt's lungs gasp and hack uncontrollably, letting him know how much they hate what he's just put them through. So far, the drug isn't doing anything for him. It's apparent to Burt that he has coughed out whatever effect was supposed to happen. By the time he's recovered, the rest of the party have entered their own la-la land. They take care to avoid any negative commotion that could ruin a good high. The self-centered attitude created by the drug has given them permission to ignore Burt's turmoil; they couldn't care less what he is going through. Even Meadow has abandoned him for another friend she feels can share her high. Watching her openly flirt with another boy is leaving him feeling as lonely as a dying calf in a hailstorm. This new and different American woman makes him feel small and insignificant. The elation he had experienced in making her happy with his ability to score the bag of pot has been replaced with the sick feeling that comes with rejection. Her whole demeanor—physical, mental, and, in some strange way, spiritual—is causing him to become a nursery of tortured emotions that are nearly impossible to identify but are nonetheless powerful enough to leave him a weak, nauseous, heartbroken victim.

Ditched by the rest, Burt continues staring off somewhere. He's frozen. It's obvious that he's uncertain of his bearings and does not know what to do next. For the next few minutes, he wanders around blindly. His face is tortured. His whole purpose in being there was to share the happenings with Meadow. That purpose has escaped him without one of equal significance to replace it. Feeling confused, unable to control his emotions and lost in his despair, he begins his withdrawal. Not sure where he is going, he only senses a need to run away. He passes Chuckie, who is still sitting in his car and waiting for another eager patron. Burt feels strangely out of place. What had been a welcome sight a half hour ago only serves to remind him how far out of his element he has strayed. Each step carries with it a feeling of emptiness and loneliness. Even Chuckie, lost in the effects of his own drugs, fails to look up and see this poor, dejected child walking past his car. There is only one destination that can offer Burt the comfort he seeks.

Like a homing pigeon, Burt soon finds himself in Micky's backyard. He's not there because he wants to discuss his painful situation. There is no other place to go, and though he may be at odds with Micky, it's familiar and predictable. Right now, predictable familiarity is the balm that's good enough.

The evening twilight is leaning toward dark. Micky is still reading. He's determined to get the last of the good light. Looking up from his book, he's surprised to see Burt back so soon. It's just dark enough that he doesn't notice his friend's forlorn countenance.

"You done protestin' already?" says Micky. The smugness of his tone reflects his mindset.

Burt remains silent under the guise of looking for a place to sit, but in reality, it's to process Micky's self-righteous taunt. He finally forms an answer. "Naw. There weren't much to it. Seems everybody was there just to get high."

"What'd I tell ya! Those people only want to get high. They don't care about all the stuff they pretend to care about. Most of them don't have a clue what they're protesting, anyway," says a self-satisfied Micky.

Burt is satisfied to sit and let Micky rant on with his sanctimonious pomposity against everybody and everything he regards as godless. Burt barely hears anything Micky is saying. His mind is off in another place. Whether he asks for these thoughts or not, they are bombarding him. He can't get his mind off Meadow. She could be the devil, and it wouldn't change his longing for her smile, voice, and free spirit. There is nothing Micky can say about her that will change Burt's aching for her.

CHAPTER 3
College

Summers begin unasked, and they end the same way. The long-awaited day when Micky and Burt will begin their college life has arrived. It's an understatement to say they're nervous. Burt has spent most of his summer scurrying around meeting people his age who don't have the same sheltered background he has. Most of these new friends are active in the anti-war movement. Micky, on the other hand, has spent his time studying the rightful war issues defending United States' involvement in this Asian predicament. How each of these eighteen-year-old young men handle their anxiousness is unique. Burt, being on the smaller side, is more apt to be unsure of himself, he looks for approval and is willing to let go of a value in favor of another if it will give him a sense of belonging.

Micky is of a different bent. What had given him high school status was his taller stature, a broad smile when it was needed, and his tendency to speak only if he had something worthwhile to say. His high school peers regarded these as superior qualities, which has left its mark on Micky by creating a unique confidence within him. High-schoolers of a lesser status generally don't hold this degree of confidence.

To Micky's amazement, his college experience is proving to be frustrating. Since his high school was a small parochial community, it was easier to be good at something there. Where he had been the only senior as tall as he is, there are now twenty, thirty, or more students who are as tall or taller. Where he had been an exceptional debater, he now faces an onslaught of people with skills matching his or bettering him. Even in his debate class, people tend marginalize anything he has to say—especially regarding politics or religion.

These secular college peers couldn't care less about Micky's Christian high school accomplishments. They have a new standard they use to measure appeal, and Micky is not a good fit. Micky is accustomed to valuing his religious beliefs, his political beliefs, and his lack of moral turpitude. This is the first time in his life he's experienced nearly a wholesale shunning of his values. Hardly anyone is paying any mind to what he thinks or has to say about anything. It's as though he's of another time, when his standards may have had some meaning. But what is becoming clear is that these standards no longer relate in any profound way and are quickly rejected. The satisfaction Micky had enjoyed while he was popular for all his grade school and high school years is quickly fading into despair. For the first time in his life, he's finding he has a stiff tongue. It's certainly not from having nothing to say, but for fear of being shouted down. In a conversation with Burt, his frustrations begin to surface.

"These guys are idiots," laments Micky. "They don't have a clue what they're talking about. It's like they hear something said by some old, worn-out beatnik like that Allen Ginsberg guy, and they buy it as though it came from the mouth of God. They remind me of a bunch of mindless lemmings running for the cliff."

Burt, on the other hand, has stepped out of Micky's sphere of influence by joining the college chapter of SDS. For the first time in his life, he is enjoying a sense of belonging to something. He's no longer counting the summer days by their names, and instead by what he's learned and the rap sessions he's enjoyed. He's emboldened by this avant-garde comradery enough to speak condescendingly to Micky.

"You gotta start loosenin' up, man—you're so uptight."

Micky has no words. It's one of the few times in his life he's been left speechless. The only thought running through his mind is what Christ had told his disciples in a similar situation: *"Don't cast your pearls before the swine ... shake the dust from your shoes and wait for those who are willing to hear you."* Struggling to remain on the high road, Micky isn't finding comfort in these words like he did when it was just a verse without the accompanying conflict. He is discovering how effortless it is to hate those who disagree with him.

Totally frustrated with Burt's actions and still shaking his head, Micky turns and silently walks away. Even though he remains unspoken, his body language says much more about his attitude toward Burt's so-called "freedom." A shade of impersonal, objective thoughts of not caring about this turn of events struggles to make its way against a stronger sense of personal rejection and isolation, all brought on by the invasion of these new-world notions.

Mikey's level of frustration demands a release of sorts—a scream, a howl, or banging his fist through anything nearby. Instead, he falls back on his pact with God that if he asks in Jesus' name, his prayer will be answered. His relationship with God has always settled around his good behavior. He's sure he has an "in" with the Almighty, especially since his behavior (at least, in his estimation) is beyond reproach. He had said the sinner's prayer when he accepted the Lord when he was ten and, in his estimation, has not needed it since.

He begins by imploring God to seek retribution against his tormentors. He even offers to do the job himself. *After all, am I not a tool in God's hands to do his work?* is Micky's assumption.

"Almighty God, you see what your faithful servant is having to go through with these godless cretins. Damn their efforts—and if needs be—damn them along with it! In Jesus' name, I ask it!"

He waits silently for a moment, hoping to experience the relief he's seeking. When it doesn't come, he entertains the thought that maybe God has also abandoned him. He's quite sure that if he works to flatter God with a few more platitudes, God will grant him his wish. What he is not aware of is the godless vacuum he is creating within himself. It's quickly filling with anger and resentment toward anyone who disagrees with him—including God. His actions are not incongruent with his religious perceptions—at least, not at this juncture. After all, his spiritual directors have rightfully demanded that their students obey God in all things. They have also pointed out those targets where disobedience to God's law prevails. It's usually against a secular group or a religious denomination with differing theological notions. What has been left out is the method to deal with these targets. Like Peter in the Garden of Gethsemane, Micky finds that swinging swords at one's enemy and cutting a few ears off trumps the painstaking effort to seek God's direction in a more realistic prayer.

There is as much lacking in the secular performances as in the religious of this age; many of the young are not seeking maturity as did former generations. Such terms as "don't trust anyone over thirty" have declared adulthood an enemy, an expression shared by a nationwide youth movement. This phrase, though held as a truth by most youth, is wrongly represented as a movement with a collective face in all its aspects. Some have rightly described this as a period of a "me generation" in which individual rights have become the prevailing obsession. It's underscored by a protest movement reflecting a premium placed on self-centeredness. It can be seen in the personal agenda each young person has for him or herself. It seems the rite of passage for many of America's youth is to demand a plethora of things that, in past times, were ordinarily earned. In various circles, the mandate varies from free education, free love, legalized dope, no war, an end to racism, abortions on demand, and a demand for as many government entitlements of which individuals can legally and, in some cases, illegally avail themselves. Many spend their time overcoming these challenges that prove to be more detrimental than beneficial. One could argue that a benefit of this behavior is that these new ideas are stretching their minds beyond its original dimension—but then, so is planning a bank robbery.

These young people have become easy targets for religious zealots like Micky, just as he has for them. In one of Micky's many tirades with Burt over Burt's insistence on siding with the protesters, he says, "Burt, I thank God every day that I'm not like these heathens. I don't know how you can side with their godless ways. It defies everything we've ever learned."

Burt is left to sort through a carefully chosen group of explanations that aren't much more than shallow talking points—they don't amount to much. This is not to say that Micky's worldview is much more accurate. In both their circles, they have become entangled in opinions and personalities stronger than their own who have swayed their young minds toward these scripted viewpoints.

"The war is run by a bunch of bureaucrats in Washington DC," Burt expounds. Then another time, he blusters into one of his favorite rants on "the imperial, industrial war complex" and claims they are running the war to line their pockets. Most of what he has to say, true or false, consists of disconnected pieces of verbiage he's heard from others. Micky, on the other hand, prides himself on his debating skills. His arguments are usually more disciplined and organized, but, like Burt, his ideas are really ones he's borrowed from others. The major difference between these two young men is that Micky claims to speak for God. What remains the same in both is how absorbed they've each become in proselytizing the other.

Rather than opening each other's eyes, they end the debate in a stalemate only to wish each other good riddance until they meet again. This is becoming more difficult because they share a dorm room. Burt will usually be the one to leave and not return until he's sure Micky has fallen asleep. On this occasion, Burt has already stormed from the dorm room, leaving Micky to debate himself. Needing to clear his head, Micky decides to go for a walk. His hope is that he can send off a telegraphic prayer to God as though God were some type of telegraphic office boy designed to get our coffee and make us comfortable, instructing Him on what he wants done with this situation.

Micky spends the next hour in a huff. He still hasn't gotten used to giving up his power over his longtime friend. His notions are limited to his own experiences. He still believes that to control others, he needs more power—even if it means invoking God to get involved. He hasn't learned that power hardly ever solves human problems. The problem with Micky is that he believes it can. He scarcely understands his own misplaced passions, much less how to master them. Instead, he buries himself in frustrating thoughts that only make his head ache.

Not used to struggling, Micky is experiencing emotional states he has no name for. *I feel like a ship floundering in a storm,* he thinks.

It's a thought that has come up on his blind side. More and more, he is discovering his high school experience had not prepared him for this. He has always had a loathing for those who have opposed him, but for the first time in his life, he is experiencing self-loathing. He has no idea what it's called; he only knows he is experiencing a new feeling. A lack of power is quickly becoming his new dilemma. He's beginning to believe that life has cruelly held secrets from him, and that he's being cheated. It makes him want to lash out at something.

It doesn't take him long to come across a likely target. A group of people has gathered around a young man playing a guitar. They're a war protest song. Before a second thought can make its way into Micky's head, he's storming his way through the crowd of pot-smoking, long-haired hippies to stand within inches of the guitar player, glaring at him. With one sweep of his hand, he grabs the neck of the guitar, tearing it from the man's grasp. Micky begins to swing it at everyone in sight. It doesn't take but a few seconds before a large young man in the audience wearing a leather vest with fringe and a red handkerchief twisted into a headband takes offense and charges Micky from behind, knocking him to the ground with the guitar flying off in another direction. Micky is facing a very large, angry guy. Now armed with nothing more than his own anger, he makes his next thoughtless move. Speed has always been Micky's strength, whether on the baseball field, the grid iron, or the track. It isn't failing him now. In a burst of energy, he rises to his feet, storms the man, and tackles the man at his waist, driving him off his feet and into a pile on the grass. From this advantage, Micky, realizing the man's size, begins to drive his fists into his face, head, neck—anywhere he believes will disable his opponent. Instinctively, he realizes he can't allow this huge man any advantage. Continuing to pummel the man, he is only interrupted when he is suddenly and violently pulled off from behind. The experience tells him he may be in for some more trouble. Struggling to his feet, he is met with a familiar face: Burt's.

"In the name of God, what are you doin', Micky?" Burt asks.

22

Micky stands wide-eyed and dumbfounded before his interrogator. Never has this friend laid hands on him. What is perplexing him even more so is how his life has come to this. There is suddenly an awareness that deep within his soul, there is a nothingness—a hollowness that's void of hope. It's as though God has abandoned him. At this point, Micky is incapable of understanding anything. Before he can answer his friend, he is met with an additional problem. The campus police had seen enough of this fiasco to know its instigator. In another moment, they have returned Micky to the ground with knees on both his back and neck, ensuring he is going nowhere. At the same moment, his arms are twisted behind his back with handcuffs lacing them together. After he's jerked to his feet, he's immediately led off to a waiting patrol car.

Burt's instinct is to advocate for his friend. "Let him go! I can get him out of here!"

Burt is caught off guard by the policeman's response.

"If you don't step back, young man, you'll be joining your friend," responds one good-sized cop.

Burt and Micky have spent the entirety of their lives in sheltered environments. This is a first for them. Neither has had as much as a conversation with a police officer, much less been threatened with arrest. Burt is stunned for the moment. His lack of options is a truth he's suddenly faced with as he's led off in handcuffs. As soon as Micky is secured in the backseat of the police car, an officer returns to get statements from Micky's victims.

"That cat's insane," is the assumption made by one of Micky's long-haired victims.

"That dude's gotta be high on acid to act like he did," says another.

The owner of the guitar is carefully inspecting his instrument. "Thank God. All that's wrong is a couple broken strings," he observes.

When the police ask if anyone wishes to press charges, they have an overwhelming inclination to say "no." This generation is enormously antipolice. Even to be caught collaborating in any way with the "pigs" (police) is to draw suspicion onto one's self as being a conservative, or worse, a "narc" (undercover narcotics officer).

Since no one is willing to press charges, the police have the option to charge Micky with what is referred to as "Disorderly Conduct." It's a catchall charge that allows them to make an arrest for varying infractions. They are considering this when Burt, in another bold effort, confronts the arresting officers once more.

"My name is Burt Wilson. I'm his roommate. If you let him go, I'll be responsible to get him back inside our dorm room without any more crap." His request is orderly, polite, and can't be more submissive or forthright. The police officers look at each other with the same thought: *Releasing him will save a bunch of paperwork.* Without a word spoken, the officers approach their patrol car. Micky's six-foot-plus frame looks dreadfully out of place locked in the caged backseat of this vehicle. It's apparent that he's praying. His hands are folded, and he's rocking back and forward, tears in his eyes as he implores God to get him out of this mess. His short hair has a decidedly disheveled appearance that's exaggerated by his dejected demeanor. Opening the rear door, the largest of the two officers bends over enough to get Micky's attention. "Young man, you have a savior. Your buddy has answered your prayer. We're allowing you to get your sorry ass out of here."

Looking as if he has just lost his best friend, Micky's eyes meet Burt's as he peers around the officer. Burt, too, has bent over to get a look at his lifelong friend. He's never seen Micky like this before: a pitiful sight of fear and confusion. It's the first time in their relationship when their roles have been reversed, and it's certainly the first time Burt has encountered such weakness in his friend. Neither of them is prepared for this change. It's leaving them a bit uncomfortable, but nonetheless, Micky will accept this development, providing he will not be going to jail.

Set free, Micky is forced to pass by his victims. Burt and the officers are keeping a wary eye on Micky as he picks up the pace, hoping he can get by and avoid eye contact with these former targets.

They remain guarded and suspicious as he makes his way through their ranks without incident.

Once out of range, Burt is emboldened to confront Micky with the simple question, "What the hell was that all about?"

Micky is quiet. He is openly agitated by the question and makes the grunting sound that usually indicates he doesn't want to be confronted.

Burt isn't willing to let him off the hook that easily. "Come on, Micky, talk to me! You know darn well that isn't the way we were taught."

Micky is clearly uncomfortable. He clears his voice, which has taken on a wobble that hasn't been there before. He shrugs his shoulders in a defensive way and, attempting to give his words a clear tone, he says, "I've had it with these people and their mockery. They mock everything that I hold sacred. They mock God, our country, our values ... I could go on and on! When I saw their open and deliberate belligerence, I just snapped!"

Burt is silent. He's had his differences with Micky, but this is the first time he's seen him go over the edge in this violent way. Without much thought, Burt says, "Mick, you gotta remember this ain't high school any more. This is a whole different world."

"That doesn't mean I gotta like it," says Micky, continuing his defensive role.

"No, you don't gotta like it, but you can't go around fighting everybody and everything that disagrees with you," says Burt with a firm tone.

"These wimps don't know what fighting is. If we sent them to Vietnam, they'd curl up like baby girls calling for their moms," returns Micky. His disgust is clear.

As usual, their differences have brought them to a stalemate. Both carry their own thoughts as they try to sleep.

CHAPTER 4
Unanointed

In the ensuing weeks, Micky digs in even deeper. His rigorous belief that his current faith and social behavior form a view that's acceptable to God is becoming more and more pronounced. This self-righteous self-assurance has become the motive behind his social maneuvering, his conniving, and his dismissive posturing against those he has marginalized as less than God's children. To Micky, this means he need not value anyone's opinions other than his own. Eventually, it becomes easy to take it another step. He not only disregards others' opinions, but also the people themselves. He scrutinizes others like a commanding officer would his soldiers, holding them to a standard even he can scarcely live up to. On the other hand, it continues to frustrate Micky that his high school status means absolutely nothing on this college campus. It doesn't help when not only his peers regard his opinions as obsolete, outdated, and archaic, but also the ever more liberal faculty members. It only continues to add to his lurking insecurities when even his professor considers his debating skills to be mediocre at best.

It's an ordinary school day. Burt is out somewhere doing his thing. In the absence of any other friends, this has left Micky alone to fare as he may. It isn't much of a stretch to decide the library is the place to go. *At least there I can catch up on my homework or even lay my head on a library table and take a nap.* It isn't long before he is well into a math assignment. For a reason he can't explain, he looks up in time to see a familiar form placing her books on a table across the room. It is a girl he had a few dates with last school year. She'd been a cheerleader while he was on the football team. They'd shared a similar status among their peers for their four years at the same high school. He notices she still possesses the same regal stature she held the last time he took her out, only now she stands out singularly because she doesn't have to compete with all the other pretty cheerleaders. It takes Micky but a moment to abandon his homework and make his way across the room. Once there, he stands awkwardly for a moment, staring at this striking female. He's overjoyed to see such a familiar form. For reasons he cannot explain, he feels a sudden wave of comfort and ease about this girl. She seems to have a pleasant air about her that only comes with familiarity.

His awkwardness ends when she looks up to see him standing there, staring at her. "Micky Murphy! What are you doing here?" is her cheerful acknowledgment. In one single motion, she is out of her chair. She throws her arms around him, demonstrating in no uncertain terms that she is thrilled to see him.

Micky couldn't be happier. "Carolyn Barnes, it is you!" She is dressed conservatively compared to the number of girls throughout the campus wearing peasant dresses and tops with no bra. She still wears a form-fitting dress with a crisp, white-collared top unbuttoned enough to suggest the possibility of cleavage. In an almost automatic, wordless motion, they pull chairs out and sit down at the table. They both are delighted to see each other. Within fifteen minutes, they have found their high school days to be the preferred comfort zone to talk over "old times." Several hours pass quickly. What is becoming readily apparent is that they share a similar fate with regard to the emerging youth culture. Neither of them is accepting of it, nor are they accepted by it. The familiar values that held them together in high school and were considered normal, everyday norms and mores suddenly stand out in contrast with the liberal views of their peers as extreme opinions that need to be obliterated. They are pleasantly discovering a welcome ally in one another. It's an alliance that arises out of a perceived necessity. High school had been the best part of their lives. Both are prepared to accept this experience as the apex of their lives and are not prepared to move beyond. Absorbed in one another, they haven't realized the library is preparing to close and is asking everyone to pack up and leave.

In the simple act of resting her hand on Micky's arm, Carolyn, nearly tearing up, says, "You don't know what a great feeling it is to find you today. I feel so alone on this stupid campus. I have nothing in common with these kids. It's just such a relief to realize I'm not the only one going through all this."

Micky responds by placing his hand on hers. "I know I wasn't always available in high school, but now I'd like to see you more." Carolyn slightly intensifies her grip on Micky's arm and brushes her Florence Henderson bangs aside. Looking up through mascaraed eyelashes, she replies, "I'd like that, Micky."

It doesn't need to be restated how thrilled these two outsiders are to discover each other in this threatening sea of liberalism. They promise to be available to each other. They are certain their shared Christian filter has given them the perception of the true God, and between the two of them, they must encourage each other with the hope that together, they will overcome whatever these anti-God people have to throw at them.

Carolyn is the youngest of three. She has an older sister and brother. Her mother is a schoolteacher, and her father is a successful entrepreneur. She has attended a parochial school since kindergarten. There is no question she is steeped in the Judeo-Christian ethics of her generation. This is perfectly natural, as fifty percent of Americans attend church every week, and ninety percent profess a belief in God. Carolyn has prided herself that despite the different circumstances here at college, she doesn't experiment with drugs and remains a virgin. She makes no secret of her disgust with the vile, gross behaviors of the many girls of her generation who embrace free love and drug and alcohol abuse. On the other hand, Carolyn's portrayal of virtue strikes others as a coolness verging on harshness and unfriendliness. Although this is also considered the natural behavior of one who feels a sense of repression, Carolyn struggles to know what to do with her emotions. This behavior results in her shrinking away from confronting her feelings and any exhibition of passion. It generally comes to the surface as anger veiled in a certain sobriety of speech and steadiness of character.

Parting comes easy now that the pair have agreed to attend a Campus Crusade for Christ rally the next day. Their level of anticipation grows as they await the moment when they will meet again. Since freshmen aren't allowed to have cars on campus, Micky agrees to meet Carolyn at her dorm and make the fifteen-minute walk to the rally together. He has opted to wear what he always wears to anything to do with church: a white shirt and tie, dark trousers, and black polished shoes.

Micky finds her ready and waiting in the dorm's lounge. Her short hair is suitably coiffed, and her attire and makeup are modest. She leaps snappishly to her feet, anxious to let the day unfold. Her strained demeanor has been replaced with a radiant smile. She had a high school crush on Micky and is happy to revisit the thrill it produced once again. He, too, is excited to have a date with a girl he considers to be on his social and spiritual level.

Soon, they are on their way. Even with this occasion being well publicized, they are surprised to find so many modest-looking kids seemingly on their way to the same occasion. It's being assembled on the same intramural field where other events of a very different nature have been held. Micky and Carolyn find the protest signs reflecting the same unrest seen at anti-war rallies disturbing. Some are especially disturbing because they attack the very core of their existences in an anti-establishmentarian way. They are especially troubled by signs that read "TO HELL WITH THE CHURCH" or "GOD IS DEAD." Others are much more inviting, like "JESUS IS HABIT-FORMING" or "GOD LOVES ALL HIS CHILDREN." The music is flowing from a Christian band calling themselves New Folk that's situated on a stage outfitted from a truck flatbed. People are pouring in from every direction. Micky and Carolyn find a suitable place to sit and wait for it all to begin. This event has the potential to impact the lives of up to a thousand young people as the field begins to swell with bodies. Micky and Carolyn are especially heartened by the size of the crowd because they had felt like two lonely people hanging on to the hope they believe only God can supply.

Soon, the music stops. The campus leader representing Campus Crusaders for Christ steps up to the makeshift stage and approaches the microphone. Suddenly, the crowd bursts into applause for this very recognizable and likeable young man. His name is Luke Gale. When the crowd finally settles down, he begins by telling the crowd how, as a boy, he had been troubled and had given his life to Christ, and how this changed his so that now he can care for every one of God's children, including each of them. He continues by informing them that God has a plan for each of them and encouraging them to imagine that each of them has the God-given power to deliver God's message of salvation that will change hearts. He says Jesus is the bridge between God the Father and his children and then tells them that they are the true revolutionaries. He says the world is in a mess, and they can change it with God's direction.

Micky has always hoped he could belong to something as big as this. With much the same feeling he had while listening to his high school commencement speaker, he begins to imagine himself giving a powerful, persuasive presentation like this. He can't put the notion that his very existence is for greatness out of his mind.

Carolyn is also captivated by everything that is going on, but her results are different than Micky's. She is just happy to see so many people turn out for this great, life-changing event. Just knowing that in her walk with the Lord, she is not alone here is enough to satisfy her.

On their walk back to Carolyn's dorm, she is especially verbose. "I can't believe how many people showed up for this. I had imagined we would be the only people there. There must have been over a thousand—it's been unbelievable."

Micky is listening, but his mind is somewhere else. Like during his high school commencement, and now hearing this powerful presentation, his dreams of greatness are growing larger. "I can't argue with any of it. It was phenomenal." He next finds himself mouthing his thoughts. "You know, Carolyn, I can see myself doing something like those guys." The words came out loud before he realizes he has said them. He's noticeably embarrassed. It makes Carolyn pause for a moment. His introspection doesn't surprise her. She has always admired Micky for his ability to lead. If there was a high school committee, he oversaw it, and it was always successful. "I think you'd be great," says Carolyn, happy she is able to share in such a supportive role. Pausing to look at her for a moment, a feeling of delight sweeps over him. This is the kind of support he's always been seeking. Little did he know that it would come from such a familiar source. Overjoyed with Carolyn's reaction, he says, "You really think so?"

Carolyn pauses for a moment, basking in the attention she's getting for her supportive opinion. "Yes, I really think so," she boldly reiterates. These words are like beautiful music to Micky's ears. Not even his parents have supported his desire to go into the Christian ministry. He and Carolyn are both satisfied with where the moment is taking them. Micky squeezes her hand a little more—not to hurt her, but out of excitement over being in the presence of such a beautiful ally and the discovery that she is solidly in his corner.

The day of togetherness for these two reinvigorated souls has come to an end. Micky leaves Carolyn at her dorm with the assurance of reuniting for lunch the next day. Returning to his dorm, Micky tries to calm his thoughts, but his mind won't permit it. He lies awake most of the night visualizing himself in roles of greatness, of preaching to thousands of eager listeners. He reinforces his formations with something he had read someplace that said to trust his dreams as the hidden gate to eternity and that dreaming is the first part of action. By morning, little has changed. His enthusiasm to put into action the contents of his dreams is still with him. He decides to cut his morning classes and concentrate on his next move. What he decides is to present himself to Luke Gale, the director of the Campus Crusade for Christ, as a willing volunteer. He is certain his passion will be regarded as an asset.

Dressing himself in the same church clothing he wore the day before, he nervously makes his way across campus to Luke's office. It's in a modern one-story office building with a chapel attached to the back. Luke Gale is a twenty-something enthusiastic Christian clergyman dedicated to the obligation commanded in the Bible to preach the Gospel of Christ to the world. Micky is quickly put at ease by this young man's generous nature. He is finding him as compelling in his office as he did on the stage the day before. As Luke slips onto a chair behind his desk, he directs Micky to a waiting chair in front of him. Settling in, Luke places his elbows on the desk's surface and presses each fingertip against the same fingertip on the other hand, giving them a steeple-like appearance. All in all, his comportment presents a rather pensive air.

"So, what brings you to my doorstep, my friend?" asks this animated young clergyman. Micky is trying hard not to appear intimidated by the importance of this talented man. Clearing his throat, Micky manages to get a few words past his lips. "I attended your rally yesterday. I have to say, your words moved me."

Without as much as a pause, Luke says, "Wonderful! What did you hear?" His smile makes one feel he is doing something right.

This kind question has come up on Micky's blindside. He'd been paying more attention to Luke's delivery style than the content of his message. In a near fit of panic, Micky's gaze begins to shoot around the room as though some angel could be in hiding in the wings ready to give him the recollection he needs. Instead, he spots the word "revolutionary" on a small placard against the wall. This brought back an immediate recall how Luke had talked about each of us need to become revolutionaries for Christ. "I was particularly struck by your use of the word 'revolutionary' regarding the Christian church," says Micky, hoping he's pulled off an adequate answer. He waits for a response from Luke.

"Good, because that's exactly the direction I wanted that message to go—to penetrate the heart and soul of the listener to begin a revolution first within themselves, and then to become a power of attraction to others who are still struggling with their own issues of living and dying," says Luke with an air of finality. Respectfully listening, Micky is quite sure Luke's message didn't get to that depth within himself. Nonetheless, Micky is nothing short of a fawning sycophant as he gazes back at Luke with a demeanor that suggests overall compliance.

Satisfied he has the attention of this young suitor, Luke poses the question again: "So what brings you to my office, my friend?"

Without hesitation, Micky says, "I'd like you to mentor me."

Without hesitation, Luke shoots back, "Why?"

"Because you have something I want," is Micky's ready reply.

"What could I possibly have that I can give you?" is Luke's puzzled response.

"I don't know what its name is, but you have it, and I want some of it myself," replies Micky in a tone that reflects frustration rather than self-assurance.

Luke's tone turns more thoughtful. "I believe what you see in me can't be gotten by absorption," he says. "Hanging around me isn't going to do much other than reveal myself—the good, the bad, the ugly. All I can do is point you to the same source of power I go to when I seek a daily reprieve."

It would be a stretch to say that Micky is grasping what Luke is saying, but he continues to be very enamored with the way Luke is saying things. There is a certainty to his words. This is what is appealing to Micky. *I don't understand what he just said, but I love the way he says it*, is Micky's thought.

Before continuing, Luke measures what he's just said to Micky against the way Micky reacts. It's obvious to Luke that Micky probably isn't hearing with an inner ear; he only hears lightly. Against this, Luke decides, "I'll be your mentor on one condition: you volunteer your time to the Crusader program."

This isn't exactly what Micky wants to hear. *I'd rather be a little nearer to his inner circle,* is his first thought. He's not accustomed to relinquishing the control over that much of his life. Where are the applause and floodlights as he scores another touchdown in this volunteer arena? At Micky's juncture in life, seeking status has little to do with being well liked and more to do with gaining some unnamed, mystical rank. Micky is more concerned with having an imposing social position. Being around the right people is what gives him the noble status he seeks. Micky recalls that being in the limelight gave him a lot of status in high school. He was always at the center of things. What Micky hungers for is not always easily gained by those who desire it: power and control! The idea of taking a volunteer role under the control of some person he will more than likely view as an inferior is not to his liking. In bearing the levers of power, discrimination is essential. Being in charge allows its bearer to hand out or withhold rewards directly. Micky is convinced that it's God's plan for him to be a leader; volunteering is not where he feels he'll fulfill this vision of grandeur. Mick is certain God is in his corner and bold to hold the opinion that it's the correct order of things. Anything less would be hypocritical.

Micky is trying his hardest to remain cheerful. This task is the hardest thing he has ever been asked to do. It's like he's lost his high school "innie" anointment; a sense of an unfamiliar weakness is lurking at his door. After all, he's accustomed to the roar of a crowd, not the silence of anonymity. It's like he's been asked to fill in for the towel boy after scoring a winning touchdown. But the one attribute he has managed to bring back to the surface is his self-confidence.

While all these differing thoughts are buzzing around inside Micky's head, Luke sits with his fingers still forming a steeple-like shape, waiting for Micky's response. "Well, what's your decision?" Luke asks.

Micky feels a jarring as though he has just been dropped from an upper floor to the basement. Stumbling around attempting to regain some dignity, he senses a returning confidence that is battling to overtake the sense of impotence that's attempting to sneak in. "I'll give it a try," is Micky's response.

Luke continues his scrutiny. "'Trying' is not the attitude that makes a good volunteer. I need more of a dependable commitment." It's clear that this is a type of conversation that Micky has never had to tolerate.

Micky is certain Luke has been the loser in this exchange by hobbling his rare and distinct talents, but once again, his confidence comes with a challenge. "Okay, you're right. I will use all that God has given me to make sure I do my best," says Micky with a renewed sense of commitment.

A smile makes its way across Luke's face. He arises from his chair, offering Micky his hand and saying, "Then I promise to mentor you with the same hardy pledge. But for now, I want you to report to my right-hand volunteer. His name is Malachi Maloney. You'll find him at the intramural field, organizing a cleanup. Just tell him I sent you, and he'll find you something to do."

With this exchange coming to an end, Luke escorts Micky to the door, closing it behind him. It takes Micky a moment to realize their conversation has ended. He stands frozen for the moment. The past proceedings are still sinking in when Luke's secretary touches his arm, asking him if there is something else he needs. A little embarrassed at his lapse of attention, he says, "Thank you, but I'm all set." With that, he makes his way back out to the street to determine the best route to the intramural field.

CHAPTER 5
The Recruiter

In his differing afternoon mood, Micky makes his way to the cleanup site. He's a little depressed because he's thinking over his seeming downgrading, but he's determined to make the best of it. He's struck by how much trash has been generated by the rally. He hardly recalls seeing any debris the day before. Paper and cans of every description are being processed and separated into different containers. It's difficult to pick out Malachi since everyone seems to be working on one form of a mess or another. His idea is that this young man will probably be commanding the operation from a command center somewhere on the grounds (because that's the way he imagines he would be doing it). Instead, it appears there is no real division of labor; everyone is working like an ant colony and moving along in a synchronized operation. Pulling a worker aside, Micky asks where he can find Malachi. The laborer responds with a hand gesture, pointing to a very tall young man with a shock of dark hair dumping a can of trash onto the bed of a waiting pickup truck. Despite his depressed mental condition, Micky makes his way across the field. He's still unsure this is not a cruel, humiliating mistake, and his every step comes with its own challenges. This low feeling of humiliation is brand new for his purported stature. *Now I know how low a snake in a wagon rut feels.*

Micky gets it over with by offering a compact introduction of sorts. "Are you Malachi? My name is Micky. Luke sent me here hoping you can put me to work."

With barely a once over, Malachi throws him a large floor broom. "Get in the back of the truck and start pushin' this crap toward the front."

Each of the dozen or so workers moves seamlessly from one task to another, speaking little. This is not the group of people Micky would have voluntarily chosen to hang out with had it not been for Luke. He finds himself judging these people by their looks, as he always has. After all, being on top of the heap of beautiful people in high school, why would he choose to hang out with this marginal crew of mediocrity? Nonetheless, the day drags on. Micky moves from one needed task to another along with the rest. With the day finally ending, he welcomes the respite. To say he enjoyed it would be a lie, but he did endure it and finish without quitting.

Malachi is taking a moment to thank each of the volunteers for a job well done. "It's a dirty job, but together we got 'er done," are his congratulatory words. "I want to thank each of you. You all did a commendable job." Micky accepts the approval but is secretly hoping his proficiency will be singularly acknowledged. Begrudgingly, he accepts the feeling that he's been overlooked and makes his way back to his dorm. Reviewing his day brings with it a plethora of unresolved irritations others brought about by not meeting his expectations. He's much like the quintessential play director who is certain the play would have been great if only everyone would have stayed in place and remembered their lines.

After cleaning up, he still can't get past the prickliness brought about by the day's events. Knowing Burt's lack of empathy for anything he's doing now days, he opts not to return to his room and chooses to visit Carolyn instead. He's quite certain he'll find a waiting ally, and when he arrives, he learns that assumption couldn't have been more accurate. More than pleased to have been placed in such high regard, she welcomes him with open arms. Women ion campus are not allowed to have men in their rooms, so she agrees to meet him in the lounge. Desiring to have more privacy, she uncovers a way through a service door to sneak him into her dorm room. She soon discovers she enjoys receiving the flattery she gains by giving her undivided attention to Micky's slights; she agrees with each of his alleged insults, from Luke all the way through Malachi.

The evening twilight's translucent glow is having an almost magical effect. The emotional impact and the attraction they have for one another is transforming into a new and unexplored region of their relationship. They are more than willing to let this magnetism lure them to wherever it is leading them. Everything about their sentiments for one another feels so right; how could any of it be judged wrong? Giving their feelings sovereignty has led them to a situation neither has the ability—nor the desire—to withdraw from. An hour later, with various items of their clothing—socks, bras, underwear—strewn haphazardly around the room, each of them sees a sobering picture of what has just happened. They're both forced to own it, as much as they would prefer not to. Clumsily reuniting themselves with their own clothing, they prefer to remain silent, with their own guilty feelings as a private accounting. Much like hoping it's possible to return squeezed out toothpaste back into the tube, they look at each other through eyes of guilt, each feeling they have betrayed themselves and God. It's more than they can handle now. For this moment, self-loathing is much larger than any enjoyment they may have experienced. Both agree that what has transpired is a mistake and can't be repeated. With a guilty silence, they say their goodbyes. Micky retraces his way out through the service entry and back to his dorm.

The very person he had hoped not to encounter earlier in the evening is now a welcome sight. Burt is sitting in their room with his homework. "How ya doin', Burt? Long time, no see!" is Micky's welcoming response.

Looking up from his book, Burt is working up a welcome smile to return Micky's surprising friendliness. "Yeah, I been busy. It's good to see you," returns Burt, closing his book. He's missed their camaraderie and is happy to see Micky taking the initiative to bring it back. Micky sits down in a chair opposite Burt. He's leaning forward with his elbows resting on his knees, hands clasped together and a pensive stare. At the same time, Burt sees something in Micky's eyes that he has never seen before. It's a subtle change, but noticeable to this childhood friend. It reflects a crack in his ever-present confidence.

"You okay, Micky?" asks Burt.

Without answering, Micky says, "I think I'm gonna drop out of school and join the army."

Burt is unquestionably taken aback. "You're gonna do what?" is all he can manage to say for the moment.

"I'm gonna quit school and join the army." Micky states this in such a matter-of-fact manner that Burt can't help but remain shocked.

"When'd you decide all this?" is Burt's next achieved question.

"Five minutes ago," says Micky. "I can't deal with what's going on in my life any longer, and I've decided I need a change of priorities."

Burt remains frozen in time, still holding his closed book. "When you plan on doin' all this?" is Burt's next question.

"Tomorrow," is Micky's matter-of-fact answer. "And it can't come too soon."

With that, Micky removes the clothing he had just put back on a half hour ago, lies down on his bed, and falls asleep.

Morning brings Burt up and ready to meet his day in the classroom. Micky, on the other hand, purposely remains in his bunk. The last thing he wants to do is debate with Burt over his decision. As soon as Burt has left, Micky is up and packing his few belongings. He next stops by the dean's office to withdraw from school, heads for the bus station to buy his ticket, boards the bus, and heads home.

With bag in hand, he's met by a surprised mother in her kitchen. "Where in tarnation did you come from?" is her uncertain question.

Micky drops his bag and gives his mother the biggest hug he's given her in years. "Well, young man, I'll ask you again. Where in tarnation did you come from?"

"I just decided I needed to talk some things over with you and dad, so I bought a bus ticket and came home," says an unapologetic Micky. "By the way, where is dad?"

"He's out in the garage tinkerin' with stuff so he doesn't have to help me put up these curtains," says his mother.

At that moment, after hearing Micky's voice, his dad enters through the door that connects the garage and the kitchen. A surprised look makes its way across his face. "What brings this pleasant surprise?" is his smiling question.

Not wanting to sound alarming, Micky decides to downplay his visit. "Oh, I just missed you guys and wanted to say hi."

By this time, his father has had ample time to look his son over. He sees the same subtle difference Burt had seen the night before. "Well, I'm so happy you made *that* decision. It's good to see you."

For now, all three are willing to let things ride until a seemlier time allows things to come to a head on their own. Meanwhile, Micky is content to spend the morning with his dad in the garage, working on a lawn mower. His mother remains in her kitchen. She's happy she has one of her children home to cook for. The conversation in the garage has circled around from the lawn mower to some of the campus activities that are making the news.

"What's goin' on with all these people rioting in the streets? When I was your age, we were fighting a war. It was called the great war. If we hadn't won, we'd all be speakin' Kraut. Twenty years later, we were in another war. We had no intentions of letting the Krauts or the Japs win that war, either. If we hadn't had that mindset, we'd all be speakin' Jap west of the Mississippi River and Kraut east of it. I was too old for that one. Then your brother fought in Korea so we didn't have to learn to speak Korean or Chinese."

Listening to his father, Micky decides this is the time to segue into his reason for being home. "Dad, I've decided to drop out of school and join the army."

There is a long, quiet pause. It's obvious this announcement from his son has come up on his blindside.

"What made you decide to do something like that, son?" It's the only thing his father can think of to say. There is a clear change in this patriarch's voice. It's true he fought in WWI and earned several medals for his valor in France's trenches, but that was him. He also recalls how devastated he initially felt when his oldest son made the same announcement at the advent of the Korean war. Trying to remain composed while his mind tries to wrap itself around this announcement, he recalls once again making a comparable announcement to his parents nearly fifty years earlier. He remembers his father's face going blank and his mother's tears. "How did you come to this decision?" is his father's next question.

Not certain how to answer, Micky mulls over his pastor's teaching on the "just war" issue, and how much he despises the anti-war protestors, and most recently his fall from grace with Carolyn. His answer would be much more succinct if he included the guilt, regret, resentment, and sadness he's directed at himself. Unfortunately, these are buried so deep below his neurotic need to be "Godlike" that they can't be exposed to the light of truth, much less confessed. "I can't put my finger on one thing, but I got a strong desire to go, dad." For the moment, it's all he can come up with. While his father is listening, he is reviewing his own passion to serve and hoping he can resuscitate enough to warrant some understanding toward his son. He realizes happiness can only occur when an accord is reached between a man and his chosen way of life. He knows that attempting to talk Micky out of this will be futile; he's got to find his own way.

Their conversation is abruptly interrupted. It's Micky's mother calling them to supper. "Don't bring this up to your mother just yet. Let me handle it," begs his father. Micky nods in agreement, happy he's gotten this far. They both head for supper. Miraculously, they manage to get through the meal without spilling the beans. As a small child, Micky recalls watching his mother agonize and worry over his older brother while he was away in the service, and how she would go to the mailbox every day, hoping to hear good news from him. She aged with weary apprehension until he came home safely.

Not quite certain how he is going to break the news to his wife, Micky's dad waits until he is somewhat sure she'll be able to handle it. The dishes are done. All that's left to do is take the evening walk they have settled on as an obligation to keep themselves healthy. Micky has obliged himself to tag along among a flurry of questions from his mother concerning his wellbeing. Remembering all the sports in which he had participated, she asks him, "What kind of sports are you doing this semester?"

Figuring his father is taking too long to make his intentions known, Micky says, "Nothing right now, but shortly I'll be getting all the exercise I can handle."

With basketball season approaching, his mother asks, "Are you able to keep your grades up and play basketball at the same time?"

Micky hesitates for a moment and hopes the best explanation will drop out of the sky and save him from going any further. Of course, it doesn't happen. Despite his father's request to allow him to handle this, he's opened his mouth and finds himself expected to qualify his last statement. "I'm joinin' the army, Ma." Those five simple words stop his mother in her tracks. Her demeanor tells the whole story of the impact this announcement is having. Her blank expression brings Micky back to those days years ago when his brother was serving in Korea. How quickly she is falling back into those old days of dread.

Seeing the less than desirable effect this announcement is making, Micky quickly attempts to defend his decision. "I believe it's my Christian duty to serve my country against those godless communists," are the words that roll off his tongue effortlessly. These words are replicated in the mindset of nearly every God-fearing Christian throughout the country.

With the most worrisome look he has seen on his mother's face in years, she finally speaks up. "Oh, Micky, does that mean you're leaving your education behind? You've worked too hard all through high school to throw it all way."

"I'm not throwing it away, Ma. I'm only putting it on hold," says Micky apologetically.

"I'm terrified you're not going to return home," says his mother with her eyes welling up in tears.

"I can only trust that God wouldn't have given me this mission if He were not going to be with me," replies Micky.

Micky's mother is not convinced that it's God's plan that's driving her youngest son, and she withdraws into herself, knowing the futility of arguing against his decision. It comes back to her how futile it had been to argue with her oldest son in her attempt to prevent him from going off to fight a foreign war many years before. Micky's father is taken aback at the abrupt way his son is handling this with his mother, but he soon shifts from irritation to being pleased it's done and behind them.

Morning arrives, and Micky's mother is up before anyone. She spent a restless night worrying over Micky's rash decision to involve himself in a war that is surrounded by controversy. In the meantime, no longer committed to a class schedule and no longer under the pressure of deciding his destiny, Micky sleeps in. He feels free for the first time in years.

By afternoon, Micky is out of the house and on his way to the recruiting office. As he enters the building, he is met by a series of posters designed to help fill the army's ranks. These encouraging handbills have been used successfully since the continental army was formed. Their purpose is to generate enthusiasm. They depict either images of purpose-driven soldiers—often carrying weapons— fulfilling a needed role or a highly colored graphic featuring Uncle Sam pointing his finger directly at the recruit while making eye contact with the entreating words, "I WANT YOU!"

Micky meets a young recruitment sergeant who's not much older than himself. He finds himself enthralled with this young man's comportment. He can picture himself in such a role. The recruiter wastes little time with introductions; he's all business. The campaigns differ from time to time and from war to war. It's this young man's job to stress the opportunities available for incoming recruits and to fit each recruit into a role the army needs filled.

He begins by questioning Micky's motive. "What makes you believe the Army is for you?"

Micky responds with an answer he believes will gain the approval of this important appearing colleague. "My father served in

WWI, and my brother was in Korea. I believe it's my God-given duty to protect this country against the tyranny of evil." Micky carefully examines the recruiter's demeanor for an approving response. Instead, the recruiter moves to the next question.

"What role do you picture yourself playing in our Army?"

"I'd like to be a chaplain."

This answer provokes the response Micky has been hoping for all along. "So, you want to be a chaplain. What makes you believe you qualify?

"I've been in a Christian school my entire school career."

"How about academic credentials? Like, are you ordained in any denomination?"

"I don't have any real credentials, and I'm not ordained."

Looking through a dossier, the recruiter says, "Since you're not ordained, I may be able to find a spot for you working as a chaplain's assistant or as chaplain's driver if you qualify after your boot camp training."

Not totally satisfied with this assessment, Micky fills out all the required paperwork. The recruiter reassures him several times by the recruiter that despite the fact that joining up is an unpopular decision, it is, nonetheless, a good one. As Micky turns to leave, he finds none other than Burt standing directly in front of him in the entrance to the recruiting center. His hair is nearing his shoulders, and his beard is weak and straggly. Micky looks at his unholy demeanor as though he were scandalizing a cathedral.

"What the heck are you doin' here?" asks Micky. He looks behind Burt to see who may be with him. Micky's voice carries a tinge of disgust; he believes Burt might be here to do some kind of protesting.

Holding his ground, Burt says, "You didn't think I was gonna let you do this without me, did you?"

After all their recent differences, Micky can't be certain of what he's hearing. Overwhelmed, with a lump forming in his throat, he grabs Burt with both hands. "Are you sure? I can't believe you're doin' this."

"I called your house, and your ol' man told me what you were doin'," Burt says. "I figured we'd been together since kindergarten, and there's no sense in separatin' now. Let's go back an' talk to the recruiter an' see if we can get in on the buddy system."

The recruiter couldn't be happier. One more recruit guarantees he's well on his way to maintaining his quota. Efficiently and proficiently, he shuffles papers across his desk for each to sign. Within ten minutes, both are told to remain ready, as they are both on the US Army's official waiting list to receive further orders.

Micky is looking long and hard at his friend, trying to imagine what brought about this change of heart. A memory of their last encounter is running like an old news reel in his head. It had ended with both holding angry sentiments toward the other. This new journey they are agreeing to embark on together may or may not have had the same ending without the blowout, but the attitude both carry now indicates they have the capacity to forgive and forget. Taking their conversation in a new direction, Micky is the first to encourage an open dialogue to rationalize the motives behind his decision.

"You're probably wondering why I dropped out of school."

"I kinda figured you meant what you said when your stuff was all gone," says Burt.

"Nothing's the same. In high school, I knew who I was and where I was going. College changed all that. Things started to happen that were totally out of my control. I felt like a square peg trying to fit into a round hole. Then I met Carolyn. We hit it off perfectly. Before long, we had compromised our Christian principles to remain virgins until we married." Micky pauses long enough to check Burt's response to this confession. "Rather than risk leading each other into further temptation, we broke off our relationship. The only thing I could think of that would give me a whole new outlook was to join the Army," relates Micky, finalizing his last statement with the kind of sigh that says he hopes the decision was a good one.

45

Burt is listening intently. He's surprised at how open Micky is being. This is not like him. He's usually much more guarded. However, despite this new phenomenon and their differences over the years, Burt has always regarded Micky's thoughts to be a bit deeper than his own. He's not sure this time. He has experienced firsthand the results of Micky's restrictive and inflexible attitudes and how it has played a major role in Micky's confusion as to where he can make himself fit in this so-called "youth movement."

Nonetheless, Burt has his own struggles. He is encouraged by Micky's ability to put his dilemmas into words. This is one of the reasons he continues to be drawn to his friend; Micky helps him clarify his thoughts and express his own quandaries.

"I was all gong ho in gettin' involved with somethin' different than what they had been brainwashin' us with in our little world. What I had hoped was gonna be the new nirvana—the age of Aquarius turned out to be another bunch of brainwashin' bull crap—only this time, it was from another direction. That Meadow chick helped me make my decision. After she stole my heart, it took me a while to figure out she and her group had no principles to lose. All they have is a bunch of slogans. They go with whatever protest the next party centers around. Right now, I'm not sure about much myself. The army seems like it could be a new start," returns Burt with his own brand of awkwardness.

Their choice of action relates the unexpressed truth that despite their differences, they still need each other. Both are experiencing a moment of peace around their decisions. They're of the opinion that setting these new goals is a positive act and will provide a sense of purpose in their lives once again.

CHAPTER 6
Boot Camp

This is merely the beginning of the next chapter of their young lives. Within two weeks, they have received their induction orders to report to Fort Wayne in Detroit, Michigan for a physical and swearing-in. Surprisingly, both sets of parents are respectful toward their sons' decisions and are being as supportive as any parent who understands the risks can be. Like all parents who send their children off to war, acceptance of the situation is the closest thing to happiness that they expect to reap.

It's five o'clock in the morning when Micky and Burt meet at the bus station, ticket in hand. They soon discover they are only two of a waiting bus load of other young men. A few, like Micky and Burt, are volunteers, but most are potential draftees who are praying that they will flunk the physical. The main topic of conversation among these pre-physical potential draftees is methods to create physical conditions to avoid the draft. One bearded fellow has two bars of bath soap—one under each arm. He hopes it will create an unhealthy sweating condition. Another is showing off the needle tracks he's made on his arms using a pin in hopes that he can convince the doctor he's a heroin addict. Another fellow named Pete is certain he has the perfect solution to avoid being accepted by any branch of the armed services. When he's asked what he has planned, he assures everyone that they will know when the time comes.

By seven-thirty, the bus arrives at the Fort Wayne induction center. They are met by a uniformed army sergeant. "I'm here to provide the best plan for you to get your physicals over and done with. All it's going to take is for each of you to follow directions," he says. They are then led into what appears to be a locker room. The sergeant orders each to stand in front of a locker, he then supplies each of them a manila packet with their name typed across the front and a padlock along with a key on a long chain. When this is completed, he continues, "You will all strip down except for your

47

socks and place your clothing along with your other belongings into the locker, lock your lock, and place the key around your neck. Carry your packet with you and present it to each healthcare worker at each station." When this is complete, the sergeant continues his guidelines. "I want you to form a line and follow me." The sergeant suddenly stops and, in a clearly irritated voice, confronts an inductee who is still wearing his underwear. "What is your name, inductee?"

"Pete Powell, sir," answers the inductee.

"Did you not hear me order you to strip?"

"I did, sir, but I can't do it."

By this time, this sergeant is in Pete's face. "What do you mean 'I can't do it'?"

"I know there's queers here, and I ain't no queer, so I ain't showin' any of 'em my naked body."

The sergeant looks Pete square in the eye with only two words, "Follow me."

Falling in behind the sergeant, Pete replies, "Yes sir." He's led to an office that says STAFF PSYCHIATRIST on the door heading. He knocks gently. The response is "Come in." There sitting behind a desk is a middle-aged man smoking a cigar. Removing the cigar from his mouth, he peers over a pair of glasses half down his nose, asking, "What is it, sergeant?"

"You might as well start with this one, Doc. I'll let him tell you why he's here," says the sergeant, closing the door behind him.

"What seems to be the problem, young man?" inquires the doctor.

"I think that sergeant's a queer, sir," replies Pete. "You ain't a queer, are ya?"

"What makes you say that?" further queries the doctor.

"I know these guys; they're everywhere. I saw a ton of 'em on the bus comin' down here. All they wanna do is look at my dick and I'm keepin' my undershorts on!" The doctor doesn't respond, rather, he begins to write things on a piece of paper laying on his desk.

"You ain't gonna kick me out sir, are ya?" There is clearly a tone of panic in his voice. "Ya can't kick me out sir! I came here 'cause I wanna kill people! I ain't got to kill anybody yet! Ya gotta let me kill somebody! I just wanna kill? Please sir, ya can't kick me out!" His voice is heard throughout the building, bringing the sergeant in at a dead run with two military policemen with him. Pete is quickly escorted out, but not before he takes the opportunity to wink at his bus mates over pulling off his foretold ruse. Both the guy carrying soap under his arms for days and the guy poking pins in his arms look on with envy as Pete is escorted to the "unacceptable for military service" room to be sent back home.

Mickey and Burt are soon processed through their physical. After they both pass, they are allowed to dress themselves and are led into another room, where they will be sworn in. Here the inductees swear to up hold the constitution of the United States and to obey orders from the president and those he has placed over them. This ceremony is conducted by a commissioned officer. It's designed to recall a sense of patriotism and to urge each of the inductees to take this opportunity to earnestly serve their country. It couldn't be truer in Micky's case. He seldom chokes up over events, but this one has him in its grip. With his back erect, he stands at full attention. With his right arm bent at the elbow, he raises his right hand. Barely able to gasp the words out without tearing up, he manages to complete the swearing-in piece.

Burt, on the other hand, is merely going through the process as though he were signing up for a volunteer job. He's not expecting much more. During the ceremony, he wonders what Meadow is doing. This infatuation with her is a persistent slice of his life, and it's refusing to loosen its grip. He wishes he could have managed better. To a large degree, he blames it on his parents' insistence that he attend a parochial school. He has always felt that because of it, he is losing out on the worldly encounters others are enjoying. His hope is that this military experience will provide him with something other than a "churchy" life. Meanwhile, he remains guarded as he watches those he perceives to be much worldlier than himself. He envies their style.

Now that the swearing-in ceremony is completed, things begin to change rapidly. They are no longer civilians but are now classified as personnel under the jurisdiction of the United States Army. There is a sudden change in the tone of those in authority from patient to highly impatient. There isn't time for thinking about anything other than what you are expected to do next. Next comes quick. All these young men are lined up and run by a healthcare person operating some sort of gun that shoots a vaccine into each of their arms. Next, they're taken to a center and tested for a type of work they'll be suited to do for the army. Micky has asked to be a chaplain's assistant, and Burt has asked to be a scout. Burt has no clue what that entails, but it looked cool in the description booklet.

A uniformed man who appears to be a sergeant, judging from his sleeve patch, comes forward and asks for a volunteer to oversee these recruits on their way to their basic training facility. Micky perceives that this is the chance he's been waiting for to prove his leadership capabilities, so he suddenly breaks ranks. Stepping forward, he says, "I'll do my best to get us there."

"What's your name, recruit?" asks the sergeant.

Pulling his shoulders back into an attention mode and in clear a voice, he says, "Michael Murphy."

"Okay, Murphy, you're in charge. You're expected to keep these hooligans in line and all on the same page 'til you get to your basic unit station. Is that understood?" says the sergeant, handing him a clipboard with the name of each recruit and their airline ticket.

A sense of pride overtakes Micky, since he has been appointed to this seeming important position over all others. His mind shoots back to when he was high school captain of every sports team he played on. His teammates always looked to him for leadership, and he was happy to display his skills. This is just the opportunity he's been hoping would come his way.

Before Micky can respond, the sergeant, happy to have this task out of his hair, has turned on his heels and headed off to another duty, leaving Micky muttering something that was intended to show appreciation to the sergeant for recognizing his readiness to take on this responsibility. Looking around, Micky sees the recruits still lingering in a formation of sorts. Taking this opportunity, he addresses them. "I expect us to all act like adults and be responsible enough to stick together and to keep me informed as to your whereabouts."

All these young men are recent high school graduates. They all remember those days when their regular teacher was absent, and a substitute was assigned to their class. Everyone can readily admit they rarely held the same respect for the "sub" as they held for their regular teacher. This well-traveled mindset is already beginning to settle in with this crew as a couple of draftees disregard Micky's appointment as their overseer and begin some horseplay. In his most responsible tone of voice, Micky approaches their seeming indifference to protocol. "You guys realize we're not expected to act like little kids, so why don't you straighten up?"

Boldly giving Micky the brush off, one of them replies, "Why don't you lighten up, dude? We're just havin' a little fun."

Before Micky can react, he's saved by the bus arriving to take them to the airport. After managing to get everyone on board, he finds the trip uneventful except for the noise level of talking and laughter. These young men have been quickly made aware that their destinies are no longer theirs to decide. The draftees are especially having problems with this part of their armed service requirements. Unlike the draftees, the volunteers are much more compliant because everything that has placed them on this bus today has been their decision. A small group of draftees has settled in the back of the bus, away from the overall population. Their conversation is less boisterous. They are definitely more engrossed in their discussion than the others. By the time they have reached the airport, Micky makes one more appeal for the men to stay together and not wander off. "We have an hour before we board our flight to Fort Dix. The plane waits for no one, so we need to stick together." As soon as they enter the terminal, a few seek out a restroom, others wander into a gift shop, and others are engrossed in pouring vodka into soft drinks from a bottle smuggled by a recruit named Al Haskins. Micky is finding his overseeing position as fruitless as trying to herd cats. A portion of these boys have little or no regard for Micky's appointment or the conferred authority that goes with it. Those who are compliant are guys who wouldn't have needed supervision to begin with.

Micky is unable to relax. Looking over what's left of his flock, he doesn't recall having anywhere near this kind of angst as captain of the track team. But then, not many of these recruits have been high school athletes or members of any organized team. They consider authority something to be avoided. With the flight time approaching, Micky makes a group effort to reorganize his crew. This is different from his high school leadership experience because there, he didn't have to work at leadership. After all, his school gave him thirteen years to amass a following. He was ranked by his peers as a school big shot. In this case, he has no rank; he's just a nobody that volunteered. Being a nobody is not a status he's accustomed to. In an all-out effort to emulate someone who has rank, he makes his way through the terminal, barking orders at those in his group. "Listen up. We only have fifteen minutes. I need to make a roll call. Go immediately to the boarding gate and wait for me there." He's getting a mixed reaction from an unsmiling ambivalence to an assurance of co-operation. Not certain whether he has rounded them all up, he is aided by the public-address system announcing the plane's arrival: "FLIGHT NUMBER 274 TO TRENTON, NEW JERSEY LOADING AT G GATE." Making a beeline to the "G" gate, he takes a quick roll call. Out of the thirty names he has on his clipboard, twenty-eight are accounted for. Micky is in a near panic. He gives each of the recruits their ticket and orders them to board. He, in turn is quickly determining that it's necessary to make another sweep of the terminal to find the two missing recruits. Burt comes forward to join him. They take opposite ends. Micky has made his way to the outside of the terminal when he spots his two missing recruits. Hollering at the top of his lungs he gets their attention as they are entering a taxi-cab. "Where do you guys think your goin? You got a plane to catch!"

Both turn and look at him as they continue to enter the cab. One of the recruits, named Darnell, hollers back, "You may have a plane to catch, but we're on our way to Canada."

It takes Micky a moment to process what Darnell had just said. In the time it takes him to figure out these two are going AWOL, they and their cab are making their way down the street, soon to be swallowed by traffic. At a total loss as to what he should do, Micky hurries to meet Burt back at gate G, only to discover that the plane has left without them. This is a moment of complete regression for Micky. The color has completely drained from his face. His mind along with his body is totally frozen. Realizing they are stranded, they automatically look to each other for some quick solution. In his entire life, Micky has never failed like this. His body has gone from frozen to shaking. "Burt, what am I gonna do?"

Burt, on the other hand, has never held himself to the same high expectations that Micky has. He shrugs his shoulders and says, "I dunno. Catch the next flight, I 'spose."

Not accustomed to looking to others for answers, Micky catches his reflection in a window. What he sees is a pitiful loser with slumping shoulders. He hates what he sees. In a bold attempt to recompose himself, he strains to pull himself erect. He has had his share of defeats on the football field but always had the luxury of sharing them with his team. This is his alone to deal with, and he knows it.

After speaking with a nice lady at the ticket desk, she assures them they can fly standby. By afternoon, two seats on a flight to Trenton, New Jersey with an arrival in the early evening become available. As can be expected, their plane is late causing them to miss the last bus to take them to Fort Dix twenty-three miles away. This glitch is being corrected by informing them to be ready for the next bus the next morning. They spend the next couple hours pacing around the terminal. They become aware of other young men their age milling around in uniforms while waiting to catch a flight home. They have completed their basic training and are on leave to wait for their orders. Micky can't help but be impressed by the comportment these men have about them, and especially by the crispness of their uniforms and the high gloss shine on their shoes. They seem to stand more erect and tend to portray a confidence he has never seen in anyone his age. With an uncomfortable inferior feeling, he's reluctant to approach any of them, he remains an admirer from afar.

Realizing they are going to spend the night, Micky and Burt select a series of chairs to line up, making them into a suitable bed. Morning arrives. After they seek out a quick breakfast, the next bus arrives as scheduled. The only problem is that Micky's and Burt's seats had been assigned on a previous bus. This means these seats on this bus have all been assigned to others, which additionally implies they'll be obliged to stand for the twenty-three-mile bus trip to Fort Dix. The words spoken to them by an officer after their swearing are coming back to haunt them. He had warned them, "From now on, if you're early, you're on time, if you're on time, you're late, and if you're late, you're as good as dead." With the heavy traffic and the starting and stopping makes the trip nearly intolerable—that is until they disembark. They are soon to understand "intolerable" in a brand-new way. The big welcoming sign reads "WELCOME U.S. ARMY RECEPTION AREA FORT DIX N.J. THE HOME OF THE ULTIMATE WEAPON." Along with a busload of fresh-faced boys, they are suddenly met by several uniformed men with wide-brimmed hats screaming orders at them in a voice none of them had ever experienced in their lives. With this unholy alliance in their face, in truth, there isn't one of them who wouldn't gladly relive the worst experience they have ever endured to escape these gates of hell.

Not certain how they are to inform this screaming, uniformed sergeant that they are a day late and not on his list, they fall in line with all these documented recruits. They are certain that when they're discovered, it will bring a misery they have never experienced. The closest thing either of them have experienced to anything like this is being late for a high school exam.

Burt looks at Micky for his reaction, only to get the full brunt of a disgruntled drill sergeant's spittle in a near insane screaming rage over not keeping his eyes straight ahead as ordered. He's a thirty-something male—imposingly trim without an ounce of fat anywhere on his sinuous frame—outfitted in an imposing, neat, crisp tan uniform, smartly set off with a forward-tilted wide-brimmed hat. Without warning, he leads them off on a near run with another drill sergeant on their sides and one at the rear, all screaming for everyone to hurry faster. When one guy breaks into a dead run, he's stopped and screamed at only one inch from his face. "Who gave you the order saying you could run?! Do you understand that only I am able to give you that very specific order?! Running at the wrong time and in the wrong place can cause casualties! Do you understand?!"

Nearly having a panic attack, the young man says, "Yes sir."

This only serves to enrage the drill sergeant further. Back in his face again in a combination of scream and growl, "Did I just hear you refer to me as 'SIR'?"

At this point, this big, strapping nineteen-year-old former football tackle doesn't know whether he should fight or flee. Instead, he freezes with his only movement being his Adam's apple as he tries to swallow and his eyes blinking involuntarily. His brain is going in overdrive in an attempt to react correctly. In a split second, his brain tells his body to do something he had learned on the football field: he lunges at the drill sergeant as though he were coming off the line. In less time than it takes him to blink, he finds himself lying flat on the floor with the drill sergeant standing over him, holding his arm in a very compromising position with his boot firmly on his larynx. In less than a minute, he is being scooped up by two military policemen who have placed him in handcuffs; they lead him off to the stockade.

It would be an understatement to say this maneuver has a major effect on those who witness it. The drill sergeant continues in a voice meant to get their full attention, and as though nothing significant has happened, says, "I take this moment to inform the rest of you maggots that the only persons you address as 'sir' are officers. I am a sergeant, and I am specifically a drill sergeant. When I give a command and ask if you understand, you will answer in your big boy voice, 'YES, DRILL SERGEANT!' Pausing only a half second, he adds, "IS THAT UNDERSTOOD?!"

"YES, DRILL SERGEANT!" It's the united response of thirty voices.

"Do you understand you are to remain silent unless given a command to respond?"

"YES, DRILL SERGEANT!"

Micky and Burt are discovering that they must listen carefully. It's imperative that their every move complies with a specific set of orders, or they will suffer the consequences. They are catching on to the army way very quickly. Next, they are being led in front of a large garbage can and ordered to line up. The drill sergeant begins, "I am giving you one chance and one chance only to dump anything you have in your possession that is illegal. That includes any drug you may have on your possession without a prescription and weapons, including guns or any kind of knife, be it a switchblade, pocket, or hunting knife. There will be no questions asked if you follow orders. If any of you decide to risk violating this opportunity, you will be sent to the stockade, tried in front of a military court, and sentenced to serve time in a military prison. Do you understand me?!"

"YES, DRILL SERGEANT!"

The process begins with one after another marching by the can and throwing out questionable objects of various kinds. With this process completed, the drill sergeant moves flawlessly to the next order of business. They are taken to get haircuts. Many of the volunteers have arrived with relatively short hair, hoping to give a good impression—but it's not regulation short. This process will take no more than a couple of minutes per recruit. The draftees are the most anxious. Their angst is high; it's as if each is expecting a beheading rather than merely a shaved head. This certainly was not something they had signed up for. They regard this humiliating head shave as just another example of a repressive government walking on their rights. As the barbers peel each head to its bony skull, they have their own methods of entertaining themselves. Burt's hair is almost to his shoulders, and his sideburns are about to engulf the entire side of his face. The barber politely asks him if he would like to keep his sideburns. Since he doesn't have enough hair on his chin to grow a good beard, he has sophomorically let them grow wild. These have been his trademark of late, and Burt can hardly believe his luck.

"Yes, I'd like to keep them," is his grateful answer.

With two quick sweeps of a clipper, both sides of Burt's face lie bare. In another exacting second, the barber has opened Burt's hand and deposits his sideburns with the words, "Here you are, sir." Despite the command for silence, a low snicker moves through the room.

Moving swiftly, they are marched to another building to be fitted for uniforms. After completing this task, they are moved to a barrack that is of a WWII vintage. Here, they are each assigned a bunk and a locker. Next, they are marched down to an area referred to as the "latrine." This is no more than a row of toilets with no dividers and sinks with overhead shiny sheets of polished steel replacing glass mirrors. Another open room at the end of the building supplies them with a half-dozen showers. Most look on with some sense of dread, while some of the southern boys viewed this as an upgrade. If the Army planned this as the great equalizer, they have succeeded.

At five thirty in the morning, they are awakened by an army cadence. Many awake startled, not readily aware of where they are yet. It only takes seconds for the realization that it's not their mother's voice inviting them to a home cooked breakfast, but that of their beloved drill sergeant. "All you maggots have two minutes to make up your beds and present yourselves outside for calisthenics."

Sitting on the edge of his bunk, Burt wipes the drool from his mouth as he simultaneously trips over a pair of combat boots he had not placed far enough under his bed. Micky isn't doing much better;

he's stumbling around in a fog and trying to determine whether to put his pants or socks on first. No one in their barrack is passing muster so far. With more prompting from their drill sergeant, shouting, "Quick! Quick! Quick! Get up and out!" Somehow, the entire barracks manages to be dressed and outside lining up for a roll call. Meantime, the drill sergeant is flipping through papers attached to his clip board. Without warning, he shouts, "ATTENTION!" Among this motley crew, there aren't two that are positioned the same. The only thing that can be said in their defense is that they are at least all erect. The drill sergeant continues. "I will call your name in alphabetical order. When you hear it, without thought or evasion of mind, you will step forward and say the word 'present.' Then you will move to my right and form a line in alphabetical order. Is that understood?"

"YES, DRILL SERGEANT!"

Within sixty seconds there is a line formed. The only recruits who have not stepped forward are Micky and Burt. The drill sergeant's total attention is focused on these presumed interlopers. As they continue to stand at attention, they brace themselves, hoping that somehow this gesture of compliance will ease any earlier infractions. With his hands on his hips and a look of disbelief, the drill sergeant approaches them. Suddenly, he explodes with expletives these two have rarely heard coming from the mouth of an adult. "What #$%& are you &%$#@ idiots doing in my barracks?"

"We missed our plane, drill sergeant," reports Micky in his loudest voice.

Pleased only because he can pass these two "jokers" on to someone else, he says, "Report to the second lieutenant immediately." These are his only words as he walks away.

CHAPTER 7
Advanced Individual Training

After meeting with the second lieutenant and enduring a royal butt chewing, they are sentenced to five days of KP duty—and that's on top of their regular basic training duties. Of the two, Micky is taking this humiliation the worst. Up until now, he's been known for ninety-five-yard run backs or setting new records for track events—and that's just to recall his physical prowess. To demonstrate his intellectual skills, he also headed the debate team and the school newspaper. He's certain that having been captain of every athletic team he's played on demonstrates superior leadership skills. This military life is where he imagined himself floating above all those who had been drafted and brought in fighting and kicking. With the tough encouragement of this drill sergeant, he sees many of these people being propelled into completing tasks better than himself. Now he's enduring the ridiculing eyes of all his peers. The drill sergeant has painted him as "the guy who went on vacation and abandoned his unit." Micky has been on many honor rolls, but at this moment, he's not faring well; he's so far removed from the type of acclaim he had imagined for himself that it's depressing him. The drill sergeant has zeroed in on Micky's self-pity. He's single-minded with his attention. With an uncompromising diligence, he scrutinizes every action Micky takes and measures it for a proper army response. With his nose no more than an inch from Micky's nose, his usual diatribe goes like this: "Knucklehead, are you just plain dumb? There ain't no room for pussies like you in my army! Act like ya got a pair or go home to your mommy! Do you understand?"

"Yes, drill sergeant!" is Micky's response.

Not satisfied he's making his point, the drill sergeant, with nose still nearly touching Micky's yells in a voice designed to get Micky's full attention along with that of everyone in the entire barrack, "DON'T LOOK AT ME, YOU MAGGOT—KEEP YOUR EYES STRAIGHT AHEAD. YOUR MOUTH AIN'T NOTHIN' MORE THAN AN EMPTY

SEWER. THE ONLY WORDS YOU WILL SAY ARE 'YES, DRILL SERGEANT OR NO, DRILL SERGEANT.' DO YOU UNDERSTAND?"

"Yes, drill sergeant," returns Micky.

"YES, DRILL SERGEANT WHAT? THAT YOU'RE A CRY BABY PUSSY?"

"No, drill sergeant, I'm not a cry baby pussy!"

"LOUDER, PUSSY! I CAN'T HEAR YOU! DO YOU UNDERSTAND?"

"YES, DRILL SERGEANT, I UNDERSTAND. NO, DRILL SERGEANT, I AM NOT A CRY BABY PUSSY!"

"THEN LET ME SEE YOUR KILLER FACE!"

Micky still looking straight ahead, contorts his face and mouth agape, and lets out a blood-curdling, "AAARRRGGG!"

"IF YOU THINK THAT WIMPY YELL SCARED ME, YOU'RE DUMBER THAN I THOUGHT. I WANT YA TO DO IT AGAIN!"

This time Micky digs as deep into his gut as he ever has. This time, out of a combination of self-hatred, exasperation, and defeat, he bellows out a "AAAARRRRGGGGGHHHHH!" that would rival a wounded moose.

"You're gettin' better. Keep workin' on it!" With that the drill sergeant turns on his heel and returns to his office at the end of the barrack. His primary mission is to destroy everything within these boys that stands in the way of making a cohesive fighting unit. By becoming the very embodiment of war, he hopes to place his recruits under enough stress to accomplish his mission at the end of their basic training.

Micky is left exhausted, but for some odd reason, he no longer feels like a punching bag. Strangely, he feels much better. It's as though he's given up his former high school status to this ego-crushing, annihilating drill sergeant; he's been freed of all his defiance. Up until now, he has held a private resentment against the army for not recognizing his exceptionality. With this drill sergeant, he's discovering it's easier to comply than fight the system. With this problem resolved, sleep comes quick—and so does morning. Micky really feels like his old self and is ready for whatever is in store today.

He's up, finished with his personal toilet task, shaved, on the field, and ready for roll call and reveille. He's preparing himself for P T. The drill instructor spots Micky already moving in anticipation and without permission: from foot to foot , rolling his head, and shaking his hands out like he's ready to start without his unit. Somewhere from the bottom of his raspy vocal cords, the instructor roars, "THIS IS MY PT, NOT YOURS, PUSSY! YOU'LL PLAY BY MY RULES, NOT YOURS! STAND DOWN, RECRUIT. IS THAT UNDERSTOOD?!'""

Micky boldly responds, "YES, DRILL SERGEANT!" He continues his fidgeting, although he lessens it to a low twitching.

"STAND AT ATTENTION, BUTT WIPE, BEFORE I KICK YOUR PUSSY ASS UP AROUND YOUR NECK AND THEN KICK YOUR FAGGOT HEAD OFF! IS THAT UNDERSTOOD?" roars the drill sergeant with the veins in his neck ready to explode. With very little emotion, Micky snaps to attention. He is finally responding to orders like he would if this were his high school football coach. Still seeing him as a high school preppie, the drill sergeant hasn't grasped that message. Instead, he announces to the whole platoon they are going to have extra PT because of "Miss Murphy's dancing episode."

The next episode is the drill sergeant producing a chair. Looking Micky square in the eyes, he roars, "HAVE A SEAT, MISS MURPHY" Once again, this is not a happening Micky is feeling good about. On the football field, he called the plays. Now he's ordered to sit during the entire PT session and watch as his platoon companions struggle with the extra PT assignment. The drill sergeant begins to explain to his companions, who are already in formation: "Miss Murphy can't seem to pay attention to details. She doesn't seem to care about any of you, so now you can show her how much you care about her by doing her PT while she takes a break." If the drill sergeant is creating this incident to nudge Micky into a sense of common responsibility among his platoon, it's having the proper effect. Micky realizes this is not going to sit well with his squad. They've had a bad feeling about him since the first day. His arrogant self-righteousness is only highlighted by his seeming comfort while sitting in a chair and watching the rest of the platoon go through extra drills because of his behavior. Seeing Micky resting while the other are given his PT is hardly the kind of scenario that attracts comrades. He's felt a kind of rejection by others in not wanting to be around him. More and more, Micky is realizing the need to click with his platoon. For the sake of getting along, Micky is setting aside his arrogant attitude toward the seemingly bizarre orders from his drill instructor—at least for the present, he is finding it easier to obey than to resist.

Burt's reasons for joining the army are not so clear cut. He had experimented with the protest movement and found it to be more party- and drug-driven than he was comfortable with. Besides, he has all sorts of guilt, regret, remorse, sadness, and all forms of unforgiveness towards himself and his parents for his shortcomings. But at this juncture, it's just easier to blame Meadow. *After all, she broke my heart.* Also, Burt doesn't have too far to fall, since his ego is on a much lower level than Micky's. The only high school tribute Burt remembers receiving was that he was a good team player. Either through cowardice or laziness, he has not developed his own talents; he's not sure where this disconnect in his conduct began or will end. Subsequently, he's accustomed to living vicariously through Micky's accomplishments and is willing to wait for Micky's next successful feat—which, despite Micky's depression, Burt is certain will occur.

Micky's next *success* is not about to begin tonight. As a further disciplinary action, Micky is selected to take the "fire watch." This is an old carryover from the days when they heated the barracks with wood stoves and needed a "fire watch" through the night to prevent the building from burning down. Nowadays, it's designed to watch for trainees roaming around without authorization or, in tonight's case, something even more drastic. It's Micky's assignment to watch for any unusual disturbances, including a fire. At midnight, he is alerted to the scuffling sound of some movement at the end of the barrack. Not certain of its cause, he cautiously makes his way in that direction in time to observe a couple of shadowy figures making their way to the stairway leading to the main floor and the outdoor entrance. The door is locked on the inside to prevent unauthorized personnel from entering the building without clearance, but it can be opened from the inside with no problem. In this case, it's a couple of his platoon mates deciding they've had enough of Uncle Sam's armed forces and are deciding to go AWOL (absent without leave). Unconcerned about disturbing the sleep of the rest of the barracks, Micky bolts after them. Unable to identify either of them in the dark, he commands them to "HALT!" They totally ignore him and continue a dead run for the exit. Quickly making his way down the darkened stairway, Micky finds himself soaring headfirst for the last half dozen steps. His next awareness is a medic hovering over him and bringing him to. It seems he tripped on something that had been left on the steps and knocked himself out as he came to a sudden stop at the bottom of the stairway. The other person he becomes aware of his is his drill sergeant standing aside with folded arms and a disgusted look on his face. As soon as the medic okays Micky, the drill sergeant, looking directly at Micky, says, "I don't know why I expected more from your clumsy ass, but from now you're relieved of fire watch. You can bet this is just the beginning for you. Get your ass in your bunk, and I'll deal with you tomorrow." Micky, still in a fog, cannot recall how he ended up in this predicament. First thing in the morning, the drill sergeant is looking Micky over. His left eye is completely swollen shut. "You're lucky, Murphy. I had other plans for you today, but they'll wait, sweetheart. Meanwhile, I'm sending your pitiful ass to report to sick bay. Is that understood?"

"Yes, drill sergeant."

For much of their time spent as trainees, the recruits march everywhere if for no other reason than to reminded them that they are no longer civilians. When they're not marching, they're crawling over, in, and out of every kind of barbed-wired mudhole, practicing the grenade throw or bayonet assault drills over and over, screaming "kill, kill," rope climbing, running obstacle courses, over-head arm walk, and piggyback running. All this occurs under the constant watch of their beloved drill sergeant, whose grating voice is never silent. Just a few weeks ago, there had been as many notions as there were recruits. This training is designed to provoke a common reaction for every circumstance that can and will arise in each of their army careers; they're trained as a common corps to obey and never question orders. Now, with the weeks wearing on, this drill instructor is successfully forming a team where everyone is on the same page; they're becoming a unit that will eventually integrate into every crook and cranny of the United States Army. He's not only eliciting a common response, but also giving them his personal assurance of their fighting skills.

Advanced individual training (AIT) is the next phase of their training schedule. At this stage, each recruit is asked to declare their preference for advanced individual training. The entire platoon has been given a dream sheet; it's designed to give each recruit an opportunity to declare what they want to do. They also are required to take a battery of tests to determine what they are apt to do best. Micky lies in his bed after lights out. He's thinking back to that moment during his high school commencement when he was inspired enough to forfeit his future to the missionary field. Micky can feel a strange sensation rocketing through his body. He fears that it may be some strange kind of sensuous sin that is invading him on his blind side, but then he recognizes it: the simple pleasure of coming to a decision.

For the first time since he arrived here, Micky is content to continue his training. It is when he falls asleep that his contentment soon turns into a nightmare. The drill sergeant enters his dream and is asking him for his dream sheet. Continuing to enjoy the contentment that he had earlier while he was still awake, he hands over the paperwork. In it is his request to work with the chaplains as an assistant. The drill sergeant receives it with a wry glance. Flipping through it, he suddenly explodes. "Murphy, what are ya some kind ah joker, what do ya think ya are? Billy Graham? You're not a pussy! I trained ya to be a killer! Forget this crap! Get out there and kill some gooks!" The nightmare is enough to bring him out of his sleep. He lies blinking for a moment. It's that period of waiting for a discernment of sorts to kick in and tell him he's only dreaming that erases all the pleasure he may have enjoyed earlier. Even after his mind has accepted this as a bad dream, he finds it difficult to fall back to sleep.

The next morning is bright and full of promise. Nonetheless, the lingering dread of having to face his drill sergeant continues to haunt Micky. Despite his recent reconciliation with his platoon and a renewed camaraderie, Micky has a daunting kind of apprehension hanging over himself. *What if he puts me in the infantry? What will I say? What will I do?* The drill sergeant is in his office and is calling them in alphabetically. It seems like it's going to be forever before he gets to the "M's."

Seeking out Burt, Micky confides in Burt concerning his plans. "I ain't surprised, Mick. You always have been a lot churchier than me," is Burt's grinning response.

Taking immediate exception to Burt's description of him as being "churchy," Micky shoots back, "Well, you need to take a good look at yourself and how much you've backslid since we graduated. You could use a first-rate confession of the sinner's prayer yourself, you know."

Burt knows without being told what his weaknesses are and has admittedly struggled with them. He takes a moment to determine how he is going to answer Micky's assault. "Well, you're right, Mick. I have backslid, and I know it, but you're so blasted full of yourself that you can't see your own shortcomings. You can ask anybody in this platoon, and I'll guarantee you they'll tell ya the same thing."

"I don't need anybody in this platoon telling me what I know is right for me. I know I got a calling. For me to ignore it would be for me to disobey God," says a miffed Micky. With that, he turns on his heel and heads back to his bunk to wait his turn. What doesn't surprise Burt is that Micky never asked him what he was requesting on his dream sheet.

The "M's" are finally called. A corporal assigned to arrange the order in which they are called finally calls out, "Murphy." After meeting with Burt, Micky's anxiety level has reached an all-time high. Entering the drill sergeant's office, he feels a lump forming in his throat and the sweat running down from his armpits to his wrists. The sergeant leaves him standing at attention as he mulls through Micky's paperwork. After his dream the night before, Micky can't help but have the feeling he's been here before. After what seems like a lot longer period than it really is, he's almost comfortable not hearing what he suspects is going to be his fate.

Still rifling through Micky's paperwork, the drill sergeant grabs his package of Luckys from his desk. With the dexterity of one who has performed this ritual thousands of times, he flips his Zippo open, lights the end of a fresh white papered fag, and allows a plume of white smoke to swirl above his head. At long last, the drill sergeant looks up from his desk. "What possesses you to believe you are equipped to give spiritual aid and comfort to our troops?"

Without missing a beat, Micky says, "Drill sergeant, I have attended a Christian school my whole school life, and believe I have been called by God to do His work in proclaiming the Gospel of Jesus Christ to sinners."

Unblinking, the drill sergeant remains wide-eyed and silent. Continuing to stare directly at Micky, he says, "I didn't ask you what you were gonna preach. I asked you what makes you think you can give comfort to a frightened soldier."

Micky is doubling down on his resolve. "Drill sergeant, I don't see how preaching the Gospel to a dying man is a bad thing."

After two tours in Vietnam and life-threatening shrapnel injuries both times, the drill sergeant continues his stare. With the decided look of a man who knows more about the work of God in men's lives than most, the drill sergeant says, "Murphy, it's not the dying I'm concerned with; it's those who are going to live and have to face life with broken minds and bodies. How you gonna comfort them?" While Micky is mulling over these words, the drill sergeant ends his dialogue, saying, "Right now, I don't believe you're worth a shit, but I'm gonna grant you your wish. For your advanced personal training, I'm going to recommend you to Religious Affairs and let them deal with you."

Micky can't believe his ears. He had been preparing himself for the worst. "Thank you, drill sergeant. I won't let our country down," he says these words with the same conviction he used to convince his coach of his winning attitude before a game. Closing the door behind him, he immediately feels a sense of joy returning to replace the expected woe.

Right away, Burt notices the pleased look on Micky's face. "Ya got what ya wanted, din ya?"

Relaxed for the first time this morning, Micky says, "Hope to tell ya, I sure did." With that, he returns to his bunk, basking in his success and still not asking about Burt's goals. But then, Burt doesn't expect anything more from Micky than what he gets. Micky has been like this since their first encounter in kindergarten, when he asked Burt if he could have a bite of his apple. Excited to have someone need him, Burt was excited to share. Burt handed Micky the apple and didn't get another bite until all that was left was the core. Their relationship has remained the same since. Burt likes to serve, and Micky likes to be served.

Finally getting to the "W's," the corporal shouts out "Wilson." Taking a deep breath, Burt makes his way to the drill sergeant's quarters. Standing at attention, he patiently waits for the drill sergeant to acknowledge his presence. He's sitting behind his desk. He's not looking up. The drill sergeant is staring at a paper containing an assessment he had made of Burt along with Burt's request. Still not looking up, he says, "It says here you want long-range reconnaissance. Why did you choose that?"

"I believe I can do this, drill sergeant. I've been a team player my entire life," says Burt.

"What if I were to tell you I was going to deny your request and place you in the infantry?" says the drill sergeant, now looking directly at Burt.

"I'd adapt, drill sergeant," says Burt.

"I believe you would, too. Well, I'm not going to do that. I think you're going to make a damn tough soldier. I'm going to approve your request, and I will challenge anybody who opposes the same," says the drill sergeant with an air of respect for Burt and his choice. Now standing, the drill sergeant makes a last comment, "I was in a recon unit myself. Do us proud, soldier." With that, he dismisses Burt.

Back at his bunk, Burt lies silent. He has an amazing recollection. As he had listened to the drill sergeant's encouraging words, a revelation had hit him. It's the kind of truth that has avoided him, just out of reach but visible. *I really don't need Micky, do I?* For the first time in his life, Burt is seeing Micky as flawed—and not just his recent flaws, but those that went all the way back to the kindergarten apple incident. Surer in himself than he has ever been, Burt takes the moment to thank God for the revelation and to ask God to continue to remember him. This is all reminiscent of Burt's simple dependence on a Divine Presence. He never got the grades in religion that Micky did; nonetheless, he has always had a simple, childlike faith in his Creator, so he says a simple thank you for simple things. His final thoughts are of gratitude for this revealing insight. *I wonder why I never saw this before?*

CHAPTER 8
A Bombshell

After thirteen years of unbroken companionship, the time is quickly arriving when Micky and Burt are to begin their Advanced Personal Training. Micky is assigned to a Religious Affairs unit in Fort Hamilton, New York. Burt, on the other hand, having earned a letter of recommendation from his drill sergeant, is being assigned to the United States Army Fifth Special Forces Recondo School Nha Trang located in Vietnam. Their impending separation is dealt without a lot of emotion, although Micky is surprised not to find Burt trotting along behind him to work with the military clergy. For their entire relationship, Micky has come to expect Burt to show up alongside him in whatever direction Micky has taken them. The full impact of this separation hasn't hit either of them at this point. Neither of them can investigate the future to even imagine how this loss of each other's support over such a prolonged period is going to affect them. After their eleven-week boot camp training, both are completely immersed in their own realizations that their own potential and self-confidence can make a better army. They both have come to the realization that they can do a lot more than they had ever imagined with what they have.

Micky has been granted a thirty-day furlough, while Burt will be immediately sent off to Advanced Training. The hour is at hand when the only thing left to do is to say their goodbyes. The confidence both have reaped from their basic training is replacing their adolescent fear of being apart. A new level of maturity is emerging; they are not allowing their different aptitudes to influence their attitudes toward each other. It's culminating in an emerging respect for their individual differences. It appears they have found peace within themselves through their individual decisions and are extending the same peace to each other. Without knowing it, this small consideration is singerly the greatest act either of them has ever performed for the other. Whether this newfound courage has overcome their fear of facing the world without the support of the other is yet to be tested, but for now, they are demonstrating their mastery over any fears of separation. They're taking satisfaction in a kind of reasoning neither had been capable of prior to their military training. It permits them to follow their individual passions without enduring each other's censure.

Taking full advantage of his thirty-day leave, Micky is opting to proudly wear his uniform on his trip home. This is not at all out of character for him; he has always enjoyed setting himself apart from others his age. Once he's home, he intends to maintain his military attitude by continuing to wear his uniform around town. The local anti-war group openly discusses him behind his back.

"You seen that Murphy dude struttin' around town in his fascist uniform. He's so straight, if you had three more like him, you could make a square out of 'em," is what one long-haired anti-war protestor commented as he is exhaling a lung full of pot smoke. Of course, these remarks are made behind Micky's back. Not one of these protestors could stand up to him in a physical confrontation. On the other hand, Micky considers them all to be the anti-Christ and has no problem confronting them head on or referring to them as "commie pinkos." He makes it clear that if he were in a position of Divine power, he'd have them all burning in hell.

Inside Micky's immediate family, a whole new sense of pride has developed; first in Micky's decision to join rather than wait to be drafted, and second in his decision to become a chaplain's assistant. On his first Sunday back at home, Micky decides to wear his dress uniform to church. Both his family's and his church's tradition is to wear one's uniform whenever possible. It almost brings about a feeling of being aristocratic. For those opposed to the war, this ritual becomes a bit blurred. It's not always that they're scornful of the practice as much as they're just plain ignorant of it all. Upon meeting the pastor at the door, Micky lets him know what his army occupation is going to be.

"I always thought of you as someone who would go into the clergy," professes the pastor.

This is the kind of anointment Micky has been hoping to get from somebody. He's hardly aware how effortlessly his sense of self-importance overtakes a major part of his currency.

Another thing occurs on this same Sunday. Carolyn is seated in a pew directly in front of him. He did not say goodbye to her before he left, nor did he write her while in basic training. Even with her back to him, she is as strikingly beautiful as she always has been. Along with this comes Micky's memory of the sweet and sour incident that sent him into the armed services in the first place. His mind is not in a good position to hear much of the pastor's sermon, as his thoughts drift back to all the circumstances of their liaison eleven long ago weeks prior. Without permission, a play-by-play reenactment of the whole affair fills his mind and sets his desire on fire all over again. Reliving the whole experience while sitting in God's house and listening to God's word being preached is creating more inner conflict than he can cope with. Guilt overcomes him to the point where he makes a pretense of having to use the restroom and excuses himself just before the end of the service. But as things always go, Murphy's law has its way. The pastor, seeing him rise, takes the opportunity to bring notice of him to the rest of the congregation.

"If you haven't noticed already, we have one among us who is going to need our support and especially our prayers. He is especially blessed because he has asked for and received his wish to become a chaplain's assistant. It's our own Micky Murphy." With that concluded, he finalizes Micky's recognition by leading the congregation in a standing ovation.

Without a doubt, this is the first time in Micky's life when he became flustered over receiving an accolade. He is desperately trying to avoid Carolyn from seeing him, but now she has turned completely around with a stunned look. She is not applauding and has locked her startled eyes with his. Only the two of them are aware that they are the only two in the whole congregation who have entirely different

71

thoughts. With his cover blown, Micky awkwardly resigns himself to sit back down for the pastor's final blessing, which ends the service.

There are enough people surrounding him with hearty handshakes and pats on the back that Carolyn can avoid an encounter. She quietly slips out before circumstance forces her into a situation she isn't prepared to deal with. Instead, she opts to return home with her family.

When the last person has shared their military experience and given him their blessing, Micky pauses long enough to let his mind shift into another dimension. He turns completely around as though he is expecting something to be there. His mind hasn't caught up with his senses; his eyes scan the nave for Carolyn even after he saw her leave. There is no harmony in his life and thus no happiness as his mind forces him to contemplate how to deal honestly with his and Carolyn's connection. His thoughts are centered but drift off toward making a life for themselves. *I don't know if I'm in love with her or merely infatuated.* Either way, she has become mentally central enough to dominate his thoughts once again. All the confidence he has gained in boot camp is leaving him; he's unsure how to deal with this kind of torment. He's at a total loss as to how to fix this, even though he is fully aware of how he screwed it up. This causes him to freeze in a situation that continues to demand a remedy.

The semester break has brought Carolyn home from college. It's the beginning of the Christmas season, and she has taken a part-time job as a waitress at Greg and Lou's diner, hoping to make enough money to begin the next semester. After seeing her at church, Micky is still wrestling with how to deal with his mixed-up emotions. Unaware of Carolyn's waitress job, he stops by the diner for a sandwich. Plopping himself down on a stool at the counter, he grabs a menu. In the next moment, he hears a familiar voice behind him: "Nice uniform, soldier." Spinning himself around, he sees the only woman in his life who he has carnal knowledge of. Her demeanor is hard for Micky to read. She doesn't look angry or receptive—maybe sad? He's not certain. It's all happening in a split second. He swallows hard as his whole body becomes flushed with a mixture of fear and guilt. Some is for the indiscretion they shared, but more for how he left her stranded to deal with it alone. Something tells him he owes her more than a goodbye. He's just not sure what to say or do. For the moment, he settles on saying, "Thank you. You look great yourself." Rather than this breaking the ice, it seems to have gotten thicker; they both awkwardly try to take this simple greeting to another level.

"Are you home for long?" she asks.

"Thirty-days. Yeah, I got thirty-days," he says, clearing his throat and stupidly nodding his head because he has no idea what to say or do next. "How about you?" he struggles to ask.

"I'm home 'til after the first," she replies, nervously tapping her pencil on the counter.

It's obvious there are some unfinished matters pending between them. It's just unsettling because neither has had this kind of an issue loom over them before, and they have no idea what to do with it. Carolyn, seeing the menu still stuck in Micky's hand, takes advantage of it as a diversion to move the conversation in another direction.

"Know what you want yet?" she asks, still tapping her pencil.

"Oh, just bring me a grilled cheese and a coke." He has relaxed just enough to notice how grateful he is to have stumbled across her this easily. He had been dreading how he was going to connect with her and was at a loss as to how to do it. While she turns to take the order to the kitchen, it gives him time to think about what his next move should be. He's quite certain the ball is in his court to come up with something; it's just mystifying him what that something should consist of. The problem is soon solved when Carolyn turns and asks with a straight face, "You want it cut with stars or hearts?"

Her humor catches him completely off guard. It takes a moment for his mind to trip over her lampoon. He's relieved enough at her wittiness to respond, "One of each."

A smile from each is suddenly replacing any words that could have been said to produce the same result. This is not to say all things

73

are fine between them, but it's an easier effort to launch a new beginning under a softer premise. Micky's fear is quickly replaced with a positive feeling. Their mutual decision to continue this opportunity to rectify their earlier unseemly behavior is gaining a momentum. Trying to deny its impact on them is imprudent. They have been engendered with the absolute that the only time intercourse is permissible is within the bond of marriage. Neither is prepared to defend the secular world's nonchalant attitude toward this holy tradition.

Micky and Carolyn agree to meet after Carolyn's shift is finished. Micky has returned home long enough to wash and wax his '57 Mercury convertible Turn Pike Cruiser. When he excitedly returns, he finds Carolyn waiting at the diner entrance. She is noticeably tired after carrying trays of food all morning and afternoon. Strikingly, it has produced a kind of relaxed beauty Micky has not seen in her. With his eyes firmly fixed on her, in a smooth move, he meets her at the passenger side with her door open. This habit is very firmly fixed in his person having been taught him by his mother on how to treat a lady.

It's a brisk December day with a bright sun and clear blue skies—rare for this part of the northern hemisphere. But with the sun lower in the sky bringing shorter days, it's beginning to cast a shadow. With no particular plan, Micky begins to drive. He finds it as difficult as he always does to initiate a conversation with the opposite sex. He generally has a disconnect with anyone who is not interested in his agenda. Until his connection with Carolyn, he found girls to be boring. This is one time he doesn't want to mess it up with uninteresting conversation. The silence is deafening. As a former cheerleader, Carolyn finds it less cumbersome to act lively, but work has exhausted her. The silence has become too conspicuous to bear. In an effort to relieve the growing awkwardness, they both burst out with words over the top of the other. This produces a giggle from each of them as they catch themselves doing it a second time. It's enough to put them

74

at ease. In a rare moment of soul-searching, Micky says, "I know we got some talking to do, but I'm not certain how or where to begin."

In a moment of intense introspection, Carolyn has teared up. With her mouth agape in a funny, twisted way and not wanting her mascara to run down her face, she dabs the corners of her eyes with a tissue. She returns to her previous silence. Looking at her disquiet and realizing how this meeting is affecting her, Micky feels an infrequent tinge of compassion. This nuance causes him to make a left turn, leading to a city park. He slowly makes his way to the edge of the river that winds its way around and through the community. Parking the car at the river's edge, he places his arms around Carolyn, hoping to demonstrate his concern and maybe be of some comfort to her in her distress. The sunlight dances from ripple to ripple as the river forces itself through a rocky formation. Experiencing this simple occasion together with the car's heater fan making a mesmerizing hum allows another silence to be acceptable. With a wordless gesture, Micky places his fingertips to Carolyn's chin, gently turning her head toward him. Once her lips are in position, he softly presses his to hers. The moment is electric as it surges a flush of pleasure through each of their bodies, raising their passion to significant highs. This is not something they are prepared for. It's coming about so soon. It's catching them both off-guard enough to wonder what this will ultimately lead to. The pent-up passion is not about to release itself without a break in its intensity. Carolyn is the one to suggest they take a walk. Hardly able to remove himself from her side, Micky hesitantly agrees.

The air takes on a bite as the orange sun lowers into the horizon. Still flushed with passion, they barely notice the cool bite of the December air. Small talk is coming a little easier than an hour ago. As they hold hands and walk, they are very conscious of considering how to become part of each other's life, and not certain where exactly or where these feelings are going to take them. Feelings and emotions are flying at nearly a Mach pace. Stopping every few steps to kiss, they can feel each other's cold noses against their hot skin. There is something they both sense as enduring within these sensations. Neither is looking on these as passing fancies, but they are becoming more certain that they are intuitions that need to be valued. They are each living with the knowledge that they have already opened a door within their relationship that cannot be closed and reopened after they have chosen their life's mate. Within the context of their religious training, they have already violated one of its long-held sacred tenets to remain celibate until marriage. It's been long understood that the meaning of things is not in the things themselves, but in our attitude toward them. It's obvious that their own convictions are struggling to compel their thoughts. Like most choices, theirs are held in the grips of passion or reason. Which of these is chosen will compel their next action. They have readily experienced living with the guilt of violating their core convictions, and they fear it's about to happen again.

Amid their passion, Micky and Carolyn are discovering they're on trial once again to either give in to the power that is saying *You both know these feelings need to be acted on. After all, you do love each other, don't you? How can something that feels so right be so wrong? Do you really want to look back on this opportunity and realize how wonderful it could have been if you hadn't been so afraid to live it?*

At this young age, they are capable of realizing that the strongest principle of their maturity lies in their choices. They have each had a similar religious training and have been strong advocates to maintain its tenets in their everyday lives. Right or wrong in someone else's belief system, theirs refuse to be compromised.

Holding her tight, Micky continues to struggle with his overwhelming desire to have everything Carolyn is, including her body. Very much aware that he's lost this battle once before, Micky is struggling with attending the lessons he learned from it. This desire demands action. There can be no happiness without action, but this doesn't guarantee happiness will always follow if the choice is wrong. Either they pull back at this point, or they suffer the consequences. It would be an understatement to say their limitations have been tested;

they are at the brink, and they know it. Whether or not they restart is up for grabs.

Carolyn, in turn, is not faring any better. She realizes that the seemingly heavenly feelings gripping her at this moment *are* going to turn on her tomorrow and become her hell. She has experienced enough already to have these authoritative second thoughts banging against the sway of passion. It's Carolyn who pushes Micky away, saying, "I can't do this again and try and live with myself. It's been too much."

In a rare moment of unselfishness, Micky realizes a potential he didn't possess several months ago. "Okay. You're right, Carolyn. I love you, and I can't, either." He pauses for a moment and then adds a bombshell. "What do you say we get married?"

This is not the reaction Carolyn was prepared for. She thought this would be the furthest thing from Micky's thoughts. This is catching her completely on her blindside, and it shows in her reaction. Even though these are moment-sized pieces of life, Micky is throwing, she didn't see this one coming. Up until now, she has been concerned not to lose herself in the passion of the moment. Now she's confronted with seizing a moment she has not envisioned. This could indeed be the panacea to end her worry of remaining celibate until marriage. This worry is draining her of her strength, and now Micky is providing a way out. After all, it isn't as though she has never met him; she has had a crush on him since their freshman year. Now his love is being thrown at her, and all she needs to do is make it her choice. She knows the only thing that will prevent her from fulfilling this dream is her. Taking a minute to process what he is propositioning, not willing to sit on this proposal any longer, she breaks out in the common language all the world understands—a smile. Venturesomely, she grabs him. Pressing her body and her lips against his, she breathlessly replies, "Yes!"

"How about tonight?" adds a clearly delighted Micky. After all, it's in moments like this that destinies are shaped. This is exactly the kind of outlook both have been looking for; it promises to end their quandary and bring happiness.

"I would if we could," says a beaming Carolyn.

This reaction is as though it is coming from a blind person who is suddenly able to see, not with merely her eyes, but with her heart. It has been said that "The most beautiful things in this world cannot be seen or heard, but must be felt with the heart."

With the inevitable indiscretion put on hold, they spend the rest of the evening with lighthearted talk and giggles. It's the kind of laughter that accompanies a decision that has been settled and is now behind them.

CHAPTER 9
Victory Belongs to the Most Persevering

Meanwhile, Burt is ten thousand feet above the Pacific Ocean in an army transport plane to Da Nang, Vietnam. The trip is long, tedious, uncomfortable, and incredibly boring. He has played all the euchre a person can stand and has finally resigned himself to sitting with his arms crossed and his eyes closed in the hope that he can fall asleep and wake up at their destination. Thoughts of home dominate his thinking. Even though he and Meadow were never what could be regarded as an "item," he can't help but let her dominate his attention. He has her high school senior photo, and he periodically stares at it as though she has become his link between home and here. It's an odd fixation, but it's effective.

Burt's mind wanders from one line of thought to another. Finally, it makes its way to questioning his motive behind asking for recon. *After all, there are so many other positions I could have asked for. Why did I choose this one?* Micky is suddenly brought to the forefront of Burt's mind. *I wonder what Mick is doing?* This thought lays bare another realization. It's a sense of alienation—a strange kind of loneliness that has accompanied him all the way through his school days. Attaching himself to Micky always allowed Burt a reprieve. To his consternation, he has witnessed first-hand how the army looked at Micky's high school successes. They had not been in the least impressed by Micky's high school resume—all that stuff stayed back in the halls of academia. Nonetheless, to have Micky jerked from under him leaves Burt feeling a kind of separation anxiety. Self-doubt has its way of raising its ugly head. The army is supplying Burt with the opportunity to meet the enemy—not only those in Vietnam, but also those lodged in his mind. It's pretty much agreed that technically, high school ends with graduation, but "technically" doesn't translate to completely eliminating it in one's personality or behavior.

This opportunity to train as a reconnaissance soldier is affording Burt the probability that he will become his own man. It has never been a secret; he has always hoped to be more like Micky. Living vicariously through Micky's accomplishments has afforded Burt the luxury of never having to develop his own endowments— that is, until now. In the insightful words from his captain spoken at his basic training graduation, "Be the best *you* you can be—everyone else is taken." Intellectually, Burt understands this, but his relationship with Micky goes much deeper. Despite their differences, when the chips were down, they have always come through for one another. Now they are apart, left to follow their individual destinies. On the one hand, Burt is adjusting to this, but on the other hand, it's proving to be a whole new world—certainly a world he never knew.

Burt is jostled awake by the distinctive screech of the plane's tires contacting a concrete air strip. Within minutes, the plane has taxied to its designated disembarking ramp. Making his way to the open door at rear of the plane, his nostrils suck in the first waft of Vietnamese air. It's made up of high heat and the pungent stench of human excrement and rot. It's night, and the sky is not a color Burt has ever seen before. It's a blue-black hue with sporadic flashes of heat lightning lighting up a surrounding field of helicopters, making them appear like giant gilded dragonflies. Burt's eyes continue to scan the landscape. He sees nothing here that has any familiar appeal. *Is this the hellhole we all come to die for?* It's an inescapable mindset. He is quickly becoming aware that the military axiom "adapt and overcome" is going to be much more pervasive than anything he's dealt with thus far.

They are quickly marched off the transport plane to waiting helicopters prepared to carry them to their designated locations. This is all done with army precision, leaving personnel to constantly deal with redundant delays. There are three soldiers already seated and waiting in the cargo hold of the helicopter. Burt hurriedly throws his gear in and joins the others in biding their time. But as all things go in Uncle Sam's military, they are soon rushing as fast as the machine permits to meet the next deadline and begin the waiting process all over again.

Within the hour, the helicopter is on a landing pad in a coastal air base named Cam Rahn near Nha Trang. Now they wait for trucks designated as troop carriers to carry them to the base. The army has an unwritten equal time rule that says the time spent waiting must equal the time spent traveling. These stops have at least permitted these four soldiers to become familiar. Burt is from Michigan, Herb "Buck" Morris is from Harlan County, Kentucky, Jim "Quincy" Standridge is from Alabama, and Robert "Bob" Kovich is also from Michigan. They're all the same age except for Buck, who's a couple years older. All four of them have had their basic training at different bases, and all four have come with recommendations from their superiors. There is an immediate sense of comradery that they hadn't had with others in basic training. Their personalities are definitely individual but also open to making team efforts. Maybe because Buck is older, they automatically give him a kind of leadership status. Even with this early pecking order, the thing on each of their minds is whether they can live up to their glowing recommendations. This concern is soon mired in getting their bunks arranged and getting fitted with new uniforms. They are now members in training of the Fifth Special Forces Division Nha Trang Vietnam.

Motivation is not a problem for any of these men. They have entered this elite training with all-star records and appear prepared to take on whatever tasks they are required to complete. It's not referred to as "special combat training" without reason. This very specialized long-range reconnaissance patrols (LRRP) reconnaissance duty calls for engaging the enemy in close combat. Only those who are prepared to kill or be killed find themselves drawn to this duty. They have passed all the entrance exams, are eligible for special training, and will have every chance of surviving. Often, this work will go above and beyond the call of duty. This training, which is often referred to as "Spartan *agoge*" training," takes risks far beyond conventional units by going deep into enemy territory, where discovery means death. While spying on the enemy in his own backyard, the "LRRPs" become the eyes and ears of a division. They are the first guys in to determine whether a platoon or a division is needed to send in the guys with the rucksacks, steel pots, and M-16s—the grunts.

On a moment's notice, they must be prepared to return fire with the weaponry of a platoon with only four to six men. Unlike other special forces, they are not to be known. Because of need, some division commanders developed conventional recon units, but they are not nearly as sophisticated or as well trained. This school is three weeks of eighteen-hour days. With full packs, ammunition belts fully loaded, and enough full water canteens to drown an elephant, they're expected to run seventeen miles every day. They were told they needed to anticipate what they may be facing by thinking like the enemy—especially when it comes to where they may expect booby traps.

Barely given enough time to recover from the daylong travel, they are confronted with the first phase of their training regimen. "Report at twelve hundred hours at the airborne field," is an order from a sergeant. *He who questions orders is the first one killed* was an axiom they learned in boot camp; it resonates with them now. Without question, they report as ordered.

To begin the program, they are required to march to the field and perform a fitness test to prove they are physically fit enough to continue. These four have no problem completing this leg of training. Something about this program also obliges one to become a drinker. Burt soon learns that airborne school is also a drinking fest. Of course, this is a brand-new experience for Burt. However, he is willing to catch on and must admit he enjoys the drinking part—it's the hangovers that he objects to.

Next, they begin learning the very basics of parachute packing and proper landing. Excellence is demanded. Indecision is viewed as the enemy of courage and must be eliminated. Every part of this program is designed to rely on their training and to build muscle memory so every phase is completed as efficiently as possible. Facing the 250-foot jump tower standing as ominous as a hangman platform, it's understood that one must become brave by performing brave actions, and "being airborne is not a right; you have to earn it." This mantra is heard over and over until the whole person becomes its truth. There is no room for mistakes, from packing the parachute to deploying a successful landing. After baby stepping through overcoming fears of jumping out of a plane a thousand feet in the air and mitigating any problems during the descent is finished, the soldier either conquers his fears or drops out. After five successful jumps by the end of the week, Burt, Buck, Quincy, and Bob are still very much in the running.

With no break, phase II begins. It's team week. It's designed to build a team where individual strengths and weakness are assessed and form a bond of trust in each other's capabilities. Burt's team includes himself, Buck, Bob, and Quincy. They are ordered to carry a three-hundred-pound log for seven miles on the first day. On another day, they are required to move a barrel full of rocks twelve miles. Then they're given a road march with full packs for twelve miles—to be finished in no more than four hours and twenty minutes. In testing their problem-solving skills, they are given a jeep with only three wheels and ordered to make it ten miles in an allotted time.

Phase III begins today; it involves engineering. They learn how to blow stuff up. It's also time to assess their readiness for combat. To accomplish this exercise, they are expected to scale their way up a nearby mountain in the dark while remaining undetected. What happens next is not expected. After reaching the top, they are met with a barrage of artillery and rounds from a fifty-caliber machine gun going off all around them. At this point, a momentary confusion takes place, followed immediately by Buck shouting, "Take cover!" Not able to discern at this point if it is incoming fire or outgoing, they dive for cover. Burt can feel his heart going at least a hundred miles an hour. *God help me if this is how to war.* This is his first thought. Then, nearly automatically, he calls out for the others' positions and begins to crawl just like he had learned in basic. It's mainly muscle memory. Buck is assuming his unofficial leadership position. "Anyone wounded?" he barks. No comment. "Sound off," Buck says with a commanding voice.

Satisfied everyone is safe, he calls for everyone to regroup. Burt has already crawled his way across a rough terrain and reached Buck's position along with the other two. The automatic weapon firing has ceased. Having been sent on this training mission with only a .45-caliber pistol, this assault is totally unexpected. They had been assured this was a secure position; having an assault on their hands now is a total game changer. Buck has morphed very quickly into complete battle mode. "We're meeting a force unit and need to move fast, but for certain we gotta get a handle on what's goin' on here." Considering they are a long-range reconnaissance patrol and are often expected to engage the enemy in close combat, they begin a strategic offense. Without question, they are aware that this is a situation where the enemy may have an advantage. Their entire training has taught them to be prepared to kill or be killed. The team has reorganized and is making some assessments. Buck is the first to speak. "I don't believe we're under attack by more than a small caboodle. There was only the one big gun. I didn't hear any small arms goin' off."

Burt agrees. Pointing to a position over his shoulder that's barely discernable in the dark, he adds, "I couldn't tell at first where the shots were comin' from until I spotted the muzzle fire comin' from that small clump of trees. I agree with you, Buck. The lack of small arms fire tells me the same thing. It's a small corps—maybe just two: one to feed the gun and one to do the shootin'."

Everyone agrees to move on to the next step: search and destroy. With a plan quickly assembled and wanting to take advantage of the small amount of darkness left, they begin making a slow crawl to gain what advantage is available over their assailants. Burt is the first to arrive at the position where he saw the blaze emit from the gun's barrel—it's abandoned. Hundreds of spent rounds litter the ground. His breath surges in rushed bursts as his eyes quickly scan the area for any movement. He spots Quincy and Bob on his left flank and Buck on his right. All four carefully assess the situation. Buck makes a hand movement indicating the need to widen their perimeter to scout for evidence of a merely pulled back enemy. Within a half hour of surveillance, they rejoin and arrive at the same conclusion: the area is abandoned. The next step is to map out a course of action. Buck is the first to speak. "I think you're onto somethin', Burt. If there was more than a couple of 'em, they wouldn't be runnin'. I think we need to follow these guys and take 'em out." The others agree.

In their world, retreat is not an option. Their thoughts quickly gather around how best to achieve their goal and take out the enemy. They rapidly map together a plan and begin a course of action. Once finished, everyone knows the place they need to fill, and every piece needs to fit into their overall strategy. Taking notice of the torn-up ground where the weapon had been mounted, Quincy points out, "We can track these guys. They had to drag that weapon up here, and they gotta drag it back. All we gotta do is pick up their trail and make sure we don't get shot doin' it."

With the mindset of fighters and their confidence bolstered, Burt volunteers to take point. He will lead them out by twenty yards, always within eye sight of the others. He can't help but feel his life being measured in the number of breaths he takes; he's never certain how many he has left. The vagueness of a lurking enemy is keeping their minds, eyes, and ears focused. They keep in mind the very specific threat made against them a couple hours ago in the uncertainty of the morning darkness. Even so, their hope is in their superior training. They're making each moment count. With the advent of daylight, they are certain that with a careful strategy, they will become the hunters instead of the hunted. Individually, their courage is strong, but it's even stronger when buttressed by the devotion they each possess for the others' wellbeing. Some may refer to this as a kind of simplistic hope, but with these men, it's more of an awareness of its truth than hope; it's an understanding without words and buried deep within the soul. There is no doubt in each of their minds that they have the skill set to succeed or die trying. With this kind of optimism providing the very meaning in their lives, they take each step believing they are that much closer to their goal.

The jungle path they are following is well worn, so it must be well used. There are definite signs indicating this seeming enemy has used this trail a considerable number of times. This is giving Buck some concern. He feels they could be walking into a trap. As he is mulling this thought over, Burt's hand waves off to the side as he barks, "Hit the dirt!" They instinctively dive into the jungle cover on each side of the road. Just as the men react, a volley of .50-caliber rounds flies over them. Burt remains low and undercover until the blasts have stopped. Carefully and slowly, he begins a crawl through a tangle of plant life in the direction of the gunfire, turning his head only enough to catch a glimpse of Bob and Quincy trailing along behind. With the assurance of their support and his lead position, Burt continues his pursuit. With his .45 in hand, he crawls a few feet only to stop and assess the situation once again and again until he is within twenty feet of where the gunfire had been initiated. At this point, a voice calls out in a hushed tone, "Hold your fire!" Burt recognizes it as Buck's voice. He's positioned himself behind a tree and called out to prevent them from sending their own volley of flying lead.

"How'd you get here before me?" says a surprised Burt, also following Buck's lead using a hushed voice.

Waiting for Quincy and Bob before he makes another move, Buck steps out from behind his jungle rampart. "I made a half circle hoping I could come up behind them." I managed to get a glimpse of them as they were scurrying down the path. But here's the clincher— they didn't look like gooks—they were too tall. Besides, gooks aren't dumb enough to try and outrun a patrol pushing a 50 cal."

Pausing long enough to give Buck's assessment a moment, Burt replies, "Well, who else could it have been?"

With the same assured demeanor, Buck says, "It's our own guys."

A look of bewilderment comes over the others' faces. Quincy speaks up. "What? Are they tryin' to kill us? This don't make no sense!"

"I don't believe they're gonna kill us, but I think they're puttin' it to us like a test of some kind," says Buck. Not even the impact of being shot at hits them as hard as this statement from Buck.

Burt is the first to respond. "These guys are probably thinkin' they're gonna make us crack. We gotta come up with somethin' to put an end to this BS."

Buck is pulling out the map they were given. "I think I know where they are headin'. They gotta stay on this path to keep that gun from tanglin' in the jungle." Pointing to a location on the map, he continues. "This is where we are right now. This is where I believe they're headin'." Pointing at a point on the map that doesn't indicate a trail, Buck goes on. "We can get off this trail, make our way through the jungle, and cut them off if we go double time."

Seeing this as a strong option, the others brace for an alternate route that will prove to be the most challenging task they've taken on during this whole fiasco. Taking advantage of a nearby stream, they resupply their canteens, dropping an iodine tablet in each to purify the water. Quickly devouring a C-ration, then check their compass position and head into the jungle. The estimation is a mile before they will overtake the opposition, but it's not a mile of open fields. It's going to be a mile of some of the roughest terrain in the region. The heat is also beginning to rise as they are now at a lower elevation than they were earlier this morning. Without a word, they prepare themselves to adapt to and overcome any difficulties that threaten to hinder their objective. Each man is willing to go the distance. Being fully engaged in their purpose gives them an unquestionable incentive to challenge the unlikelihood of overtaking their nemesis and neutralizing it regardless of the physical difficulty. They're in the best physical condition they've ever been in, and they're pushing their limits to get through the heat, rock, and jungle overgrowth. If the enemy is proving to be rated as a ten on a scale of one to ten, the jungle is proving to be a twelve on the same scale.

Before an hour has passed, they come across an open area that exposes the trail. Just as they had expected, four American GIs are struggling with an oversized .50-caliber machine gun. Still well concealed, the four pursuers stop for a moment. Each gazes across the open field through field glasses. What they are observing is the other four setting up another parapet for the big gun. From where they stand, it appears to be a sergeant and three enlisted men. A smile comes across Buck's face as he watches these opponents preparing to terrorize himself and his three comrades once more. Delighted they have succeeded in catching this break, they remain concealed like stealthy voyeurs. Still smiling, Buck says, "These guys don't know what they're in for. I've got a plan that will ensure we get our next stripe." The others are all ears as he explains what he has in mind. Convinced Buck has a workable plan, they're eager to get started. Buck leaves them with one more of his sayings that he credits his grandfather for originating: "The results we achieve is gonna be directly proportional to the amount of effort we apply."

The plan begins by taking some of the water they have left to make mud. They apply it all over any exposed skin. This seemingly insignificant gesture is enough to give each of them a chilling appearance. The next step is to surreptitiously crawl through approximately six hundred feet of elephant grass to an area behind these antagonists. Each of them has assigned themselves to one of these opponents. Successfully reaching the target area without being detected, they regroup for the next phase. They are now behind and within twenty feet of their objectives, who have clustered around their gun. It's difficult to hear what they may be saying, but their low chortle makes it clear they are enjoying what they are doing. It's obvious they are expecting to see this group of initiates trying to sneak down the trail and are prepared to throw another harrowing encounter their way.

Buck is using finger gestures to count down from five. As soon as the last finger goes down, the four of them blast out of the undergrowth all together with a battle cry designed to waken the dead. In a coordinated fashion, each grab their designated mark from behind with a .45-caliber handgun against his temple, barking, "ON

THE GROUND, ASSHOLE!" It's clear this troupe has been caught completely by surprise, finding themselves face down in the dirt at the hands of trainees. Their hands are quickly bound using their own belts. They are completely disarmed. Buck is the first to jerk his oppressor to his feet. It proves to be the sergeant leading this debacle. There is no doubt this crew is shocked at how quickly they went down. They never expected this turn of events that has them so unquestionably held helpless by a foursome of neophytes; they realize these mud-faced warriors are no longer under their management in any way. Not able to use his hands, the sergeant is coughing and spitting in a near futile attempt to free his mouth of the dirt that had been driven in when his face hit the ground. The others aren't in much better shape as they are also jerked to their feet, stumbling.

"Y'all make one wrong move, and y'all gonna go through life with no nose, 'cause I'll blow it off your stupid face. Y'all get what I'm tellin' ya?" says Buck, pressing the barrel of his .45 against the nose of the sergeant.

It would be an understatement to say this sergeant hasn't regained any type of "sergeant decorum." There is no doubt he is fully aware that he is now completely at the mercy of this squad of novices. This defeat is pressing hard against the craws of these seasoned soldiers. This sergeant is frantically aware of the consequences he will certainly undergo if word of this turnaround reaches his captain. Regaining a small portion of his dignity, the sergeant makes a very respectful plea. "You boys know that I am only doing a job my captain ordered done. What's it going to take for this all to go away?"

Hearing this truly humble plea, Buck pulls Burt, Quincy, and Bob aside. After a quick conference, they return. Buck takes the lead. "I want you to write in your own handwriting what happened to you today by the four of us—and sign it along with these other goons. I'll then hold it 'til I see the glowin' report you write our captain about the more than professional way we met our challenges. Also, we want your recommendation that we receive our sergeant's stripes. Make sure you use a lot of words like 'valor', 'courageous', 'boldness', 'fearlessness', an' maybe 'gallant'—I've always liked that word."

Listening to this reasonable request, the sergeant gladly agrees. Loosening his bindings, Burt comes up with a pencil and the blank side of his map. The sergeant readies himself to begin his atonement. Buck is looking over his shoulder as he begins. The sergeant makes his first sharp-tongued objection. "I can't do this if you're gonna stand over my shoulder!"

"I just wanna make sure you get the words 'totally duped' into the concession."

The sergeant stares at Buck with that look that says *How'd I ever get tied up with this guy?* All the same, he regains his focus and takes the next twenty minutes to complete the document. As he hands it to Buck, he seems to feel the same worry a student feels when handing in a test. The sergeant obsequiously stands aside while nervously blinking as Buck reviews his summary. Finishing his appraisal, Buck produces a big smile and a slap across the sergeant's back, saying, "Ya done good, Sarge! Couldn't've done it any prouder if I'd wrote it myself." With a stern look, Buck folds this acknowledgement and places it in his pocket, saying, "Y'all gonna get this back when we get our stripes."

They've said everything that needs to be said and have come to a quick, conclusive agreement to go their separate ways. By late afternoon, Burt, Buck, Quincy, and Bob return to the base, ready to give an accounting for what they were intended to believe was enemy fire. The sergeant and his enlisted men come in from another direction and are also expected to spend the next hour before chow filling out a report detailing their account.

Within a few days, all reports are in and have been reviewed. Burt, Buck, Quincy, and Bob find themselves being ordered to report to the captain's office. After being escorted by a corporal into the captain's presence as a single patrol unit, they make a smart salute, after which they are told to stand at ease. The captain is behind his desk with elbows resting on its surface, fingertips touching fingertips, staring first at one and then another of them. Finally, he forms some words. "I've been in this army for twenty years. In that time, I have reviewed hundreds of reports involving men doing what you men are doing. I've yet to see a summary as glowing as this one. Either you're God's gift to the United States Army, or you've pulled off one of the smoothest scams I've ever encountered." With these words spoken, the captain ceases speaking and continues to stare at these depicted supermen with a suspicious eye. Not seeing anything in their demeanor to cause him to substantiate his suspicions, he moves on. "If my sergeant didn't have such an impeccable record in dealing with these matters, I'd throw your asses out of here and consider this whole matter as so much BS. For the present, I have little choice other than to turn this report over to the review board. With all that's been included in this, I doubt there will be any problems in your promotions to sergeants."

It's all the team can do to maintain a demeanor of military decorum while they listen to this captain. As soon as they are dismissed and out of earshot, they let out a whoop that can be heard in Saigon. When they arrive back at their barracks, they're not surprised that the sergeant and his three enlisted thugs are waiting for them to return.

"Okay, wise guy. Ya got what ya wanted. Now I want what you got," is the anxious demand from this impatient sergeant.

"Yeah, yeah! Don't wet your pants 'til the water comes. I got it right here," Buck says, retrieving a folded map from his hip pocket.

Belligerently, he snatches the paper. Quickly and wordlessly, he unfolds it to verify its authenticity. With nothing more than a "Hurumphh," he holds the flame from his Zippo to the underside. In a couple seconds, he drops the charred remains at Buck's feet and walks away. Buck takes a moment to kick the remainder of the ashes around the floor before jubilantly high-fiving his crew once again.

CHAPTER 10
Angola

Carolyn has met strong opposition from her family in bringing up her and Micky's nascent idea to wed before he ships out to Vietnam. Micky isn't getting a much better reaction from his family, either. This puts the ball firmly in Carolyn's and Micky's court. "This is a real bummer," laments Carolyn. "I can't believe my family sometimes."

"Ya, tell me about it. I'm not getting any cooperation from my parents, either. They say we hardly know each other. I told them I've known you since we were little. Still sticking to their guns, they blew my argument off."

They are sitting in Micky's car at their favorite spot down by the river. It's here, alone, where they are inclined to let their passions get the best of them. Micky still has a couple weeks left before he's shipped out and deployed in Vietnam. Micky's been rolling something over in his head for the last couple days. After a session of heavy petting in which things have definitely heated up, he says, "What do ya say we just elope and let the chips fall where they may?"

Barely able to say "no" any longer to her scandalous desires, with a flushed-red face, Carolyn gives way, saying, "It sounds good to me, but how do we make *that* happen?"

This is the moment Micky's been waiting for. In a heartbeat, he has picked up her agreement. "Do you remember Darrel Traub from our class?" Without waiting for her answer, he continues, "He knocked up Jan Jackson our senior year. They eloped one day without anyone finding out about it until they were ready to tell. When her parents discovered she was pregnant, they had a cow until they showed them their marriage license."

Carolyn is listening intently. In all truth, if anyone had told her a month ago she would be having this conversation, she would have dismissed them as being out of their mind. But this evening, this possibility is working its way around in her mind in a way she had never imagined. "What if we get married like that and people think it was because I was pregnant?" she protests.

Mustering up a very cavalier voice, Micky says, "What do we care? We're not in high school any longer. Let 'em talk."

Carolyn finds it comforting to let Micky take the lead on this. In some ways, she feels it's traditional. Thinking back to Darrel and Jan, her only question becomes, "Where did they go?"

"Angola, Indiana," is Micky's authoritative answer. "We don't need blood test or a three-day waiting period. We can leave tomorrow morning, be there by noon, married by twelve-thirty, and back home in time for supper."

"Does this mean that we're engaged?" she asks in a voice too feigning to take seriously.

Pausing long enough for the thought to take hold, and with a little knowing smirk, Micky says, "If you can't wait long enough for me to buy you a ring, I'll say, "Yes indeed, Miss Carolyn, we are truly engaged."

Carolyn finds she is willing to follow Micky's lead to the point where she lets him take their passion a step further than she has prior to this conundrum being solved. They both have a wordless accord thus far that it's probably okay now that they have decided to get married. With the evening coming to an end, they reach a decision that despite this stronger commitment to one another, they need to marry as soon as they can arrange it; they have discovered after the fact that the guilt of unmarried sex is still there. Under their post-orgasmic scrutiny, their nineteen years of Christian influence is not so willing to be compromised; engagement is only engagement, and marriage is still marriage.

After a restless night, their realities come to the forefront—it's a mixture of apprehension and excitement. *Apprehension*, in the sense that this determination is a clandestine effort to circumvent the wishes of their parents—and *excitement* in the idea of daring to go forward with an unconventional approach to something as divine as marriage.

Under the guise of going to the city to Christmas shop, Micky stops by to pick up Carolyn early enough to meet her father leaving for work. A few pleasantries are exchanged. The feeling of being a thief suddenly overwhelms him. *I'm stealing his daughter.* It's truly a disturbing thought. Faced with this reality brings on a smudgy feeling of dishonesty. Nonetheless, as soon as Carolyn appears behind her father and, complicit as Micky is in this deception, it brings about a feeling of camaraderie with their dishonesty. Knowing they have the full support of one another, the decision he and Carolyn made to go it their own way is quickly reinforced and just as quickly followed by a dispassion for their parent's concerns.

He has a tank full of gas and the hundred and thirty dollars he has managed to save over his lifetime tightly packed away in his pocket. She forces a nervous smile as he opens the drivers-side door for her. She hops in moving only far enough to allow him to drive. Taking a deep breath, she snuggles close to him for security, bolstering her determination to follow through with their scandalous fiasco. He, in turn, puts the car in drive and his arm around her shoulders. Their journey begins.

This mixture of uncertainty creates an environment between anxiety and excitement. As the miles drone on, watching the countryside roll by creates a momentary sense of peace. The uncertainty suddenly roars back with the appearance of a highway sign announcing, "Angola, twenty miles." Micky can feel an anxious sweat trickling down his sides. Carolyn is nervously fussing with her hair and makeup. The hour of decision is here. Entering this strange town renews their feelings of being not much more than interlopers crashing in for an even more questionable purpose. There is almost enough uncertainty to feel as much wrongness as rightness in their decision. What had seemed so right in the throes of passion is now being scrutinized by daylight. Before embarking on the final leg of their resolution, they agree to have lunch. Micky swings the Mercury into a drive-in advertising twenty-cent hamburgers. Barely aware of what it is they are eating, their thoughts scatter throughout their meal. To say this period of life is their biggest separation from their high school phase is a correct assessment. Unlike Micky's military training and Carolyn's college experience, where others played a role in their decision making, this piece of their lives rests completely in their hands.

With lunch complete, there is only one piece of business left undone. They both know what it is. Finding directions to the city hall is easy enough. Much of the economy of this small Midwestern town is centered around those young people finding their way here to be married as quickly and efficiently as possible. Carolyn is perfectly willing to let Micky weave their way through the bureaucracy surrounding this ceremony. All that's special about this event is that they have to wait for all the legal weeds to be parted before any smiles are allowed. When they arrive at city hall, they are met with several other couples waiting in line for their turn to "tie the knot." Finally, it's Micky's and Carolyn's turn! With all the legal forms filled and refilled, with all the "t's" crossed and all the "i's" dotted, an affable magistrate appears. Introductions are quickly completed, and they get down to the business at hand—getting married. Within five minutes they have completed a pair of vows that are expected to last them a life time. "Anti-climactic" may be the word for what Carolyn and Micky are experiencing. They were run through like an assembly line. It's probably more acceptable to Micky than to Carolyn. It just doesn't meet her standard of a special day. Nevertheless, they are pronounced man and wife and are experiencing a measure of elation over *that* success.

The trip back home is much less tense than the drive here. Carolyn would have liked more ceremony but is willing not to quibble about it. Micky has other ideas. He had seen a sign on their way in this morning promoting a lodge called the "Old Log Inn." Silently biding his time, he spots the marquee once again. It's a rustic-looking lodge with individual cabins. When he pulls the Mercury onto the drive leading to the office, it catches Carolyn totally by surprise. "What are you doing?!" is her immediate reaction.

"Oh, I thought since we got up so early and have been on the road most of the day, we could use a little rest," Micky says with the same sly little smirk Carolyn has become acquainted with on several other occasions.

"Oh, my gosh! We are married, aren't we? I'm still not used to it," says Carolyn.

"Maybe this will help," says Micky, reaching into his glovebox. He produces a small box. "Last night, I confided in my mother what we had planned. At first, she was resistant, but then conceded. She surprised me by producing this." With that, he opened the box to reveal two rings: an engagement ring and a wedding band. From their design, it is apparent that they are a high-quality set. "My mother said these belonged to her grandmother, and she wants us to have them as a special wedding gift."

Carolyn stares at the rings and then back at Micky. Her eyes are beginning to moisten as she takes the box in her hands. "They're beautiful!" she exclaims.

Micky takes each of the waiting bands and slips them onto her finger. They fit perfectly. In a moment of delight, Carolyn throws her arms around Micky's neck, declaring, "I love them, and I love you."

This is truly the moment they both have been waiting for. It's becoming real, and more real by the moment. With these rings on her finger, Carolyn is feeling much more complete in her new situation. When Micky opens the car door to register them into a cabin, Carolyn leaps out along with him and boldly accompanies him to the registration office, all the while flashing her ring finger in a display of self-assurance.

After paying the five-dollar registration fee, with key in hand and without the fear of burning in hell for eternity, they make their way to their cabin with the full intention of consummating this relationship within the boundaries of their Christian faith. Within seconds of closing and locking the door behind them, they are tearing at each other's clothing in a near frantic attempt to get naked. Without keeping track of time, it could be said the estimated time for this first round may have been about sixty seconds. For this young pair of novices, this may as well have been a daylong marathon, considering the amount of energy they've expelled. Things slow down now, and they are making a determined effort to engage each other in a conversation other than intimate talk. This lasts only so long before nature once more has her way. There does appear to be a much more relaxed atmosphere surrounding this second round—enough for Micky to bring out his little smirk once again and ask, "How far is it?"

"How far is what?" asks Carolyn with an innocent concern to her voice.

With the resort's marquee displaying "The Old Log Inn" clearly seen through the window, still maintaining a smirk, he plays with Carolyn, asking, "How far is the old log in?"

Not being as slow-witted as she pretends, she gives him a little slap, saying, "You can't help being naughty, can you?"

The day has been one of resounding emotions of lows and highs. Thankfully, it is ending on a high note. This hour spent in the Old Log Inn is an hour out of their lives that will be recalled again and again.

With the day ending and Micky and Carolyn returning home with no evidence of Christmas shopping, they have decided to meet with both sets of parents and come clean regarding their real purpose in leaving so early in the morning. Micky's mother had been given a heads up and, as it is in many husband and wife teams, she couldn't keep the secret from Micky's father. They willingly give their blessing despite their initial disapproval. When meeting with Carolyn's parents, they are totally in the dark. Carolyn's mother indicates in a sad way how she feels cheated out of sharing in her daughter's wedding. The question now arises: where will they live for the next few weeks before they each must return to their commitments— school for Carolyn, and the army for Micky? After seeing Micky's room full of athletic trophies and dust, Carolyn would prefer to live at her parents' home. Her parents agree, and they set up a workable housekeeping agreement.

CHAPTER 11
Out of the Womb

This past year has brought with it challenges these newlyweds have never explored. It's as significant as the first year out of the protection of their mother's womb, except the womb, in this instance, has been spread well over a nineteen-year gestation period with both of them born into a family, then in the public and parochial school system, and finally in a wedding and the armed forces for Micky and college for Carolyn.

Once Micky completes his "Advanced Individual Training" as a chaplain's assistant, he will find himself in Vietnam as quickly as he can pack his bags. For Carolyn, being a newlywed with her husband absent after being together for only two weeks is guaranteed to bring challenges into her life she never knew existed.

Like every present, it soon becomes a past. The two weeks fly by, leaving Christmas and the New Year celebration a memory. It's barely the amount of time a young married couple need to adequately acquaint themselves to each other—especially when under the roof of a parent. But like all newlyweds, if they don't have something to compare it to, it's all new and everything is up for examination and consideration. By the time their two weeks are spent, even if they were required to live in a tent, under a bridge—anywhere—if they could do it together, it was better than having to report back to school or the military.

To fulfill his requirement to become a chaplain's assistant, Micky has received orders to report to Fort Hamilton in New York for four weeks of Advanced Individual Training (AIT). The school had been moved from the now obsolete Fort Slocum to New York for reasons only the military understands. When he arrives, he finds himself once again confronted with a rigorous time schedule—it's almost like being back in boot camp. After thirty days of civilian life, this school is significantly designed to reorient him back into a military mindset.

The first basic requirement for a chaplain's assistant is to have ten weeks of basic training in soldiering. He's finished with that task and ready to move on. One of his primary duties lies in protecting the life of the chaplain. Since chaplains don't carry weapons, the assistant is required to be trained in the use of firearms. Micky scored well enough on the firing range to qualify for the position. He's also required to learn English grammar, typing, spelling and punctuation, religious history, and the roles and responsibilities of army chaplains.

Micky discovers that he is being trained in many different religious traditions and practices and how to serve the chaplain in their differences. There is much more of a conciliatory attitude toward their differences than what he has grown up with; that is much more of an ecumenical attitude than his denomination practices. This kind of toleration is not something he has been taught to abide in his denominational upbringing; he's beginning to wonder if this choice is doable. He can easily recall some of the scathing diatribes his denomination has held against those Christian denominations that disagree with them. As in most occupations where the subordinate isn't given options to choose what he will do or not do, he's under oath to follow orders. Those in authority are quick to remind him that he is here to follow orders rather than organize a debate.

This is not sitting well with Micky. Had he been aware how much of himself he would have to give up when he joined, he may have had second thoughts. It isn't just some of his "church notions" he's had to reevaluate; it's also finding someone who cares that as a high school quarterback, he had scored four touchdowns in a single game—and that was only a year ago. "The coach said I was the best quarterback he'd ever coached in his career—there's films of it. I was treated like royalty, and all I had to do was play football. I was good at it!"

Micky is finding himself yearning for that kind of attention again. *If only these people knew what I'm capable of if I'm given a chance.* Micky's frustration is creating a mindset that would enjoy seeing his nemesis suffer like he is. It isn't much different than a quest for revenge over a bruised ego. *I'll show em. They'll see!* In truth, it isn't so much that he wants to destroy them. He longs to be a hero again—he wants an encore, and he just wants them to invite him to their party so he can carry out his yearning.

Micky's attitude is coming out sideways. It's putting him at odds not only with his command center, but also with his fellow soldiers. He spends much of his spare time writing letters to Carolyn describing the officers that thwart his efforts as "idiots." He hopes to find a friendly ally in her as a devoted wife. She doesn't disappoint him. Wanting his attention as bad as he wants the attention of others, she takes great pleasure in accommodating him by taking his side. "They just don't know you like I do, Micky. I know full well what you are capable of—I watched you do it for all those years through school."

Carolyn was a four-year high school cheerleader, and to date, this is the high point of her life. But the occasion for this to occur again ended with a walk across a stage to receive a handshake and a diploma along with the assurance that she is equipped bring the world to its knees. Initially being the first to marry among her crowd—and, of all things, to the captain of the football team—has given her distinction. Without Micky, she finds herself alone and without the support of her cheer squad, and with Micky in the army, she is undergoing a struggle with self-doubt. When he was at her side as the husband, she could show off; this gave her the prominence she hungers for. Without Micky's presence, a sense of completeness is absent. With an unsure future, Carolyn finds it easy to delight in her former celebrity high school standing. Taking comfort in these lonely times by recreating her glorious past gives her an identity she doesn't wish to lose. She hasn't experienced these kinds of isolated feelings since her first day in kindergarten. At least for the present, she has opted to stay at home and take classes at a local junior college instead of returning to the state university.

Even with Micky successfully compiling enough credits to receive his certification and guarantee a place in the chaplain's assistant program, he feels he has not received the respect he was expecting. His "challenging" reputation along with being short tempered with people whom disagree with him have preceded him and continue to be the main source of his disappointments. One of his sergeants lovingly told him he was "an arrogant ass" and had to "earn respect in this man's army." Micky chooses to view this as an "idiot's sarcasm" who probably never got beyond ninth grade. He's always viewed himself as an athletic scholar or a scholarly athlete who is quicker, cleverer, and more authentic. Not to be getting the commendations from his superiors as he had anticipated has done nothing more than create another source of bitterness. He'd expected that after spending his formative years in a Christian school, these present instructors would have become aware of his above-average knowledge on how one can best serve the Lord.

With his five weeks of AIT completed and no other choice than to prepare to leave for Vietnam, Micky makes the necessary arrangements by phoning Carolyn and his parents to say his final goodbyes. His call to Carolyn was heartily received. "Oh, thank God you called. I didn't receive a letter yesterday, and I thought the worst—that they had shipped you out before I could say my goodbyes. I want to let you know how much I love you and need you to come back."

"You don't know how much I miss you, too. Just hearing your voice makes me want to jump through this phone and kiss you. I was hoping to have a week free before flying out, but it didn't happen. They're building up a massive force and are short of men everywhere, so they're rushing us along to fill the gaps."

Not fully understanding the reality of Micky's information, Carolyn changes the subject. "I have something else to tell you." It's the same excited voice she uses when she tells her friends about her new stereo.

Hearing her excitement, with the full realization that there is no chance to be there with her pulls even harder on Micky. He swallows hard to hold back the quiver that's forming in his throat.

"What do ya got, sweetie?" he manages to spit out while wiping the moisture forming in both his eyes.

"We're gonna have a baby!" she says.

There is a momentary pause on Micky's end. The processing path this information is traveling has hit a dead end. Micky is sure, but hoping he's unsure, of what he has just heard her say. He's trying to figure a way of having her rephrase what she just told him in so many plain words in a different way—one that doesn't seem so undeviating. "Are you sure?" is all the words he can think to say.

Her voice has taken on a different tone now—one of uncertainty—not uncertainty about being pregnant, but rather about how Micky is receiving this information. "Yes, the doctor told me I'm between two and three months along."

There is another pause on Micky's end of the line. Still attempting to deal with this new development in a way that will make him sound less stupid than he already feels and feeling a hot flush across his face, he unbuttons his top shirt button and forms the words, "How can you be two months pregnant when we've only been married a little over a month?"

Now the pause is on the other end. "Well, it must have happened that first time we got together at school," Carolyn says with a bit of reluctance in having to admit the outcome of that moment of indiscretion. There is no other explanation; science has tracked the fetus back to its conception.

Micky's brain has finally caught up with his next words. "You're right." His following thoughts forming more words are, "Have you told your parents yet?"

"No, I wanted to tell you before I tell anyone else."

There is yet another pause as Micky digests what is being said. "Maybe we should wait a while before we open that can of worms."

Considering how he and Carolyn are going to live with the fact that a baby formed out of wedlock is coming, he adds, "Let's not give any unnecessary fodder to wagging tongues."

Suddenly, Carolyn's upbeat news has taken on a dark side now that Micky has decided they should conceal what should be a joyous happening.

Still looking to Micky for a course to follow, she becomes much more dour. What she had hoped would be a shared joyous occasion for just the two of them is now taking on the characteristics of an intrusion that's demanding to be dealt with in a depressing and guilt-ridden manner.

Carolyn's voice has turned to a sob as she forces some words. "Aren't you happy?" It's a plea for gladness that's riddled with sadness.

Still attempting to get all considerations dealt with in a practical way, Micky's being summoned to set aside his anal pragmatism and deal with this update with the ears and heart of a loving, caring husband. Not having a clue how to do this, the only recollection he has of the duties of husbands and fathers is his relationship with his own father. Quickly, he asks himself *How would my dad handle this?* Before he is satisfied he can speak with something of an assurance, he astonishes even himself. "Let's rethink this, Carolyn. I'm overjoyed with this news. My main concern is, how are you able to deal with being pregnant before we were married without me there to support you?" He's as surprised at finding these caring words as a man digging in a pile of horse shit would be at coming across a pony.

Just hearing his concern has lifted Carolyn out of a seeming pit of despair. Now she knows she has a partner who's willing to go the distance with her. "I realize I'm gonna have to deal with this without you being present. I think I can handle it if I know I have your support," she says with some newfound grist to her words.

"You have my undying support. I have no doubt you will do the best job you know how to do. You didn't make the honor roll at school because you didn't know what needed to be done next," says Micky with what he hopes are his father's reassuring words coming through him. "I know God will look out for both of us if we keep Him in our hearts," adds Micky.

"Micky, you always know what I need—that's why I married you," says Carolyn.

"I know what all three of us need is for me to come back," says Micky with a tone of resignation to both the good and bad possibilities.

"Write to me, Micky. Always let me know how you are so my mind doesn't start makin' things up—promise me?" says Carolyn.

"I promise," says Micky. The reality of this new development has made its way into his very being. *I have more to lose than I ever dreamed I would have.* It's a brand-new awareness that has become a dominant thought—one that has never, in his nineteen years, been anywhere near him. And now it's his life.

After hanging up with Carolyn, Micky calls his parents. His father answers the phone. "Dad, it's me, Micky."

"Yeah, I know who ya are. What ya callin' about—ya broke and need bail money?"

Knowing his father's sense of humor, Micky plays along with him, "Yeah, I got caught stealin' dead flies from blind spiders."

They both have a chuckle in appreciation of a common son and father bond they carry together. "I'm calling to let you know I passed my tests and am going to be deployed tomorrow morning for Vietnam," relays Micky.

"Who's that on the phone?" is another voice Micky hears in the background. He immediately recognizes it as his mother.

"Micky, your mother knows I'm talkin' to you. She ain't gonna let up 'til I give her the phone. I want you to keep your head down and stay safe—ya hear?"

Before he can hand the phone to his wife, she grabs it from his hand. She's saying "hello" before the phone ever reaches her mouth. This is her youngest son—her baby—and she never lets anyone forget it—especially Micky. It doesn't take but a splinter of a second for her to shift into high gear motherhood. "Have you put weight back on? When you were home, you were skin and bones."

"Yeah, Ma, maybe five pounds or so," says Micky, knowing full well his mother's relentless ways when it comes to how well he's eating. The conversation soon gets around to why he is calling. Predictably, his mother begins to cry. He knows what he is doing hurts her, and he tries hard to keep her from hearing the fear in his own voice, but the die is cast, and there is no turning back. His fate is waiting for him several thousand miles across the Pacific Ocean. The only thing left to do is go forward into the unknown, meet it, and hope God's hand is below him, ready to catch him.

CHAPTER 12
Mission Accomplished

Burt has been given sergeant stripes along with his three "battle buddies" Buck, Bob, and Quincy. None of these young men were individually outstanding in high school. Not one of them considered himself to be part of the "in" crowd or in any way a leader. The common denominator among these young men is that they more often see the world as inadequate. Individually, they have never had the resources to change things. Without a lot of words to explain their relationship, they are finding that as a team, they can make up for their individual deficiencies and move forward using each other's strengths. With each mission, each of them has multiplied his experience. So far, as a team, they have proven to be very effective. After each successful or unsuccessful mission, they meet to give an honest assessment of each other's performance with the idea of always finding ways to make improvements. This keeps them very much in tune with each other's strengths and weaknesses. They prefer to work with their strengths, but are always aware of those weaknesses that can be eliminated or turned into strengths.

These four men have distinguished themselves over and over. They are good at what they do and, in turn, they like what they do. They have found a niche in the army that can't be found in the civilian world. From their numerous missions, they have returned with information that has saved lives and valuable military assets. Buck has retained his leadership position only because he has the respect of each team member and always placed their wellbeing ahead of his own. But then, this could be easily said of each of them, by each of them. They have truly made themselves battle buddies in every sense of the word. Recently, a fresh-faced second lieutenant right out of college had the bright idea of not having four sergeant E7s working together and attempted to split them into other teams. That was until they made it known to him that if he attempted such a maneuver, they would make certain he would meet with an accident he couldn't recover from.

The mess hall provides a common space for soldiers who normally wouldn't be involved with one another to interact. Today is a normal day there. Some who were here yesterday are in the field and not present today, and others have been killed and had replacements flown in. Talk varies as different experiences are hashed over. Usually a conversation will center around how much time each of them has before they go home.

There is one guy who is making a point of crashing the table where these four recon guys are sitting. It turns out his name is Wayne, and he comes from the same hometown as Quincy. Pulling out a chair he sits down placing his tray on the table. He's thin and looks drained of energy. His uniform sleeve has a distinct outline of sergeant stripes that appear to have been ripped off. He and Quincy carry on a conversation about the mutual people they each know. Finally, Wayne gets around to why he had come over to this table specifically. "Last week, you guys did the recon on a mission I was sent out on. You guys really messed up." The blood has drained from Wayne's face, giving him a zombielike appearance.

These words have definitely gotten the attention of these four as Wayne continues, "You guys reported all's you saw was a small platoon. What we met was a whole damn battalion. My second lieutenant, who don't know shit from ice cream, ordered us to move forward and engage. When I saw what we were up against, I ordered my men to retreat. They had us out gunned ten to one. The SOB had me dressed down and demoted, no thanks to you guys." With that, he got up and left leaving these four to digest what has just been said. They remain quiet, alone with their own thoughts. The only thanks they expect is that the work they do is done well. It's too late to turn back and undo what had obviously been a screw-up on their part. Remaining quiet, they finish their meal and return to their bivouac. They try to stay as secretive as possible so that spies working as laborers would never know the unit even had a long-range reconnaissance patrol (LRRP). It's upsetting in one way that their identities have been found out, and even more so that they have botched a mission. They are quickly realizing that they could only learn so much in Recondo school. Most of what they are learning now is coming from experiences they have shared with the jungle and each other.

Most recently, they have been assigned to a reconnaissance mission that will take them into the jungle near Laos. They must carry enough food to maintain themselves and, if needs be, enough ammunition and firepower to give the impression that they are an entire platoon. It's the kind of mission placing them in the jungle long enough to gain an upper hand on the enemy. They prefer to do this up close by visually making contact—hopefully never to be seen. They become the eyes and ears of an entire unit. The commanders depend thoroughly on the information they bring back to the unit, which determines whether a platoon or a division is needed. This mission has as its primary focus where the enemy may be storing munitions as well as what kind of patrols they may be initiating and always on the lookout for snatching an unwary enemy combatant to interrogate.

While preparing for their Laos expedition, the team requisitions all the materials they'll need along with a helicopter to drop them off in the jungle. This whole way of life is becoming a normal routine for these men. With nothing to hear other than the whooping sound of the blades rotating overhead and the roar of the engine, the men are left alone with their thoughts. Looking out over the head of the door gunner and out the open sides of the helicopter, Burt's mind drifts back to what his life had been during his high school years less than a year ago compared with what he is doing now. A satisfied little smile crosses his face. *I never imagined I would find my place in life livin' in a damn jungle.* This kind of life would have been puzzling a year ago, but now, despite all its fear-producing enigmas, Burt finds it challenging and exhilarating. He has developed survival skills. To say these latent aptitudes didn't begin on the little league ball team as a kid and then later as a high school athlete would be one-sided. After all, he did make a basket from nearly mid-court once. But now, because of his army training and a natural propensity to cheat danger, he has taken what could have remained a high school high point to another level. He rarely thinks of home anymore and hasn't looked at Meadow's picture for weeks. Buck, Quincy, and Bob have become his family.

Riding in the seat beside the pilot, Buck is watching the terrain below. (He's also building a report with the pilot who will be extracting them in a few days.) It's a beautiful mosaic of different tints of greens and browns where rice paddies and jungle are sprinkled together, causing them to create a medley of colors. Within minutes, the entire topography changes to a mountainous jungle—the kind of terrain in which an enemy can find hundreds of places to hide, lay out booby traps, and disappear into an underground tunnel in a wink. Burt's thoughts drift to some of the other challenges they've faced, but his attention can't help but return to the mission at hand. *Boy, this one is going to be some kind of humdinger.* Motioning for the others to prepare to disembark soon, the pilot makes a false landing about a mile from the intended position. This game of cat and mouse causes the enemy to rush toward that position, allowing the pilot to focus on a bare spot on top of an otherwise jungled mountainside. Without touching down, the pilot hovers a couple feet off the ground, allowing all the equipment they tossed out to remain intact. The disembarkation is as routine as the terrain allows.

To be as secretive about their location as possible, they need to work fast and economically. To get all their equipment off the ground and out of sight, all four work with as much precision as the circumstances permit. These men have achieved so many successes because they like what they're doing and are anxious to get on with it. Among the four of them, they believe that the best defense against an advancing enemy is the trust within their team. They've developed an unusual certainty about each other's capabilities that's rarely experienced among ordinary infantryman. All they need to do to know where they stand is look at one another. Buck is the leader, Bob mans the radio, Quincy is point man, and Burt handles the artillery— namely, the claymores and C-4 packs. In some cases, Burt changes off with Buck as rear guard. If they should lose a member due to his being wounded or slain, the others are trained to take his place.

Within thirty seconds of landing, with one eye watching their chopper roar away and the other on the terrain around them, they quickly meld into the jungle. Once they're under the jungle canopy and hidden from snipers, a sigh of relief is their reward. Enemy snipers wait in trees throughout the jungle with only one objective: kill as many Americans as they can. It's a chance these covert adversaries are willing to take before they are discovered and shot out of their perches.

Having their coordinates down to begin their operation doesn't mean this LRRP unit is able to maintain their positions to the letter. As in the past, they are relying on visual geographic markers to move back and forth to their extraction location. They talk in near whispers, since they have no idea how far into enemy territory they've ventured. The enemy may already have point men in position to monitor their every move. Until they become more certain of their surroundings, they will err on the side of caution. The usual hand signals they learned in Recondo training and those they've worked out between themselves make up most of their communication.

Very slowly, they begin their reconnaissance operation. Each man has accepted a task to scrutinize what may lie within their immediate perimeter. With these small special forces patrols, the army has opted to sacrifice manpower for stealth. Finding the enemy and following them far behind enemy lines is a risk far and beyond what is expected of conventional units. Getting caught could mean months of torture, interrogation, and death. To reduce the chance of being seen before they see the enemy, the team adopts a camouflage ploy. Along with the others, Burt has built a nest of jungle plants around his helmet, and blackened his hands and face with burnt cork to look more like an end man in a minstrel show. The only body parts not subject to camouflage are his white eyes and pink tongue. There is barely an inkling that there may be a human being hidden behind all this. Looking at the others, he can't help but imagine them as a team of deranged jungle hermits.

With a slight finger gesture, Buck motions the men toward him. Before initiating a mission, it has been their agreed tradition to invoke the Divine. They gather around with bowed heads and arms and hands on one another's shoulders as they quietly recite the Lord's prayer together. This openness is not a strange custom; this was a common locker room practice before a high school team left for the field. When they finish, Buck taps his watch and whispers the time to return, adding, "Stay alert, stay alive." Each gives a knowing nod. Each man knows the direction he is to go, as well as the directions of the others. The quieter they become, the more they can hear. The jungle has its own way of signaling the presence of an intruder—it becomes quieter. Crawling on their bellies, they make themselves as low as possible and slowly move out. The jungle is gradually accepting this respect by returning to the steady chatter of its countless animals. They are undergoing what they need to do to become one with the jungle and operate only a few feet from the enemy when necessary. This requires nerves of steel and faith in a power greater than themselves who they trust to provide the discernment they need at these times.

The designated time of return brings them back to their small base camp. They are satisfied that the enemy is not directly in their backyard enough to let their guard down and begin to discuss what they individually have to report. Quincy is the first reveal something. "About a quarter mile from here, I came on a path. It looked pretty well worn, so I hung around long enough to see what was goin' on. The longer I hung out there, the more things were comin' to light. I started catchin' the smell of them damn fish they eat, and then I hear 'em chatterin' and laughin' so I know I'm damn close to somethin'. I hunkered down and crawled about a hundred yards 'til not only was I smellin' the little bastards, I could see 'em. They was about a dozen of 'em gathered 'round a damn hole in the ground. I knew right then and there they was a bunch of them damn tunnel rats. They was goin' in an' outta there like a bunch of ants. I laid there watchin' 'em carryin' on for at least a couple hours. Far as I could figure, they was a patrol unit—'bout a dozen of 'em."

None of the others have gleaned anything nearly as significant as this report, and they are totally engrossed in Quincy's account. Each is evaluating what this information means for their objective. Intelligence is always primary in these missions, but there are other objectives that can prove to be very beneficial as well. Conducting ambushes is also a priority if it can neutralize an area and make it safer for the grunts to establish a foothold. Buck is quick to assess what could be done with Quincy's account. "Y'all think you could get us up to that position without bein' seen?"

Quincy shoots back a look of surprise. "Course I can. I got there an' back in one piece, didn't I?"

The next hour is spent going over more of the details surrounding Quincy's encounter. A strategy is worked out and agreed to. They know what they could be in for. It's no secret that these north Vietnamese soldiers are on their own turf and are more than worthy opponents when it comes to using the jungle to their advantage. Nonetheless, with all of them on the same page, they slowly and cautiously begin to retrace Quincy's near crawl to the enemy position with each fulfilling their assigned station. The jungle is thick and unforgiving, making it difficult to carry much more than their M60 and ammunition, a coil of rope, a sheath knife, a canteen of water, a few C-rations, a first aid kit, a supply of C-4 explosive, and a few claymore mines. This all must be arranged to prevent them from sounding like a bunch of Irish tinkers stumbling about the jungle. There is nothing in nature that replicates a metallic sound of metal on metal. In the jungle, these foreign noises will bring normal animal sounds to a halt as they wait out its originator. Quincy is filling his role as point man with his eyes on high alert for any movement and ears open for any disturbing changes in jungle sounds. It's also important to decipher the origin of smells. from humid jungle odors to human odors such as cigarette smoke or cooking smells.

As if this were not enough concern, all of them support the others in watching for booby traps. Burt is the rear guard to make sure they won't be caught in an ambush with their pants down. He is also doing his best to eradicate any visible trail by ensuring that much of the vegetation twisted by their boots is lifted back to its original form. This process slows them, but living minimal traces of human footprints improves their chances of remaining undetected. The enemy patrols are no strangers to tracking in the jungle and can find vegetation that's been disturbed and track it back to its originators with the patience of vipers.

This team cannot have lingering reservations about what they must do. Each must perform his job faultlessly, not only for themselves, but also for each member of the team. They have quickly become aware that 99 percent of the time, they will be clearly outnumbered. But with each incursion, they are coming to rely more on their skills with a new confidence. These are traits that are absorbed without a lot of conversation. It's an understanding that doesn't need a lot of words; it's more important it's lived. It's a heavy challenge for young men who spent their last year on a high school football field only to find themselves in a Vietnam killing field a year later. The shared experience of living with the reality of danger forms the ties of trust these men have shaped with one another. Sharing these dangers ensures them they are living life 100 percent.

The day is wearing on. It is taking four men much longer to cover the same distance as Quincy covered alone; the larger the troop, the more cumbersome jungle travel becomes. By afternoon, the temperature is well into the nineties. Their supply of water is slowly dwindling. Quincy, who is still point man, suddenly stops. He warily signals the others to get down. All four drop to their bellies. They are on high alert with hearts pounding and breath quickening. In a moment, the reason becomes clear—they have come within a few yards of a trail. It's being traveled by a group of Vietnamese men who are haphazardly carrying their rifles on their shoulders. It appears to be a patrol unit making its way back to camp. It's clear they feel quite secure in their surroundings. They are making no effort to quiet their chattering. A similar security is coming over the LRRP patrol; they realize they are here undetected. After snaking and twisting through the jungle for the past few hours without a single incident, this occurrence is loaded with emotions: fear, hate, and excitement are all savagely coursing through these nervous young men. These are no cakewalk patrols. The same rules apply: keep your wits about you, stay alert, be ready to report what you see, remember what you hear, and think before you act.

As the enemy patrol makes their way down the trail and out of sight, Buck makes a hand signal to the others to make their way to his location. With cat-like stealth, the others soon join him.

Keeping his voice to a whisper, Buck begins with, "Everybody okay?" A nod from everyone is all the assurance he needs. Aware they have the upper hand, with intelligence-gathering remaining the primary objective, they continue to whisper, "We need to get fix on these guys. They all got North Vietnamese uniforms. They look like they could lead us to their command post if we keep an eye on 'em."

"I'm pretty sure these gooks are part of the same group. I recognize a couple of 'em," whispers Quincy.

"How far you figure we are from where y'all spotted their camp?" asks Buck, still keeping his question to a whisper.

Raising his head up enough to crane his neck around. "Probably 'bout a hundred yards that-a way," whispers Quincy, slightly leaning his head in that direction.

Considering everything Quincy has to offer concerning what he saw earlier and the objectives of this mission to report combat patrols, enemy caches of weapons, conduct an ambush if it presents itself, locate command posts, capture enemy documents like maps, and—with a little luck—snatch an enemy officer to interrogate (a live prisoner can offer information that can't be gotten from a dead man), Buck gives the signal to move forward. Agreeing to stay off the trail, they choose a jungle course where they can keep it in sight. The heat and the thickness of the foliage would stop an ordinary soldier, but these aren't ordinary men. Patiently, they stealthily crawl under, over, and through everything the jungle is able to throw at them. Within twenty-five minutes, they have reached the same location Quincy had reached earlier. They're looking at the same crude bunker built around the entrance to what appears to be an underground tunnel. Making no signals, Buck leaves each man in position to make his own assessments.

What they are seeing is the worst enemy that a military camp can experience: boredom and idle time. Its results are apparent adversaries not paying attention. Remaining undercover, these four feel a sense of safety and calmness as they continue to watch the ant-like comings and goings of their foes as they go in and out of their underground lair. A time comes where not even a guard is left posted above. Buck takes advantage of this opportunity to gather the team. Slowly and silently, each makes his way to where they can remain hidden but have an effective pow-wow. In a whisper, they begin letting each give an account of what they have perceived. Each has similar accounts with a few peculiarities the others hadn't noticed. Burt reports how from where he was located, "I notice these guys ain't pissin' and shittin' in their bunker. They're usin' the jungle about three yards from where I was layin'. I didn't take time to see if I was layin' in it myself—you guys smell anything?"

With a smirk, Bob says, "I can't tell the difference. You always smell like shit anyway." This produces muffled guffaws from all of them including Burt. Savoring the moment of levity, Buck nevertheless brings order back to this tiny jungle community.

With the atmosphere quickly changing back to serious-mindedness, Buck asks the question, "You see any officers comin' to your latrine?

Burt contemplates the question for a moment, "Yeah, there was a lieutenant. He took a dump earlier, but I haven't seen him since."

This gives Buck pause. He finally pronounces very softly, "We're gonna get that guy—hopefully with his pants down."

With the daylight beginning to wane, they take advantage of the shadows to strategically reposition themselves in pairs around the perimeter of this enemy outpost. The plan is for Burt and Buck to remain at the latrine location while Bob and Quincy place themselves in a place where they can gain access to the entrance of the tunnel. Without being certain what can be lying under them, they know from some of their other exploits that these tunnels often turnout to serve as weapon caches.

The night goes by with each of our pairs taking two-hour watches. Burt's watch is uneventful. During middle-of-the-night watches, Burt meets his aloneness. It's different than loneliness. Loneliness is always accompanied with a kind of anxiety. Burt finds his aloneness is accompanied by a feeling of contentment; he can't imagine anything other than always being here, where he is, forever in the moment. This makes it impossible for him to imagine his own death.

With daylight forcing its way through the jungle canopy, it's coming down to zero hour. They have prepared themselves to be ready to act as soon as these nemeses begin to stir. A few enlisted men have made their way out to do their thing, but no officers yet. Burt and Buck are positioning themselves to take out the first officer that has at least his pistol hand busy gripping his hanging pistol. Burt is lying with Buck not more than a few feet from this outdoor privy. They've completely covered themselves with jungle vegetation, so someone would have to step directly on them to become aware of either of them. From Burt's vantage point, he can see a man unstrapping his pants not more than a yard or two from where he lies. He seems to be hunting for an unused spot to take care of his business. Another thing coming to light is that this man is about to dump on Buck. It's further apparent that as an officer—and a captain, at that—he's claiming his right to privacy. Unlike the enlisted men, he's come alone. When his pants are down around his ankles, Burt is up with a rush of power; he slams this officer's midriff with the vigor of a striking cobra. The force knocks the wind out of the man, leaving him gasping long enough to for Buck, with a knee on his chest, to stuff a rag into the man's mouth to prevent him from hollering. With the precision of a trained assassin, Burt flips the bare-butted soldier over and lashes his hands together with a piece of rope he's prepared for the occasion.

Quincy and Bob have been anticipating their moment. The second they see Burt and Buck neutralize their quarry and with the timing of a guillotine, they prepare to strike the entrance of this underground labyrinth with a grenade attached to enough C-4 explosive to level a ten-story building. The pin on the grenade is pulled and tossed as it thumps its way downward to a depth that guarantees the explosion will effectively seal the entrance to this cavern until the day of Armageddon. BAAAWWOOOM! With dirt showering down all around them, these four men are quickly making their way into the camouflage of the jungle along with their captured captain, who is still stumbling with his pants dragging along by one leg behind him. They realize any explosion like this is definitely going to get the attention of any enemy positions around the area. Before they can assess its origin, it's time they begin to make their way back to their extraction point.

The helicopter has become the lifeline to these LRRPs. The most reassuring words a pilot can utter to an LRRP is, "We're comin' to get you!" To ensure they are coordinated with the helicopter pilot, Bob is on the radio arranging the details. Never has a pilot said he would not come. To become sloppy now would prove to be ill advised. They are still deep in enemy territory, so they are utilizing their hit-and-run maneuver and hoping they have confused the enemy for long enough to get to their extraction point. These boys are much huskier than they were a year ago, and full of the kind of bravado that comes from knowing your pretty good at what you do. With these young men returning home—if they do—the characteristic the civilian communities will find most disturbing is the kind violence they have routinely given themselves over to. Right now, right here, it serves them well. This enemy officer is fully aware that despite the youth of these soldiers, it would be to his disadvantage to attempt an escape. He is blindfolded with hands bound, naked from the waist down, and wearing a noose around his neck that's capable of tightening to the point of strangulation, should he attempt a break.

The pilot needs at least twenty to twenty-five minutes to reach them, providing he doesn't encounter a resistance along the way. If he should happen to encounter the enemy, his door gunner is prepared to return an overwhelming amount of firepower with a vengeance. His door-mounted M60 machine gun and the rockets mounted to the sides of the helicopter are usually enough to deter an enemy onslaught—providing it can be located.

The team must out of harm's way, especially with the much coveted enemy captain in tow. To evade as much trouble as possible, they hide in a little grove of mountain trees short of the extraction point. All the while, Bob mans the radio. He's sending the coded coordinates to the pilot while being careful not to expose their location. Turning his wrist over and exposing the iridescent dial of his Bulova, he notices it's only nine hundred hours. With a little luck, they'll be back at camp in time for a late breakfast at the officers' club. War is hell only if you're losing.

CHAPTER 13
Chaplain Gohrke

With all his training completed and his goodbyes over and done with, Micky finds himself ordered to Vietnam by way of the USS Pickaway, which has been refitted as a troop carrier. With all that he's been through since high school—boot camp, advanced individual training, marriage, and learning he's a father—he has yet to develop the individuality and complexity he lacked as a high school hero. Life had been so much easier in high school. Many of his classmates envied his popularity—they didn't want to be *like* him, they wanted to *be* him. He had never found it necessary to develop anything within himself mentally, physically, or spiritually beyond a high school level. Even his "calling" to become a missionary has its roots in his adolescent ego. Everything Micky did from elementary school through high school was orchestrated to promote his "Big Man on Campus" award his senior year. No one could argue that this experience hasn't fostered Micky's tendency to believe that this is all he needs to succeed in life. He's convinced that his ideas are up to standard to spread the Gospel of Jesus Christ to the heathen world if he's given an opportunity. He's also convinced he's supporting a just war and is willing to devote his time to the military as a chaplain's assistant to meet both these ends. *After all, wasn't I near tears listening to our pastor give us our graduation address?* In his own words to Carolyn (who is willing to sit at his feet and blink her eyes at his every word), he stated, "While I'm in Vietnam, I'd like to write my own high school biography. I believe a major publisher would find it overwhelmingly unique."

Micky's military experience has been anything but satisfying. His insides cry for attention—warranted or unwarranted—because he got used to it in high school. All this failure has caused Micky's frustration. He worked hard in school to calculate what would move his status forward, and now having all the rules change has caused his demeanor to become hostile and aloof. This has resulted in a preoccupation with thoughts of home, where his high school conduct still gives him status. There are still plenty of his schoolmates around that remember his record-breaking sprints, or how he saved the football team from a loss with his eleventh-hour touchdown.

Micky has found his way to the deck as he has every evening since he's boarded. A flood of cool air hits him. He finds it overwhelmingly refreshing. The night is clear, and the stars are bright. *I wonder if Carolyn ever looks at the stars* becomes his momentary fixation. In reviewing his and Carolyn's relationship, he's particularly drawn to her weaknesses and how much she finds her strength in him. It's much like she did in high school. *This* is the kind of stuff he and his buddies could talk about endlessly; what women were supposed to be like, and what kind of crap you were and weren't going to put up with in a woman. He knows that by going to Vietnam, he is not as effective in living out these predilections, but things can wait. *I've only signed on for thirteen months. This time next year, I'll have a wife and a child waiting for me.*

Happy to be coming into port a week later, he can't help sharing his frustration in a letter to Carolyn: *I'm beginning to feel as though I've been born and raised on this tub! I'll be happy to be anywhere but here!*

Da Nang is Micky's port of entry. After disembarking, he is loaded onto a troop truck and begins the final leg of his journey to the base. The truck winds its way through narrow dirt roads that are not acquainted with the large military vehicles that are intruding on them. Micky had seen scenes on the news that showed people along the roads welcoming American soldiers by waving flowers and American flags. He's not seeing any of that here. He's a little more than disappointed.

The outlying Da Nang countryside is a typical third-world community in its simplicity and lack of aesthetic appeal. The roads are composed of a reddish dirt. They seem to sprout miserable buildings along their edges, occupied by even more dour-looking humans that have been sentenced to push or pull every type of conveyance in the hope of making their cumbersome lives a bit more manageable. Micky can't help but notice the starkness of his new surroundings; the dirt is a boring color he's already tired of seeing. This is a new low for Micky. He's already downhearted, and being thrown into an environment that is as poor and despondent appearing as this drops him into a new low. He's feeling there is no yesterday and no tomorrow, and he's been condemned to an everlasting now—like being in hell.

After what seems like an endlessness journey, he arrives at the base. Just as challenging in appeal is a sign with the simply written words CAMP EAGLE. The perimeter is surrounded by scrubby-looking jungle foliage that has no visual attraction in any of its odd-looking forms, and it's speckled with strange-looking tombstones that give it even more of a look of desperation. It has been a cemetery for countless more years than it's been an American airbase. Micky's first impression screams inside his head: *What have I gotten myself into? This is the most miserable-looking place I have ever been to in my life!* Unlike the native inhabitants, the only commonality he perceives when referring to the soldiers is *At least these people look like me.*

At his drop point, Micky is met by a corporal who's been instructed to get him to the chaplain's office. Fighting with a backpack that's been digging its straps into his shoulders, he struggles to keep in step behind this single-minded courier. This corporal is devoted to army protocol. Much to Micky's bewilderment, the soldier seems content in this environment. Despite the temperature being well into the high eighties—enough for perspiration to soak through what had been Micky's crisp, clean uniform only hours before—this soldier looks as though his starched shirt just came from the laundry. This heat is also enough to intensify the humidity, which intensifies the strange odor this country assumes. It's an odor that Micky has never encountered in the fresh breezes of Michigan's Great Lakes. The chaplain's office is located in the heart of this conglomeration of huts referred to by the enlisted men as "hooches.'" Realizing he has come to the end of his journey, Micky is left standing alone in the middle of a small reception room. With what feels like a dry tongue, Micky swallows hard and, with a nervous sigh, makes his way to the door at the end of a short hallway. The words across the door are a plain block type. CAPTAIN DONALD WARDWALL CHAPLAIN UNITED STATES ARMY it plainly reads. It's the chaplain's headquarters. Without further ado, Micky softly knocks on the door with one knuckle. "Enter," says the voice from the other side of the closed door. It's clearly not a pleasant voice—it has a harsh, impatient edge to it. Entering and saluting smartly, Micky says, "Private Michael Murphy reporting for duty, sir."

Looking up from some paperwork on his desk and over the top of a pair of reading glasses, he casually returns Micky's salute. "At ease, private …. What'd you say your name is, again?" It's the same impatient voice.

"Murphy, sir! Private Michael Murphy," repeats Micky as smartly as with his first encounter.

"Okay, Murphy, so you're my new assistant. Good! I need you to do something right away. Your first duty is to get me to the airport before I miss my flight. I've got my R&R (rest and relaxation) coming up, and I don't intend to miss it. I've had it with this base's bunch of drunken reprobates. You'll find a jeep out behind—oh, here, take these bags with you. Put them in the jeep," says Chaplain Wardwell.

Micky forgets his loathing for this place for a moment; it's quickly replaced with an anxious desire to make the right impression. Micky hustles around bringing the jeep to the front of the building. He promptly makes his presence known to his impetuous chaplain. "Okay, sir. I have your bags on board and the jeep is ready to get you to your flight, sir."

Barely acknowledging Micky's confirmation, the chaplain begins his departure with a quick stride. Micky reacts by attempting to out-stride him to get the door open for him, but before he can reach it, Wardwell is already swinging it open and making a hasty exit. He lets it swing back to meet Micky. A couple more strides, and the chaplain is in the jeep's passenger seat. He's unquestionably on a full-court press to get out of Camp Eagle. Once they're in the jeep, an explosion rocks the atmosphere around them enough to feel a shudder come through the ground. "Damn heathens! They're at it again. They never stop. I gotta get outta here for a while," protests Wardwell.

This is Micky's first confrontation with the reality of war. The enemy is sending rockets into the base from an undisclosed area outside the base perimeters. It's enough to cause Micky to recoil and nearly jump out of the jeep.

Clearly agitated, Wardwell says, "These pagans are gonna be the death of me yet. I don't have time for their crap. Just get me to the airport. I got an R&R coming, and I'm in no mood for their shenanigans. They can devastate this dump without me."

Micky slams the jeep into gear, nearly throwing himself out the open side. Desperately trying not to aggravate the captain, he tries to recall the route he traveled to get here. In his attempt, he roars out through a makeshift road built by the military in time to meet with another incoming rocket that lifts his jeep nearly over and lands him, jeep and all, in a water-filled ditch. Without a second thought, he slams the jeep from third gear into first gear, keeping their momentum going forward. It works. He directly rockets the jeep, himself, and his passenger back onto the road. Once they're back on track to the airfield, the chaplain begins to scold Micky. "Where'd you learn how to drive? Didn't they teach you to bring the jeep to a complete stop before you put it into first gear? You can get a court martial for a stupid trick like that. When I return, we'll deal with you."

To say the least, this entire incident is putting Micky into an emotional tailspin. This is hardly the introduction he had expected. To add to the turmoil when they arrive at the airfield the chaplain's plane is making its way to the runway. "Step on it! Don't let that plane out of your sight 'til I'm on it!"

Without a second thought, Micky throws the jeep into second gear and floors it, hoping to wind out a little more torque. It works, and the jeep lurches forward.

They notice the back hatch is not closed on the C1. This gives the chaplain hope that he can still overtake the plane. He orders Micky to give chase. With the gas pedal at its max, Micky overtakes the C1 in just a few seconds. Wardwell is using hand signals to coax Micky closer and closer to the open hatch. By now, Wardwell is standing up in the jeep and grasping his duffle bag with one hand while he's grasping the top of the windshield with the other. With the jeep gradually inching closer to the open rear hatch, with a burst of energy, Wardwell propels himself from the jeep to the floor of the open hatch just as it's beginning to close.

At this point, it's hard to determine which of these two individuals is the most relieved—Micky to have this ordeal over with, or the chaplain, who at last is leaving this "Godforsaken" camp behind him for a few days. On his way back to the base, Micky can't help but reflect on his introduction to Vietnam. He recalls how his Advanced Individual Training instructors emphasized that the chaplain's assistants are there to assist the chaplain in every way they're asked to bring spiritual aid and comfort to the American soldier. This chaplain's behavior has baffled him beyond any kind of sensible explanation.

After returning to the base, Micky is taking it upon himself to spend his time in the chaplain's office and do what he can to make himself useful to some of the other chaplains. One especially has caught his attention: a Lutheran chaplain. Notwithstanding the army's high regard for the Lutheran chaplain's outlook on discipline, respect for separation of church and state, and their high-quality education, Micky finds their religious behavior more guarded than that of most other Protestants. They've remained Catholic, but some synods are not quite Catholic enough to fellowship with Roman Catholics or, for that matter, with Lutherans of a different synod. He finds it interesting how Lutherans are sacramental, much like Roman Catholics, but they guard their communion against any chance that a Roman Catholic or any other Christian may stray to their altar and attempt to partake.

Chaplain Captain Keith Gohrke, a thirty-three-year-old graduate of the Concordia, Saint Louis class of 1961, is referred to as "Padre" or "Sky Pilot." He seems to be cut from a different cloth. He's well loved by the Lutheran boys as well as many from other denominations. Padre Gohrke is just old enough to command respect from these young eighteen- to twenty-year-old grunts. He has chosen not to marry at this time; he lost an older brother to the war while he was in seminary and, in memory of his brother, has dedicated his ministry to soldiers in need of spiritual comfort. While pointing a finger toward Micky and swooping up a small zippered case from his desk, Padre Gohrke says, "I've got a call from the field hospital. They have a couple guys they've just medevacked in from the front. They're in bad shape and are asking for me. I need you to get me over there."

In a flash, Micky salutes and heads for the jeep. Assisting this chaplain in meeting an obligation is exactly what his training has directed him to do. His is not to question an order but to complete it as efficiently and effectively as he can. With directional aid from the Padre, they quickly arrive at their destination. With the resolve of one who has a definite purpose, Gohrke exits the jeep and makes his way to the infirmary. Knowing his way around, he quickly spots the two wounded soldiers. One has just been prepared for surgery. The hand on his left arm is fragmented, leaving only a bloodied bone. A wound in his side is exposing what appears to be a torn stomach. From the looks of his wound, Gohrke presumes he's going to lose more of his arm. "How you doin', soldier?" asks Gohrke. His voice is soft but confident—characteristic of one who is certain.

"I've been better, Padre; do you think I'm gonna make it?" asks the young man. It's clear he's agitated.

"These docs are some of the best I've seen. If anybody can get you back together, it's these guys," reports Gohrke with the confidence of one who knows. Taking advantage of this moment, he continues, "What's your name, soldier?"

"Matt, sir." The voice is weak, and hardly audible.

A reassuring smile makes its way across the chaplain's mouth as he forms these words, "Matt, I want you to remember, you have a Savior who loves you and has promised never to leave you or forsake you, no matter what may befall you. This loving God has promised to be with you through the valley of the shadow of death. I want to reassure you that this is a truth you can rely on." With this said, Chaplain Gohrke presses his thumb against Matt's forehead, tracing the cross and reciting a prayer: "May Almighty God, the Father, the Son, and the Holy Spirit bless and keep you and keep your faith fast until you stand face to face with our loving God on the last day."

Micky is amazed by how much calmer this wounded soldier has become. He realizes he is witnessing something he has not experienced in his Christian life; the love flowing out of this chaplain is warm enough to heat the room. Micky is not comfortable with this kind of emotion. He considers himself a pragmatist and is not prone to sentimentality. Meanwhile, Chaplain Gohrke has moved to the other wounded man, offering a similar hope. At this juncture, Micky can't help but be drawn to the simplicity that possesses this man in comforting the souls of these seriously wounded men. There is a power of attraction within this chaplain that he has never witnessed in any clergyman he's been acquainted with. Micky's academic Christian education was designed to take advantage of the free grace from God like a child receiving free stuff from a parent; it isn't a stretch to understand his lack of a giving concept.

After driving the chaplain back to his quarters, Micky is finally shown his quarters. He is bivouacked behind the headquarters, where he can be summoned on a moment's notice. It's not a bad room. He's sharing it with two other chaplain's assistants. Since they are not held to the same schedule as ordinary enlistees, their job description is to be at the beck and call of the chaplain they're assigned to. For Micky, at least for the present, it's Chaplain Gohrke. Chaplain Gohrke is doing his best to initiate Micky as to how he likes to conduct his worship services—especially after Micky let him know he had took piano lessons as a young kid. Gohrke has ordered him to begin to practice on a small, antiquated portable organ powered by batteries. Gohrke loves to include liturgy in his services, has provided Micky with practice sheets, and frequently involves himself in Micky's practice sessions— he loves to sing along. "For all our gracious God has given us, there is a richness to giving back our best," says Gohrke of the liturgy with a tone of reverence.

Gohrke, frequently holds counseling sessions for soldiers who often are scared, or have gotten a "Dear John" letter from home, or have moral concerns regarding the war. Being in Gohrke's presence daily is making it more and more difficult for Micky to disregard the chaplain's unpretentious way of presenting Jesus' simple message of salvation to those lonely souls who are fighting either fear or boredom. The old phrase *There are no atheists in foxholes* is proven regularly enough in this war. Often, the days are monotonous. They drag on as though there is no war, only to be suddenly interrupted with the most terrifying moments of their lives. Without a doubt, more than eighty percent of the men have a high regard for the chaplains. They trust them as spiritual counselors who often prove to be their only link to a reality that is resilient enough to keep them from going over the edge. With his connection to the chaplains, Micky is becoming privy to more and more of the soldiers' sentiments about the way the war is being conducted and, much to his surprise, is finding himself directing them to Chaplain Gohrke's discussions on the pros and cons concerning the war. Much of this is being fueled by new recruits who are more aware of what's going on back in the States. They come singing anti-war anthems fed by rock and roll singers who are having a big impact on the culture.

Gohrke rarely minces words. Micky has heard him challenge soldiers who feel they don't have a moral obligation to fight in this war by saying, "Let's deal with the reality of our situation. Whether we like it or not, we're here, and our choices will eventually come to this: If we all want to get out of here alive, then we must begin to look out for one another. That guy sitting next to you wants to get home as bad as you do. That requires each of us to fight just as hard for each other. Our welfare is going to depend on how well we hold true to this certainty, even in the intensity of combat. That means we are going to fight for everyone in the platoon—not just for ourselves."

Micky finds his stock answer about this being a just war challenged by moderating opinions like Chaplain Gohrke's. Micky walks a fine line; he is still troubled when he can't connect to his fellow soldiers. In a conversation he initiated with Gohrke, Micky confessed, "Since I've been in the army, I don't feel as though I've ever been able to relate to my fellow troops. I see them having a brotherhood with each other that I don't have. I envy the way you deal with tough situations. You always seem to have the right answer. I'd like to have that ability."

Gohrke takes a few moments to study what Micky has just owned up to, and then he finally says, "Micky, I have no clue what gifts God has in store for you—I'm still discovering my own—but I do know this: unless you thank Him for those He has already given you, you'll never get more." In typical Gohrke fashion, he moves on to something Micky can change without waiting for Micky's response: "I told a group of men going on night patrol I'd have a worship service for them. You sounded like you got the liturgy down pretty good, so let's get going, and ... bring your little organ along with the rest of the stuff."

"Yes, sir," is Micky's only response as Gohrke hurries to get his service book and at least a stole as a vestment. Something about the Padre's conversation lingers in his thoughts. *Maybe I haven't been grateful.* This revelation has come from a father confessor he's come to admire. Micky ponders this revelation differently than he would if it were coming from anyone other than Gohrke. With a different attitude, he fills the small trailer hooked behind the jeep with his portable organ and a small altar the chaplain likes, along with a dozen or so chairs for seating.

The enemy has frequently crept within range of the base and will not hesitate to raise havoc by lobbing in rocket grenades—usually at night, when they can quickly meld back into the darkness. There are riflemen sent out to meet this threat several times a week. When there is an immediate danger like this and these soldiers are exposed to this kind of peril, they are much more willing to fight an enemy who violates the safe haven of their base; those who are called to go on these night patrols in an effort put a stop to these incursions are much more inclined to follow orders than they are when they're asked to charge over some obscure hill—especially if it's a hill they already cleared the day before.

Micky is busying himself with his duties. He's found a little clearing off to the side of the hooches where Chaplain Gohrke can hold his service discreetly. Gohrke likes to be close enough to the larger population that they can join in if they feel compelled, but not so close that he appears presumptuous to those who don't. At least in this setting, he very seldom—if ever—has been inclined to grapple over differing theological difficulties. Rather, he has taken on a more open ecumenical approach, mingling military ends with theology. His intention is to meet the spiritual needs of these young soldiers as soldiers. He regards denominational bickering as a worthless luxury.

Chaplain Gohrke explains his position, saying, "Under normal conditions regarding human interactions, we can agree that certain scriptural situations should be met. But we are being called on to respond to extraordinary circumstances. This is not the time for any of us to attempt to take on a pious morality as to what our Christian responsibility toward our enemy may be. Today we must understand that we are not at the mercy of fate. In spite of our stupid, rebellious inclinations to involve ourselves in wars, our God is still in control. In spite of our rebellious and sinful nature, He knows exactly what He is doing. What each of you must do in this mission is to place yourself under His care. Trust that regardless of the outcome, this good and gracious God has your individual fate in His hands. If you get angry, get angry with your enemy over how he treats your brother. And always remember your brother next to you wants to live as badly as you. Watch out for one another. Blessed is he who lays down his life for his brother. When you come back, I'll be here to help you pick up your pieces."

When Chaplain Gohrke completes the Communion liturgy, he further adds, "This is Jesus' table. Our Savior invites those who trust in

Him to share the feast he has prepared. Any of you who trusts Jesus as your Savior and wishes to receive the Body and Blood of our brother Jesus in Holy Communion, come forward."

As Gohrke is communing the last man, a familiar sound rings out. It's the crack of a sniper rifle. No one is certain where it's coming from, but it's suddenly certain what the object of its aim has become. The communion cup is ripped apart by the impact of the slug, spilling its contents. This small congregation of men lies prone in a group. Not willing to risk detection, one shot is about all the enemy is willing to risk. Micky has been outfitted with a military-grade .45-caliber sidearm and an M-16 rifle, all for the protection of his unarmed chaplain. Realizing he is just as defenseless in this situation as those with no weapons, he lies motionless. Still lying on the ground soaked with consecrated wine, Reverend Gohrke can't resist the moment and says, "Christ is still shedding His blood! Look how he took that last shot for each of you. We have a good and gracious God."

CHAPTER 14
Prisoner Camp

Several hundred miles south, Burt is preparing for another mission with his crew of Bob, Buck, and Quincy. They've been called to a nearby command center for a secret meeting with the field commander. They must be transported about ten kilometers to a secured field post. It's going to involve passing through an outlying village that's been suspected of harboring Viet Cong guerillas. The road leading into the village is more of a narrow path than a road. The only vehicles forcing it to widen are American military vehicles. This morning, it's clogged with Vietnamese workers heading for the surrounding rice paddies, many of them donning wooden poles across their shoulders with two buckets of human excrement hanging off their ends. Dumping them onto the rice paddies is both convenient and beneficial as a readymade fertilizer (American GIs have labeled these as "honey buckets"). The road is full of people with hand-pulled carts carrying anything that can be bought, sold, or utilized.

The troop transport truck is a military deuce and a half with an open cockpit with a driver and an armed escort. This morning, the driver's assignment is to get these four recon guys to this outpost. He is maneuvering this truck around everything that can be used as a hand-driven conveyance when a boy no more than ten or twelve years old steps into the pathway and opens fire with an automatic weapon. The driver is hit immediately, causing the truck to come to a sudden stall after going through a couple of death throe–like jerks of its own. All four passengers are on their feet with weapons in ready defiance against this saboteur. Burt is summarily emptying his clip into the boy. The boy is thrown in every direction by each cartridge ripping its way through his tiny torso. By the time Burt's last round has successfully finished its retribution, Burt is standing over the mangled, bloodied body in a near hysteria, yelling, "Get up! Get up, ya little bastard! I wanna kill ya again!"

The escort is already on his radio, calling for support. The mayhem is not over. The hysterical mother of this boy is already on the scene, screaming things in Vietnamese. A group of men place the boy on a cart and disappear into the village. Burt has no time to recover; the escort has moved the wounded driver to the side and turned the truck around. Within a couple minutes, they are met by a support team from the base. The wounded soldier is medevacked back to the field hospital, the truck is re-outfitted with another driver, and they get back on the road.

Once the team arrives at their destination—an outlying jungle base—they're led into small conference room and asked to take a seat. The commander in this case is a major—Major Roger Liktag, to be specific. Like a bull, he charges through the door; the four pop out of their seats and stand at attention while he takes a seat at the head of the table. "At ease," he barks. He begins, "Gentleman, your reputations for getting things taken care of has preceded you. We have a problem, and I'm confident you are the four who can solve our dilemma. We are missing six men. They, were sent out along with their platoon two weeks ago on a mission that was fairly routine. The problem we're facing is that they're all accounted for except these six disappeared without a trace. Currently, one of our Vietnamese regulars has come forward with a story we can't substantiate. He's claiming they're being held in a jungle prison camp. What we want is for you four to search for this camp and verify this guy's credibility. As a matter of fact, I'd like to send him along with you men as a guide."

Buck is the first to question this latter decision, "Sir, I can speak for all of us on that point. I believe it to be a reckless decision. These gooks ain't trusted as far as we can throw 'em. For all we know, he'd lead us straight into an ambush."

The major is contemplative for a moment, then speaks up. "I want those men found as soon as possible."

"I know, sir, but takin' that gook along ain't gonna do nothin' but be a pain in the ass. We'd have to keep one eye on him an' the other on all his slant-eyed cousins. Given half a chance, he'd lead us right into a booby trap in a heartbeat."

The major is aware he is in command, but he is also aware that if this Vietnamese man was forced on these men, he may not come back. Since many of the Viet Cong guerillas don't wear uniforms, it's become nearly impossible to differentiate soldiers from civilians. If there is even the slightest chance this informant is lying, this project will absolutely fall into a "free kill zone" category. In a growing number of incidents, rather than take a chance that these are merely innocent civilians, American soldiers are inclined to kill anyone who looks or acts hostile, including women and children.

Realizing he doesn't want to create a "push comes to shove" moment over this seeming informant, the major backs off and shifts into another dark side of this fiasco. "Okay, there is another problem. This camp is reportedly over the border into Laos. We aren't supposed to be in Laos. These cretins know how to play this game—they're crafty. They put these camps in places they believe we won't venture. Our men have no military secrets these people want, they don't want anything more out of these men than to break them, forcing them to tell a story of how bad the Americans are treating the Vietnamese people—it's all for propaganda BS. The American news media can't get enough of it."

The four are listening intently. Buck takes the lead. "You get us out near this place, and we'll find it. It may take us awhile, but we'll find it. I know you can't guarantee us you can give us all the support we need, but you can make certain if we find this place you'll do everything that can be done to get these guys outta there."

With a stare that can only be regarded as honest and forthright, Major Liktag declares in a firm tone, "That's the whole damn purpose of this operation. I'm going out on a limb with every general above me. Nonetheless, I'm willing to put my ass on the line—that's exactly why I asked your commander to give me the best he has. Like I said, gentlemen, we aren't supposed to be in Laos. I can only promise I'll do all I can to support you even if it means my rank. You find these men and report back to me. I'll get a team of special forces to get them out of there."

The energy is beginning to build between the four of them. This is the kind of assignment that produces an equal level of tension and anticipation. How some men look at assignments such as this as a challenge and want to begin as soon as possible remains a mystery to those of a gentler nature. Burt is reveling in the attention this major is paying to their abilities. For the first time in his life, he has become good at something. Back in high school, if it hadn't been for his relationship with Micky, he would have remained a nobody. But now he has come into his own. The four of them have built a reputation that exemplifies the army's mission of building men who work together as well-oiled machines. These four have been given assignments that demand split-second decisions and have demonstrated an exceptional ability to succeed where others would have caved. Their boot camp experience, their Advanced Individual Training, and the number of victories they've managed to survive is living proof that the human brain can be re-wired.

The exceptional ability these men convey is second only to how they do it. They must haul all the equipment they need out in the jungle for days at a time—often over a week. Food and water alone is a challenge, never mind the amount of firepower needed to ward off nearly any kind of attack long enough to be successfully extracted.

The next morning, Burt, Buck, Bob, and Quincy are being helicoptered due west toward the Laotian border; they're barely above treetop level. As usual, the roar of the helicopter motor prevents any kind of flowing conversation, leaving each man with his own thoughts. Burt fights any thoughts that take him home to reflect on what his parents may be doing. He knows better than to allow Meadow to enter this sphere of thought, as she has a way of pulling on parts of his maleness that must only remain as obscurities if he wants to survive. These are all luxury thoughts that must be suppressed. They can only grow to be unwanted distractions that will interrupt the kind of work they've given themselves over to. These men regard

God as force behind them and unquestionably behind their decisions. "How else can we explain our continuing success?" Burt asks.

Vietnam is approximately the same size as California. It can be traversed in a couple of hours. The helicopter pilot is the same guy who's flown the team for several of their missions. They've developed a close brotherhood, and they always share with him in their victories. At the moment, he's paying close attention to the topography below. Suitable landing sites can be few and far between in this part of the world. The jungle is dense, leaving only places where no vegetation grows on bare, projecting rock as precarious landing sites. The pilot is very aware of how quick and precise he needs to be to ensure a success of his own. Never certain where the enemy may be lurking makes his odd maneuvering questionable at times. It's been found to be effective to make fake landings to confuse any potential adversary activity in the area. After several of these, a suitable site is located. As usual, this must be done as quickly and precisely as humanly possible. The rotary blade kicks up every conceivable piece of dust, making their disembarkation even more precarious.

Their equipment precedes them as they quickly pitch it from the open doors a few feet to the ground below. This is summarily followed by Burt and Buck jumping out one side and Bob and Quincy from the other. The routine is down to the second as they grab their equipment and make a mad dash to the safety of the jungle. It's not possible to distinguish which of these men displays the strongest presence. They appear to be equal, operating as a single unit. Each is burdened with a hundred or more pounds of equipment. As heavy as these packs are, it is remarkable that these young men do not stoop. They are strong and eager, yet they possess a noticeable degree of patience when it's required. They are each in amazing condition despite the amount of beer they've had between missions. Along with these backpacks, each man carries a telescopic M60 rifle that's never away from his reach. All this combined indicated remarkable level of endurance.

When the team reaches the safety of the jungle overgrowth, it's time to begin their strategy. This assignment has been entrusted to them, and they are hell-bent on fulfilling it. Once they're able to coordinate their maps with what they remember of their view from the air, they agree to begin their trek. They must remain ever wary of booby traps. The Viet Cong are amazingly clever when installing these deadly devices. Some are as simple as a weak cover of tangled tresses laid unnoticed over a pit with sharpened slices of bamboo stakes ready to impale a falling victim; others are bungee cords stretched to hold sharpened spears ready to impale other unwary victims who might be walking through the jungle. The whole purpose is to plant a fear of what lies in store in the mind of every American soldier who might be bold enough to ignore these threats. Consequently, the team holds everything as suspicious until proven otherwise. These four hold a substantial acquaintance with the VC's tricks; they've been extensively trained to know what to look for, in addition to their firsthand experience.

They particularly recall one of their *real* training sessions when they were exposed to a VC-held area. One of the trainees unwarily fell through the cover over one of these pits and lay helplessly screaming on a bed of sharpened stakes that sliced their way into his body. When the others heard his screams, their first impulse was to rush to his aid. The seasoned instructor shouted orders to prevent the others from going to the poor guy's assistance. With careful inspection, they discovered that the VC had anticipated this reaction and surrounded the area with pits to trap unwary would-be rescuers. The need to successfully complete the mission and survive to tell about it has a foothold in the psyche of each of these collaborators. Their expertise keeps them both sharp and diligent.

Leaving a cache of ammunition at their expected extraction point is advisable; it lessens their burden and guarantees them adequate defense should they need it. They carefully count out just enough ammunition to hopefully hold them through a short-run firefight until their rescue helicopter arrives. Nevertheless, this certainly doesn't compromise their abilities to carry on with their mission.

They also are united in how they intend to move through the jungle—always slow and in sight of each other. They prefer to stay off any trails, as these are usually patrolled. With each carrying a small, state-of-the-art hand-sized radio, they've worked out a simple but effective communication system using only the on/off button in a series of near silent clicks. This scheme is designed to keep them all from encountering an unforeseen danger that only one of them has become unaware of. It's been a life-saver in the past and is readily depended upon. It frees them to cover more territory than if they were moving in a straight line. The major drawback is getting themselves and their loaded packs through the unforgiving jungle tangle. As slow as it is, they remain focused, following an agreed strategy.

The first day is uneventful. Finally coming to an end, they regroup and happily slip their backpacks off their tired shoulders, rehydrate and eat a dehydrated ration, and quietly discuss what they plan to do the following day. Burt agrees to take the first watch. Other jungles he's been in have a myriad of night creatures expressing themselves with all kinds of unfamiliar sounds. This jungle is pitch black and has an eerie silence that incites his thoughts to randomly bang around and bounce off the walls inside his head. He doesn't possess an emotion he can identify. There is a contentment in this kind of situation; it's not a loneliness as much as an aloneness that gives him contentment. *This is the first time in my life when I feel like a first-class version of myself.* This thought gives him satisfaction each time he finds himself alone in the jungle. When his watch is up, he sleeps like a dead man.

Morning arrives. The brief contentment he enjoyed during his turn at watch has quickly been replaced by a familiar awareness of hunger. With a minimum of noise, each man efficiently takes care of his bodily needs, always keeping the environment within the scope of his attention. This foursome is mentally, emotionally, and physically prepared to meet the day, regardless of the circumstances. They are obsessed with doing this kind of work and have insulated themselves against the regular soldiers, who are often overheard referencing them as a "bunch of cowboys." These young men have found peace within themselves amid danger. They believe they were born for this kind of work and have found their true selves. In less than twenty minutes after they rise, they are as fully organized to resume their trek as the environment permits. With all this concluded, they gather for a simple prayer, have a quick pow-wow to review today's strategy, and are on their way.

The early morning daylight is struggling to find a path to the jungle floor. The best it can do this early is to give a golden crown of sunlight to the tops of the trees. Although the temperature will soon rise in direct proportion to the rising sun, these same trees that held yesterday's heat have released it gradually through the night while awaiting today's sun to replenish the loss. There is no lack of monkeys and jungle birds in these trees, and they're ready to scold any competitors who threaten their private domain. The trick in this part of the jungle is to move in concert with the animals. This is a requirement if they expect the animals to give an alert to warn of other human intruders. It involves finding a rhythm of movement that is acceptable to these local inhabitants.

By noon, the temperatures have risen substantially. By chance, they come across a mountain stream of water making its way through a tangle of rock and fauna. More than ready to take advantage of it, they release their packs and take turns at watch while the others lie prone in its coolness. Having had his turn in the stream, Burt feels a sensation he hasn't felt since leaving the States: a chill. It's brief but loaded with his recollections of Michigan winters. He recalls how the city had flooded a ball field and allowed it to freeze, turning it into a skate rink. It was a great social event for young people. He recalls how willing he was to become an obsequious sycophant for any girl who asked him to tighten the laces on her skates. He recalls kneeling in front of her bare shin, staring at the faint remnants of last summer's tan, and noticing how it was accentuated by the whiteness of her skate.

Now Burt's eyes catch something struggling to free itself from a tree limb lodged in the stream. Making his way over to it to get a better look, he finds a hat and quickly retrieves it: almost black, with a floppy brim. Giving it a closer look, it turns out to be a Viet Cong military hat. By this time, he has the attention of the other three. This find automatically shifts their attention from enjoying an unexpected pleasure to the reality of their surroundings. Each of them is responding in exactly the same way; they seize their rifles and scan the jungle. Never satisfied that the enemy isn't lurking just beyond their scope, they spend the next sixty seconds searching every opening the forest provides. Seeing nothing that suggests they may be in imminent danger, they gather around the newfound artifact. With anxious eyes, Buck continues scanning their perimeter. Simultaneously, he runs his fingers over the soggy material. In a near whisper, he says, "Chances are this washed from upstream. Charlie (a slang term for the Viet Cong) may have some form of stronghold above us."

The others nearly replicate Buck's reaction and sentiments. "This is a ready water supply for any kind of settlement. I suggest we follow it for a while," says Burt. Within minutes, they have a consensus, have shouldered their packs, and are on their way. The course is rough and steep in some places. The water rushing over the rocks produces enough background noise to prevent them from hearing anything else. A mutual concern over this dilemma splits them into two groups: Buck and Burt on one side of the stream, and Bob and Quincy on the other. They have also agreed to get back into the jungle just deep enough to hear other sounds but still see the stream.

The day wears on with nothing significant to report. But as evening approaches, each man is experiencing a super awareness. This is not a new phenomenon. An unknown energy has influenced each of them equally in the past. It always comes when they are about to encounter a new confrontation. Along with this heightened awareness is an obsession to continue until each of them becomes mindful of its source. In this case, Burt is the first to be tipped off. *That's tobacco smoke I smell.* Lifting his nose a little more, he verifies it. With nearly a knee-jerk action, he is prone on the ground and signal clicking his radio transmitter. Buck has belly crawled to within twenty feet of Burt. Burt gives him a hand signal by putting his two fingers together and touching them to his lips as though he's smoking a cigarette. Buck lifts his nose enough to catch a whiff, signaling his detection. Bob and Quincy are on the other side of the stream. They detect an enemy close at hand. Relying on their past experience, they are expected to begin to work their way to the other side. Once again, they are all together. A plan is yet to be worked out. After making an assessment as much as can be made before darkness sets in, they conclude that they know the location of the cigarette smoker and are closing in on that location. The dusk is turning to night. They have an advantage. They all are in possession of state-of-the-art night vision scopes. This gives them an edge on the enemy, who is not in possession of this technology. The only drawback is that it gives off a faint glow, allowing an astute enemy to become aware of their location. They're willing to use only one scope discriminately manned by Buck, and they feel it's worth the gamble to unequivocally determine if this is their target.

As night spreads across the jungle making even the shadows disappear, these four have devised an action to formulate a truer assessment of this situation. They agree to spread out to create a wider construct. Since Bob is the last man to position himself, it's his responsibility to signal his readiness. In concert, they begin to guardedly crawl in the direction of the trailing cigarette smoke. After a slow, deliberate movement forward, Burt is the first to report his discovery. Using the click signal, he spells out the word "l-i-g-h-t-s." What's captured his attention is a faint light from a jungle lamp that emerges through the leaves, creating a flickering display. By all accounts, it's at least a hundred yards out. This heads up has gotten the attention of everyone on the team. Certain they are onto something more than a lone camper, they continue to cautiously crawl forward across the jungle floor. These men have not only the enemy to be concerned with, but also everything that lives and crawls on the jungle underside. This includes every kind of ant, spider, and snake that takes offense to anything crawling over their domain. Buck is next to make contact. He is within fifteen yards of a lone human lighting a cigarette. Taking advantage of this person's mistake in compromising his vision by staring into the flame, Buck quickly puts his eye to his night scope. What he sees appears to be a guard. The man is armed with a carbine slung over his shoulder. Buck recognizes this carbine as the Soviet SKS carbine/semiautomatic Chinese copy used by the Viet Cong. Not risking being located, as soon as the man extinguishes the flame, Buck quickly turns off the scope. Using his radio, he signals "C-h-a-r-l-i-e" to the others. This alert instantaneously raises the awareness of those who are still probing around in the dark. Rather than risk detection, Buck stops where he is. A wrong move, a twig snapping—almost anything could cause enough curiosity on the part of this guard to prompt him to investigate further.

On the other hand, Burt is in position to move forward and investigate the source of this unexpected jungle light. *It's nothing nature can provide, so it must be from a human source* is his prevailing thought. Unaware of the number of guards or their locations, he cautiously moves forward, keeping his attention on each thing that could potentially compromise this mission. In a short period of time, he's on the edge of a clearing. He's looking down at a small complex of hooches with this single lamp burning brightly on a pole in the center of the clearing. Risking detection, he nonetheless places his scope to his eye. What he sees next is not a sight he can take comfort in: a series of cages, approximately four feet square. In each of these is a human form cramped against the sides in various positions of discomfort. Suddenly, Burt becomes aware that this is the very object of their mission. This is indeed the prisoner-of-war camp they've been seeking. Scanning across the area, he suddenly focuses on several other humans bound with ropes hanging in various positions from what appear to be meat hooks secured in the surrounding trees. Some are bound wrist to ankle, and others are hanging from wrists bound in a backward position. This is guaranteed to slowly, painfully dislodge their arms from their shoulders.

Meanwhile, Buck is keeping a wary eye on the activity of this guard only a few feet in front of him. This guy seems overly trustful of his conditions and his surrounding and makes no bones about clearing his throat, chain smoking—and now snoring. This is the break Buck has been waiting for. Very slowly, he begins to get to his feet. Employing his night vision scope, he finds his way back to their rendezvous point. Bob and Quincy have already arrived, and Burt isn't far behind. Bob and Quincy made their way to the back side of the camp and viewed pretty much the same thing as Burt, with one exception: they came across a path that went deeper into the jungle. Not certain where other guards may be posted, they opt to stay put until a better assessment of the situation presents itself.

Convinced they have uncovered the mystery of the missing six soldiers, they agree to get as much rest tonight as they can. Sleeping intermittently between watches is all these four expect for the night. They've agreed that the first thing they must do with the pre-dawn period is to return to their voyeur's undertaking. "We gotta figure how many of these slope heads are mannin' this camp an' where they're placin' their guards. This is gonna tell what kinda mess we're getting' ourselves into," says Buck.

This is an agreed assumption. It's gonna be a daylong assignment. They've agreed to report back after dark with any information they find to be crucial. Each of them has chosen his assignment. Burt guardedly makes his way back to a location where he can remain hidden and still gain an optimal amount of information. Light is giving the camp a more complete appearance. There is an aspect of forlornness clouding this place that the night vision scope can't portray—only daylight can render the full truth of this hellhole.

Looking through his scope, Burt can follow the depths human depravity will go to, to seek retribution against a fellow human. By any civilized standards, these jailers are heartless in their treatment of these prisoners. (It's been noticed by others at other times that the veneer of civilization is very thin and is quickly eroded in times such as these.) What Burt is seeing firsthand is a group of enemy combatants approximately his own age making life unbearable for another group of fellow human beings. In doing so, the hate and anger has given birth to torture methods that are barbaric in any book. In the past, Burt has struggled with himself in not giving himself over emotionally to wild, uncalculatable misgivings. This situation has a much more personal element surrounding it than anything he's encountered thus far. What he's viewing are tortures that even in his wildest imagination are beyond the pale of his worst demented state. He is watching a guard wave a live rat by its tail in front of a bound, kneeling American prisoner. He then places the squirming rat in a bag, places it over the prisoner's head, and ties the bag tightly around his neck, leaving him to scream and squirm helplessly on the ground. The same guard commences to kick this hapless prisoner unmercifully.

The men in the four-by-four-foot so-called "tiger cages" are also released just long enough to clean their excrement off themselves. They're then tied at the wrists and interchanged with those hanging from the meat hooks. Some are hung upside down in enclosed in metal closets with a guard beating on the exterior to prevent sleep. Those who've been cut down are then dragged—conscious or unconscious—and stuffed into the empty cages. This enemy isn't interested in torturing these prisoners to gain information from them—rather, they are either seeking retribution for what they have perceived to be American atrocities against them or trying to force the men to give signed statements denouncing the United States.

Burt is watching with the anger of ten men. He had thirteen years of parochial schooling, and never once did he doubt the existence of God. Every fiber in his being is screaming at God to intervene in this event and put an end to it. His academic Bible lessons have not prepared him to meet this kind of corruption of the human soul. Being forced to watch his fellow Americans beaten and humiliated hour by hour only to be subjected to yet another unimaginable torment is reducing him to the level of one of these tormentors. His own desire for vengeance is becoming insatiable. As the hours go by with the absence of God becoming more conspicuous, Burt's childhood Christian faith is evaporating into the beastliness of his surroundings. By the end of the day, he is emotionally drained and spiritually bankrupt. He feels no connection with the civilized world or with God.

At last, it's time to regroup. Making his way back to their rendezvous, Burt is finding he's become a different person. *These animals don't deserve to live. What's more, I'm going to make sure they don't.* A latent cynicism is overtaking him. Buck has already returned. Soon Bob and Quincy come sneaking in, with Burt following soon after. There is a different kind silence between them. It's a silence that is unlike anything from any other operation they've shared thus far. It's the kind of silence that's difficult to bring words into. They've all shared the same powerless experience while watching their own undergo ruthless cruelty at the hands of men they could kill with their bare hands. Trained as they are in patience and stoicism, they are not prepared to sit watching idly as six of their own are having the life deliberately crushed out of them.

Hardly able to keep his voice down to a whisper, Burt is the first to comment. "I don't believe there is a God. No God sits by and lets this happen to his people! If we wait around for God to free these guys, they'll be dead!"

The silence continues; each finds it difficult to process what they've experienced. None of these men are willing to regard this aspect of war as a normal facet they can ignore. The problem remains that they are under orders to report what they find back to Major Liktag. Buck reminds them of their obligation to follow orders. "We ain't out here freelancin'. We're out here to do a job, and by God, we're gonna get it done."

Quincy breaks his silence with some new information. "I followed that trail behind the camp to a place that looks like sleepin' quarters. I only could account for no more than eight men mannin' this whole place."

Buck looks at Bob, waiting for his report. "I held my sights on all of 'em at one time or another. I had my finger on the trigger. It took everything I got in me to keep from blowin' their damnable heads off."

Buck is getting the drift that he may be outnumbered regarding how to handle this situation. It certainly isn't a lack of anger that pushes him to challenge their insubordination. "We gave that Major our word we'd find this prison camp and report back to him and I think we oughtta be men of our word."

"We can be 'men of our word' and bring these guys home just as well," says Burt. "If we wait for anyone else to act in this situation, those guys won't last long. If you guys don't go in there, I'll go it alone."

Buck realizes he is facing a near riot of angry comrades. "We ain't gonna barge in there like maniacs. If we gonna do this, we gotta do it good n' right. We gotta get a plan together. Let's get a couple hours of sleep and think on it a bit."

With a turn at sleep and a turn at watch, they each manage to get a few hours of sack time. This gives them enough of a stretch to get themselves together and become mentally organized enough to make a comprehensive plan.

Bob is the first to speak. "They only got one guard at that bunk house. I could've taken him out anytime I wanted."

Buck has gotten little sleep. He's gone over several ideas and has settled on one. "I want to get us all in position like we got 'em surrounded. When y'all get where ya need to be, click your radio. We all gonna start throwin' lead on 'em like we're a whole damn platoon."

This is what Burt and the rest of them have been waiting for. They pull out as much ammunition as they could carry and begin to sneak out, making as little noise as possible in to what is becoming familiar terrain. Burt can feel his lungs heaving in anticipation of what is to become of all of them. This is no time to be wondering if this is a good idea; they've all committed themselves. By daybreak, they've positioned themselves in such a way and determined how they're going to begin their fireworks. When each is set, they click their radio along with their identity clicks. This gives Buck the assurance that they are in their proper positions. When he signals back to them, they all commence to fire at once from all directions. The guards are the first to be taken out, and then anyone in sight. The enemy is caught completely off guard. Some try to run for cover, only to be mowed down. Bob sprays the bunk hooch using the automatic mode on his M60. As the bullets make contact, they throw debris in every direction. Two more come scrambling out with multiple wounds and collapse as they are hit by Quincy on the opposite side. Taking advantage of the enemy's confusion, Bob dispatches a grenade into the bunk hooch. The straw and mud are blown into the air, and the walls begin to collapse under the force of the explosion. Two more come crawling out through the dust of the explosion, screaming and cursing in Vietnamese. They are immediately dispatched. It's become a free fire zone. Every human in this camp who is not an American is considered an enemy combatant and killed. It's become clear the enemy has been overly confident in the supposed security of their hidden jungle torture prison.

Burt can hear the bullets from Bob and Quincy tearing through the brush overhead. Aware of the need to stay low to avoid being hit by "friendly fire," Burt remains hunched down behind a tree but still able to fire his cache of bullets. Being only four in number, they are nonetheless succeeding in displaying a force much larger than the four of them, resulting in total confusion and decimation of the enemy. The enemy has not returned one shot. Equipoise in battle is nowhere close to describing this total annihilation. Taken totally by surprise, the enemy lies mangled by the overwhelming barrage of gunfire.

Buck and Burt are the first to present themselves to the American captives as liberators. The release them from their cages and cut down those who are hanging from the tree-borne meat hooks.

These men are hardly able to stand, naked, and covered in filth, but the look of relief in their faces is clear; the hope they find in this dark day is evident from their smiles, weak as they may be. Burt had made it a point to ensure he was the one to kill the guard who had placed the hood with the rat inside on the American prisoner. He is also making it a point to remove the rat bag from the prisoner's head. The poor guy's entire face and head is riddled with rat bites. He then places it, rat and all, over the head of the deceased guard and ties it securely around his neck. The final body count is twelve—four more than anticipated.

All four of the liberators are on the same page. "We gotta get the hell outta here fast," says Buck. He realizes they must rely on their training and experience to ensure an effective ending. They hardly have the luxury of allowing their freed prisoners to regain their strength. Letting each take their fill from a canteen of water is the best they can do under the circumstances. The prisoner who had been hanging backward from his bound wrists has no feeling in his arms but is able to stand and walk. Two of those who were in the cages are unable to stand at this point. The other three are weak but able to assist those other three as much as possible. They're in a terrible world, and all of them know it. Their primary source of energy at this juncture is adrenaline and youth. Burt's ears are still ringing from the gunfire, but he's ignoring the uneasiness for the greater and more immediate need to get everyone out of this ordeal and to a safer place.

Quincy has been able to scrounge a couple small bags of rice from the wreckage. Bob has cut some poles and given them to those who are struggling to walk. Burt is also able to recover the prisoners' clothing, including boots; they had been stored in a small storage hooch along with their dog tags. This is all accomplished in less than half an hour. Picking through the clothing worn by the dead camp officer, he's also been able to recover some documents written in Vietnamese. Folding these, Burt places them in his rucksack to present to Major Liktag.

The team focuses on moving out of Laos to an extraction point in Vietnam. For all practical purposes, these men are in the sovereign country of Laos without permission. It's a zone the United States military can't infiltrate without creating an international incident. Experience and training are telling them what to do, but only their confidence in their abilities is allowing them to move forward. If this skirmish had a narrative or a point of view, it would read that despite the ramifications, *the end justifies the means.* There isn't one of these four men who wouldn't do the same thing over again. The relief and the willingness of these rescued men to do all they can to involve themselves in the process of their liberation despite their injuries and the determination of the American soldiers to rescue these prisoners demonstrates the attitude American soldier's resolve to never abandon their own. There is always an element of uneasiness in war. Everyone is anxious to get out, but not at the expense of completing a necessary task. These men need the protection of some clothing—and especially boots. With a concerted effort, the team gets the prisoners into pants and shirts and puts boots on their feet. Their legs are far from strong, but with a good amount of determination, a stout staff, and some aid from the others, these liberated prisoners are ready to begin the trek out. They have the desire and the willingness, and now—because they've put themselves in the hands of these liberators—the knowledge they'll need to survive.

CHAPTER FIFTEEN
Dengler

Micky has been outfitted with an M1 51 quarter-ton truck with a trailer—commonly referred to as a Jeep. His primary job is to chauffeur Chaplain Gohrke. Since chaplains don't normally carry weapons, Micky is also commissioned to be his bodyguard; he's been issued a .45-caliber sidearm and an M-16 rifle. Today, Gohrke has decided to make his way to the front some ten kilometers through the jungle and mountain passes. He knows the need for spiritual comfort is stronger in the battle zones than on the base.

"When things are going well, there is little demand for God— it's when everything is going to hell that these guys need the spiritual comfort only the Gospel can bring," says an impassioned Gohrke. Besides, those chaplains who are not willing to serve in war zones quickly lose credibility; the men like to see their chaplain's valor exceed their own.

Micky's Christian school background focused a lot on behavior: no smoking, drinking, cussing, or sex before marriage. The behavior Micky sees displayed in others have led him to take on a self-righteous attitude toward his fellow soldiers. Some of his high school debate team topics had been to defend his Christian principles against the modern, permissive culture of the day. Without discerning a significant way of approaching Chaplain Gohrke seemingly overlooking certain immoral behaviors in those he's ministering to, Micky risks taking advantage of having Gohrke trapped in the jeep to question Gohrke about his Christian sentiments.

"Sir, do you mind if I ask you a personal question?" asks Micky. They're at a point in this trip where Micky feels confident enough to keep his eye open for any unforeseen dangers and hold a conversation.

Gohrke looks at Micky with one of those pastoral expressions that welcomes any member of his flock to engage him with anything on their mind. "Certainly, Micky. What's on your mind?"

"Sir, do you condone the behavior of these soldiers in their open violations of God's law?"

A little puzzled at the question, Chaplain Gohrke asks, "What do you mean, Micky?"

"I mean, these guys are drinking every chance they get. They're smoking dope or screwing every Vietnamese hooch maid that passes through their door."

Gohrke pauses in thought for a moment. "Tell me, Micky: do you believe you are a sinner?"

"Of course I'm a sinner?" says Micky.

Gohrke pauses once again, then forms this question: "Are you willing to tell me one of your behaviors that you regard as a sin?" It's the type of question that only one who is comfortable in his own skin can ask.

Micky is noticeably caught off guard by the forthrightness of Gohrke's question. His first reaction is how to deal honorably with the unexpected turn his question has taken. His next reaction is to try not to stammer and attempt to sidestep Gohrke's unwelcome probing. Then a third thought tells him that despite his attempt to dodge the question, he's safe because he can't recall anything he's done wrong anyway. With a serious, no-nonsense look, Micky boldly declares, "I used to sin when I was little, but since I gave myself to Jesus, I haven't found it necessary to sin anymore."

Gohrke gives him a knowing look that tells Micky he's not buying his story. "Let's leave my question open for the time being. In answer to your question regarding the behavior of your fellow soldiers—no, I don't condone anyone's sinful behavior, including my own. But if I'm to take another man's inventory, I must be prepared to use the same measuring stick on myself." Pausing for a moment of thought, Gohrke continues, "What I want you to consider is this: what in a man's life experience will bring him to sin? Last year. you had little classroom tasks to consider these kinds of questions using your pen and paper. Today, you are facing the realities of life. I also want

151

you to consider what you think the purpose of the Christian cross is and who it was intended to benefit."

The time of being in a safe military zone has rapidly changed. The subject of conversation quickly changes to their immediate predicament. Micky has heard from some of the other soldiers how unsafe the area they are about to enter can be. Since the chaplains don't carry arms, Micky is very much aware of his role as Gohrke's bodyguard. With all seriousness, he asks, "I think this is the area I heard could spell trouble for a lone jeep traveling without support—are you certain you want to continue?"

Without a pause, Gohrke says, "Our Lord has brought us this far, and I'm certain He can finish the job if He wills."

Micky got his answer point blank. He checks his sidearm and the availability of his M-16. Without further question—and in case it isn't God's will—he floors the jeep, driving like he's been stirred by something from hell. Looking over at the seat next to himself, he sees Gohrke hanging on with both hands, saying nothing. This tells him his driving has Gohrke's approval. After half an hour and a million bumps in the road, they arrive at the war zone. They are abruptly faced with a dilemma. The officer heading up this platoon has been wounded and has been helicoptered out. The sergeant that's left in charge is combat green and near a panic stage. Pulling the chaplain aside, the sergeant explains his fear. "Our second lieutenant was hit with mortar round. There ain't another officer here, so that just leaves me. This is my first combat experience, and I don't feel qualified to lead these guys."

Gohrke recognizes the overwhelming stress in this twenty-year-old's face. With compassion, he says, "I'm a captain, and I've had military training. You stand down, and I'll give you a hand until they send a replacement. Just catch me up on where you find us with the enemy."

"Thank you, sir. You don't know how relieved I am. I'll do everything I can to help you keep this mission goin'," says the sergeant. They spend the next half hour going over where and how this platoon can be the most effective in rooting out the enemy.

Gohrke realizes immediately what's needed. "You say the enemy is in front of us and you've been pushing them back into the jungle. Do you have any patrols watching our flanks?"

"No, sir, we don't at the moment. We've been spending a lot of our time medevacking our wounded out of here."

Gohrke takes a second to look around. He is viewing a tired platoon. They've been in the field for days, relying on air drops to bring in needed supplies. If that weren't enough, they've lost their commander. Seeing all he needs to see, Gohrke says, "What we need to do immediately is send a scout team out to make certain the enemy isn't attempting to 'horseshoe' us in. If they manage to do that, it wouldn't take much for them to close up the end, and we'd be surrounded. We got to make sure that if we're going to fight, it's going to be on our terms."

The sergeant is relived and content to take chaplain's orders; he couldn't be more eager to rustle up a couple patrols, providing he doesn't have to make the orders. Just as he's beginning to bring a team together, an enemy rocket comes screeching in. It catches the entire camp's attention. Two men are hit by the full force of the rocket. They're down and not moving. Until now, the Americans have been the pursuers. Chaplain Gohrke shouts out the order to man positions. His suspicion that their flanks could easily be compromised has come to fruition. The enemy has pulled them into a vulnerable place. The artillery is coming in from three sides: the front and right and left flanks. Getting the sergeant aside, Gohrke assesses the situation: "They'd be coming in on our rear if they had enough men. I think they're stretched out about as thin as we are. We need to get patrols out there to find where they're firing on us and take it out. For now, the Americans are returning around after round from their heavy .50-calibers and sending every bit of jungle underbrush that's hit flying in the air like it exploded. As usual, the enemy has underestimated the overwhelming firepower backing the American soldier. With this backing, the patrols begin to move out. They're armed with M-16s, as much ammunition as they can carry, grenade launchers, and a strong desire to find the enemy and wipe him out.

After the .50-caliber machine guns have done their work the jungle is extremely quiet once again. Micky finds himself in a foxhole along with a guy who last week had been the focus of Micky's attention. He was one of those "sinners" Micky had been telling Chaplain Gohrke about an hour earlier. Now he's facing his accused in a foxhole with the necessity to look out for each other. Micky cannot recall a time in his life he felt this vulnerable. With not another thought on this young man's sins, Micky discovers they are sharing a common need for one another. The name stenciled across his fatigues reads DENGLER. Under these circumstances, knowing each other's names isn't that important. What's important is without thought to race, color, or creed, there is an immediate bond developing between them to stay alive. They both remain crouched together in the hole, waiting for someone to tell them what their next move is going to be.

Micky is as frightened to die as is this young man. Being in the presence of another human sharing the same fear offers only a limited amount of comfort, but it is nonetheless a real need—or, put in stronger terms, a *craved* need. Concerns about race, color, creed, or the kind of sinner sharing your angst have no place in this crisis. The common need of one another for one another creates a remembrance and a special bond that lasts a lifetime—even if they never meet again. To add to the misery, a torrential rainstorm has blown in. It's coming down in buckets. The dirt in the foxhole is turning to a greasy slime, drying like scummy wax, and sticking to their already grime-covered fatigues. They have remained wordless to the other, alone with their individual apprehension. Certainly, neither are accustomed to this kind of anxiety, but just having another human to share what life they have left is enough for now.

The patrols have been out for hours looking for bodies as well as enemy combatants. The remainder of the platoon remain in position, hunkered down and awaiting a possible ambush. The hours go by. The rain finally subsides. Micky and Dengler have remained silent with only their own fearful thoughts to occupy their minds. With the immediate danger seemingly past, Micky is the first to break the silence. Extending his hand, he says, "My name is Murphy—Micky Murphy. I'm the chaplain's assistant. He pronounces this in a way that's generally reserved for royalty.

"Well, it's damned good to know I'm in good company if I'm gonna face my Maker," Dengler says smiling and extending his own hand along with a bit of irony. "My name's Allen Dengler. I knew you was the chaplain's assistant 'cause I seen ya together around the base."

They have found that "common bond" all soldiers find together when they enter the fighting fields—a mutual agreement to set aside differences and a desire to survive. Still in their shared foxhole, Micky and Allen divide up a meal of C-rations interspersed with small talk about themselves. From time to time, gunfire is heard around their perimeter, causing them both to return to a pensive silence of waiting and seeing. They are certain it has to do with the patrols sent out to rout out any lingering Viet Cong fighters. All of this awareness brings with it a healthy degree of uncertainty that ensures they will not be caught unawares once again.

One by one, the patrols return. They are busy reporting and conspiring with the intervening officer, Chaplain Captain Gohrke, and the sergeant. The camp has begun to relax, with men beginning to venture out of their foxholes. The sun has come out immediately, heating things to a muggy milieu. Meals of C-rations and shared cigarettes are making their way throughout. Some are cleaning the mud out of their weapons. Others are removing some of their rain-soaked clothing while swatting an onslaught of jungle parasites stirred by the rain and the scent of blood. Micky is keeping an eye and ear open to the chatter among the men regarding the past few hours.

For now, Chaplain Gohrke has finished with his military business and is seeking out Micky to begin to set up the portable altar and ready the communion ware. As lead officer and as the chaplain, Gohrke is in a position to make a special call to worship for the entire

155

platoon, including a special provision of Holy Communion for those who desire it and are still on guard duty. There are only a few things in life capable of bringing a man's bottom up to meet his crisis. Fear of being killed is undeniably one of them. In this situation, the entire platoon has been tenderized enough during the past few days of combat to show up for services, including Dengler, an acute backslider and practicing sinner. In the absence of an immediate danger to worry him, Micky is quickly returning to his well-worn road of judging sinners. He has been around the Lutherans long enough to know they don't pass Holy Communion around to just anyone who walks through the door. He's interested to see how far Gohrke is willing to go with his generous invitation. Meanwhile, his thoughts meander around to who among this bunch he believes is worthy enough to receive this Holy Supper. He's especially watching how Dengler is behaving during the confession of sins part of the liturgy. *This is one of those guys who thinks he can sin all week, show up on Sunday telling God how sorry he is, and then start all over again the following week. And he's just fine with it.* This has been a staple in Micky's thought for much of his life. He knows he can sort out the worst of the sinners much better than Gohrke.

After a short homely describing God's grace like drinking a fine whisky, with an emphasis on *it must be taken straight*, and using the words of institution, Gohrke begins to consecrate the bread and the wine to become the body and blood of Christ. Finishing this, he renews the same invitation for all of them to come and partake. Micky participates by distributing the host in the form of consecrated bread, while Chaplain Gohrke distributes the chalice. Micky is nearly incensed beyond words when Dengler follows the faithful to receive the body and blood of Christ. Despite his feelings of well-being with Dengler when they were both faced with death in the foxhole with enemy rockets pouring in and their need for each other, his self-righteous attitude once again follows the well-worn path of no resistance. Begrudgingly, he places the host on the tongue of this known reprobate. He then watches self-righteously as Gohrke cheerfully gives him Christ's holy blood to drink without a moment's hesitation.

The men are still standing in a group while receiving the chaplain's words of God's blessing when once again a shot rings out. In a flash, the scene changes from contemplation to terror. The initial reaction is to hit the ground immediately, weapon in hand, prepared to defend oneself. They all hit the ground, save one man. Dengler seemingly hesitates for a half second before collapsing to the ground alone. Micky knows exactly what has happened. He's experienced it before. A sniper has taken advantage of the lull and fired a shot, striking Dengler in the forehead and killing him instantly. Micky's first reaction is pure shock and a fear for his own life. While Gohrke—and everyone in the vicinity except for Micky—has run to the aid of this fallen warrior and with the .50-calibers ferociously returning fire, this aftermath has become a surreal incident. Micky watches from the sidelines as if this were a movie in slow motion. This whole incident doesn't fit one high school religion test he had taken, nor any athletic event in which he had participated. This is beyond the pale of anything he has experienced in his life. His mind is anxiously treading sand like a stuck bulldozer; he's unable to clear any of it out of his head. It's as though two realities are continuing to clash; his old high school reality and this strange, aberrated reality are attacking his expectations. He is finally able to settle on an agreeable conclusion: *This must be God's seeking His retribution for Dengler's sinful life.* His thoughts of shared aims surrounding his foxhole experience with this young man have been completely and subjectively replaced by his conceit.

With Gohrke's voice yelling at him to get a medic, Micky finally gets ahold of himself and remembers his job is to be the number-one assistant to this military chaplain. He doesn't have to go far, since the medic is already in the congregation and heading to Dengler's side. Meanwhile, the attending guards overwhelmingly reply with .50-caliber guns spraying the jungle with rounds so close a nit couldn't survive. The scene moves very quickly from chaotic to organized ·

chaos. A patrol is organized and sent out to verify a miss or a kill for the sniper. The guard detail had spotted the faint flash from the sniper's rifle and handily took him out. They are back in an hour, dragging what's left of the dead sniper. Headquarters demands a body count. They are very specific about this to the point that men have been extracting an ear from each kill rather than dragging a bunch of bodies about.

This kind of carnage is new to Micky. In Micky's world, the word "kill" had only been used metaphorically during a sporting event. This is as far removed from anything he has ever experienced or ever imagined he would experience. Little by little, the religion he has learned in Christian school is eroding under the realities of war. He has always regarded God as blessing him, making him not given to sin like most other people. But recently, where he has always been so certain about his and God's relationship, a bewilderment is beginning to overtake him. More and more, he's beginning to see the way the corrupt world is having its way and less and less God having His way. This war is far, far removed from the shelter his church had provided. Often, his church life had removed him from the snares of Satan's world rather than pushing him to meet and overcome them. It's a design by which some American parents choose to keep their children safe. Unfortunately, while it may make them temporarily safe from Satan's snares, it doesn't necessarily make them mentally and spiritually strong. This strategy has had limited success in modern American culture and doesn't do well at all in a war zone. Many remain frightened children who are unable to do anything very good or very bad. While some run toward the noise, others remain hunkered down in a foxhole, doing nothing more than not running way; they're satisfied to do their thirteen months and get the hell out of here.

What had originally been planned as a day trip for Micky and Chaplain Gohrke to and from the fight zone has turned into a week. Nonetheless, they remain to serve. It may be outside their military job description, but Gohrke feels it's his duty until another combat officer can be brought in to replace him. He's pulling double duty as the senior combat officer as well as his heartfelt commitment to council and share hope with those who languish.

The day finally arrives for a fresh new senior officer to arrive—and fresh he is. He's a newly drafted college boy who through his ROTC training has been promoted to the rank of Second Lieutenant. The sergeant is almost as despondent as the day Gohrke began helping him out. "Padre, I hate to lose ya. You were sure an answer to my prayers. I'm not lookin' forward to our next skirmish with this newbie."

"I want to tell you something, sergeant; I couldn't have done alone what you and I did together. You're a good combat leader. You do the same for this new guy and I know things will go well. Oh, and by the way, don't forget to say prayers for this newbie—he's sure to need them."

Gohrke makes his last rounds among the men. There couldn't be a stronger bond between himself and this rag-tag platoon of warriors. Hands can be warmed on the love coming out of this chaplain. Some are near tears as he makes his way from soldier to soldier, blessing each of them.

Micky is taken aback with all the attention this man of God is getting from these men. Still yearning for those glorious schooldays of a by-gone era when he was the center of everyone's attention, his mind fills with envy and jealousy. It's to a point where it shouts out, *What about me! I'm with this guy. I'm the one who set up everything you guys needed to have a decent worship service! Don't I ever get any thanks!* Although, he has been a football, field and track star, undergone weeks of combat training and several more weeks pertaining to his Advanced Individual Training, he feels very ill prepared for this kind of life-threatening misadventure. His rather naïve "Just War Theory" hasn't been thought of in months.

With everything in place, the time finally arrives. Chaplain Gohrke and Micky are set to return to the base. For Micky, this occasion hasn't come soon enough. He has had the jeep loaded since morning and it is now noon. Lingering in the war zone with life-altering events happening way to often to suit him, Micky's survival only guarantees he's lived to endure the harshness of war to begin another day. Aware of having to retread the same dangerous road he traversed a week ago, he has the jeep's speed at maximum capacity. Gohrke is just as silent about his driving as he was on the way out. And just as phenomenally as before, they make it through this enemy-occupied area without a mishap. The conversation once again turns to Micky venting his frustrations.

"I don't get it. I can bust my butt doing everything I'm asked to do and never get any acknowledgement for it, while you seem to be reaping all the glory." Realizing what he's just blurted out to his superior makes him wish he could put those words back in his mouth, but Micky's naïve compulsion overrides his ability to remain silent.

Gohrke's surprised look at his driver's animosity is telling. "You're right. I have been remiss in expressing my gratitude for what you do for me. I want you to know it's *certainly* appreciated."

This confession on the part of Gohrke is even more confusing. Micky doesn't have a clue where this conversation is going or what it's going to come to. On the other hand, this chaplain is cognizant to this young assistant's weakness; he has had him under his tutelage long enough to recognize very few of his strengths and many of his shortcomings.

CHAPTER 16
Hard-hitting Extraction

A four-man reconnaissance team had been sent into Laos to locate a clandestine prisoner-of-war camp, gather information on it, and report back to Major Liktag. The concern had been for six American soldiers believed to have been taken prisoner by the Viet Cong forces operating on the Vietnam side of the border. These six men were reported to have been taken into Laos to a clandestine jungle prison. The four-man patrol unit has located the prison camp but, due to the nature of the situation, they have disregarded orders and have attacked and decimated the camp to save the prisoners from what they saw as a certain death. At present, there are ten American soldiers on the wrong side of the border: four recon soldiers and six freed grunt prisoners. If they are apprehended in violation of the Laotian border laws, the United States will abandon them rather than risk an international incident.

Buck is taking command in his usual no-nonsense approach. "Let's get this show on the road!" With that said, Buck, Burt, Bob, and Quincy all readjust their backpacks up on their shoulders to shift the weight. This allows them to be of some assistance to one of the recovering prisoners. They begin cautiously as they make their way down to the creek bed. They had followed this same stream for several miles before they discovered the prison camp. Now it's time to make their way back down the rough terrain and begin the trek back to their extraction point.

There is no panic among them other than a mild desperation to have Laos behind them as quickly as possible. The entire area on either side of the creek is wet and soggy. It has a sponge-like consistency when it isn't all rock. Water squirts from either side of their boots as they slog their way along, causing a slurping sound with each lift of their boots. Buck is walking point. The trick is to be as perfectly attentive to everything around them as possible. Accumulating six more men in various stages of distress could compromise their mission. From sheer weariness and weakness, a couple of the salvaged captives wobble and fall; they need nearly constant support. These shattered soldiers would rather rest, but they dig down deep inside and manage to get to a sitting position, take a deep breath, and then stagger to their feet once again.

The whooshing wings of bright colored birds going from tree to tree ahead of them warn everything in the bush of the presence of these jungle interlopers. It's not the best scenario for a stealth operation but it's going to have to do despite their threatening situation. These unfettered prisoners cannot be held to the same level of competence as their rescuers, even in their best condition. One of the men begins to hallucinate, believing that Burt, who had taken charge of keeping him moving, was one of his tormenters. Burt is obliged to pin the frightened man down to keep him from running into the jungle. This is another noisy disruption that is ill timed for a surreptitious escape. Even though time is of the essence, a full effort on the part of everyone in the party finally settles this tormented soldier into enough of a confidence to resume plodding on.

They slog along for another hour before the same soldier slips back into another hallucination. As fear gnaws like maggots at his brain, it takes everyone's effort to prevent him from running off. Once more, Burt pins him to the ground and waits for the poor man to calm down. With little fight left in him, the weary soldier is suddenly jerked back into reality as abruptly as he left it. The man's courage is peppered with a desperation, but he remains compelled by a greater need to survive and manages once again to pull himself together. At this juncture, there is little pain in death; rather, life has become laborious, while death means rest. Nevertheless, there remains an innate desire to live.

Feeble and weak from starvation—too feeble to be of any assistance—the rescued prisoners trudge on. The amount of ground they have covered since mourning is about four miles. It's now afternoon. After checking the map, Buck concludes that they have crossed the border and are now back in Vietnam. It doesn't remove the danger, but it does renew their confidence in being extracted when the time comes. There are also other considerations. Because of the nature of reconnaissance, Buck's team is not well acquainted with being hunted. Generally, they are the hunters. But because of the enemy's losses, they are certain the chances of getting away with this escapade without a chase is next to nil. The nature of this war suggests that it's unwise to wait too long in one place; they need to be on the move. The judgement of the team is to make use of the daylight by getting as close to the extraction site as possible. Unfortunately, the six rescued men are still not able to make their way without assistance. With this constant problem, the recon team is having second thoughts about how much further they can push these men. With only a few hours of daylight left, the team finally acknowledges the inevitable: they can't push any further.

Buck calls a quick meeting. "I think we need to split up. We stand a better chance of not bein' found if we ain't all in a bunch. Me and Burt can take three of these guys an' Bob, an' you an' Quincy take the other three. We'll get back together in the morning an' make a plan to get our asses outta this shindig."

The six liberated men can't be more relieved. They have pushed themselves beyond any sane limits. If it were not for their army boot camp training mixed with an American fighting spirit encouraging each other on, none of them would have survived the day. But now things have slowed to where after a dinner of C-rations, they drift off into a sleep that's fully ready to harvest their individual nightmares.

Another night is completed. It went without a hitch. The rescued soldiers are more rational this morning. The emancipated prisoners rub their emaciated muscles, attempting to prod them into action. Youthful vigor is a companion of strength and remains strong as only youth is strong. They are inclined to imagine they might make it out of this bad dream. Though these men are alone in their thoughts, they aren't lost. They have the full support of Buck's team. They are together, traveling back on the same marked trail the team made a few days before, and they are now within a half day of reaching their extraction point.

They are still in Viet Cong territory. Everyone is aware of the enemy's fierce bite and the necessity not to overstay. Buck's team is cautious but unafraid as they organize the way out. "Whether we think we can get out of this mess or think we can't, both can be right, so let's stick with we can," coaches Buck. "Let's move it out."

Within minutes, they are back on the trail. The jungle is its usual noisy self. The six additional soldiers are determined to hold their own this morning. They're far from recovered, but their physical and mental faculties are much improved. There is a measure of real hope as they find new strength in this early morning beginning.

Burt is looking over this entourage of men his own age. He feels an overwhelming sense of obligation to their wellbeing. When he compares his life this morning with his life six months ago, that former experience floats across his psyche as surreal. *This* has become his natural way of life. Each of these freed prisoners owes his freedom to the tenacity of Burt. After all, it was Burt who insisted they not risk leaving them at the mercy of their captors and merely report their findings back to the major.

Burt is focused entirely on surviving just this leg of their mission and will meet the next leg the same way—one piece at a time. He's taken point this morning. For him, life is only available in the now. These newly acquired reconnaissance skills have produced an elevated meaning to his life. Burt's world demands greatness in purpose as well as in action, and so far, things have gone much the way they have for nearly all his missions. In his former life, he could procrastinate without much consequence, but today a lack of vigilance is the difference between life and death.

The jungle is thick, and the trees quickly devour Burt's thirty-foot lead. His strides are long and purposeful as he stealthily moves around, under, and through the underbrush, all the time aware of any telling change in the environment. A perpetual sweat has already soaked his fatigues. The effort has even now afforded him a kind of breathing rhythm that supplies his muscles with the oxygen they need to push through to a stage beyond weariness. With the right concentration, the right resolve, and the right need, greatness can be achieved—and greatness is what is needed today. Burt's mood is optimistic; he's full of self-assurance and hungry for whatever the jungle can throw at him, and content enough to hum a quiet tune. It's at times like this when, despite his anger toward God, he is inclined to renew his relationship. It goes deeper than a feeling—it's more like an awareness.

Burt's aim is to reach the extraction point without a hitch. As he begins to plod through the bush, he feels himself moving through spider webs and damp leaves. Travel could be much easier if they stuck to the trails, but that is where the enemy is encountered, and today is not a good day for that. With visibility limited to whatever mother nature is willing to yield, it's better to stick to a compass, anyway; trails have a way of meandering and taking them off course.

Burt forges ahead, battling everything but the Viet Cong. The terrain is changing, with sprouts of vegetation popping up along with a noticeable decline in elevation. Even the air is becoming heavier as the jungle becomes thicker. The undergrowth remains dense and is having an easier time fighting its way through the spongy composition of rotting leaves. This snarl of trees, vines, and insects would make anyone other than Burt more aware of the amenities of civilization, but this is the very type of environment he's grown to love. Despite its difficulty, he finds a splendor about it that he has never felt in the modern world. Every step is urging him to pick up the pace as the mountain races downward. His second thought is to remain vigilant and go at a slower, more cautious pace to prevent an enemy surprise and allow their new guests some time to recover a bit more. He sidesteps here and there to avoid impassable tangles and recheck his compass bearing to ensure that they are still on course. At last they have reached the lower plateaus and, according to their map and compass, are within a mile of the extraction site. Even so, nothing seems familiar. Burt has been concentrating on their location, their pace, and any unfamiliar changes in the jungle noise. Occasionally, the jungled mountain will flatten out on its way down. They've come to such a place. To a mountainous jungle terrain its equivalent to a desert oasis. The freed soldiers couldn't be happier. This is the first real break they've had since Burt set the pace earlier in the day. But Burt is in no mind to enjoy it. He's more concerned with the possibility of a surprise enemy attack while encumbered with six emaciated soldiers who are physically and mentally running on fumes.

Everyone is uncomfortably warm, with only the harsh, raspy sound of ten men breathing raggedly. The jungle has suddenly become dead silent. The trees that are normally alive with animal life are noiseless. Everyone's eyes scan their perimeter; they don't know what they expect to see. It's the kind of silence the jungle maintains when it's waiting for it knows not what; it's the kind of quiet that it isn't at ease. While the remainder are content to rest, watch, and listen, Burt goes into his stealth mode and begins to belly crawl toward a location he senses is suspicious. He's left his heavy backpack behind and is moving with only a rifle. This freedom allows him to move faster and with less exposure. Still, nothing seems familiar; it's too quiet. His eyes scan first to the right, then the left, and then straight ahead. He sees trees, more green trees—some old and large, others young and scrawny and struggling for a random ray of sunlight cutting between the leafy canopy—all in utter silence. He finds himself probing alone in this solemn temple, searching for those who will pervert its sanctity. He ignores the mild itch left by an earlier insect bite and the stinging sensation caused by his salty sweat penetrating the many scratches on his bare arms. His concentration is totally focused on his mission to investigate his suspicions.

Suddenly, there is a faint sound in the distance, breaking the jungle silence. Burt's eyes and ears are wholly fixated toward the interruption. Burt is certain he can hear voices. They're not the lower intonations of westerners' voices, but rather the higher-pitched inflections of the Asians. After hesitating for a moment to analyze his next move, Burt opts for stillness. The slight sounds of metal canteens clunking on other hardware tells him these are likely to be North Vietnamese soldiers on patrol; they're better equipped than the Viet Cong fighters, who often are left to live off the jungle. Soon, his suspicions are verified. Watching for any movement, he's not more than twenty feet off a path as a patrol of six uniformed North Vietnamese soldiers slip by, leaving him unnoticed. At this moment, a new consideration becomes apparent to him: *If we're gonna get out of here, we're gonna have to deal with these rats!* Their movements suggest they're too much at ease to suspect any Americans to be in the vicinity. Not exactly certain what this handful of scouts may represent, Burt begins his trek back prepared to report his finding.

As he crawls over beds of decomposing leaves and twigs along the jungle floor, the pungent smell is all too familiar. He senses a oneness with it; he's spent much of his life these past months becoming acquainted with all its features. He is even aware of the taste of the different kinds of dirt that coat his lips. He feels wonderfully alive in the moment, despite his circumstances.

Making his return approach to the small gathering of his fellows, Burt is struck by its familiarity. It looks like a safe haven as they remain lazily slumped on the ground unaware of the close proximity of the enemy. Buck is staring intently at Burt as he enters their circle. "Well, what ya got to report?" inquires Buck. There is no mistaking the intentness in his voice.

"A patrol of gooks passed by. There was six of 'em. I don't know where they were going. Right now, I don't know if they're ahead or behind us," reports Burt.

It's an all too familiar report in this war. Fighting it is half knowing what's going on; the other half is conjecture. There are hundreds if not thousands of miles of hand-hewn tunnels honeycombing the entire country that permit surprise attacks and quick disappearances.

Buck is taking stock of all the variables. "We're runnin' low on rations. We ain't got enough to make it through another day. We ain't doin' much better with water. Our PRC (radio) has just enough juice to make a pickup call. We gotta get to that extraction site an' get our sorry asses outta here pronto!"

Burt is listening conscientiously. He's already seen the enemy and knows they're not here for a picnic. "If we get caught before our Huey can show up, we'll be up a creek without a paddle. They'll never be able to land with a bunch of firepower goin' off at 'em," pronounces Burt. "Once they see that dragonfly comin' in, they'll be lookin' for an opportunity to take it out. We gotta play this smart if we're all gonna make it.'"

They spend the next hour going over different setups. With time running out and nothing written in rock, they prepare to move as cautiously as possible and play it mostly by ear. The six freed grunts are catching on as best they can. They're not used to this kind of clandestine warfare. They're more accustomed to lying in a foxhole and hoping they don't get killed. None of these six have done anything particularly courageous, except that none of them chose to run. Even at this juncture, each is attempting to become less of a liability and more of an active participant in their rescue.

Soon, they're moving through a thinner part of the jungle without trouble. Buck, Bob, Quincy, and Burt all recognize it as an area they negotiated a few days before. At this same moment, Burt sees movement up ahead. With a hand motion, he puts his crew flat to the jungle floor. He looks hard at the area where he distinguished the movement. It was nothing more than enough of something to interrupt the light traveling through a tiny opening in the underbrush. Then the strange movement occurred again. This time, Buck also sees it. Not certain if be man or beast, they remain quiet and still hidden by the jungle undergrowth. Within a few minutes, this strange phenomenon has occurred in several different areas. During this pause, they are all preparing their M60 rifles in position. The movement is by all calculations moving in a direction in line with Buck's team. Before long, this obscured cluster of shadowy movers approaches a thinner part of the jungle. Burt recognizes them as the patrol he had encountered earlier. There are only six of them, but they are on a route that will put them on top of this covert team of Americans in a minute. The enemy patrol has unknowingly shortened the distance between themselves and the Americans. Burt knows what he must do—and he must do it quick. *BLA-BLA-BLA-BLA:* all four M60s throw six enemy bodies along with trees, brush, and anything else that may have been in their trajectory into the air, letting gravity slam it all back to the ground as so much scattered debris.

Buck is now satisfied that things are settled enough, so he gives a hand gesture to move forward. Knowing time is of the essence, the ten Americans anxiously put enough distance between themselves and the half-dozen dead North Vietnamese soldiers to warrant Buck's motion to stop. Unfolding a map and checking a compass bearing, they conclude that they are around the area of their extraction site. Bob wastes no time in scaling a tree to give them a better view of the terrain. Monitoring from his thirty-foot perch, Bob motions toward a direction on their right flank. In a short time, they are at the site.

All of them are aware that the disturbance they created with the gunfire will inevitably produce a larger endangerment from the North Vietnamese army. The entire crew his on high alert. This sense of urgency has raised their adrenalin levels up along with the expectation that this will be enough to accommodate any crisis. Since Quincy's radio still has enough juice to place a request for extraction, he places the call and stresses the urgency of their situation. The return call assures them that they can oblige in a short time. Buck has decided they need to be as close to the landing site as they can be while retaining the ability to conceal themselves. Having had similar experiences in the past with extractions, the reconnaissance team is aware that the enemy will attempt to overwhelm the sight in the hopes of disrupting the operation. Meanwhile, they retrieve the cache of ammunition they had left in anticipation of this happening and set up a perimeter to prepare to defend themselves against the inevitable clash with the North Vietnamese.

Their eyes and ears are trained not only on the surrounding terrain but also on the horizon. The time seems to drag like it always does in urgent situations. In time, Hueys' unmistakable turbulences are rapidly becoming noisier as they close in on the extraction site. The horizon produces two of these flying machines in column. They appear, resembling two huge dragonflies. There is a sense of relief among the team as well as a high degree of apprehension about having to reveal themselves. Because of the weak condition of the freed prisoners, the plan is to prepare them to extract first. Meanwhile, the recon team creates a gunfire distraction to hold off the Vietnamese if needed. In seconds, the expected response from the waiting enemy begins. They are throwing everything they have at the incoming helicopters. One of the Hueys pulls out of range while the other comes in to hover a few feet off the ground with the expectation that these men will overcome the distance and quickly get aboard. This maneuver shortens the time they are in this high danger zone and allows for a quicker descent. Quincy and Bob are quickly shepherding these men to the hovering helicopter amongst the clumps of dirt thrown into the air by enemy bullets. Bob suddenly goes down, along with the soldier he is assisting. It's obvious that they are either dead or grievously wounded. All the while, the helicopter door gunner, Burt, and Buck are returning gunfire into the surrounding jungle in the hopes of creating as much distress among the enemy as possible so they'll retreat. Operating alone, Quincy has managed to push the remaining five men on board. With a wave to the anxious pilot to lift off and in a hail of bullets, Quincy immediately hits the ground and begins to crawl to his fallen comrade. Bob has been hit by a bullet in the chest and is obviously dead. With his adrenalin still overwhelming any sense of danger to himself, he checks the other soldier. This young man is taking his last gurgling breath as he, too, yields to his injuries.

Buck and Burt helplessly watch this entire disaster; one of their own has fallen, and the other remains in mortal danger. Meanwhile, the Huey is making a turn to return to the base, when the unthinkable occurs: it begins to spin out of control. It seems the tail rudder has been destroyed by enemy artillery, causing the aircraft to jettison toward the ground in a final burst of flames. All the negative possibilities they had gone over and hoped to divert are plummeting toward them at Mach speed. They can't overcome the tremendous amount of firepower the enemy is able to throw at them. The remaining chopper can assess many of the problems this ground team is unable to overcome. They respond with their rockets straddled on each side and the door gunner's mounted .50-caliber machine gun. This gives Quincy the opportunity he needs to get back to cover. Things are changing so fast. Despite their training and experience, they can't hold this enemy back any longer. It's hard to imagine all these trees surrounding them are full of men intent on only one thing: killing them.

The second Huey is circling over the treetops and pulls back out of range once again. Seeing this abandonment, the remaining team members are resigned to meet their Maker but not without throwing the last of their ammunition at the enemy. Suddenly the air around them is interrupted by the sound of a much larger aircraft—it's a C1-47. Its roaring engines monopolize every other sound around including the artillery. This aircraft is outfitted with a compilation of motorized guns mounted off the rear assembly. In the common vernacular, this gun ship is referred to as "Puff the Magic Dragon." Its guns are capable of shredding everything behind them. With no ammo left, Buck, Burt, and Quincy are resigned to meet the enemy with nothing more than their knives or their bare hands just as the C1-47 begins to unleash its capabilities. The sound is deafening; the huge guns tatter, grate, grind, and chop every living and nonliving entity in their path without discrimination. If these three survivors hadn't been fortified behind a solid rock formation, they would have been disregarded as casualties of friendly fire. The bullets ricochet off the rock and smash everything around them. The whole of the demonstration is over in less than a minute. There should be nothing left of an enemy. These three recon guys have only one thing in mind for the moment—it's *How we gonna get Bob outta here.* After a few minutes of lull, the three cautiously venture out from behind their stone fortress. They are having the first moment of reflection seeing Bob lying unmoving in his own spent pool of blood. The other soldier is also laying face up with a stopped stream of coagulated blood forced from his perforated lungs, now mixed with the dirt beneath his head. Still alone with their thoughts, the sound interrupting their reflections is the whirling sound of the Huey returning to bring them back to the base. This reconnaissance team can step away from the emotional impact of dire situations. This situation is a new test to challenge their internal grist to overcome the fallout surrounding one of their own fallen comrades. For the moment, they put the need to morn their loss on hold and focus on what their next move will be. They need to get the Huey back and get Bob, the other dead soldier, and themselves safely on board so they can get out of this hellhole.

The Huey is directly overhead, beginning its descent. The first shot caused Burt to flinch as the spent bullet whizzed by his head. He's not even certain he heard it over the noise of the helicopter. Was it really a shot or merely some debris the helicopter stirred up? Glancing around at the others, Burt sees in their reaction they also experienced something. The helicopter is only twenty feet above them. With all his strength, Buck is lifting Bob upright as best he can. Quincy is holding the soldier in a similar fashion. The expectation of a trouble-free landing is suddenly interrupted by a whistle sound and a thud followed by a sound like someone just struck a huge sheet of metal right next to them.

The next awareness Burt has is of his confusion. He is having trouble breathing, and he seems to be lying on the ground. The chopper is no longer descending. In his confused state, it appears to be ascending. His thoughts are again cut off, and he awakes to being loaded into a helicopter along with as many wounded as can be crammed into this waiting helicopter. He becomes aware of blood beginning to swirl into an opaque texture inside the cabin, splashing against everything in its path. What catches his attention is Quincy's limp finger seemingly tracing a downward trajectory through the milky that's substance now coating the wall. It slowly comes to rest on the deceased soldier he had been holding. Rather than focusing on his wounds, his mind settles on this as an odd phenomenon. He spots what appears to be Buck sleeping next to him. He thinks it's peculiar to see Buck sleeping that way. As quickly as everyone on board is secured, the helicopter lifts off, turning sharply around toward a field hospital. In less than fifteen minutes, they're landing among a group of green tents with huge red crosses embossed across the top of each one. Within minutes, they're evacuated and rushed into one of these tents. Before long, these wounded warriors are finding their bloodied bodies probed by field doctors in an ongoing battle to save limbs and the lives of otherwise dead men. Doctors working under less than ideal conditions to stabilize these wounded combatants slash away clothing and dead flesh without discrimination. The flesh from the calf of Burt's right leg has been shredded, exposing the bone. A large portion of his buttock has been torn open, and his gut is open enough to leave intestines hanging off to his side. These field surgeons are patching wounds that can be stitched and working together to save as much of limbs as they can with the hope that a better facility will complete the task. As soon as he's stabilized, along with several other severely wounded, they're summarily airlifted from this field hospital in South Vietnam to a fully equipped army infirmary in the Philippines.

When Burt wakes, his first remembrance is a strange experience he had while in transport. During his extraction, he expected to die, but he suddenly had a mystifying awareness of another presence. It was not a presence that instilled confusion, but rather one of calmness, communicating with plain words he could hear clearly and understand amid all the noise and chaos. The voice was strong and concise, saying *I'VE GOT YOU!* The words were so powerful and firm that from this point on, Burt becomes indifferent to his life-threatening wounds. For a reason that's only been communicated to him, he knows he's going to be okay.

The harsh, deafening sounds of battle have been exchanged for the quiet swishing sounds clothing makes as its wearers go about their duties around him. It's a strangely disarming sound. Burt's dilated eyes are open, suggesting he's fully conscious and not experiencing any alarm over his condition—but then, morphine can do this. This savagely wounded young soldier can barely whimper through the quieting effects of the drug. It's doing its job. Long gone are the days when a half bottle of whiskey and a stick clamped between the teeth would be the only reprieve a wounded soldier could hope for. For this situation, whatever has happened or is happening is way outside Burt's ability to bring anything to mind. There is no yesterday or tomorrow; he is only conscious of the moment.

CHAPTER 17
R&R

After a harrowing, life-changing week, Micky is actually happy to get back to Camp Eagle. A few of Dengler's comrades are aware of his death and are approaching Micky about the circumstances. A soldier named Kenny who is from Dengler's hometown and went to high school with him appears to be the most distraught over his fall.

"What can you tell me about Allen? How'd he end up gettin' killed?" is Kenny's fraught concern.

In his nineteen years, Micky has never even thought of such a troubling question. He suddenly feels very, very inadequate. To concern himself over such disturbing circumstance is a brand-new phenomenon.

"He was taking part in Gohrke's church service when a sniper put a bullet through his head," pronounces Micky.

It's obvious Kenny is taking the loss of a school mate and fellow soldier hard.

"We came in on the buddy system, went through boot camp and AIT together. Both of us joined 'cause that's what we thought we should do. I can't believe those bastards got him! I'm beginnin' to hate this damned war."

A few others begin to join in. Another soldier named Jim picks up where Kenny left off.

"I got drafted. I didn't have much to say about it. I never have bought that crap about the Commies takin' over the US. Hell, we can't manage our own people. How them Commies think they're gonna do a better job?"

Another soldier named Roland chimes in, "If them damn Commies were ever able to make it across the Pacific and land in California, they'd damn well never know where the shots were comin' from. We got more guns in my county than we got people."

This talk continues on for a few more minutes until Kenny says, "The only thing I wanna do right now is get drunk." With that, he opens a foot locker that's filled with beer. He cracks one open and hands it to Micky; it's a liquid that has never passed Micky's lips. Before he can think of an excuse why he can't drink it, someone else suggests they make a toast to Allen. The rest agree as each of them grabs a beer. Micky, still not able to find words strong enough to avoid having to make the toast, lifts the beer to his lips and takes a swig. He's surprised by its effervescence. It doesn't taste that bad, and so far, there are no lightning bolts from heaven. He has always prided himself of the fact he had gone all the way through school without ever tasting alcohol of any kind. So far, it's had no ill effects. Feeling no different, he takes another sip. He's more concerned with how this experience is going to affect him and is taking it on as a project that needs to find an ending. He has somewhat removed himself from the rest of the group as he's becoming more serious about challenging it further. Still no change in how he feels. This time, he lifts the can to his mouth and in several large gulps consumes the rest of the beer. Setting the can down, expecting either the devil to grab him and pull him to the depths of depravity or he'll begin to hear angels sing. It's a different experience from anything he has ever undergone. The first thing he notices is how numb his lips are beginning to feel and how the numbness is gradually making its way across his entire face, and traveling through his entire body—arms, hands, legs, and even his feet. This is followed by a slight giddy and somewhat euphoric feeling. For reasons only known to Micky, his mind has wandered to that beer-filled footlocker. He's not asking himself any serious questions about his changing behavior. At this point, the only question he has is *why did I ever think that something that can make me feel this good could ever be bad?* Without a second thought, he makes his way to the beer-filled trunk and grabs another beer. He then makes his way across the way to the rest of the group with a new sense of community. He actually feels as though he can socialize with the rest of the group now. *This beer is like a miracle. I can't remember feeling this good since my tenth birthday party when I got my dog* is Micky's new thought. He cracks his second beer with the intention of that being all he'll want. No sooner is that one consumed than he finds himself at the same foot locker, reaching for another. It isn't long before an overwhelming desire to take a nap overcomes him. Without leaving for his own hooch, and before he realizes what's come over him, he lies down on the floor and passes out.

It's the next morning before Micky wakes. He's fully clothed and in his own bed with no idea on how he got there. With very little recollection of the day before, his first concern is the violent headache he's experiencing. Making his way to the infirmary, he explains his situation to the nurse. She gives him a couple of aspirins and instructs him to "lay off the booze." These words from this medical person and her straightforward no-nonsense directives blow his cover. He was hoping he could pass off his condition as some kind of jungle illness.

Regarding his driving duty, Micky is eternally grateful that Gohrke didn't need his services. The rest of the day is spent in recovery. By late afternoon, he makes his way to the mess hall to try and eat a little. What isn't clear is how the stuff that had made him feel so good could be the culprit for his condition.

He's met by Kenny and Joe coming in behind him. They're both wearing a wry grin.

"How ya doin' there Micky?"

"I'm doing okay, but one thing I got to know ... how did I get from your hooch to mine without me knowing it?" says Micky with an air of curiosity.

The two soldiers begin to laugh.

"We put your sorry ass in a wheelbarrow and dumped you into your bed."

Frightened to ask any more questions for fear of the answers, with his thoughts in one dimension and his feet in another Micky drifts over to an empty table where he can be alone to clear his head. His mind drifts to Carolyn. *I miss her so much. I wish I was done with this damnable war.* Between his apparent hangover and missing Carolyn, he's barely able to eat. Yearning to be alone, Micky returns to his hooch. His roommates are on assignment leaving the room to himself. His mental condition has quickly deteriorated from the gung-ho soldier who was convinced in the "just war theory" to a sobbing product of his decision. Whatever confidences he had built in high school are all but evaporated. To Micky, it seems all his aspirations to become a notable leader have dissolved leaving him feeling powerless. He recalls how his teammates relied on his expertise on the football field and how as the captain and anchor of the track team he led his team to a championship. His passion for life has been altered from an overly confident young man to that of a whimpering failure. In a fit of uncontrollable weeping over his situation, Micky buries his head in his pillow to muffle his wailing, *Why God, why? I've tried my best to be obedient to your wishes. Is it because I got Carolyn pregnant out of wedlock that you're punishing me? I promise I'll do better. Just don't punish me anymore!*

Micky wants nothing more than to change the way he feels. He recalls the euphoric relief he had experienced the day before when he was drinking Kenny's beer. He has reached a place in his thoughts where he no longer holds high-minded ideas about Vietnam being a just or unjust war. He just wants to stay alive long enough to get out of here—to any place but here. His remembrance of the escape the booze previously gave him is enough to get out of bed and make his way to Kenny's hooch. His desire to change the way he feels gives him enough optimistic anxiety to make it happen. With the newfound hope that Kenny will be able to accommodate his need, Micky is all but indifferent to the dire surroundings he found intolerable a while before. Kenny has returned from the mess hall and is lounging on his bunk, studying a girlie magazine. When he looks up, he is surprised to see Micky.

"Hey, Micky, what ya up to?" asks Kenny. There is a clear look on Kenny's face that spells curiosity.

Micky feels desperation making its way back into his person. He isn't quite certain how those who have made drinking a normal part of their life approach the need he feels at the moment. Micky feels clumsy but knowing he needs Kenny. Until this moment, he has regarded Kenny a hopeless sinner. This feeling has not been merely set aside, but replaced by his overwhelming need for Kenny's help. At the moment, Kenny is his only link to changing the desperation he's experiencing.

"Doing okay, I guess."

Still struggling to maintain a sense of calmness on the outside despite the nervousness inside, Micky clumsily asks, "Hey, Kenny, you got any more of that beer?"

Kenny, being the opportunist that he is, quickly replies, "No, but if I had a jeep and a trailer, I know where we can get more." Micky jumps on this. "I got use of a jeep and a trailer," he promptly responds.

"Well, I guess we've solved a problem," replies Kenny. "How fast can you get it here?" is his next question.

"Five minutes!" is Micky's anxious response. This new purpose is giving Micky a reason to begin to feel better. Within fifteen minutes, Micky has returned. Kenny is all smiles. It's obvious he's pleased he's found a new partner in his booze business. Kenny wastes little time hopping in the jeep. He feels a rush of importance, as he's about to be chauffeured. The only drawback is that the jeep and trailer are known to support the chaplain's work. Nonetheless, with this newfound purpose, it's a perfect decoy to remain under the radar of any military police who may oppose hauling alcohol willy-nilly around their jurisdiction. With the ease of someone who has a history of this shifty kind of hustling, Kenny directs Micky across the base to the officers' club. Once there, Kenny tells him to wait in the jeep and then makes his way to the back door. Micky can see him conversing with another soldier and handing him what appears to be a small container. Returning to the jeep, he points his finger in a direction and says to Micky, "Pull around to the door over there." It appears to be a service door for loading and unloading goods. Without question, Micky drives to the location, backing the jeep and its trailer to the open door. Kenny and the other soldier begin to load the trailer with cases of beer. It's a surreptitious undertaking. It turns out the soldier in charge of the officers' club has a hankering for opium-soaked marijuana. Micky sits in wonder. He had no idea of all the clandestine scheming that went into getting a few cases of beer—four, to be precise—and a big bag of ice for cooling the warmish brew. A portion of his self-righteous, judgmental attitude has crept over him once again. With a critical eye, he watches the sum of this devious transaction. Despite the fact he personally initiated the whole affair, he continues to live in a delusional world of denial about his personal wrong doing. *My focus is only on getting a few beers for my nerves.* This is Micky's way of separating himself from any immoral or illegal schemes that are brewing between Kenny and this unknown soldier.

The deal has been consummated: the illicit cargo is covered with a tarp to prevent unwanted eyes from detecting the true nature of the freight, and Kenny is back in the jeep. Still feeling notable, Kenny flippantly points in the direction he wishes Micky to drive. Micky suddenly becomes aware of soldiers noticing him—the chaplain's assistant—driving the base's most notorious hustler with a load of something that needs covering. By the time they have returned to Kenny's hooch, Micky's nerves are barely holding him together. He's never put himself in this kind of jeopardy before. They quickly unload the ill-gotten booty, pack it into Kenny's ready supply of footlockers, and envelop each with a hardy provision of ice. It doesn't take long before word gets around. Kenny is ready to sell out at fifty cents a beer, but not before Micky has consumed his fill of the magic elixir. This time, he manages to drive himself back to his hooch and put himself to bed.

Morning arrives with one of Micky's hooch mates shaking him awake. "Wake up. Chaplain Gohrke wants you in his office. He doesn't appear to be in a good mood."

Micky's feet hit the floor. He has the same headache he had yesterday morning along with a lingering alcoholic haze. Struggling to find a clean field outfit, he haphazardly puts himself together. What he labors with the most is remembering anything about how he managed to get to his hooch after spending most of the day at Kenny's. Still in a state of confusion and queasiness, he makes his way to Gohrke's office. Desperately attempting to act normal, it's obvious he is either acting recklessly or is unaware of his state of unreadiness. Gohrke sits behind his desk, staring wordlessly at Micky. It's difficult for him to put language to what he is looking at. Micky is standing before him, attempting to salute and stand at attention. His shirt is untucked, his shoes appear to be on the wrong feet, and his legs are unsure. Without warning, he staggers forward and manages to catch himself before he collapses across Gohrke's desk. This causes Gohrke to shove his chair back and spring to his feet. Micky manages to catch himself. With the same clumsiness a drunk has during a sobriety field test, he attempts to start over by getting himself back on his feet so he can stand at attention and pull off a regulation salute. This time, he is successful only in sprawling across the chaplain's desk and knocking everything onto the floor. With all this happening at near warp speed, Gohrke is still wordless. His next action is a reaction: he quickly goes to the rescue of his prodigal assistant. Having had some experience somewhere in his ministry with this happening, it is all coming back how to deal with it. He grabs Micky from behind, drags him to an empty chair across the room, and smartly dumps him onto it. Micky sits dumbfounded, as a drunk does when his frontal lobes no longer supply any useful information. All Micky is becoming aware of is that he is emerging into the worst day of his life. His condition the past few days is not anything he has ever dealt with. To begin a day this way is not something he imagined he would be dealing with, even in his wildest dreams. To look at this as though it were just another milestone in life is not the kind of dramatic role he wishes were playing out just to experience the end. The idea that he could fake his way through this ordeal has suddenly come to its end.

Gohrke is finally forming some words. "What in the world has come over you, soldier!?

Micky draws in a deep breath and exhales it in the form of a sigh. His emotions are running in every direction. He has a conglomeration of guilt, remorse, self-condemnation, embarrassment, and a million others he can't identify.

"I don't know, sir. I think I got some kind of jungle sickness," slurs Micky in one last attempt to deny the actualities.

"That might be if the jungle is brewing beer, because that's what your sickness smells like," replies Gohrke. "So, what I want you to do now is to go back to your quarters get yourself cleaned up, get some breakfast, and report back to me at ten hundred hours. We've got a full day of work to finish."

Once again, Micky gets to his feet. With as smart a salute as a drunk can put together, Micky replies in his boot camp voice, "YES, CHAPLAIN CAPTAIN!"

Gohrke can't help but roll his eyes and dismiss him.

Micky stumbles his way back to his hooch. All the way, he is castigating himself. *Next time, I'm only going to have one. I don't know what I was thinking. I must have drunk a lot to get in this condition.*

The first person he meets is Kenny. Kenny is waiting in front of Micky's hooch. He's nervously smoking a cigarette. He's already heard about Micky getting in trouble. What brings him here isn't a burning desire to help Micky. The look on his face tells another story. He says, "Ya didn't tell the chaplain where ya got the booze, did ya?"

Micky is sober enough to understand Kenny's concern; besides, Kenny's his supplier, and he doesn't want to do anything to jeopardize their relationship.

"No, I wouldn't do anything like that," says Micky in a very offended tone.

"You damn well better not. We got a good thing goin' here. I don't need no chaplain snoopin' around. He could ruin a good thing, ya know," says Kenny. With the toe of his shoe, he butts his cigarette into an imperceptible mixture with the dirt. Looking at Kenny now with eyes of a differing concern, he says, "You look like you was rode hard and put up wet, boy. You feelin' all right?"

"Not really," says Micky. His hands are shaking uncontrollably as he attempts to put his boots onto the correct feet.

Reaching in his pocket, Kenny pulls out a small medicinal bottle. Handing it to Micky, he follows with instructions, "Here, take a snort of this. It'll help ya with them shakes."

Barely able to hold the bottle, Micky asks, "What's this stuff?"

"It's anti-hangover medicine—it'll stop them shakes ya got goin' there," says Kenny with an air of authority.

Unable to open the bottle by himself, Kenny relieves him of it long enough to unscrew the top and hands it back into Micky's still shaking hand. Micky places it near his nose. After taking a whiff, he asks once more, "What is this stuff?"

"It's a cough syrup with enough codeine to settle them shakes ya got goin'," reports Kenny. "Go ahead and take a couple slugs—you'll see I know what I'm talkin' about."

Hesitating for a moment, Micky looks at the bottle one more time with the expectation that the bottle may want to give its opinion. When none came, he tipped the bottle back and let the thick potion slide down his throat.

"If this works for ya, let me know. I can get ya a bottle for about ten bucks," says Kenny.

As promised, Micky's shakes leave him. He's cleaned up and has a little food in his gut. As he's preparing to meet Gohrke, he can't help but think, *I'm sure glad Kenny showed up with that medicine. I don't know how I could have gotten by without it.*

Gohrke meets him with a wary eye. "You look much better, Micky. I hope you learned something."

Wanting to put on the best face he can with this superior, Micky agrees, "Oh, yes sir, I sure did learn a lesson."

With that behind them, they make infirmary rounds and put a service together for another platoon that's preparing for a mission. Nothing more of the incident comes up for the rest of the day.

At the end of the day, after dropping the chaplain at his quarters, Micky makes his way over to Kenny's to thank him for helping him get his head back together earlier.

"I don't know what I would have done if you hadn't helped me out with that medicine this morning," thanks Micky.

"Think nothin' of it, kid. Just glad I could help ya out. If your still in the market for a bottle of your own, let me know, 'cause I got an extra one," says Kenny. Reaching into his footlocker, Kenny pulls out a cold beer. Handing it to Micky, he declares, "Just to show ya my heart's in the right place, have a beer on me."

Micky can't think of a reason to say no. *One sure isn't going to hurt me* is his prevailing thought. Returning Kenny's generosity with a gracious smile, he gladly accepts Kenny's kind invitation. In a short time, he finds himself kibitzing with a few other soldiers who happen to stop by. He's marveling at how easy it's become to socialize where he never thought it possible. This is the first time since he joined the army that he's enjoyed this kind of comradery. Not wanting it to end, he finds himself willingly buying another beer. The evening wears on with Micky finally stumbling his way back to his hooch.

Going to bed in an alcoholic blackout, Micky wakes still fully dressed to a pounding headache, a queasy gut, and the shakes. What he discovers—without remembering how it got here—is a bottle of Kenny's magic potion on his night stand. Remembering the difficulty that he had the morning before, he manages to get the cap off and tilts his head back, allowing the contents to run down his throat. Within a few minutes, the codeine has found its way to his brain and is giving him the relief that he's hoping for. The shakes stop and bring a sense of irreverence toward his circumstances. His thoughts are centered around himself. His ultimate concern is how he's going to maintain this newfound lifestyle.

With very little outward distress, he makes his obligation to Chaplain Gohrke, picking him up with clean combat fatigues, but with less than a ready-to-go-to-work attitude. What Gohrke notes in particular is Micky's lack of interest in his performance, and a kind of lethargy he hasn't seen in him until the past few days. Sitting back, Gohrke takes a long, unsettling look at Micky's demeanor. His eyes have a blank lifeless look to them. There is an unusual indifference in

Micky's behavior, it's something strange when compared to his nearly obsession with detail.

"You on some kind of medication, Micky?" Gohrke asks. His questions are always forthright and to the point, with little or no hesitation.

Even in Micky's tranquilized state, he's taken aback by Gohrke's bluntness. Gohrke has a way of intimidating truth from people. But not ready to acknowledge his new-found epiphany of a near magic hangover medicine for fear of Gohrke's disapproval, he lies. "No sir, not at all."

Still staring at him, Gohrke mouths a grunt: "Urumph."

Gohrke's stare has a truth accompanying it that can easily cut through Micky's codeine haze. This is enough for Micky to feel a tinge of guilt. His thoughts take him to a very uncomfortable place that people go when they aren't accustomed to being deceitful—more guilt. Despite the codeine effect, Micky is struggling to keep up his Christlike demeanor and, he knows Gohrke knows he's lying. What Micky thinks and what he says are already are at odds enough to throw up a red flag.

For Micky, life is quickly shrinking down; his obsessions with alcohol and codeine are his ultimate concerns. *This is what I need to get me through this hellhole. I know I can quit anytime I want. I know once I get out of here, I can become a great thinker. I mean who has had as much stuff thrown at him as me.* This has become his reasoning for continuing. Where he has, until lately, written to Carolyn a couple times a week, now he hasn't written in a couple weeks.

He has become Kenny's main courier and picks up whatever Kenny is promoting—beer, pot, cocaine—with the chaplain's jeep. This is done in exchange for whatever elixir Kenny is promoting to get everyone through another day. There is never a time when Micky doesn't think, *All of this will pass someday, and I'll become the important philosopher I always believed I am.* He believes this in spite of his defiance against sane living. Chaplain Gohrke has given Micky his own category. He calls it the elder brother or prodigal son syndrome. Gohrke has taken note how Micky's self-righteous attitudes have shifted from the self-righteous attitude of St. Luke's elder brother in the parable of the prodigal son to becoming the prodigal son himself. It's as though the elder brother within him could no longer endure his own conceit and remain sane, so he creates the prodigal as a pressure release in the hope of keeping his sanity. Regardless, his deficiencies remain. Micky is merely shifting from one form of self-centeredness to another and from a sin higher in his nature against love itself to a different form found lower in his nature: railing against his own body.

The unusual part of Micky's story is how quickly he can switch from his physical and mental reliance on drugs and alcohol as the "prodigal son" back to his role as the self-righteous "elder brother" in his attitude toward others. He has accepted his behavior and believes that because he *thinks* he is righteous, he *is* righteous; no matter how flawed others find his behavior, he has devised a way to imagine it is righteous. This behavior results in him thinking he's on the same level as divine thought—including when he's inebriated. The history of the world is made up of persons with the same rationale, who ultimately fail.

For Micky, the weeks and months role by without a break. The day finally arrives; he has earned some R&R (rest and recreation) time. He can't prepare himself for this liberty quickly enough. Those leading a normal American life back in the States may look at this break as an ordinary weekend at a resort. As small a token as this may be for enduring danger or periods of boredom, these young men who've been awarded this five-day pass may as well have been awarded paradise. It's a long-awaited break from the perils of war and Micky's mundane tasks alongside Chaplain Gohrke. He's put in for Hawaii.

During one of their many hours of downtime, while sharing a joint with Kenny, Micky laments the change in his plans. "My first plan was to put in for Hawaii, hoping I could get Carolyn there, but the doctor won't give her permission to fly because she's too close to her delivery date. I had to take the next available slot: Bangkok."

"It's cool, man, I been there. The booze and drugs are everywhere—it's a paradise compared to this rat hole. You can even rent a woman for the whole time you're there. Just make sure you got plenty of rubbers, or you could end up with that Russian disease goin' around down there on the streets." Kenny is almost as excited about recalling his escapade as he was about being there.

This last bit of medical information has caught Micky unawares. "Not that I'm going to be hooking up with a woman, but what's this Russian disease you're referring to?"

Kenny looks at him with a wry little grin as he hands him the last of the joint, saying, "It's called 'Rot-cha-cock-off'."

This little one-liner along with the Asian reefer he's smoking catches Micky just right, giving him one of the rare laughs he's had in months.

By the next morning, Micky has checked out with travel orders in hand. He's been to the base center to turn in his firearms and is now in a Huey flying to Cam Rahn Bay. The pilot has a little routine he follows when he's coming into that base. He always flies low over the beach area with the intention of catching a nurse or two sunning topless. These are small preoccupations that make an otherwise repetitive flight a little more motivating.

Micky expects to take full advantage of every moment of his R&R. When he arrives at the reception center, he begins by ditching his jungle fatigues in a locker and switching into khakis. He learns his flight will be leaving later in the evening. This gives him an opportunity to wander around and check out the local scenery. Even though he is still in Vietnam, this change of conditions makes him feel like he is at a resort. Spotting a bar, he decides to stop for a drink. Since his entire drinking career has been centered around what he and Kenny have been able to barter for from the enlisted men's and officers' clubs, it's been beer. Now, he is facing a bar with every kind of bottled alcohol that one could imagine. Micky doesn't want to risk ordering a drink he knows nothing about. Instead, he plays it safe and orders a beer. One leads to another, and another. Soon, he is stumbling about, attempting to get to his flight on time. By some miracle, he manages to board his plane. It's a six-hour trip. Without a moment's hesitation, Micky plops into his seat and promptly passes out.

Six hours later, Micky is shaken awake by a stewardess. Coming to, he struggles with reality. He has no idea where he is or how he got here. The inside of his mouth feels like he has cotton for a tongue. He immediately has a need to gag. This begins his quest to find the plane's washroom. Slamming the door behind him, he retches his guts into the toilet. This is hardly the first time he's had to deal with this difficulty, but it's the first time he's out of a familiar element. Digging his hands around in his pockets, he finds his bottle of codeine and chokes down a swallow. The thick solution has a very familiar taste and, in a few minutes, proves to have a familiar effect. Taking just a bit more for good measure, Micky runs some water in the basin and splashes the cool liquid on his face. With outside pressure from a persistent knock on the door prompts him to make the best of the circumstances, he opens the door to face the captain. It seems he's the only passenger left on the plane. Getting his things together, he makes his way to customs behind a group of other soldiers. He's beginning to feel the euphoric effects of the opioid. Once he's there, his small bag is searched, along with his pockets. What is immediately brought into suspect is the half-filled bottle of codeine. Not able to show a doctor's prescription on the bottle causes it to be confiscated. This sudden seizure of this indispensable treatment is putting Micky into a state of apprehension. Nonetheless, things are not stopping for Micky; procedures move the whole group of soldiers to a bus, where they are taken to an R&R center. Here, they prepare themselves to listen to a two-hour lecture on what they can and cannot do in Bangkok.

It's explained how each person is a guest in this country and is at the mercy of the local police if they choose to be a scofflaw. The military can have their hands tied if the soldier gets in serious trouble, although everything that can be done will be done. The soldier is also expected to have his ID and orders on his person at all times. With this finished, no one goes anywhere until they have a sanctioned hotel room or apartment and a list of contact numbers. At the end of this lecture the military has provided a rental facility to rent street clothing and a bus to transport them to their home away from home.

When they've been supplied with everything they are going to need, it's time to leave the center. Micky has decided on a small hotel room with a shower. In the outdoor space between the center and the bus, the smell of city hits Micky full force. The odor of rotting fish, raw sewage, and burning garbage permeates the air, hanging over the city like a huge pair of dirty socks. *I welcome the Vietnam smell over this garbage heap any day,* is Micky's unexpected thought. It's an unpleasant affront that makes him want to gag all over again. He's hoping the smell is temporary, but much to his displeasure, it doesn't dissipate much once he's in his room. This is not the R&R experience he was hoping for.

This sudden change in environments is having an adverse effect on Micky emotionally. *I wish Carolyn were here. I miss her so much.* This disappointing thought rampages his emotions with a loneliness he finds disheartening. Regardless of his feelings, if the military hasn't taught him anything else, *adapt and overcome* comes back to mind. Micky has taken this to heart and has chosen alcohol to help him cope through the unpleasant circumstances of military life. This is not exactly what this slogan was supposed to inspire in an adherent. Be that as it may, he is quick to exchange this feeling of loneliness for the warm sense of wellbeing alcohol initially provides.

Micky recalls an advertisement in the lobby for a brew named "Sangsom." The poster with the concoction splashing over a sparkling glass of ice has caught his attention. His mind is telling him, *This is just the remedy I need. I'll feel a lot better.* He is still certain his actions will bring him happiness. He pushes the guilt, remorse, regret, sadness, and unforgiveness all under his next drink with the hope that it will stay away. Acting on this premise as his best thinking, he calls down to the bar to have a bottle sent to his room. Within minutes, there is a soft, unobtrusive knock on his door. Answering, he finds himself face to face with a pretty young Thai girl about the same age as himself. She strikes him as very attractive. With her pearly white teeth, welcoming smile, shiny black hair, and crisp white blouse accented against her olive-colored skin and dark, thigh-length skirt, she appears classier than the base's Vietnamese peasant girls used as hooch maids.

In her best English, she says, "Hallooo, Meestaaa Meekaaa. You oordoo sangsoo? Urr?" (Hello, Mister Micky. Did you order Sangsom? Yes?)

Micky stands dumbfounded before this very feminine young woman. It's been months since he's had any female interaction. He has always expected the next attractive female he would see would be Carolyn. This liaison is catching him on his blind side. He just stands rigid, blinking, without a word.

"Yes, I did. Just set it here," he says, clearing his bag off a small table.

Boldly and assuredly, she steps into the room and sets the tray on the table, all the while continuing to share the same unrelenting smile.

Micky is noticeably uneasy with his beautiful intruder. His next group of words come out in a staccato of nervous utterances. Clearing his throat, he manages to say, "How much will that be, ah … ma'am … ah … miss?"

Continuing her positive demeanor, she says, "One hunerr-feefttee bahh. (One-hundred-fifty baht.)"

Trying to make sense of the dollar to baht exchange, Micky fusses with making what should be a simple transaction. Sensing his uneasiness, all the while good-heartedly laughing, she says, "Laaa meee hell you." (Let me help you.)

Carefully picking out the correct amount, she hands him back his change. But she doesn't end it there. "Yoo wan guide companio foww few day. Oneee cos hunerr bahh. I happee do eee foww yoo," she happily adds.

This is exactly what Kenny had tipped off him could happen and what Micky was positive would have no effect on him. His mind is in a swirl, as he is well aware what this entails. At this very moment, he doesn't know if he is more excited or nervous about his whole turn of events. Still staring and clearing his throat a few times, he is trying to find an answer. One part of him is saying, *You're married. You shouldn't do this. You need to stay true to your vows.* Another voice, along with a yearning for female companionship, is shouting, *This isn't going to hurt anyone because no one is ever going to know. It's only passing. Besides, I'm so lonely that I need someone to care about me, even if I have to pay for it.* Under the continuous influence of alcohol, Micky's frontal lobes are in no condition to espouse anything beyond his baser nature.

"How much is that in American dollars," he finds himself asking.

Still with an embracing smile, she says, "Thaa owneee tweteee Amaacaaa dollaa day."

Micky has found his ability to fight off this kind of temptation has all but abandoned him. In one foggy minded morning in Bangkok, Thailand, he makes his decision, saying, "That sounds like a good deal."

With even a larger smile, she says, "Yoo maay vay goo deecisioo. I haa contrak maay meee yoo gull. Yoo sigh? (You make a very good decision. I have a contract that makes me your girl. Will you sign it?)"

Micky looks at this very beguiling young women, realizing that for a measly twenty dollars a day, he can have his needs met. His only thought is *Where do I sign?*

A very congenial gentleman has been listening outside the door. His affable smile is nearly as infectious as the young girl's. In his hand is a typed paper. Extending his hand to Micky, he says, "Myyi naaay Chakrii. (My name is Chakrii)." He next points to the young

191

woman, adding, "She myyi eeemployee. Hull naaay Anong. (She is my employee. Her name is Anong.)" After the introductions are complete, Chakrii hands Micky the paper he's holding. It's written in English and basically says that for twenty dollars a day, Anong is to be his guide and companion. Micky takes a moment to scan it, in another moment he signs it.

Chakrii folds the document, along with the money for Micky's remaining visit, places it in the pocket of his very formal dress shirt, shakes hands with Micky one more time and disappears. This leaves Micky and his new concubine to themselves.

With her persistent smile, Anong says, "Yoo waaa massaaa? (You want a massage?)"

Micky pours himself a drink. "I'd love that, Anong."

CHAPTER 18
Homecoming

Burt has been left sedated as he continues to undergo one surgery after another in the hopes of saving as many of his limbs as possible. The military has drafted young surgeons right out of medical school with the promise of paying off their educational debt in exchange for their service. What these young surgeons lack in experience is made up with bringing a host of new procedures capable of saving many more casualties than in any previous war.

A little more than a week has passed before Burt discovers he is the only survivor left on his recon team. As his condition begins to stabilize, his sedatives have been cut back, resulting in a more profound awareness of the loss of his teammates and what it means. This awareness is beginning to have a greater impact on his outlook. As his physical body heals, the rest of his person—mind and spirit—falls into disillusionment followed by a gradual but ever deepening depression. To imagine reality without fulfilling his calling as a warrior and to adjust to having the closest men in his life torn away so abruptly has left Burt's mind and spirit wounded more severely than any physical wounds.

His unhealthy mind grinds on, and the healthcare workers hardly notice. They are the best in the world for treating nearly untreatable physical wounds but nearly unaware of the mental wounds these warriors suffer. Burt's mind travels backward because it's the only reality he has; he finds it too cloudy to look forward. Recalling the fateful day brings his thoughts to the moment he heard the thud next to him, followed by the explosion. *What could I have done? What did I leave undone?* His eyes stare straight ahead as he recalls the events of that day and tries to imagine a way to correct his errors and bring back his teammates. He can't bring himself to admit they're actually gone forever. *I'm sorry, guys. I know I missed something and let you down. Just give me another chance, and I'll make it up to you.*

Burt's stay in the Philippine hospital has gone from months to nearly a year. He's physically able to be released and is also honorably discharged from the military with enough medals and ribbons to fill the chest of his dress uniform. However, the ominous direction of Burt's thinking continues uncontested. He is well on his way back to the States after over a year's absence with little to no expectation of anything. Since the army has rejected his willingness to be reinstated, his only plan is to return to his Michigan hometown and drift into some kind of life. The plane he flew in on is scheduled to land at Los Angeles, California. The captain announces they will be landing in minutes, thanks everyone for choosing his airline, and says he hopes they had a relaxing flight. Along with a nearly full plane of soldiers, he begins to clap let out a "WHOOP!" Some of these military men are on a thirty-day leave, others have served their stint and are being discharged, and still others, like Burt, have been wounded and are making their way home. The plane lands without a hitch. Each soldier holds himself responsible for his duffel bag, including Burt. He's still on crutches with a prosthetic foot on one leg and must wait for the other to heal before he can have that one fitted. Even so, he slings his duffel bag across his shoulders like he always has and makes his way to the down ramp.

What Burt and the other soldiers are met with once outside the plane is unimaginable. There are young men their age with long hair and scruffy beards along with young women with long tresses of their own who are wearing peasant dresses adorned with colored beads that hang about their necks and rest on braless breasts covered with scanty blouses or men's T-shirts. What happens next is certain to linger in the memories of these soldiers for the rest of their lives. The crowd begins to jeer, calling them "baby killers," with some even going so far as to spit on them. This is hardly the reception any of them expected. Once in the air terminal, some of the soldiers rush into clothing shops in the hopes of changing into civilian clothes. After stripping out of their uniforms, some dump them in garbage cans.

After months of jungle fighting, Burt is not easily intimidated. While holding himself up on one crutch, he lands a punch squarely in the face of a spitter, breaking his nose. The poor dope is grasping his nose with blood running between his fingers as he screams like a baby girl. Up until now, security has been ignoring the protestations of this unwashed pack. Once physical contact is made, they have been instructed to detain the perpetrator. In this case, it's Burt. Security immediately ushers him off to a room to wait for the police to come and make an arrest. They have also called an ambulance to tend to the protester's broken nose.

When the police arrive, they listen to the airport security explaining what happened. They quickly arrive at a decision. Within minutes, the police read Burt his Miranda rights and place him under arrest. They explain to Burt that he has violated the civil rights of the protester by attacking him and declare that they are taking him into custody. Burt, still not recovered enough to fight the police, surrenders without a fight. He has been trained to bring the fight to the enemy and is now being arrested in the country that taught him that skill. They subsequently have sent him home with the expectation that he will restrain that ability.

The police are somewhat sympathetic but are having their own issues with the media as to how they are handling people who are practicing their civil rights to protest. They have become much more guarded and likely to follow protocol. They are treating Burt with all the consideration they are allowed. Regardless, Burt is housed in a cell with a whole group of reprobates. His crutches are taken from him, since they are regarded as potential weapons. This decision makes a simple thing like use of the latrine nearly impossible for him.

The other men in his cell have been arrested for crimes involving drinking and driving and are trying to sleep it off. Others are there for disturbing the peace, domestic violence, and a number of other petty crimes. An inmate across the cell sits quietly staring at Burt. Burt pays no attention to him. He's frustrated beyond his breaking point and would sooner be left alone. The inmate elects to single Burt out to ridicule his uniform. "Hey, general!" he scoffs.

Burt doesn't look up or acknowledge the deriding comment. It's obvious the man is inebriated. He continues to eyeball Burt; Burt continues to ignore the inmate. "Hey, general, I'm talkin' to ya."

Burt doesn't acknowledge the man in any way but continues to sit back with his head against the cell wall, eyes closed, with his arms folded against his chest.

The man rises and makes his way across the cell until he's directly in front of Burt. Burt's head is still against the wall. The man pokes Burt in the chest saying, "I'm talk—"

The man is unable to finish his sentence. Burt has grasped the man's shirt with both hands, pulling him quickly forward to a level where his face meets Burt's forehead. In another split second, the man is lying on the cell floor, spurting blood from a broken nose with Burt's hand grasping his throat and paralyzing his airway. His smashed and bug eyes indicate he is not going to survive if it's left up to Burt. In the next moment, Burt is being pulled away by a much larger man who had been monitoring the whole situation. Burt's bully is content to lie on the floor, gasping for air. His face is beginning to swell. It's apparent his cheekbone has been crushed along with his nose. Without a word of sympathy from anyone in the cell, he crawls back across the floor to his place on the other side of the room.

The large man who saved the bully's life continues to hold Burt, all the time repeating, "It's ain't worth it, man. It's ain't worth it, man. Just let it go. I been where you're at, and believe me, this ain't worth it."

With the resolve of this stranger to stay by him, Burt eventually recovers his composure. A sense of calmness is slowly replacing the rage he felt toward his circumstances. A familiar sense of comradery with this man seizes Burt at this time. He detects that this man must be a veteran.

The man continues to talk with Burt, soon verifying Burt's certainty that this man is someone he can trust. "You just gettin' back from Nam, ain't ya?" the man asks.

"Yeah." It's all Burt is able to say. His brain has gone numb. It's obvious to the stranger that Burt is under a kind of strain that he's familiar with.

The man goes on to say, "I got back a year ago. I ain't doin' much better than you. I get pissed at everything, then I start drinkin'. I'm sittin' here with you 'cause gettin' pissed and drinkin's gettin' the best of me."

This entire fiasco has spanned all of two minutes. Other than the bully suffering from some ugly face wounds, everything is nice and calm with the rest of the cell mates. Burt's self-announced guardian warns everyone to mind their own business or they're going to have to deal with him. When the guard finally becomes aware of the bully's wounds, he's taken out for treatment. His unsupported claims that he was beat up rather than tripping and falling as the rest of the cell mates stated are discounted.

For Burt, the night seems to never end. His mind refuses to shut off, couple this with the disturbances initiated by police bringing in fresh offenders every hour, all denies him sleep. When morning finally arrives, a breakfast of coffee, toast, and oatmeal is made available. Then, like a well-oiled machine, the cell is gradually emptied. One by one, they're led off to meet with a magistrate. Eventually, a guard comes to the cell, carrying Burt's crutches. He's escorted by a turnkey for his day in court. The magistrate is in a small room seated behind a raised desk. Burt is led to a podium where he is asked by the presider to identify himself. With the court protocol completed, the magistrate reads the charges filed against him and asks him how he pleads. Burt pleads not guilty but is then dressed down by the judge for reacting with violence against a person initiating a non-violent act. He's fined forty-five dollars and ten-dollars court costs and released.

Burt has been away from the States long enough to have a major shift in his thinking. It seems like a lifetime ago when he was involved with Meadow and the hippie war protesters. Now, he has a loathing for all of these activists. Understandably, he isn't looking forward to what's between here and home, and for that matter, what may be waiting for him when he arrives. He spends the rest of the day at the ocean running different scenarios around in his head. This has resulted in an inordinate yearning to be back in the Vietnamese jungle. *I miss it. It's the only place I've ever felt was for me.*

In the past twenty-four hours, Burt has had a trying flight back to the States, the mishap with the "spitter," and the jail experience. Without much thought, he rents a hotel room where he can shower some of the jailhouse stink off and get some sleep. He arranges with the desk to get him up in time to get to the train station for his trip home to Michigan. Burt awakens at five a.m. to the sound of a telephone. Not realizing he is no longer in a hospital and hearing the ring of a telephone for the first time a very long time, he's momentarily startled. He has opted to wear his uniform despite the hassles it invites. Not wasting any more time than it takes to fit his single foot prosthesis, he calls a cab. The train station is no more than a five-minute ride. He pays the driver, exiting once more into a world he has spent his blood defending but is not making him welcome. After buying his ticket, he has an hour to kill before his train arrives. Making his way to the station restaurant, he looks around to determine where the fewest people are seated. Since his past couple encounters, Burt has a growing suspicion about exposing himself to the public. He is satisfied with an end stool at the counter. It isn't long before another man takes a stool next to him. He' an older man, about the same age as Burt's father. Burt feels encroached upon, since there are many other open seats at the counter. From the demeanor of this person, Burt is conscious of his interest in something about his injury, his uniform, or just himself. Hoping not to encourage any further scrutiny, Burt opts to look straight ahead at his newspaper. However, the man continues his surveillance. He finally speaks. "You been to Vietnam?"

Burt would prefer to ignore this man but not to appear rude, he answers his question, "Yes, sir, I have."

The man remains silent for a longer period than is comfortable. He then says, "My son went also. He's coming home today on the train."

Burt notices something sincere in the man's voice, forcing him to respond more amicably, saying, "I'm happy for you."

Just then, a uniformed marine taps the man on the shoulder. Without a goodbye, the man gets up and leaves with the marine. Burt finished his breakfast and opts to wait on the loading platform rather than sit inside. He spots a bench and takes advantage of its close proximity to the tracks. Making himself as comfortable as he can on a railroad waiting bench, he notices the man he had been speaking with previously is busy loading a large wooden box into a hearse with a couple of marines. It hits him like a hammer between the eyes what the man meant when he said his son was coming home today. It takes him back to his own feelings about losing Buck, Bob, and Quincy. What makes him feel the sorriest is how these men whom he depended on and who had depended on him were jerked out of his life. *I just know if I could have done something different, we'd still be together.* Burt looks off in the distance making the best of any spiritual connection he may still have with these dead comrades. *We were damn good, though, weren't we?*

In all the time Burt spent in the Philippines recovering, he was able to recount his experiences with only a handful of men. The opportunities were often temporary. Men were moved in and out of the hospital according to their physical condition. How the war affected them mentally was not a military concern. There are no programs available to rewire the wiring they had completed on these eighteen- and nineteen-year-old young men during boot camp, their AIT, and especially after combat. It is entirely Burt's responsibility to have a comprehensive discussion with anyone regarding his mental wounds. These men may or may not talk freely among themselves, and they find it impossible to include others who haven't experienced how unnerving combat can be. Civilians readily see physical wounds but miss how these experiences have wounded these soldiers mentally and spiritually. This group of battle-worn soldiers comprises a small percentage of all the soldiers in the theater—maybe five percent—the rest are in areas of support for the guys in the field, making sure they have everything they need: food, water, ammo, and quick evacuations for the dead and wounded.

The time arrives when Burt must board the train. The rail personnel are going out of their way to accommodate this wounded soldier. A porter has grabbed his duffel bag, while another helps him with the steps. As much of a struggle as it may be for him and everyone else, Burt has requested to be placed on the top tier of the passenger car. The workers are willing oblige him because of his handicap. The car is relatively empty; he finds this seclusion a comforting forbearance. The windows are phenomenal in that they give him a panoramic view of the entire landscape. Along with the swivel tilt-back chairs, he can't ask for any other amenity. In its serpentine winding through the mountain foothills, Burt is taken aback by the lead engine in its seemingly effortless task of dragging the entire train along behind it. He spends a good share of his time either dozing or visually acquainting himself with the vastness of the country for which he has lost so much of himself. For Burt and many other teenage boys, they cynically refer to the time they are spending in Vietnam as their "senior trip." Like Burt, very few had strayed out of the borders of their own state before finding themselves across the Pacific Ocean, fighting a war for people they could never trust and who resented their presence.

The train speeds its way to the west like a steel behemoth eating its way through mountains, prairie lands, and now into the green forests of the great lake states. Peering out the window at the thickness of this foliage awakens that longing to be back in the womb

200

of the jungle. Every forest the train speeds through is an area Burt sees as a region he could easily adapt to.

Awakening to the sounds of the conductor announcing the rail station, it's the end of the line for Burt. Straight away, he gathers up his belongings, to be met again by the rail personnel to help with his disembarking. They have all been kinder than any other people he's encountered so far. Once out of the rail car, he's on his own. He's only ten miles from home and with a little luck, he can hitchhike and be there in a half hour. Slowly making his way to a small restaurant across the street from the rail station, he hopes to get a lunch. So far, since his discharged, he has never tired of American hamburgers. This is going to be the planned mainstay of his lunch. Looking forward to a quiet lunch, his pattern is to try and find a seat where he won't encounter Vietnam questions from well-meaning and some not so well-meaning patrons. Spotting an empty booth way in the back, he hobbles down the aisle only to be met by the most unlikely person he had expected to encounter: Meadow. As big as life, she comes out of the kitchen carrying a food-filled tray for a table across the room. Their eyes lock at the same moment. A startled look of surprise shoots across both faces. Meadow hesitates for a moment. She has a moment of decision and hustles on with her order. This has left Burt with an adrenalin rush, the likes of which he hasn't experienced since he left the combat zone. With only muscle memory to guide his otherwise disoriented body to the booth, he plops himself down. The next thing he knows, there is another waitress standing over his table with a pad and pencil, asking him, "What can I get for ya?"

Barely getting his wits about him, Burt orders a cheeseburger with everything. Unexpectedly enmeshed, his eye catches Meadow avoiding him, taking another path to the kitchen—still not verbally acknowledging his presence. After taking his order, his waitress leaves him to himself. Burt is left thinking how he carried Meadow's senior picture all the way through every encounter and would find solace in looking at it at night before he would go to sleep. It wasn't as though they had such an endearing relationship before he left, but he used her as his connection to every endearing thing he had left at home. His back is to the kitchen door. Every time he hears it open, the adrenalin flushes over him again, but still, she remains secluded in the kitchen. With his meal finished, Burt is prepared to be on his way. Struggling to his feet, he gets his duffle bag over his shoulder and his crutches under his arms. Once more, the kitchen door opens, and he's face to face with Meadow. The words flow out as though they are pouring from an overturned jug, "Hi, Meadow. How ya doin'?" These are words he would often recite as he studied every aspect of her picture.

She doesn't answer but remains staring at him for an uncomfortable moment. Finally, she breaks her silence. "You get hurt in Vietnam?"

Hearing her voice now makes him remember how when he would look at her picture by any light the jungle would provide and how he would then hear her laugh. As insignificant this exercise may be for anyone else, for Burt, it made him okay with the world. To her question, he gives an immediate response, "Yes. I lost my feet."

With the same expressionless look, she gives him a hard stare along with the words, "Well, baby killers like you deserve it." With that, she walks away, leaving Burt shocked to his very core. These words cut into him deeper than taking a surgeon's knife with no anesthesia. Trying to make sense of such a heartless comment, he stands expressionless. In an unwelcomed flash, it takes him back to those high school days when he was striving to fit in someplace but always got it wrong. As much as he would like to imagine he had left those days behind, this feeling of rejection popped up like the scary things that lived under his bed in earlier times. Nearly every encounter he's had since his arrival back in the States has been a rebuff of one sort or another. His mind tells him, *You don't belong here any longer. This is not your world.* This snub from Meadow has put him over the edge.

Once on the road, there has become a change in plans that results in a change in directions. The urgency to get home has turned into an urgency to get into the woods and never come out. Burt is anxious to get away from any further contact with the outside world. During his stint in Vietnam, he began to close himself off from the rest of the world; now he feels a desperate need to complete it. It's not a world he can understand any longer. *God abandoned me in Vietnam, and now people are rejecting me in my country.* The determination he had to get home has turned toward the hunting shack his grandfather owned in northern Michigan. He needs to get there.

CHAPTER 19
Alcoholism as a Marijuana Deficiency

Micky's R&R has come to an end. To help protect against soldiers inadvertently being declared AWOL, the army has initiated a team to remind on-leave soldiers that they are to report to a bus that arrives at a specified time to return them to the R&R center. Micky is not available when the bus arrives. Along with another soldier, the driver has Micky's room number and makes a call to remind him of his immediate obligation to board the bus. They get no response. The next step is to make a personal visit to his hotel room. They knock at the door, there is yet no response. They identify themselves and call out his name, demanding he open the door. Still no response. Frustrated, the two-man team finds a cleaning lady. They bribe her with an American dollar to unlock the door. What they discover is straightforward: a room full of empty Sangsom bottles and two passed-out naked people laying on the bed—one male and one female.

To be certain the soldiers are in the right room, they examine an ID lying on a table in plain sight, along with a folded paper lying next to it. When these are examined, they identify its owner to be one Michael David Murphy, with a photo matching the naked man lying on the bed. On further investigation, the folded paper proves to be a list of Micky's orders.

Now that they're certain they have the correct person, time is of the essence. There is not a minute to waste; the flight back to the base leaves with him or without him. Subsequently, the duo is adamant in an attempt to rouse Micky enough to pull on a pair of khakis and a shirt. While one soldier picks up everything that appears to belong to Micky, including the rented clothing. The other struggles to help Micky get his shoes on the right feet. The only positive thing that can be said of Micky during this entire fiasco is that he is trying to be as compliant as his condition will allow.

With the efficiency of men who have had to go this extra mile from time to time, they manage to get Micky on the bus. Micky's dim mind is not in good enough working order to get himself back to the base under his own effort, so for the first hour, he's completely dependent on anyone who will lend him a hand. When the second hour is in full force, he's tearing through all his belongings searching for his bottle of black-market Taiwanese codeine. Little does he know, the duo that got him this far left all his alcohol and drugs back in his hotel room. Up until now, his desperation has been measured, but when Micky discovers his codeine is not with him, he begins to lose what little composure he has left. His condition leaves him shaking uncontrollably. His attempt to get some food inside himself leaves most of it falling back to his plate. He isn't doing much better with a glass of ginger ale. Looking at its brownish color, he muses to himself, *If this was whiskey, I know I'd feel a lot better.* Left with the shakes and no place to get relief, Micky has no choice other than to go cold turkey.

Within twenty-four hours, Micky is back on the base. After finding Kenny, he's scored a bottle of codeine and is feeling much better. On the other hand, regardless of how Micky feels, his performance as the chaplain's assistant is left wanting. Gohrke is far from sympathetic to Micky's progressive decline into alcoholism. This brings about a confrontation. In no uncertain terms, Gohrke pronounces, "Murphy, if you don't get a handle on this booze problem, you're going to be up for a section eight. I can't have you driving me around while you're half in the bag."

"Yes, sir, I know sometimes I've gone a little overboard, but it's nothing I can't control," says Micky sheepishly. With Gohrke's stern admonition, Micky takes the lashing to heart with a new resolve to mend his ways. He sees alcoholism as the problem of someone with a weak will. *I know for certain that's not me. Any time I've set my mind to something, I've accomplished it.* He manages not to drink for the whole week. *I knew I could quit anytime I wanted to,* becomes his prevailing thought. By the time the weekend rolls around, he's so proud of himself that he decides to look up Kenny. As Micky relates his Bangkok experience, the two of them immediately connect. Slapping Micky on the back, Kenny is reliving his own Bangkok experience with

Micky and saying, "What'd I tell ya? I told ya that place was hot!" They spend the next hour sharing experiences.

What Micky opts to bring up next is the self-conscious issue of how Gohrke dressed him down for his drinking. He's not sure why he's bringing it up with Kenny—maybe it's to reinforce his belief that he doesn't have a drinking problem. Kenny looks at him with a knowing look. "Hell, man, all's you gotta do to get off the booze is to smoke weed. That's what I do, and it works great."

Micky is all ears. As much as he's tried to convince himself he doesn't have a drinking problem, this sounds like it could be just what he needs. "No kidding! If that really works, I need to give it a try."

With that option confirmed, Kenny reaches under his mattress producing a bag of pot. "We can't smoke it here. Everybody can smell it." Pointing over his shoulder, Kenny continues, "We can drive over in that old cemetery. Nobody pays it no mind." Climbing into Micky's jeep, they make their way along the parameter of the base to a grouping of ancient stones marking the graves of a long-forgotten tribe. Very methodically, Kenny takes a pipe he keeps just for this occasion. He carefully fills it and then lights the bowl, sucking in its rough contents. Micky has never smoked as much as a cigarette, yet allowing himself to be introduced to another drug has become ordinary. Nonetheless, he feels a little anxiety; maybe it's an excited feeling. He's closely watched Kenny and feels he knows what to do. Taking the pipe, he cautiously puts its stem between his lips. Taking a small amount of smoke, Micky pulls it down into his chest cavity. Its harshness brings an immediate reaction, making him cough. Looking on with a grin, Kenny says, "You'll get used to it. It always does that the first time."

Monitoring himself for an expected effect, Micky doesn't feel a change. Still holding the pipe and believing that at least his lungs know what to expect, he takes another hit—only this time, it's a much bigger hit. The harshness is the same, but he's holding it in longer. All of a sudden, a strange euphoric sensation creeps across his body. It's a different kind of pleasure than the alcohol he's become so acquainted with, and much more intense than the mild effects of codeine. Kenny takes his turn while keeping an eye on Micky's response. All Micky is able to say is, "Wow!"

When it comes to turning someone on for the first time, Kenny has the zeal of a Pentecostal TV preacher. "I told ya, man, this is great stuff!," is his laughing response. They finish the bowl and Micky is amazed how well he drives. He's much slower and less hyper than when he's drinking.

After dropping Kenny off at his hooch, Micky becomes aware of a tremendous thirst. It's developing very quickly and is very demanding in its intensity. Deciding to stop by the enlisted men's club for a beer to quench this strange unrelenting thirst, he drinks the entire beer in less than a minute, immediately ordering another, then another and another.... It's in unwise moments of decision—be they drunk or sober—where destinies are shaped. In a couple hours, Micky climbs back in his jeep and speeds off. The very curve he had the mishap on his first day while driving a chaplain to the airport presents itself once again. Only this time, instead of an enemy ordnance flipping his jeep, he is the ordnance. The mishap knocks him unconscious and breaks a few vertebrae. When Micky wakes up in the infirmary with no recollection of the events leading up to the wreck, he realizes he must have been in a total alcohol blackout. The first thing he is aware of is Chaplain Gohrke standing over him, saying a prayer. "I don't need that," is Micky's first response.

Chaplain Gohrke wags an affirmative nod and says, "You're going to need every prayer you can get and a few miracles besides to get you out of this mess." Mickey listens with an oblivious ear. With no recall, these words from his boss are only slightly disconcerting. He can't imagine he's done anything serious enough to warrant what Gohrke is referring to as a "mess." Within the hour, the doctor and an MP give him a full presentation as to his physical condition and the charges awaiting him when he gets out of the hospital. Micky is truly shocked when he becomes aware of his fate.

"Private Murphy, with the swelling in your broken vertebrae, you may not walk again," reports the presiding surgeon. "We've done what we can here, but you're going to need more specific care. I'm going to have you evacuated to our military hospital in Da Nang."

Waiting for his turn, an MP with the insignia of lieutenant on his uniform, carrying a set of charges gives way saying, "Private Murphy, your actions constitute a court martial offence. These charges will be more specific when you're deemed capable by your physician. I suggest you ask for council. It's my opinion that you're going to need it."

Micky has been sedated in the hopes of preventing him from going into alcoholic DTs. Along with having no recall, he's been drugged enough to also not be concerned about what he has just heard.

Before the day is complete, a medical helicopter is summoned. Micky and several other seriously wounded combat soldiers are evacuated to waiting beds in Da Nang. Micky is put under the care of a neurologist. A week has lapsed, and he is free of the DT concern. A more aggressive action can now be taken to address his broken vertebrae. He is assigned to a physical therapist with a regimen of activities to be completed. Military council in the form of a captain is also meeting with him today regarding the charges against him. "I would highly suggest you do everything you can to get a handle on your alcohol problem. The court is ready to have your hide at your present standing. You can avert some of its wrath by attending some AA meetings. Micky is listening to his council only as a strategist listens to a plan of action. "I will comply, but I believe this AA stuff is a waste of time. I don't feel I have a drinking problem. I've proven to myself that I can quit anytime I want to."

To reemphasize, the captain states his wishes more as an order than a request. "I don't give a damn what you feel soldier, I want a signed paper for every AA meeting you attend—do you understand me?!"

For the first time since his last drinking encounter, Micky is having a second thought: *I know I can do this myself, but it probably won't hurt to at least see what this AA stuff's got to offer.*

The next time his doctor makes a visit, Micky relates to him how he would like to contact someone connected with Alcoholics Anonymous. His doctor assures him that his staff will make a call for him.

Micky does not hesitate to mention, "It's not because I think *I* need it. My council is adamant that I do it. I'm only following orders."

He's speaking with the doctor who treated him for his back injury and is also the guiding hand that prevented him from falling into the throes of the DT's.

Before the day is over, a staff sergeant is standing at the foot of his bed, looking directly at Micky. It startles him for a moment. He's a short, older-looking man—older than one Micky would expect someone who's still in the military to be. He has the demeanor of a man who is concerned. He makes the first move. "Are you Private Murphy?"

"That's me. What can I help you with?" says Micky warily. The first thing that runs through his mind is that this man wants to question him about how he wrecked a military jeep.

The man continues his friendly gaze, adding, "Maybe I'm here to see if we can help each other. My name is Joe Billings. I'm an alcoholic. I only gotta get through this year to get my twenty in before I retire. I was wonderin' if you could give me some pointers on how you stay sober. The doc tells me you been sayin' you do it on your own. I just need to stay sober long enough for me to get my pension. They been threatenin' to discharge me with a section eight if I get drunk one more time."

Micky is dumbfounded, to say the least. For the first time in his military experience, he is confronted with a person asking *him* for help—someone who needs *him*. This appeal brings with it an unwelcomed awareness of his own poverty; he has absolutely nothing to offer this man. The only thing that comes to mind is what his legal council ordered him to do. "All I know is, I been ordered to attend AA meetings. If you can get me there, I'll go with you." Micky feels a sudden bond with a man he had not met until two minutes ago. A sensation is overtaking him that's similar to the one that had grasped him during his high school commencement when his pastor's words had stirred in him an overwhelming need to serve God. He felt so much closer to God than he does now. It seems so long ago. The result is this man asking for help in his brokenness suddenly exposes Micky to his own neediness. *I can't give anyone something I don't have myself.* This thought haunts him. His thoughts have shot back to how his life has changed—and not for the better. *What have I done to myself?*

Within the hour, Joe has arranged to transport Micky to his first AA meeting via wheelchair. He looks around the room at what appears to be a room full of losers. It would be a major undertaking to describe the embarrassing humiliation Micky is undergoing. These are the very types of people he has snubbed all through his high school year; in his estimation, they are all weak and hollow. Micky undergoes a sinking feeling of despair. *Has my life truly come to this? There must be a mistake.* He's finding it difficult to bear under it. *I don't belong here.* It's enough to cause him to change his mind and leave, but then he spots a captain shaking hands with some of the others. A different thought begins to entertain him; *this guy must be the leader.* He hopes that this will upgrade what otherwise seems to be a horrendous experience. The captain approaches Micky with an extended hand introducing himself, "Hi, I'm John. I'm an alcoholic." Micky can hardly believe the daring nature of this admission. The thought that races through his mind is this guy must be incredibly brave or incredibly stupid to admit to something like that. *Doesn't he know that stuff can wreck his career?*

Micky self-consciously extends his hand long enough to feel a firm, confident grip—hardly the grip of a looser. Then, even more surprising, the captain finds a chair and sits down between two privates. This is hardly the end of Micky's surprises. Joe suddenly speaks up. "Hi, everybody, I'm Joe. I'm an alcoholic. Let's open this meeting using the serenity prayer." Micky is becoming even more confused, as it seems Joe is acting as a chairman. What comes next is something that places Micky in the spotlight. Joe begins, saying, "Before we pick a topic, I'd like you to meet a newcomer. His name is Micky. I think we should all share our experiences, strengths, and hopes with him today."

There is a resounding response from at least a dozen men and women, saying a simple, "Hi, Micky."

In that simple salutation Micky is experiencing a feeling he has no words to describe, it's something he has never felt in his life, it's a feeling of acceptance and forgiveness. By the end of this one-hour meeting in Micky's life, he has experienced an eye-opener. Never has he seen such bold, forthright honesty—such Divine common sense. These people possess a confidence he has only held for himself in his imagination. He has discovered a safe place where, not only can he knock on the door of the truth concerning his own imperfections, he can enter the room and ensure a fuller, safer, nonjudgmental evaluation. The miracle for Micky is he has developed as much of a thirst for this new knowledge as he has for the booze. Even with this new insight, the battle is far from won. With the help of the medical profession, they have successfully prevented Micky from going into the DT's, thus ensuring there isn't a single cell in his body that craves alcohol. But this does not eliminate the power of an overwhelming manifestation of a mental obsession to drink.

Over the next two weeks of his hospital stay, Micky has attended enough meetings to better understand this mental obsession to change the way he feels with a chemical is an attempt to fill his acknowledged "spiritual void." He has become aware of how far he has fallen from the standards he had set for himself and how powerless he is in reshaping his life in physical, mental, and spiritual ways using his own willpower. Joe described it in so many simple words: "Micky, if you continue to attempt to pull yourself up by your own bootstraps, all you'll do is continue to jerk your legs out from under yourself and land on your drunken ass. Like the rest of us, you been damn well acquainted with a lower power; you need to reacquaint yourself with a higher power—one that's big enough to fill the hole He created in you for Himself in the first place."

After several weeks of therapy and daily AA meetings, one of the most obvious changes that's taken place is Micky's release from the denial that hung onto his soul and falsely assured him that he is capable to cope with his drinking and drug problem on his own. Another idea Micky has painfully become aware of is how unexceptional his drinking career has been—it's shared in so many ways by the entire recovery group. Originally, he had hoped his case was so unique that it would be impossible for him to recover, which would allow him to continue drinking. Now he discovers he's merely a garden-variety drunk. At this juncture, the group informed him he can leave anytime he wishes, and they'd gladly refund his misery. (The common experience is Frank Sinatra's song "My Way" has become the loser's national anthem.) With just enough sobriety to remember he has a military court martial charge hanging over his head is enough to give him his second thought.

Micky's turning point is evident in the respectful way he has begun to treat hospital personnel. He's much less arrogant and demanding. He has also begun to wheel himself around to some of the other patients, forbearingly listening to their fears and concerns. "I know I don't have as much to share as some of the others, but I've been told I need to share what has been freely given to me," Micky is overheard saying these words while comforting another wounded soldier. This is the kind of life Micky would have like to have picked for himself but found himself short of the power to carry it out. This reflects the fact that something has entered his life that has not been there in recent times. Joe sees it as the same miracle within Micky as he does within his own life. It's a freedom from the bondage of a self-centered life. Joe assures Micky that he's on the right path as long as he continues to go to meetings and follows the twelve steps of AA. "Next to God, the most important word in this program is the word 'continue'," Joe says.

Micky has long ago forgiven Joe for tricking him into going to his first AA meeting. It seems Joe has already had several years of continuous sobriety. Joe's response is that it really was not a trick and that he needs Micky as much as Micky needs his support.

The day arrives when the doctors have done all they can do to correct Micky's back. He's being sent back to his unit with very few restrictions as long as he remains a chaplain's assistant. If that should change, a reevaluation would have to be done to determine his military suitability. He also is being sent back to face his court martial charges. His legal council is pleased with each AA chairperson verifying Micky's attendance and supporting his progress.

Micky spends his last day thanking all those that have been a part of his recovery—both physically but also mentally and particularly spiritually. The past few weeks have been a turning point for Micky. What he has concluded is that over most of his life despite his parochial school training, he has had a skewed relationship with God on several different levels. He spent much of his time believing he was getting God's approval for being Mr. Wonderful and God was blessing him for being a good boy but by his own admission of late, "I really had no idea that all God wants of me is to love his other children the way he does. I'm just beginning to learn how to do that. I got a ways to go." Over the course of his life, Micky has categorically done much to sabotage his Christian principles; he has left himself totally at the mercy of the failing strength of his own ego leaving him a victim of his own human condition.

Joe is in a position to meet one on one with Micky before he leaves. "I ain't here to debate anything about your church education. I figure they can handle where your souls gonna end up but AA's here to save your ass. So, all you need to remember is that there is a God, and it ain't you!"

The real test is about to begin. Micky is on his way back to his unit. Tension is definitely a part of this trip. He finds himself reciting the Serenity Prayer several times during this transition. He feels as though he's been on a retreat, and the day has arrived when he packs up his belongings and heads back into the same world he had left behind, only to discover the *same* challenges are still there, awaiting his arrival. Micky is aware that his problems are not going away, but he is hoping the past few weeks have given him the insight he needed. His prayer is simple and straightforward, asking for wisdom and discernment to know how to react to the court's decision. "And God, I need *You* to strengthen me not to drink over anything that comes my way." A calm begins to come over him each time he does this. For the number of times he's finding it necessary to repeat this exercise, he's realizing his human condition is very reluctant to give up the reins of control over the direction his life wants to take. Nonetheless, as slowly as Micky is finding a pathway to himself, this is the first time in his young life that he's dared to make such introspections—good, bad, or ugly. All through Micky's high school career, he prided himself on never giving up on any challenge, but he finds himself saying, "I've got to give up on drugs and alcohol. They've kicked my butt."

Micky's return to the base is not bringing out his best feelings. A knot is forming in the pit of his gut despite his pleading to God to remove it. He's already missing the support system he had back at the hospital. The reality of what he's up against takes another swipe at him as the bus passes by the motor pool, where his wrecked jeep is still awaiting repair. To add to an already discouraging situation, the rest of the base still smells as bad as it always has. Soon, he's dropped off at the chaplain's headquarters.

The first person he runs into is Chaplain Captain Donald Wardwell, the chaplain who had threatened him with court martial charges for the first incident he had with the chaplain's jeep. Wardwell didn't say a word to him but didn't hesitate to give him a disdainful look. Micky saluted him nevertheless. He knows it's not all over yet, he has yet to face Gohrke. With this thought haunting him, he suddenly finds himself standing before a very familiar door. Gently knocking, he hears a very familiar voice saying, "Come in." Borderline between timid and quietly respectful, he slowly opens the door, enters

214

and salutes announcing, "Private first class Michael Murphy reporting for duty, sir."

Putting Micky at ease, Gohrke stops his paperwork, spending the next few moments looking Micky over. "Well, Micky, you look a lot better than you did a few weeks ago. The last time I looked at you in the hospital, you were the color of hawk bait."

"I still don't remember too much about that whole incident, sir," reports Micky sheepishly.

"Have you learned anything as a result?" asks Gohrke. The forthright way this question is presented suggests it will be best to have a convincing response.

"Sir, I can't tell you how much I've come to realize. I've discovered more about myself in the past few weeks than I have in my entire life. I feel a lot closer to God than I ever have," says Micky. There is no doubting the sincerity in his voice.

Gohrke pauses as he considers how well incorporated Micky may be in this new union with his higher power. Continuing his assessment, he adds, "Remember this, Murphy; the devil doesn't care how close you may feel to God, as long as you're not."

No sooner is this portion of Micky's and Gohrke's tête-à-tête finished than two MP's appear in the doorway. Barely finished with his superior, he is taken by surprise with this interruption. One is holding up a paper. He is the designated spokesman for the duo. "Are you Private Michael David Murphy?" is his unbending question.

His response is open and transparent. "Yes, that's me."

"I have a warrant for your arrest. Will you please turn around and place your hands behind your back?"

Without as much as a question, Micky readily complies. He is handcuffed and led off to a waiting military jeep. After he arrives at the military stockade, the next few minutes are used to process his charges. He is then led to a holding cell to await a hearing. An hour later he finds himself before a commissioned officer holding hearings in a court room setting. Since his charge is less than a capital offence, he is given the option of having a summary court martial. This will be before a single judge without access to legal counsel. Micky wants this behind him as quickly as possible and readily agrees to a summary court martial. The officer, using the official, monotone voice of one who has this operation down to a routine, says, "In that case, Private Murphy, this court will hear your case immediately. How do you plead?"

"Guilty, sir."

The guilty plea is accepted. In the next few minutes, the official legal protocol for this action is met and concludes with the reading of the sentence. This officer of the court has sentenced Micky to rat patrol for a week around the base's garbage dump. This involves patrolling the area for rats and exterminating them. The rats in this part of Vietnam are not small; they grow well over ten pounds and are ubiquitous. Unlike the other enemies US forces deal with who can be stopped with rifle fire, grenades, howitzers, and conventional military weaponry, these frenzied rodents charge mindlessly forward, breeding as fast as they're eradicated. They have razor-sharp incisors and have been known to chew through plastic-coated communications wire, lead pipes, and even steel fences. These predators are relentless in their pursuit of food. Everyone on base has dealt with these monsters in one way or another. The very thought of these voracious hordes crawling around their hooch and over them while they're sleeping is enough to horrify even the toughest battle-hardened soldier.

Micky is given a .22-caliber rifle and a box of cartridges. It's not a military-issue rifle; rather, at some point, a soldier surrendered his Bangkok souvenir, and it eventually found its way to the rat brigade. There is no clean or neat way of taking on this duty; Micky must crawl around the vast piles of garbage to root out the rats. The first day, he kills fifty large rats. Disposing of them proves to be no problem. The Vietnamese workers around the base are eager to take them—rat meat is high on the menu of the Vietnamese people. It's reported to be quite flavorful and akin to the taste of chicken or pork. American soldiers have never considered placing them on the menu as a way of controlling their population and gladly leave that experience to the Vietnamese people.

CHAPTER 20
Skeeter

With over a thousand dollars of mustering out pay left in his pocket and a determination to get to his grandfather's hunting shack in northern Michigan, Burt has taken a bus to Traverse City. From there, he has managed to buy a secondhand motor scooter and has driven himself along with as many supplies as he can carry to the remote shack along the Platt River. After months of combat and many months in the hospital recovering from the physical wounds, Burt has been left alone to deal with the war reels that are still running in his head. The losses of his combat team and of purpose in his life have taken a toll on him. He can describe each of his combat missions as though he had completed them yesterday. His stay in the hospital was his last connection with the kind of men who "give a damn" about this kind of stuff. Now, he has only himself. There is no one who has his back; he's all alone to rehash these moments. Thinking about his lost comrades is a painful, lonely exercise. It seems the devil is hell-bent on destroying what's left of him.

The cabin was never intended to be a year-round residence; rather, it had originally been designed to merely get its occupants out of Michigan's inclement spring, summer, and fall weather. It is primarily built from discarded lumber and bundles of heavy, greenish tar paper covering the roof and outer walls. It has a hand pump that needs priming and a wood stove that serves a dual purpose: heating and cooking. The cabin's musty smell may be offensive to some, but to Burt, it's the smell of the sheltered place he remembers as a young child. His maternal grandparents would bring him here for the long summer months during his grade school years. He spent long hours learning how to fish and hunt with his grandfather. Unfortunately, both grandparents died the year Burt was thirteen. His father and mother never appreciated the shack's incongruity and have hung onto it only as an investment in riverfront property. No one, including Burt, has visited since the death of the old people.

The key to the padlock securing the door is in the outhouse hanging on a nail where it's always hung. The padlock is rusty on the outside but still working like it's supposed to on the inside. Today, the old shack has purpose once again in sheltering its guest. The first few hours have passed, and Burt is finding a wonderful remembrance in nearly everything he sees and touches. The wood pile he and his grandfather stacked is a little worse for wear; the seven-year-old wood that's been left to the elements isn't as full-bodied as it once was. Nonetheless, it's good enough to start a fire in the cook stove. One thing Burt has noticed is that the Michigan woods have a different smell than the jungle. The omnipresent odor of decaying vegetation is missing. It may be the only thing Burt doesn't include among his reasons to love the jungle. *I wish things didn't have to get old and die,* he thinks. Today, he is prepared to call on the survival skills he acquired both at the knee of his grandfather and in the military. There is nothing one can consider a modern convenience in this two-room structure. Everything his grandparents supplied the shack with was secondhand and, in some cases, nearly used up. The lamps are kerosene, and a few old candles have been stashed in various places where they can be reached when needed. Delightfully, he discovers he's grown into the closet full of clothes belonging to his grandfather. *I have grown into my grandfather's clothes—imagine that.* He spends the rest of the day reclaiming every wonderful thing he reminisces about regarding this place. This is the most content he's been since leaving the jungles of South Vietnam.

His handicap of two missing feet with only his right leg's prothesis fitted and his left tibia in the healing process necessitates the use of crutches, and it also inhibits any chance of returning to combat. With this option completely out of the question, Burt finds acclimating to his latest life is taking a good deal of adjusting. He has to keep reminding himself that this is not a war zone and doesn't require a constant alertness; the quiet is really the forest's norm.

Burt's thoughts wander from his glorious days in the jungles of Vietnam to a resentment for the American public that has demonstrated contempt for his service. What Meadow had said to him continues to haunt him. It's easy for him to believe that if he can stay away from the public, he can find the kind of contentment he felt in the jungle out here. Looking to the sky, he says out loud, "Buck, Quincy, Bob … I sure do miss you guys. We were sure somethin', weren't we?"

The days begin to add up. Burt realizes he has been here for nearly a week. For the lack of a sentinel keeping watch at night, he's still finding it necessary to block the door with his bed. It just lets him sleep better. He has no idea who this enemy may be, but then, he never knew who it would be in Vietnam. Daytime isn't nearly as unnerving. Today turns out to be a beautiful day with plenty of Michigan summer warmth. Without notice, the weather changes from this bright, balmy day to an unexpected torrential downpour. Without warning, Burt is disconnectedly finding himself back in the jungle. Buried somewhere deep in his psyche, his mind has suddenly turned to a distorted reality. He throws himself on the ground and begins a resolute crawl as if searching for an enemy. The storm has become a trigger that's throwing him into a flashback to his days as a recon operative. With the single-mindedness that comes with his former tasks, he remains focused on this nonexistent enemy. As suddenly as he went into this hallucination, he snaps out of it. Half of the wetness burnishing his body may be from the rain, but the other half is from sweat. With the rain still pelting his weary body, he gathers his wits enough to crawl back to his abandoned crutches and make his way back to the shelter of the shack. Shaken by the realness of this illusion, he crawls into his bunk. Pulling himself into the fetal position, he begins to sob, wailing a bloodcurdling yowl. He feels the loss of his three comrades in an emptiness and screams at God for making him live. "Why, God do You punish me this way? You told me 'I have you'! But you've taken everything I've lived for! Why don't You let me die?" The abandoned feelings Burt experienced while witnessing the brutal treatment the American prisoners of war were undergoing have intensified. He no longer senses any comforting connection to a higher power, but he senses the full force of a lower power trying to take what it can from the rest of his broken soul. He's exhausted and dispirited. He sees himself as so emotionally fragmented that *all* thoughts leave him without hope.

The joy and relief that were Burt's on revisiting his boyhood refuge have taken a turn and twisted into a daily drudge of struggling to survive. This struggle is not limiting itself to threatening him only spiritually and mentally; it's also taking its toll on him physically. He's continually lost weight from a poor diet and doesn't appear to be capable of making any attempts to rectify a change. Still living in his past, the present world of reality is slipping away. Between spending his remaining "mustering out" pay on necessary supplies and losing or misplacing some of it, Burt has found he's nearly broke, with very little food left. Hunger is forcing him to ride his scooter into Traverse City in search of a handout. His mind is a blur.

He never imagined this problem. He was certain that if he could get to the shack, everything would work out. Now his certainty about anything is sliding away, with no direction other than down. He's become despondent enough that just finding someplace he can get a handout will have to do. On a previous trip, he had noticed a Salvation Army church. His remembrance is that they are usually ready to give a helping hand to anyone who needs food or shelter. Parking his scooter in front of the building, Burt rehearses what he is going to tell them in the hopes that it will be enough to get some food. The lady behind the office window looks up from her work. *She looks friendly enough*, he thinks to himself. "Ma'am, I'm wondering if you folks could help me out. I'm just out of the army, and I've run out of money. I don't have enough to get a meal. Could you spare enough for me to get a few groceries?" This plea is empty of any honor or dignity. Instead, it's the honest plea of a broken young man.

The lady behind the window barely gives him a second glance, not because she is calloused, but because she is well acquainted with the underbelly of the culture. In a pragmatic tone, she states, "We don't have money for you, but we can help you out with some food.

Our pantry is open tomorrow between noon and five o'clock." Reaching behind her, she opens a refrigerator. Taking out a small brown lunch bag, she hands it to Burt. "This has enough to get you through today. Stop by tomorrow, and we'll see how we can help you out." Her smile displays a window into the kind soul she is ready to share with those unable to find their own.

With his crutches securely under his arms, Burt extends a hand long enough to secure the bag without losing his balance. Happy to get this far, he gives the bag a couple little lifts. It's got a nice heft to it. He's far from being particular what food combinations it contains, providing there's plenty of it. After eating army C-rations for weeks at a time, he couldn't be less fussy about what satisfies his hunger. This little act of kindness by this lady has lifted his spirits—that is, until he leaves the building. Going to retrieve his scooter, he finds nothing but an empty space in its place. His heart sinks. What little boost his spirits had just welcomed suddenly comes crashing down. The kind of dread he is experiencing is more anger than any other emotion. But at the same time, Burt is also experiencing a sense of powerlessness. His injuries have left him vulnerable in a way he never felt in the war jungles of Vietnam. All he can do is let out a sad sigh; not a sigh of resignation, but rather a sigh of frustration. *What the hell can a cripple like me expect to do to take care of myself?* He sees his destiny is to become an angry old fool with nothing inside but bitterness and resentment.

Surveying Burt's disappointment is a grizzled man leaning against a fence. He's holding a bag of Bull Durum tobacco in one hand and curling a rolling paper in the other. He's ready to fill the paper when he finally speaks. "Them local boys cobbed your scooter."

Looking about in disbelief, Burt stands speechless. Once again, he's feeling very alone. These kinds of assaults are more distressing than his time spent in combat. *At least there, I had my team. We had weapons. I could retaliate. Here, I feel helpless, like I have no weapons to fight back with.*

Burt needs not say a word for anyone to see the utter defeat come across his face. With little more than a stare, he takes a deep breath, shrugs his shoulders, and begins to hobble off toward he doesn't know where. If this were not enough, a distant clap of thunder threatens rain once again. The grizzled old man gives him one more holler. "You lose them feet in Nam?" This very verbose stranger is seemingly inviting himself into the private world of Burt's wounds.

The question stops Burt in his track. Not certain if this is going to be a repeat of his earlier encounters, he remains motionless with his back to the questioner. Risking a recap, he decides to let the chips fall where they may and answers, "Yeah, as a matter of fact, I did."

Pulling a pant leg up, the man says, "Korea, 1954." There, attached to a stump, is a prosthesis indicating a similar wound. It's definitely an older design held together with duct tape and certainly a lot less high-tech than the model Micky's been fitted with.

Not certain what his response should be, Micky says, "It's a bitch, ain't it?" Gazing intently at the man, he can't help but see the anguish in the man's eyes. At this point, his mind is painting a similar picture of himself in a few more years.

Taking a deep drag on his hand-rolled cigarette, the man gives him a knowing nod of agreement, then poses still another question, "You're new around here, ain't ya?"

"Ya, I guess I am now since my scooters gone. It's leavin' me stranded. I got a place back on the river about a half hour away. Sure as hell don't look like I'm gonna get there usin' these crutches," answers Burt. "By the way, can ya tell me where's a cheap place to stay tonight?" Burt enquires.

"Depends on whether you got gear. If you got a sleepin' bag stashed somewhere, there's a pavilion that's covered from the rain down by the lake. But if you ain't got no gear, then you can stay in the church basement with a bunch of drunks snorin' all night keepin' ya awake," reports the man with the superiority of a specialist.

Mulling over these options, Burt opts for the pavilion. "I like the idea of sleepin' outside if I can get a sleepin' bag."

"Go back inside an' ask 'em for one—just make sure you ain't gettin' one with a bunch of chiggers," says the man with the same air of authority.

Burt has had nearly every kind of jungle pest chew on him with impunity. "I ain't gonna worry too much about that as long as it does the job." Burt returns to the same window he visited only minutes ago along with his new request. Exercising the same sense of efficiency, the lady behind the window, says, "Give me a minute. I've got one drying on the line." In a minute, she returns with a freshly washed sleeping bag and a piece of binder twine in her hand. "You can roll it up and tie it with this if it makes it easier to carry," says the lady with a satisfied smile that her forethought will prove to be a safe bet. Burt thanks her once again and makes his way back outside.

With a swirl of smoke engulfing his entire head, the waiting man pinches the burned off the end of his cigarette using a nicotine-stained thumb and forefinger and carefully places the remaining butt into the Bull Durum bag. His face twists itself into an approving gap-toothed grin. What few teeth he has left are nicotine stained and staggered like a carved pumpkin. "Ya done good, kid. Follow me, I'll show ya a good place to stash it 'til ya need it." With a quick motion of his hand, the man signals Burt to follow him. By means of his crutches, and his amiable companion with a distinct limp from an ill-fitting prosthesis, together they amble their way to a nearby bridge crossing the Boardman River. A well-worn path angles itself along the grassy bank until it breaks into a graveled floor free of any plant life under one end of the bridge. It's taking a little more effort to navigate this slope than Burt is used to but by using the same determination he had employed facing difficulties in the army, he avoids a mishap. With the same nicotine-stained finger, the man points up toward a ledge on the bridge's underside, referring to Burt's sleeping bag, he says, "You can pack 'er in right up there. Ain't nobody gonna bother with it." Burt finds following orders from this older vet is a trustworthy gamble and makes the choice to follow his directions.

Watching Burt struggle to balance himself without toppling in to the river, the old vet gives him a helping hand, asking, "Hey, kid, you gotta name people calls ya?"

"Burt. People call me Burt. What about you? What's your name?"

"Skeeter! Been goin' by that name for so long, I forget I gotta name my ma give me. Skeeter's good enough for me, though," pronounces Skeeter, displaying his signature grin. "By the way, kid, do ya like drinkin'?"

This question takes Burt by surprise. He hasn't had a drink since the last time he celebrated with Buck, Quincey, and Bob. Skeeter doesn't wait for an answer before he's shoved his arm up to his armpit into one of the hidden crevasses under the bridge. A GIQ (Giant Imperial Quart) of beer seems to materialize in his hand. His nicotine-stained fingers prove to possess a deftness that only years of practice can produce as he uncaps it on a sharp edge of the bridge's undergirding. Devoid of the slightest need for coaching, Skeeter lifts the bottle and throws his head back as he prepares to gulp as much of its contents as he can before he needs to come up for air. Satisfied for the moment, he hands the bottle to Burt. With the bottle firmly in his hand, Burt looks at it for only a moment. A compulsion suddenly grips him; it's almost as though sharing this ritual with this old veteran is the kind of celebration he needs to keep his Vietnam life alive and to the forefront of his being. He suddenly realizes this is exactly what's been missing. *The only place I ever excelled was in Vietnam. If I'm going to keep it alive, I need to share my times there with guys who need to keep their war time alive.* Without a second thought, Burt puts the bottle to his lips and mirrors the same technique as Skeeter. This nearly wordless rite connecting these two broken souls is definitely a bonding moment linking them by their similar experiences and wounds—and maybe even more so by those wounds they aren't aware of. It's the closest thing to a religious sacrament that these two fragmented human beings can do to connect to each other's dejectedness. The rain has begun, making it an easy call to remain under the bridge and share a sack lunch and beer. In this strange alliance, Burt is beginning to feel a renewal of power that he felt with his war comrades. Blow by blow, they spend the rest of the afternoon rehashing wartime experiences, reliving and (in some cases) embellishing what may have proven to be a less dangerous moment. Soon running out of beer, they scrounge in their pockets for loose change and come up with enough to replenish their beer supply. Evening arrives only to leave them in their sleeping bags, alone in a different battlefield with their own tangled thoughts combating unfamiliar webs of newfound fears.

CHAPTER 21
A Work in Progress

With his sentence completed, Micky is reunited with his chauffer/bodyguard obligations under Chaplain Gohrke's leadership. One thing he can be certain with Gohrke is that his schedule will be packed. Gohrke has once again insisted on visiting the wounded in the infirmary. Micky has a new sense of the important role this chaplain performs when he engages with these often dispirited soldiers— especially when dealing with the complexities of living with their wounds. Today, he is listening with new ears to the strength behind Gohrke's encouragements. This kindly chaplain is seated at eye level with a young man who's not more than eighteen years old. He's listening with the sincerity of one who is willing to give this soldier one-hundred percent of his attention and time.

"It's not every day I see someone with your wounds, but what I'm certain of is that these doctors will do everything within their power and their God-appointed skills to make sure you heal. What I'm just as concerned about is what you may be doing to overcome your fear of how you're going to live with these wounds." Even with the wounds this young man is enduring, his eyes turn toward Gohrke. Aware he has hit upon an overriding worry dominating this wounded spirit, Gohrke continues. "I want to share with you a secret of a successful and meaningful life in spite of your physical condition." It's apparent this young man's attention is focused entirely on what this chaplain is going to say next. "I want you to pray this prayer with me for just a moment. Will you do that?" The young soldier nods, and Gohrke begins, "God grant me the serenity to accept the things I cannot change. The courage to change the things I can. And the wisdom to know the difference."

"If you surrender yourself to God using this prayer, you will discover a new strength beyond your own. You will find you have connected your spirit with God's and despite your physical injuries, I guarantee you won't find your heart suffering similar wounds."

Aware he has connected this young man's spirit to God's spirit, he leaves him by placing his thumb securely to his forehead, tracing the sign of the cross, he recites the words, "May Almighty God, The Father, The Son, and The Holy Spirit continue to bless and keep your soul safe in His hands."

A new connection is evolving between Gohrke and Micky. It's causing Micky to see himself in a whole new light. Instead of his focus directed toward gaining people's attention because of an imagined superior status, he is taking a fearless moral inventory of himself. As difficult as it is to objectively look at his own failings, he is beginning to recognize his self-centeredness, which he always considered an advantage. He is now able to see it for what it is—a shortcoming. Another change for the better has been a heartfelt introduction to a higher power, beginning with Joe Billings. Joe introduced him to a God that was capable of condescending Himself to the needs of an alcoholic—not as a prosecutor, but as the generous source of strength behind his recovery. Another first for Micky is the visual demonstration of how unselfishly this chaplain gives of himself to serve his higher power. Through these experiences, he is beginning to see how God uses humble servants like Joe and Gohrke to be His hands, feet, and voice. At the moment, with this wounded soldier, he is witnessing something in Gohrke that is so beautiful that it cannot be described any more than the fragrance of a rose can be described. What he is witnessing is the kind of love he can warm his hands on. Overwhelmed by an indescribable peace, Micky stands stunned at the change that is overcoming him. It's as though when a teacher is needed, they are presented.

Tirelessly, Gohrke spends at least another hour comforting these young men whose wounds have changed their dreams. Almost all have life-changing injuries like blindness, missing limbs, head trauma, spinal cord injuries causing paralysis, burns, skin diseases, and so on. What Micky is observing for the first time is how Gohrke has the ability to zero in on just what kind of spiritual message each of these men need. With the energy of one dominated by a power greater than himself, Gohrke finally ends his hospital rounds. His next mission has already been prepared in his mind. He calls on Micky to prepare to make a trip by helicopter to a jungle platoon that has been routing out an enemy that is occupying a village as a stronghold.

Arriving at the helicopter pad, Micky quickly and efficiently transfers all the items Chaplain Gohrke has listed to take with them. In a matter of minutes, Gohrke has finished with the flight manifest and is boarding the Huey. It's obvious he's anxious to get to this village. Word coming from other pilots is that this village is under siege by a seemingly out-of-control platoon leader. Despite this distressing state of affairs, Gohrke is prepared to meet the challenge. He has discovered the door gunners new M60 mounted to the floor. He's produced a big smile as he attempts to shout over the combination of the engine noise and the flopping sound of the rotary blades, "Hey man, this is quite the gun, you just get it?"

"Yes, sir. It's new. It's lighter than the 50cal, but just as deadly and it doesn't interfere with the operation of the Huey. You wanna shoot it?" the gunner inquires.

Gohrke has come from a long line of hunters and has been around guns his entire life. To miss an opportunity like this would be out of character for this Minnesota country boy. Even though it is traditional for chaplains to let others deal with weapons, he is more than capable to use a weapon if it comes to defending his life or the life of an American soldier.

"You don't have to ask me twice," say Gohrke, sporting a grin from ear to ear. Placing himself in the gunner's seat, he commences to fire across spans of vacant rice paddies. Each round can be accounted for, as it creates an eruption of water that's propelled across a backdrop of the water-filled rice paddies. After several seconds of uninterrupted gunfire, he's satiated. Relinquishing the seat, he graciously thanks the gunner.

Within twenty minutes, the Huey has found the war zone. The pilot barely lands long enough to unload Chaplain Gohrke, Micky, a small field altar and communion ware, and a few supplies. Once they're on the ground, Gohrke makes his way directly to the field commander. His name is First Lieutenant Graham Watson. He's an ROTC graduate from Michigan State University. He arrived in Vietnam less than a month ago. This is his first command. According to the chaplain's manual, Chaplain Gohrke's first obligation is to provide free exercise of religion and to provide spiritual and pastoral care. Through rumors of unethical conduct, he has concerns over this young, green lieutenant's ability to stay within the moral and ethical principles of the majority of religious standards. Introducing himself, Gohrke makes a point of presenting himself as a staff officer; he's not there to undermine the lieutenant's military command. Nonetheless, Gohrke is relying on his presence to act as a deterrent to any violations of international laws, general orders, human decency, and religious mandates as prescribed.

After Gohrke's initial meeting with the lieutenant, it's obvious that both men find themselves between a rock and a hard spot. The lieutenant's frustration is evident as he attempts to provide Gohrke with an overview of the situation facing his troops. "We're more than certain this village is providing Charlie (the Viet Cong) cover. Whether or not there are innocent civilians in this fiasco is no longer my concern. I can't take the chance of losing any more of my troops over holding back in an attempt to sort the good guys from the bad. We need to annihilate the entire village as soon as I can get a C-130 in here."

Gohrke, on the other hand, is convinced the moral and ethical lines can be drawn in this situation. "I have no intention of standing between you and a legitimate military operation, but in the same token, I don't expect to witness any unnecessary killing of enemy civilians. I'm finding it disturbing that you're finding it indispensable to wipe out an entire village to eradicate a smaller population of enemy combatants." He is hoping it will not be necessary to have to report the unnecessary killing of civilian villagers, or rape or torture of enemy civilians. So far Gohrke continues to find this young commander's demand unsettling. The call to wipe out an entire village because the enemy is using the civilians as human shields seems to him excessive. However, it's not reasonable to expect Gohrke's personal feelings to eliminate all immoral or unethical behavior. In cases like this, the commander, not the chaplain, holds the power to make military decisions.

The next equally significant concern Gohrke has for this mission is the soldiers. The old axiom stating that "there are no atheists in foxholes" proves to be true more often than not. Before any missions of great danger, Gohrke's services are attended much more vigorously than when things are free from anxiety. Today is a day of high anxiety. As soon as soldiers see Micky beginning to set things up, they begin to wander in. The looks of concern are easy enough to pick out. This group is comprised of young men who have barely begun to live and are now being asked to risk their lives in a fight they are never certain they can win. Gohrke takes a moment to look over this less than tested group of novice warriors. He says a private prayer. No one here is more convinced than himself that nothing less than faith holding out its hand in the dark is their hope.

Satisfied that he can begin, he states, "I will never leave you or forsake you." Gohrke pauses for a moment to determine what kind of response this verse from scripture is establishing in this little battle field congregation. "I want to talk to you about the ramifications of that statement. Deuteronomy 31:6 says, 'Be strong and courageous. Do not be afraid or terrified of them,' and I don't need to remind you there are a lot of *them*, 'for the Lord your God goes with you; He will never leave you or forsake you.'

"When I was transported in this morning, this was the single truth from scripture that laid before me and the one that I wish to lay in your path before you take one more step. The most often spoken directive by God in the Bible is, 'Fear not!' Of all the commands He has directed, He has given nothing more than that. 'Fear not, I will never leave you or forsake you.' When mankind was removed from the Garden of Eden, separated from God, a tremendous fear accompanied this eviction. For the first time, man realized he was alone. He realized he had done something that on the surface seemed irreversible. From this seeming death sentence, God had to constantly remind his creation not to be afraid because of our single act of disobedience. Nonetheless, this has single handedly produced the most deep-seated emotion we have as humans, *fear*, and God has to constantly remind us that He is still with us. It's said over eighty times in the Bible to 'fear not'. This doesn't mean we don't feel fear, it just means it doesn't need to command us. It does not need to decide how you act or decide what you believe about God. 'Fear not', God says. It doesn't make a difference what comes at us or what the situation may be, God says, 'fear not." We may *feel* afraid, but I need not *be* afraid. We need not let *fear* control us. We need to know there is a power much greater than our fear or our enemy who has promised to 'never leave you or forsake you.' God is telling us that He will get us through. When you think of all the bad things that could have happened to you and hasn't, you can thank God for sending His warrior angels to protect you. On the other hand, since you're going to heaven when it comes time for you to leave this world, you need to know that nothing can harm you where it really matters. I want you to know you're being delivered right this minute and when the time comes, you'll be delivered permanently. So today we can rest in the safety of our gracious God." Looking over toward an area behind the men, Gohrke takes notice of a soldier manning an M-16 in defense of this many men out in the open. He gives him a salute of thanks. The soldier salutes back.

Afterward, Gohrke stays with anyone who would like to have more prayer time. One by one, they begin to return to their stations. With this time in the field finding its own ending, Gohrke gives Micky the okay to begin to take down his little field altar. Just as he finishes, they hear a hissing sound against the relative quiet of the surroundings that ends in an explosion. The natural response is for everyone to take cover. Even though this platoon has fortified itself decently using the available terrain, this is the unmistakable work of an enemy rocket hoping to strike enough fear and terror in the

Americans to cause them to hunker down, allowing a strategic adjustment to go unnoticed.

The lieutenant is at his wits' end. Mortar fire once again comes from the protection of the village. With the sweep of his hand, he orders the radioman to come forward. In an exasperated tone, he requests the C-130 gunship. "Make it Puff the Magic Dragon," he adds. "We need this village gone," With this final dispatch, he draws all his sergeants to his side giving them the order to organize a retreat far enough back to avoid being hit by friendly fire. The men can't be more relived. The enemy has been harassing them for days from the relative safety of the village. Many of the villagers have already left for safer havens leaving behind suspected Viet Cong sympathizers. The enemy is well informed of American concerns about preserving the safety of civilians; they push this to its limits. What they are never sure of is when the Americans' primary concern for the safety of their own soldiers kicks in. They are about to find out; the distant sound of the big C-130 is producing a doppler effect as it churns its way toward the village.

Gohrke has been secretly hoping he would be gone before he would be forced to make judgement calls on the what he is about to witness. The platoon has successfully withdrawn as the huge plane passes directly overhead. In another second, the explosive sound of a hundred cannons leaving the most devastating display of firepower trailing out of every seeming surface of this huge plane begins to destroy anything and everything behind it. Micky is awestruck. This is a demonstration of firepower he has never personally viewed but had only heard about. Rather than be awestruck, Gohrke is torn once again, as he has been on several other similar occasions. The prevailing haunting question is whether he is to subordinate his religious identity to a military one. Military logic and religious values are often times at odds putting chaplains in contradictory situations; how do you square the Biblical imperative to "love your enemy" in a wartime situation or to "thou shalt not kill." Combat has a way of challenging these lessons. With the deed now completed in this instance, his role switches from prophet to priest, and to one of being present to those in need of pastoral care. "I'm not like the old testament prophets. My primary concern is not to council commanders on the moral ethics of their decisions. I'm more concerned about my availability in assisting them in picking up the pieces of their bad decisions."

This whole mêlée is over within five minutes. The thought that there is nothing resembling life left in this path would be an accurate observation. The lieutenant appears to be as awestruck over this devastating demonstration of this unique American war machine as the rest of the platoon. Gohrke is struggling with his own feelings of awe. It's suggesting his God has suddenly become too small compared to American military might. *Lord, how am I to battle this thinking?* becomes his silent prayer. Like many other chaplains in difficult war times, he remains conflicted. On one hand, he's grateful the enemy is compromised, but he's also grateful that none of the men are shouting or cheering this destruction. Instead there is a quiet resolve. He finalizes his struggle with a compromise: *The need to fight a war cleverly tempered with mercy is not a bad thing.*

Mickey has his own perceptions of what's happening. It's a long way from his classroom where pen and paper ruled: here, it's flesh and blood that's just as likely to be his as someone else's. It would be a misconception to say there is not a youthful drive to remain alive among these soldiers would be a misconception. The miracle that has taken place in this war is the majority of these young soldiers, who know little of dying for flag and country are willing to die to defend one another. At the same time, to say there is not an element of self-serving inaction by some to allow others to be sacrificed in their place is also a misconception—although this group is in the minority. Another singular miracle is Mickey's reaction. He is equally amazed at his own about face. He's coming more and more to a oneness with the sacred words of scripture that say those who are willing to give their lives for the sake of a brother are blessed. He has grasped this lesson more by example of his fellow soldiers' interactions than from the words alone. He remembers his once smug attitude toward others, including Gohrke. Today, he is truly one with his comrades, and his first regard is for the wellbeing of his chaplain.

"Are you okay, sir?" Gohrke is coming out in the open as the smoke and mayhem clear, leaving a distinct vision of what has taken place. The smells filling the air are a mixture of cordite, and burning houses, and smoldering green jungle.

Gohrke, amazed at Micky's genuine concern, responds with, "Yes, soldier, I'm fine. Thank you for asking."

Returning to his deliberation, Micky stands quiet in wonder, gazing in the direction of the massacre he's certain has taken place in the village. His concern has shifted to the chances of survivors needing medical attention. Remembering where he had seen the medics assigned to this platoon, he seeks them out. Pointing in the direction of the likely massacre, he asks, "What's your concern for any likely survivors in there?"

The senior medic is a sergeant who is willing to take the question. "We'll do what we can when the lieutenant gives the order to advance."

The lieutenant's first thoughts upon surfacing from this ordeal are not about how many survived this ordeal, but rather about how many are dead. "Get me a body count," is his first concern.

The sergeant quickly organizes the platoon to enter this demolished village as safely as possible. It had initially been the home of farmers who would have been just as content with any form of government, providing they could farm their ancestral rice farms in peace. That's all come to an end. Caught up as pawns in a war between those who champion power as the meaning of life, they have served their purpose and have paid the ultimate cost.

Small teams are organized to begin the inch-by-inch, slow, methodical search of the remains of this enemy stronghold. Lieutenant Watson's wish is to move at maximum speed with regards to the safety of his men and perform a low-level, quick hitting approach. One primary concern is to be ever aware of the enemies ever present punji pits with stakes intended to do maximum damage to anyone venturing unaware. These stakes in themselves rarely killed anyone, but they are often coated in poisons or even feces in the expectation of creating debilitating infections.

Riflemen are at the front of this forward movement are riflemen. With a wary eye for any movement, these seasoned soldiers cover each other as one after another advances into what is purported to be enemy territory. So far, there are no bodies, and no one fires on them. Suddenly an American soldier bursts a volley of shots at what appears to be a pile of foliage. Another soldier flanking him does the same. Like so many brave soldiers that run toward the chaos, several more join them. The fracas continues with shouts from different men to be cautious of what they refer to as "spider holes." These turn out to be wooden boxes laid underground in a slanted position with a trapdoor camouflaged with dirt and still-growing plants so enemy soldiers can lie there unseen. Others are a series of trapdoors that are all connected, leading into underground tunnels. By maintaining radio contact, several of these unseen "spiders" can efficiently work together to surreptitiously attack an unaware American patrol. All they need to do is prop open the trapdoor and release a volley of gunfire. They then lower the lid before they can be located. This team is fully aware of these underground fighters. They have dealt with the tunnel combatants throughout this entire campaign, and have often been frustrated by their enemy's sudden disappearance. Since the danger from sniper fire coming from trees has been compromised by the leveling firepower of Puff the Magic Dragon, these teams can concentrate on ground-level surveillance. With a renewed determination to prevent this tunnel system from thwarting their efforts, these American teams are specifically trained to be on the lookout for any ground movement.

The advancing teams have dropped to a crawling position. More shots indicate another enemy engagement. This is an indicator that the enemy is still viable—to what extent is unknown. What is known is that this network of tunnels has allowed the enemy to control when and where employments will take place. This latest development has changed the landscape enough to give the Americans an advantage because there is much less underbrush. This massive foliage has been a major advantage for the enemy in concealing these openings. Under these new conditions, this jungle foliage is smoldering, and these intense ground fires have used enough oxygen to either force these tunnel combatants out or suffocate if they remain underground. Either way, the military advantage has shifted slightly in favor of the Americans. Lieutenant Watson is being kept informed as to what can be expected. A number of these spider holes have been compromised without an American loss. Word is coming back to Watson that a major tunnel entrance has been discovered outside of the village. At the moment, the lieutenant is leading a team into what had been a village. They discover a lot of fire damage, but very few bodies. This is an indicator that much of the village had evacuated prior to the attack. The question is whether the evacuation took place as they heard the C-130 approaching or whether most villagers slipped out over the past week. If it proves to be the former, it indicates that they are hiding in the questionable safety of the tunnels. This is one of Chaplain Gohrke's concerns. Hoping not to involve himself with any more military decisions, he is willing to step back and not make an assessment unless something clearly immoral begins to take place.

Without the peacetime luxury of clearer choices, Lieutenant Watson decides to move the whole platoon forward. Even though Chaplain Gohrke and Micky are not considered part of the combat detail, they are required to press on with the platoon for their safety. As they begin an uncertain advance, Micky is taking his role as Gohrke's bodyguard much more seriously. He is focused and attentive to any new developments. Gohrke, in turn, is watching for the uplifted hands of the enemy that indicate a surrender. He is hoping that rather than shooting them, this young lieutenant will accept the gesture and follow protocol. He doesn't have to wait long. The report of a larger underground refuge has reached Lieutenant Watson. After a quick assessment, the lieutenant orders that a grenade be thrown down the tunnel entrance. The explosion concludes with the muffled sound of screams coming through the partially caved-in opening. Soon, the hair on top of someone's head pokes its way through the loose dirt created by the exploding grenade. A woman extends her hands above her head. Next comes a child who is gasping for air. Twenty-two suspected enemy combatants and several village women with children are extricated from the rubble. They are truly shaken. In spite of the fact that no one else is coming out, Watson can't assume there aren't holdouts who are unwilling to surrender. Rather than risk the lives in his command, he gives the order to seal the entrance using C-4 explosives. As they go through the task of throwing packets of the substance into the entrance of this sanctuary, three more suspected combatants emerge with their hands above their heads. So far, the lieutenant is following protocol. He doesn't have an interpreter in his platoon. If the next question he asks remains a negative, they will be required to call in an interpreter. To each of these detainees, he asks the same question: "Do you speak English?" There is no positive response. At his point, it's time to take the next drastic step. The lieutenant gives the order to seal the hole. If there are more opponents who remain there, they have been given ample time to surrender or die. Lieutenant Watson is not about to risk an underground ambush by sending his men to determine if anyone is still hidden in some unknown recess of this bunker. After clearing the area, the detail sets off an explosion that no sane person would wish to be near. The tears flowing from the woman with the child who initially emerged indicate that it's probable that someone who was close to her chose death rather than surrender.

Chaplain Gohrke has decided to stay in the background. He continues to walk that fine line between being a moral example during questionable times and maintaining a relationship with the soldiers on the battlefield—particularly when it regards the safest way to deal with an enemy. Nevertheless, the men look to him to define a bridge between these dual obligations. In a discussion with a soldier asking the question, "Is God on our side?" Gohrke was heard to answer, "I'm not concerned whether God is on our side. Rather, are we on God's side?" However, to expect a chaplain's presence or ministry to be enough to thwart atrocities is unreasonable. Considering the inordinate amount of adrenalin that's flowing through these men and creating anxiety, it's not beyond reason to understand atrocities are possible—especially when there is no discernable physical differentiation between friend or foe, bad things can happen.

Lieutenant Watson is committed to doing what he knows is army procedure in dealing with these prisoners. After thoroughly searching each detainee, he has placed a guard detail to contain them. His next action is to call in another squad to remove them along with the bodies of those caught in the firestorm.

Without a markedly obvious oversight in any of the lieutenant's decisions, Chaplain Gohrke is satisfied to leave the military protocol to the military. Convinced he's fulfilled his mission, he calls in his request for a Huey to transport himself and Micky back to the base.

Micky has had the opportunity to observe all that's happened. He's been especially attentive to the dynamic between Gohrke and the lieutenant. The cocksure attitude Micky exhibited a few weeks ago has been replaced by a much humbler demeanor. He is actually humble enough to become teachable. But as things go on the base, the tedium of an uneventful day has a way of messing with the minds of these youthful soldiers. Micky is not an exception to this phenomenon. On this particular day, Chaplain Gohrke is catching up on some paperwork and has given Micky the day off. After a leisurely morning, he decides to check in on his old drinking buddy, Kenny. Things haven't changed much in Kenny's world. He's been transferred to a supply job that gives nearly as much time off as he works. He still runs his booze and drug business pretty much at his convenience. Always happy to see an old customer, he greets Micky with a friendly handshake, saying, "Well I'll be go to hell, look what the devil dragged in! Where ya been keepin yourself?"

"The chaplain's been keepin' me humpin', but he gave me the day off," replies Micky.

Reaching around to one of his signature footlocker-coolers, he grabs a couple beers, handing one to Micky. Micky is caught unprepared. He thought this was going to be a visit of little consequence, but now he's looking at having to decide. "No thanks, Kenny. I quit drinking," declares Micky. He realizes his voice is not as strong as he had hoped, but he's hoping this statement will be sufficient to ward off any further discussion. But Kenny isn't ready to accept such a feeble declaration. "Hell, kid, one beer ain't gonna kill ya," pronounces Kenny, thrusting the beer even more vigorously forward.

Not fully realizing the power his need for others' approval has over him, Micky feels a gush of self-consciousness come over himself. Not as prepared as he imagined himself to be, he reaches out and takes the beer, accepting Kenny's estimate that "one beer ain't gonna kill ya." He is sure he can curb any desire for another. With the cold beer in his hands, his mind quickly affirms that he will have this one beer with his old friend and be on his way. The cool effervescence of the beverage across his tongue and throat is a familiar companion. With a smile, he says, "Well, I do admit, it sure hits the spot."

They spend their drinking time discussing everything that's wrong with the army and their desire to have it behind them. This discussion shortly leaves Micky with an empty bottle. Automatically, Kenny places another of the enticing beverages in Micky's empty hand. Micky's less than vigorous fortitude has eroded even further along with his frontal lobe. The ease with which this decision has made its way into Micky's brain reflects a mindset that declares it perfectly sensible to have another. The afternoon rapidly wears on with Micky once again consuming enough beer to float a battleship. Leaving Kenny, he returns to his jeep. With the turn of the key, he's soon ripping through the base as he always does when he's had too much to drink. Suddenly, seemingly out of nowhere, he's faced with a full-size troop carrier demanding a good portion of the narrow road.

Despite his drunken condition, Micky reacts as well as he can to remove himself from a head-on collision. "JESUS CHRIST, YOU WANT THE WHOLE DAMN ROAD?" he's provoked to shout. A voice as clear and concise as any he's ever heard replies, "YES, MICKY, I WANT THE WHOLE ROAD!"

This whole affair causes Micky to pull off to the side of the road, shaken. In his struggle to process what has just happened, there is reason to view this entire happening as a result of his inebriation. He cautiously finishes the drive to his hooch, parks the jeep, and makes his way to his bunk. The alcohol predictably has its way, and he almost immediately falls into an alcohol-induced stupor. His superficial rest is soon interrupted by the same clear voice he heard on the road. "YES, MICKY, I WANT THE WHOLE ROAD!" Despite his alcoholic condition, Micky finds himself sitting wide-eyed in the middle of his bunk. This voice has once more attacked his consciousness. It remains just as clear and concise as it did during his first encounter. Its insistence to be heard makes it difficult to let it pass as an alcohol-induced aberration. Whether he is ready to deal with this new reality or not, it isn't being sympathetic to his condition. This alcohol problem has him baffled by how powerless he is to conquer it. The effects of an afternoon of drinking haven't thoroughly run their course. The haunting prospect of having to start his AA program anew after he was sure he had it licked comes over him in a big, dark cloud of depression. Real guilt and anxiety plague him. Real disgust shakes him to his core. After another hour of bedridden recovery, a rebellion in the recesses of his gut fashions itself in the form of retching, perspiring, and realizing he had not gotten out of bed to urinate. If this were not enough, he has the shakes so bad he can't hold a glass of water without spilling much of it.

Micky renews his resolve to do something more than pay lip service to staying sober. "God, help me. I can't do this alone," he moans. Along with this latest reality, the guilt and remorse over his slip grow heavier within him. Resorting back through his conduct, Micky is aware this voice has nothing to do with the oncoming truck on the road as much as it does with the head-on crash with the truck-like future that's waiting for him if his behavior doesn't change. The certainty of this sets off a chain reaction of deeper guilt and remorse. What makes this so personal is that the voice actually calls him by name. There is no apparent way of reversing any of his behavior with Kenny. Micky is buried in shame. *I was so sure I could just have one and leave. I had no intentions of getting drunk.* This is so different from all his high school problems. He recalls how he could hunker down and overcome any difficulty coming his way by sheer willpower—this one is much more cunning, baffling, and powerful than any sporting event or math test he mastered.

As usual, Gohrke doesn't let too much get past him. Earlier, he had taken note of Micky's condition when he nearly hit the building with the jeep. Not wanting to deal with a drunken Micky, Gohrke stays clear of him for the rest of the day. This is standard practice for Gohrke. He's dealt with enough of the human condition when it's sober without pushing his own limits in dealing with a drunk. But this does not end his concern for Micky. He realizes the necessity of the first step of AA, which states that men like Micky must admit a powerlessness to resist a single drink. Gohrke's further realization is that he is powerless in the face of Micky's powerlessness. This is why, as Micky reports for duty the next morning, Gohrke has a surprise waiting for him. Having had an entire night to get himself pulled back together, Micky attempts to act as though nothing is amiss with him. His attire is wrinkled enough to appear as though he slept in it, and three of his belt loops have been completely missed.

"Private first class Michael Murphy reporting for duty, sir," is said with the hope that his salute will not be watched closely enough that observers will notice that his hand—as well as his entire body—is shaking.

Gohrke gives him a little salute and motions him to a waiting chair facing two other soldiers. Micky, I want you to meet Sergeant Ted J. and Corporal Don W. These men are from Alcoholics Anonymous, and I believe they have a chair waiting with your name on it." Turning to the two soldiers, Gohrke says, "Gentlemen, I relinquish my office. Take as long as you need." With that said, he turns and walks out of the room, closing the door behind him.

Micky has an unmistakable look of remorse as he takes his seat. Within seconds the tears begin to flow. The two men are far from sympathizing with Micky's slip and are more than willing to lay out some tools he can use to prevent this from reoccurring—that is, if he's willing to pick them up. A transformation of Micky's character has begun. He's turning another corner but remains a work in progress.

CHAPTER 22
Elizabeth Carolyn Murphy

With the TET offense in full force, Gohrke is up to his neck in pastoral care. The number of soldiers in need of spiritual support has exploded. In the midst of this, Micky recalls how his earlier mentor, Joe Billings, had encouraged him through example to share his experience, strength, and hope with anyone in need of spiritual encouraging. Joe was convinced that the center of Micky's problem isn't alcohol and that it's merely a symptom of an underlying problem. Joe was certain the human condition of selfish self-centeredness is at the root of all of Micky's drinking. He further assured him that if he made a habit of unselfishly caring for others, this would remove the desire to drink. Fortunately, Micky has taken to heart much of what he has learned and found an outlet for this quality of counsel in assisting Chaplain Gohrke. Often, the soldier who has found himself unable to cope with the Vietnam environment has turned to alcohol. When this method fails him, this soldier will rarely seek out the chaplain as his first responder. He usually will turn to another drug, hoping this will be the panacea that allows him to continue. In contrast, Gohrke's past experience in dealing with problem drug users or problem drinkers is one of disappointment. More often than not, he finds himself getting frustrated with the alcoholic. He doesn't hesitate to share his feelings and the church's inadequacy when it comes to this special area of ministry. As a result, Gohrke has patiently watched Micky's progress in the hopes that requiring him to deal with those who struggle with addictions will be more fruitful.

Initially, the kind of relief these troubled soldiers hope to get is often the same kind Micky experienced, but recovery requires engaging someone who is undergoing the same struggle. This gives Micky an opportunity to assure the sufferer that he is not alone, and that recovery is possible. Micky is reassured that each time he is called on to share where his own alcoholism has taken him, where he is now, and what he's done to get here with another alcoholic plays a major role in his own recovery. When asked, he readily admits that "It's definitely halted my own progression into a relapse." This formerly egocentric, arrogant bigshot is actually displaying a certain strength and integrity in a humble admission that his life has been primarily cruel, cold, and delusional. It speaks to the fact that Micky has recognized his problem and has accepted the path of recovery as the one he is willing to embrace. As he looks back on his experience, he knows his goals from beginning to end have changed drastically—it's been a 180-degree turn. Joe Billings had experienced one of Micky's turning points where Micky announced he felt like he had been "born again." Joe listened to him for about two seconds before he hit him with the following perspective, "Micky, you ain't been 'born again.' You hardly been conceived. The biggest thing in your life right now is to watch out for is a miscarriage, or in your case, an abortion." Micky thought about this as Joe had continued, "From what you tol' me about your bigshot days back in high school, you never tasted the sadness of the sinner. Your heart had never ached with hopelessness. As long as you was sittin' on top of the heap of success, it was easy for you to hand out penance for everyone besides yourself."

Providing he makes it through alive for a few more weeks, Micky's time in Vietnam is beginning to wind down. During this experience, he has undeniably undergone a range of episodes that have impacted his life in various ways—some bad and some good. His scope is undeniably turning toward home, but he would like to leave knowing he has made an impact by supporting his fellow soldiers. Micky looks every bit the healthy recovered alcoholic who has readily admitted he can never successfully drink again. Not only that—he has accepted the fact that if he does, he may not have another recovery in him. This prospect leaves him with several options, should he actually attempt to try and drink again. For all intents and purposes, what will be waiting for him is jail, insanity, or death. He can't help but reflect back on that distant day in his past when he decided to enlist. In retrospect, the Vietnamese haven't been anywhere near the enemy he has been to himself; he's brought himself closer to the brink of death than any other entity, and that includes the Viet Cong. In a moment of review, Micky is heard to say, "If 'Charlie' had done to me what I've done to myself, I would have killed him." *God, I can only thank you for letting me hit rock bottom* becomes his silent prayer.

He has been chairing an AA group using the conference room at the chaplain's headquarters. This is all done under the auspices of Chaplain Gohrke. Today, Micky is looking over the group of a dozen men who are desperate enough to have given themselves over to this twelve-step program as a path to recovery. Some of his old prideful ways are fighting to gain a foothold again; he's looking over this little group of despairing men as though he is personally bringing them together and delivering them up as his personal offering to God. Unfortunately, his old ways of wanting to be important and to stand apart from others are always his *first* thought—thank God he now has the tools to allow a much better *second* thought to prevail. It's a testament to himself that he is still only one among equals. If he has any God-given strength and hope to share with these men, it's only in union with others sharing their God-given strength and hope with him. He has become tenderized enough by his own shortcomings to become willing to pass on the familiar watchwords handed to him— such as "easy does it," "live and let live," "one day at a time." Since the early days of AA, these seemingly trite sayings have had the power within their essence to keep a sufferer on track to recovery.

There remains one more happening Micky has been waiting nine months to experience. At last, it has arrived in the form of a letter.

"Murphy!" calls out a corporal in charge of mail duty.

He's waving an envelope. Expecting his usual weekly letter from Carolyn, he notices that the handwriting is not hers, but recognizes it immediately as that of another. Tearing it open, his head and eyes move side to side, quickly scanning the lines. His whole demeanor changes from an inquisitive one to an outward display. With no reservations, Micky is on his feet, pumping his fist in the air:

"YAHOO!" It's a cry that could be heard beyond the DMZ. It's a letter from his mother announcing the birth of his first child, a nine-pound baby girl. If in the final arrival the child proves to be a girl, he and Carolyn had agreed on the name of Elizabeth Carolyn Murphy. Carolyn is required to spend a few days in the hospital before they agree to release her. According to Micky's mother, Carolyn will continue to stay with her parents until he comes home and the couple establishes a home of their own. In spite of his negligence in writing to Carolyn every week, she has proven to be a long-suffering wife patiently waiting his return.

After all the congratulations are finished, Micky sits alone for a few more moments, staring at a letter that has changed his life even further. Just the idea of being a father is hardly a reality in practice; it remains only heartfelt until he can return home to fulfill his role.

These late circumstances well up emotions he has not felt earlier in this Vietnam assignment: a mixture of gratitude that he's remained among the living and a yearning to be back home. Along with this is the growing occurrence of an uncertainty. Here, Micky has acquired a support group. He's become comfortable exposing his own alcoholism and subsequent neurotic impulses to test it. The trust that has developed among his recovery group has occasioned a transparency he hadn't had back in the world. Through a true miracle, he has learned to be a listener and a learner—especially when interacting with those he once held as inferior. Many of his old reservations that prevented him from engaging with others in an open and truthful way have begun to evaporate. In this environment where life and death are dealt out every day, all the veils of pretense buttressed by alcohol or drugs have been scrapped. The exchange has been for a life that deals with getting down to causes and conditions surrounding a sober life. It always surprises him when he finds himself learning a truth from someone who he would have dismissed as substandard a year ago. Instead of fearing that this revelation will throw him into the pits of ruin, it seems that over the past few months, he's happily joined the human race. He can only hope this new life will follow him home.

A recent conversation another soldier conveys the following to Micky: "My goal was to stay sober all week. I've been sober two weeks now."

Remembering his own first two weeks of being sober, Micky can't help but congratulate the soldier. "That's commendable— something to be grateful for—but not nearly as vital as what you've become because of it. You've gained something inside that you didn't have before. Obviously, it's evidence of a power greater than you who is working inside you. Don't forget that this happened one day at a time, and don't forget to say thank you. I might add, continue to invite this power greater than you to stay with you for another day."

For the first time, without a further explanation, the soldier knows exactly what Micky is bringing to light. It's the same message that was given to Micky. It's a simple message that says *to remain sober himself, he needs to give that same message away;* he's learning how he can stay sober by giving of himself to others.

CHAPTER 23
Born Again, or Just Conceived

Micky's back injury has become chronic. At first, it would respond to ibuprofen, but recently, the pain has kept him in bed all day. His last visit to the base infirmary was by ambulance. He couldn't get out of bed unassisted, and even then, the pain was excruciating. The doctor is not encouraging during this recent visit. Looking directly at Micky, the doctor says, "You've got yourself a couple herniated discs. There isn't a thing we can do here. Presently, you're no good to the army. I'm going to recommend you for a medical discharge."

Micky hears the doctor's words but is more interested in the shot the nurse is giving him. In a few minutes, the effects of the shot not only numb the pain but bring with it a euphoric sensation. "What is that you just gave me, Doc?" Micky asks.

"Just a little morphine to take away the pain and let those muscles relax," replies the doctor.

Micky's pain is quickly reduced, and it gives way to another consideration—Micky's addiction. "Doc, I can't afford to let these drugs take me places I don't want to leave. I'm going to have to find another way." At this juncture, the doctor's recommendation is that he should be discharged. Whether the morphine or the news of Micky becoming a father is the primary determiner in this case, either way, Micky is more than ready to change directions and head back to the States.

Concerning this new medical development, Micky wants to be the first to inform Chaplain Gohrke. The chaplain's office is directly in front of his hooch, so it's not out of his way to stop in. Gohrke is just coming out of his office when he finds himself confronting a solemn-faced assistant.

"Can I talk to you for a minute, sir?" Micky asks. His voice has taken on a somberness that Gohrke hasn't seen in him. Recognizing there is something strange pressing on this young soldier's mind, he pauses just long enough to process what is clearly a changing dynamic. In the next moment, he is motioning Micky back toward his office. Once inside, Micky respectfully waits for Gohrke to arrange the setting he prefers. In this case, Gohrke arranges two chairs facing each other. It's similar to the setting he favors when taking a confession. Motioning Micky to one of the chairs, he takes the other. Micky begins by revealing his latest medical results and the action that's been taken to discharge him. They talk over this new development and Gohrke implores Micky to be certain to follow through stateside with medical treatment through the VA.

After assuring Gohrke that he'll seek medical treatment, Micky takes a moment to change the subject. "There's something else I want to discuss with you, sir. It's another shift that's taken up a lodging in my mind. I remember back in high school how confident I felt becoming the track and field captain or how self-assured I was when I became the debate team captain. What's happened to me? How have I failed? Now I feel like I'm just another broken-down nobody."

Gohrke attentively listens to everything Micky is pouring out. With the gravity of one who can relate to this very human dilemma, Gohrke benevolently takes his turn at addressing Micky's quandary.

"You spoke as though you are experiencing a turn in your life you don't believe you deserve. You have intimated to me that you attended a Christian high school, so the wisdom I'm going to impart to you will be in that setting."

Gohrke begins, "Do you remember the Christmas story?"

"Yes, sir," replies Micky.

"Do you remember that part where the angel Gabriel came to a little, young, nobody Jewish girl and told her how even in her nobody-ness, God had seen her as the somebody who would bear his Son?" Not waiting for Micky's answer, Gohrke continues, "Well, that task's all been taken care of, but there are many, many places where you can become God's hands, His feet, and His voice and become the somebody God intended you to become before you were born. You'll discover it all in helping to heal his hurting and broken children."

Micky is listening, dumbfounded. He came into this meeting looking for sympathy but is now being charged to quit feeling sorry for himself and become useful to God in service to his other children.

Seeing he has captured Micky's attention, Gohrke continues. "I've watched you do something with your fellow problem drinkers . I've labored with them with no results. I've watched you minister to people with alcohol problems where I've never been able to. It's just like that last step you guys in AA take, where it says you start practicing the principles of your program in all your affairs—do it! And I don't mean that you become so heavenly that you're of no earthly good—leave that to those who *won't* be changed—I mean that giving of yourself to 'the least of these' makes you a somebody."

Micky is listening with the ears of someone who is likening himself to the man in the story of the Good Samaritan, who found himself beat up and lying helplessly in the ditch but is now being unselfishly ministered to by this kindly cleric using simple words of truth. His desire to be seen as a victim is slowly dissolving.

"I guarantee you, soldier, before this day is over, if you look, God will put more in front of you than you can accomplish," says Gohrke with a knowing smile.

Gohrke is paying close attention to the body language of this despairing pigeon. Micky is becoming uneasy. Gohrke knows he's given Micky a lot to digest, but he wants to hit home a point he believes Micky can recall when he gets himself buried in his own funk.

"Micky, do you recall that Biblical story of Jesus raising his friend Lazarus from the dead?"

Micky nods his head.

Gohrke continues, "If you recall, after Lazarus came out of the tomb, Jesus ordered his disciples to unwind the strips of burial cloth surrounding him."

Micky nods his head again in agreement.

Gohrke makes his final point. "Micky, God will use his Word to bring people back to a life worth living but still needs you to help with the unwinding."

Gohrke never disappoints. Micky has gotten much more than he had bargained for. He has much more on his plate to contemplate than had anticipated. The hard work of introspection he learned in AA is now challenging him in a new way. It's to help not only the alcoholic, but every one of God's children who needs the sip of cool water called kindness, forgiveness, patience, understanding, humility, or good temper.

Micky's thinking has begun to change, but it's like his old AA mentor Joe Billings told him once, "You ain't been born again, Micky. You only been conceived, an' maybe you gonna abort before you born again, brother."

This is also true of Micky's thinking. Joe went on to remind him, "You jus' can't think your way into good actin'; you gotta act your way into good thinkin'."

All of this stuff is swirling around Micky's head when one of his AA buddies shows up at his hooch drunk and crying over his slip. He wants Micky's help. Saying a silent prayer, Micky invites him in. Gohrke is right; it's already beginning.

CHAPTER 24
No Ticker Tape Parade

With the paperwork finally worked out, Micky's short time has been used up, and he's ready to go home. The plane is loaded with many other soldiers who are leaving the Vietnam theater—some to finish out their time on a base in the States, and others, like Micky, to muster out and go home. They are taken to the airbase, where they are loaded on to a Northwest Airlines passenger plane destined for the States—specifically, Travis Airforce Base in San Francisco. They experience a momentary sense of weightlessness as the last wheel leaves the runway—they are safely in the air, heading for home. There isn't one silent voice on the plane as each soldier lets out a whoop of elation. Eight hours later, the same elated "hurrahs" are sounded again as the plane touches down on American soil. Sixty uniformed soldiers leave the plane, ecstatic to have finally finished a very dangerous eleven-month stint in a war zone and have come home alive. The first thing to greet them is a fresh ocean breeze that's a far cry from the stifling stench of Vietnamese breezes. As Micky disembarks, he's overcome with emotion. Looking toward the heavens, he mouths the words, "Thank you, Lord. I'll never complain about anything again."

What they are not expecting is the reception they are receiving once they're in San Francisco. While on a layover, Micky and two other soldiers attempt to catch a cab for the downtown area. Cab after cab passes them by. Annoyed, they finally settle on a bus. In the process of boarding, a pretty young girl their age is disembarking. Looking at their uniforms, she stops midway and then purposely bumps into them, says, "F*** baby killers," and storms off in a bluster. Somewhat stunned, the three of them brush it off, find seats on the bus, and continue their trip.

What has become noticeable in their yearlong deployment is how fat everyone seems to be, and also the growing number of long-haired, bearded males. There were always some in deference to the

Beatles, who wore longer hair, but now it seems a herd mentality has stampeded into the male culture. A downtrodden, demoralized demeanor has become the look of the day. This difference makes each of these short-haired soldiers feel intimidated, as though they have been left out of a cultural transformation. These three male Vietnam veterans returning in full-dress military uniforms in downtown San Francisco stand out like three flies in a bowl of milk.

Each one have their own thoughts concerning these circumstances, but they retain one common understanding—the one that held them together in Vietnam. Without a word spoken, they know they have one another's backs. Still blazing with the excitement they held when they landed, they enter a small downtown restaurant for a bite to eat. Taking a booth, they continue their jubilant small talk as they wait to be served. After twenty minutes, it becomes apparent that they are being ignored; other latecomers are being waited on. Believing it to be merely an oversight, Micky takes the initiative. Leaving his seat, he overtakes a waiter and asks, "Can we get some service? We have a plane to catch."

With a subtle look of disdain, the waiter replies, "That booth is closed due to contamination."

Turning toward the booth as though he had missed something, Micky says, "Contaminated with what?"

Continuing his same contemptuous look, the waiter says, "You!" He walks away, leaving Micky stunned. The official military newspaper, *The Stars and Stripes*, gave brief editorials on what to expect from some of the anti-war protest actions of the country's youth, but no one expected it to be so rude—especially to men and women who have risked their lives in military service—and so widespread.

Making his way back to his table with his waiting comrades, his face tells more of what transpired than words. All he says is, "Let's blow this dump, they're not going to serve us because we're soldiers."

The others are just as bewildered. It only takes a moment to have this bewilderment turn to frustration and settle on anger. Each of them flips a few chairs as they make their way to the door. What had been a joyous homecoming an hour ago is quickly turning into a hateful aftermath.

After Micky and his two fellow GIs decide the least divisive place to wait in San Francisco is back at the air terminal, they sit quietly brooding over the change in the country over the past year. They are unable to understand where they fit in in a country that has turned on them, so they continue to chew over the events. It's as though their country is blaming soldiers for policies that can only be determined by political leaders—it's the quintessential American habit of "shooting the messenger." It's apparent this generation are becoming expert marksmen—they're indiscriminately shooting their own wounded.

Within hours, this planeload of returning survivors from Vietnam permanently breaks apart as each GI makes his way to his own destiny alone. It's a strange feeling. For the first time in a year, these warriors have to depend on just themselves. In all that time, they always had someone who had their back. Micky is on a plane destined for the center of Michigan with no thoughts other than getting home. These plans fill what otherwise would be only lonely reflections on the closing of a formative part of his life. For now, the ultimate source of his happiness is to see his parents and reunite with his wife and new daughter. For now, this is enough.

As he arrives at the air terminal, still wearing his dress uniform, Micky feels the tension. It's a university city with an ample segment of active anti-war protesters. Without incident, he is able to hire a cab to carry him the remaining thirty miles home. It seems like the cab is going excessively fast, but Micky notices the cab is only at fifty-five miles per hour. This can only be compared to his jeep, which rarely saw forty-miles per hour. After a year in jungle terrain, the Michigan landscape of deciduous trees are a welcome sight. He can't recall the jungle trees ever losing their leaves. This random thought quickly leaves him as his cab enters his hometown. It's a seventy-degree day: perfect for this time of year in Michigan. The lawns are manicured—not a common sight in Vietnam. The homes look exceptionally large compared to the small Vietnamese homes, which are often not much more than grass huts. The other strange phenomenon is that the town seems devoid of people other than those in automobiles. Despite the miles of sidewalks, there is no one on them. They seem to be a vestige left over from another period. This place is so different from Vietnam, where there are people milling around the villages all day long.

Micky has not phoned his wife; rather, he wants to surprise her. Alerting the cabbie to drop him off a block away, he's chosen to walk the last block to gather his thoughts. He finds himself shaking a bit as he pays the cabbie. His eyes immediately fix on the house on the next corner. With excited thoughts racing wildly through his mind, he slings his duffle bag over his shoulder and begins the short trek. The only movement in sight is a pretty young woman pushing a stroller on the opposite side of the street. He recognizes her immediately. It's Carolyn. He stops dead in his tracks, staring. For the moment, he seems paralyzed, unable to do anything other than stare. She looks incredibly beautiful. She stops. As she bends over the stroller to attend to her commuter, her fingers trace a path around her ears, placing her hair out of her face. There is a beautiful maturity about her that Micky hadn't remembered seeing a year ago. Remaining still, he continues to relish a picture before him that for the past year remained an event he could only fantasize. Emotion begins to overtake him, with his eyes welling full of tears of happiness. With a singleness of purpose, Micky begins to walk into the street.

A man wearing an army uniform with a duffle bag over his shoulder walking down the center of the road can't help but catch Carolyn's eye. In the time it takes her to process what she is looking at and extract her tiny passenger, she grasps who is walking down the street.

"MICKY!" is her only response. With her small bundle cradled in her arms, she runs toward him. In the middle of the street and in front of the entire neighborhood, they meet in an embrace that is long overdue. This incident brings a spontaneous applause from a few bystanders. Still impervious to anyone other than themselves, they continue to kiss, embrace, hug, kiss, kiss. This continues until a car from each direction is forced to stop. A couple horn honks forces a step back into enough of reality to get them out of the road and onto the sidewalk. Unwilling to let each other go, they hang onto each other giving little heed to the shouts from the irritated drivers.

"Why didn't you let me know you were coming home?" shouts Carolyn, hanging onto the baby with one arm and wiping the tears from her eyes with the other hand.

"I wanted it to be the surprise it's turned out to be," admits Micky.

"Well, you certainly managed that," says Carolyn.

Their attention finally journeys to the prize Carolyn has been holding dear during this entire reunion. She is cradling this treasure in such a way there is no mistaking it to be anything less than a very special gift for Micky. Slowly, Micky begins to uncover the light blanket surrounding the bundle. Inside is the sweetest little face Micky has ever seen.

"Izzy, meet your daddy. Daddy, meet your daughter," says Carolyn, quickly adding, "I hope you don't mind that I've shortened Elizabeth to Izzy?

"No, not at all. She's beautiful like her mommy," says Micky, deferring to Carolyn and not taking his eyes off this little child.

Over the next few days, Micky begins to establish new his ties with his wife and daughter, and her proud grandparents.

CHAPTER 25
The Church Session

Over the past week of Micky's homecoming, he has contacted his parents. His father told him how proud he is of him; they even have a little party celebrating his safe return. This morning, Micky lies in bed, staring at the ceiling. He hears the voices of the people in the house, the shower being turned on, a phone ringing, the footsteps of the person answering it, and traffic in the street. He realizes how foreign but how familiar these domestic sounds are and how safe it feels to be wrapped in them once again.

Now a few more months have passed, and the realities of close living with those who have been distant is beginning to wear on the family. Carolyn has been patient with Micky's frequent quiet moods. Given what little she has heard from other women whose husbands have returned from war, she expects that there will be times like this. The readjustment period—if it occurs at all—takes a long time. After all, the military employs sophisticated mental and physical methods to prepare these young men to fight in uncivilized conditions but does nothing to rewire them to return back into a civilized community—other than pay their fare back home. The loved ones of these troubled men have just as much difficulty adjusting to them as the GI has adjusting to his home environment.

After a late breakfast following church on Sunday, Carolyn puts Izzy down for a nap. After the initial welcome home celebrations, she and Micky are still a little uncertain about their relationship. The few weeks they had together before Micky left for Vietnam hardly defined their marriage. Because of Micky's back injury, he hasn't looked for work. Consequently, they are obliged to continue living with Carolyn's parents. Micky, Carolyn, and her parents are anxious for the couple to find an apartment and begin their lives together. At this juncture, Micky has not gone into detail about his back injury; coming back from Vietnam medically discharged with a drunk driving injury hardly stands against those discharged with a war injury. So far, he has avoided discussing too much of the particulars—especially with either set of parents. Nonetheless, Micky's recovery program is unbending in its insistence to become forthright in lieu of deception. He feels he can do this with Carolyn first and, if necessary, eventually include the parents—the *how* and *when* part is the dilemma.

Noticing Micky's sudden mood change and not wanting to push too hard where she hasn't been invited, Carolyn measures her intrusion. "Are you all right, Micky?" she asks, sitting down next to him and holding his hand.

"Yeah, I think so," says Micky. Despite his hedging, there is no questioning the fact that he's preoccupied. He has some things he wants to get off his chest, and he isn't sure how to go about it. It doesn't feel as if there is a breath of air in the room. It's disturbingly quiet.

"I don't believe you," says Carolyn. The tone in her voice is new; it's more matter of fact and has a distinct quality of trust. Carolyn is giving the impression that she is emotionally strong enough to listen to his story without becoming judgmental. It's a characteristic that Micky finds reassuring enough to consider making a candid disclosure surrounding his injuries.

"Carolyn, a lot of things have changed with me since I left last year. I'm not sure I even know where to begin."

She remains quiet, staring at him with the demeanor of one waiting for the next chapter.

"I got in trouble with alcohol and drugs while I was there." Micky remains quiet. He's watching Carolyn to see how this admission is resonating. Carolyn remains quite stoic—at least on the outside. Inside is another story. This unbecoming admission from a man she had wed because he *wasn't* a drinker or drug user is unmistakably cascading over her like a fountain of foul waste water. She takes a long, deep breath, letting it out in a controlled flow.

"Are you trying to tell me that I must get used to you being drunk and high now?" asks Carolyn.

"No, not at all. I got in with a bunch of guys in AA. That move saved my life," answers Micky. In saying it this way, Micky is trying to show that he has taken the lead in getting help. He has fully embraced alcoholism and drug addiction as diseases but accepts the burden of responsibility to get treatment for the disease. He must be "all in" for treatment.

"As long as I've known you, Micky, you've always had an incredible amount of willpower. Can't you just quit all that on your own without getting a lot of other people involved?"

This question follows the anxiety Carolyn underwent involving the idle tongues calculating her pregnancy period against the number of months she'd been married. With Micky's confession, she visualizes another scandal brewing in their life.

Micky contemplates her question for a moment, not because the content has given him second thoughts, but because he wants to convince her that this disease isn't subject to "willpower." Hoping not to sound overly defensive, he begins by saying, "Attempting to treat this disease by will power makes as little sense as the person who attempts to treat diarrhea by will power. It takes a condescending God and every other human that He has sent to help to bring about a reprieve."

Not certain she understands what Micky is saying, she nonetheless, makes the strong determination to remain the wife that took a vow to remain together through sickness and health. The past year has not been easy for her, either. She and her mother clashed more than once over her lackadaisical attitude toward her wifely and motherly responsibilities. Her journey from high school cheerleader to wife and mother in a year hasn't been a ride in the park for Carolyn or her mother. Micky's absence and inability to bear his part of the responsibility of parenting has left Carolyn and both her parents exhausted. Everyone is ready to have this little family out on their own.

With this part of the conversation concluded, Micky moves on to tell Carolyn the next phase of how he managed to get the back injury while driving drunk. Opting to wear Micky's confession like a loose garment, Carolyn can only respond by saying, "I hope you've gotten all that out of your system and left all that and any other bad habits you may have acquired right back there in a big pile." With just a smidgen of a smile, she goes on to say, "Goes to show you what can happen to you without me there to keep an eye on you."

"I guarantee you, you don't ever want that job," replies Micky.

The next day, Micky decides it's time begin to look for work. His old way of thinking is not ready to completely die. He finds that part of him is still concerned with what other people may think when it comes to what kind of job he'll find. He was voted "most likely to succeed" by his high school classmates. Thanks to his AA support group, he's managed to put aside his old way of always letting pride and ego get the upper hand. But those guys are the guys he left behind in Vietnam, where no one knew him. This is his hometown, where everybody remembers what a star he had been on the athletic field. To find himself looking for any kind of work that will put food on the table is humbling. He is also concerned with who will become aware of him attending AA meetings; this is also very humbling. The thought of some people shunning him where he had been such an important figure is disconcerting.

Not certain where to start, he decides to start at his church because his old pastor might be in a position to give him a recommendation. After all, Micky had been one of their standout students. He called ahead to speak with pastor, but his call was intercepted by the church secretary, Mrs. Lipton. Micky forgot what a nosy woman she is. He recalls how, in the past, she had taken it upon herself to keep pastor informed of any member she perceived to be in violation of church rules. She is tricky in her own way and seeks to gain as much knowledge as she can as to the nature of someone's desire to have a meeting with the pastor.

"Well, Micky, I did see you in church Sunday. I'm happy to see you have returned from war unscathed. Can I inform the pastor concerning what you may wish to speak with him about? This information always gives him an opportunity to prepare to be of the best service to you."

Aware of her underlying nosiness, Micky says, "Oh, it's really nothing important. I just want to touch base with him now that I'm home."

He can hear the let down in her voice. This kind of generic message is not the stuff she had been hoping for.

"The pastor has a two o'clock open this afternoon," she reports in her bland voice of disappointment.

Remembering an AA meeting he wants to attend in the basement of a nearby church and knowing he'll have plenty of time to work in both, Micky agrees. Meanwhile, he has the rest of the morning to fuss with Izzy and annoy Carolyn with his military way of making beds. He's surprised at how quickly he is applying himself to domestic chores. It may have something to do with military preparedness, but for the present, he's not digging too deep into anything. He remains grateful for small gifts and is satisfied with merely contributing to his family's good mood.

Since Micky's return, Carolyn feels she is under pressure. She feels compelled to prove to Micky that she's a well-organized wife and a competent mother to their daughter. Consequently, differences aren't always dealt with when they occur; instead, they more often get buried, which allows them to come out sideways at inopportune times. This morning is one of those mornings. Carolyn's is upset with Micky's apparent of her life. He can feel the tension but is attributing it to all the readjustments they both are facing, especially with him not being employed. To a degree, he's correct in expecting a little patience with the job outlook; he doesn't feel he's had enough time between his discharge and today to find employment. Not certain what he can do that won't risk reinjuring his back, the VA (Veterans Association) has been all but useless in making appointments. This limits any chance for compensation he may be due.

While preparing to get his day started, he notices Carolyn's extra quiet demeanor. Pulling her aside, he places his arms around her. "I know things have been hectic since I've been back, but I want you to know I'm going to do my best to make things up to you."

"I know you are. It just seems I've been under my parents' scrutiny, and now I'm under yours," says Carolyn.

Surprised at her charge, Micky steps back. Looking her square in the eyes, he says, "I know how you must feel. I'm going to do everything I can to get us our own place." The military has trained him for a lot of different things, but his training left out the adjustment it takes to come home. These are areas he'll have to work through on his own.

One of these areas is to remain on track with his recovery program. Today is only the second AA meeting he's attended since returning. He's still concerned about who might see him. He's well aware how judgmental people can be in small towns, after all he had been one of these people himself. Now the shoe is on the other foot. With the help of a new AA sponsor, he's attempting to make the adjustments to civilian life without needing to take drink. "Don't think it hasn't occurred to me a few times," he admits. His new sponsor is a man referred to as Bob A. Bob is a no-nonsense AA sponsor who is reluctant to put up with any whining on the part of his sponsees.

Meetings traditionally last only an hour, so it's become their tradition to meet at a local restaurant for lunch after the meeting. It's born out of a desire to extend the camaraderie and the laughter developed in the meetings. Much the same as his fellowship in Vietnam, Micky is enjoying his time with these fellow recovering alcoholics. He's known some of the older members for most of his life, but because of the anonymity of the program, he was never aware of their struggle. This anonymity works well as long as the participants agree to keep who is at a meeting and what has been said anonymous. These meetings are posted as "closed," which denotes that it's open only to recovering alcoholics and closed to the curious.

This does not mean the curious are completely thwarted. This bears true with people like Mrs. Lipton, the church secretary, who operates as a one-woman grand inquisitor for the good of the church.

She is also taking her lunch break at the same restaurant. With the demeanor of a true detective, the subterfuge of her intentions plays out in how she pretends not to notice anyone. Her condescending attitude toward the AA people suggests that they're the pariahs of the community. Her pharisaical behaviors culminate in her thanking God that she is not like these people. Micky realizes she has spotted him, and she will be seeing him again in about another hour. He can only imagine what she will be reporting to the pastor.

As hours come, they go. It's time for Micky's appointment with the pastor. He enters the church office to the patronizing greetings of Mrs. Lipton. "Hello, Micky," she says in a sugar-coated tone. "I'll let the pastor know you're here." She presses the button on a desktop intercom. "Micky Murphy here to see you, sir."

"Send him in," returns the intercom's bodiless voice.

"The pastor will see you now," she says, still maintaining her syrupy, sing-songy tone.

Micky makes his way across the room to the door held open by the still smiling Mrs. Lipton. He's imagining that she'll have her ear to the door as soon as she closes it.

The pastor still maintains the "expressiveness" Micky had been enamored with when he spoke so eloquently at his high school commencement. He's out from behind his desk to offer a hardy handshake and a chair. "I noticed you in church last Sunday with the rest of your young family. You two certainly make a good-looking husband and wife team," the pastor expresses.

"Thank you, sir," says Micky. "I just recently returned from Vietnam. That's the first time I've been inside a church since I left."

"Well, you can be certain we all thank God you're home safe. What can I do for you today, Micky?" asks the pastor. With these platitudes rushed through, it's obvious the pastor is attempting to stay on a schedule.

"A couple things. One, since I have been a chaplain's assistant in Vietnam, I would like to serve in some capacity in the church—like maybe a teen Bible teacher. The other thing is, I wonder if you would write me a character reference letter that I can use to show potential employers."

The pastor stands silent for a moment. His face no longer is expressing the same enthusiasm. "Well, would you tell me a little about your past year in combat?" asks the pastor.

"I served as a chaplain's assistant. It was my responsibility to set up a field church and to serve as the armed guard protecting the chaplain," explains Micky.

"That's all very commendable. What kind of social life did you practice?" the pastor asks.

"I'm not sure I understand the question, sir. Did you ask what kind of social life I had?" This last question is the one Micky was hoping he didn't need to get into.

"Yes. Since you're asking for a teaching position and a character reference, I'm asking you to tell me what your character has been like over the past year."

Micky studies the question for a moment and then says, "The life in the military is something that would be difficult to talk about in civilian terms. Things get skewed very quickly there. Right and wrong often get obliterated on a battlefront. In a military setting, if the same consideration is given to black and white issues observed in a civilian church setting, it could get a person killed very quickly. My boss was chaplain as well as a military captain. His responsibility is to ask the tough moral questions: whether this kind of active participation is allowable from a Christian moral perspective, and how does it set with a military objective," answers Micky as succinctly as he dares.

The pastor is maintaining a more poignant look that says this is not what he is asking about. He re-cocks and goes about his questioning in a more straightforward direction. "I guess what I'm asking is what have your personal habits been over the past year. Have you abused alcohol, drugs, or sex?"

This direct questioning isn't catching Micky on his blind side. He was expecting it—especially after seeing Mrs. Lipton. After all, she is known as a gossiping busybody, and he *was* cajoling with practically every recovering alcoholic in town—there is no denying it. Nor does he wish to deny it. To even imagine it would not be stuck in the pastor's ear is absurd.

Micky is annoyed with this line of questioning; his reply reflects it. "Sir, if you are asking me if I sinned over this past year, I will have to tell you I have probably committed every sin known to man, and maybe a few more. Am I proud of that? The answer is no—no more than I've ever been proud of my sinfulness. But I will tell you this much: I've since taken a fearless moral inventory of my shortcomings and have included along with this an admission to God and another friend of mine the exact nature of these wrongdoings."

This sudden forthrightness on Micky's part has caught the pastor off guard. He was certain he was going to have to dig harder and deeper to bring out this kind of admission. Hearing this admission so tersely from Micky's lips, the pastor is ready to move on to the next phase of his inquisition. "You have asked me to give my attention to your character in areas in which, by your own admission, it has not been up to par. To be perfectly honest, at this point, I will respectfully decline until I am able to observe your actions and reactions in a more direct way to assure myself of a solid change."

With these last words, the pastor is extending his hand once again to Micky to signal that the meeting has ended, but he wishes it to end on a friendly note. Since arriving back in civilization, Micky has noticed how everyone is out for themselves. It's not like Vietnam, where everyone has everyone else's back, regardless of race, color, creed, or the number of sins they've committed. In Micky's experience, this pastor is only looking out for his own reputation. He's not willing to take the risk of someone discovering Micky's sordid Vietnam past and challenging him on his decision to place Micky in positions of trust. Micky shakes his hand, but his mind has quickly readjusted his high opinion of this man's character. *I don't believe you need to worry about losing your character. You don't have enough character to lose,* he thinks. Turning immediately without a word, Micky pushes open the door, nearly knocking poor Mrs. Lipton over. It seems she's had her ear to the door for Micky's entire session.

CHAPTER 26

Micky is getting a full taste of civilian life. He's finding it as brutal as the war and just as unforgiving. He has managed to pick up a few part-time jobs, but not enough to allow him and his small family the independence they need. What he needs is clarification from the VA about the extent of his injuries. No employer is willing to take the risk of a previous injury without a clear medical report. Since it's a wartime injury, the VA is the only agency designated to perform this function. The Michigan offices are no more or less efficient in handling the flow of returning veterans than any other in the country; they're all understaffed, underfunded, and grossly inefficient. After making phone calls and sending handwritten letters to no avail, Micky is planning to go directly to the VA office and present his grievance in person.

Micky's parents have a '66 Pontiac Bonneville belonging to his mother and, because she is the perpetual parent, she relinquishes it to Micky's family, providing he use it to look for work. Today is the day he has decided to make the trip to the Traverse City VA. He hasn't had any satisfaction from the downstate offices and is hoping that the smaller number of returning veterans in the northern area of the state will allow this office to provide a timelier service. He hasn't been in this part of the state since he was a young boy. Burt had invited him to visit his grandparents' cabin back in their grade school days.

Shortly after Micky's return, he had asked Burt's parents what had become of Burt. Startled at first and visibly distressed over what fate held in store for his old friend, they gave him the only information they had received from the neighbors around the old cabin. "Then he just plain disappeared," states Burt's father, with tears welling up. "We don't know what happened to him. He never even let us know he was home. We know he's hurt, but we don't know how bad."

Micky listens. He feels from his own experience that this stateside disappearance of his old friend was more than likely caused by the government's abandonment of care. While in Vietnam, he had heard of others who came home and had lost themselves. *I'm one of them*, he muses. *The military would not have let this happen while we still were able to carry a gun. They use us up and dump us out.* Without a clear idea of how all this can be sorted out, Micky is beginning to see how this battle is playing itself out in the returnees. His old determination to be a winner is resurfacing in this unseemly set of circumstances. He makes a silent commitment to himself and to other vets that he will work tirelessly to reconstruct broken veterans.

On his way to Traverse City, Micky thinks: *Our wiring has gotten all screwed up. We need rewiring. One thing is clear: I have become aware from my AA recovery program that the absence of God in a person's life is the absence of freedom. That old Bible truth, "With God, all things are possible" is somehow the answer.* Willing to fight this new kind of battle, Micky begins to sing the ex-slave's song "Amazing Grace."

Amazing Grace, How sweet the sound
That saved a wretch like me
I once was lost, but now I'm found
Twas blind, but now I see.

Twas Grace that taught my heart to fear
And Grace, my fears relieved
How precious did that Grace appear
The hour I first believed.

Through many dangers, toils and snares
We have already come
Twas Grace that brought us safe thus far
And Grace will lead us home
And Grace will lead us home.

Micky's own bout with the devil has tenderized him enough to realize that God, as he is coming to understand God, must play the dominant role in any kind of meaningful recovery from PTSD (Post

Traumatic Stress Disorder). It's clear in Micky's mind that this is the most successful approach, but how all this is going to come about is yet to be worked out.

Coming down the big hill south of Chums Corners, Micky's mind drifts back to happier days when he and Burt would be coming down the same hill with Burt's grandparents, looking forward to their upcoming visit to the Traverse City Zoo. Things have changed along the way. What had been open land is now dotted with commercial enterprises. One thing remains in place: the buffalo are still grazing over the same landscape.

After stopping for directions, Micky finally arrives at the VA office. Finding a parking space is just as challenging as finding the address. Luckily, a spot becomes available two blocks away. Taking a deep breath, he begins his trek. He can only imagine how frustrating it must be for all the other vets with more serious injuries.

The office is full of men, some still wearing various parts of their military uniforms. Most have adopted long hair and the bearded trend of the day. The small waiting room is taking on a familiar smell of overabundant testosterone from young men. It's a smell that permeated every indoor facility in Vietnam. Micky had forgotten this detail until this moment. He hasn't been in the company of this many veterans in months. It feels welcoming—or at least familiar—in any number of ways. Selecting a seat, he prepares for a long wait. Two hours later, his name is called, and a lady hands him a questionnaire. After Micky completes it, forty-five minutes have passed, and it's time for the office to close. All of the vets who are still waiting are told to come back the next day. Preparing for the best but expecting the worst, Micky folds his questionnaire and sticks it in his pocket.

He walks out the door, and his eyes lock with the eyes of a disheveled, bearded guy with shoulder-length hair who is hobbling to the door on crutches. "BURT?!" is all that Micky can say. They both stand with unblinking eyes aimed directly at one another. Burt is taking a little longer to process who it is that's standing in his way. It suddenly dawns on him that it's Micky. Still not blinking nor changing expression, he slurs, "Micky, you ol' sombitch. How the hell are ya? I ain't seen ya in a year."

In this momentary stare, Micky recognizes an insufficiency in his closest friend that is brand new; he sees that his old friend is drunk. Burt had never touched alcohol all the way through school. "I'm doing fine, Burt. How about yourself?"

"Oh, shit, Mick, I ain't doin' worth a damn. Can't ya tell?"

"I think you may have had a bit too much to drink today," says Micky.

Throwing his head back in laughter, Burt says, "Hell, Micky, I've had too much to drink for a few months already. I'd buy ya beer, but I ain't got two dimes to rub together."

"That's okay. I can get by," says Micky.

Burt is here for an appointment. He drank his time away an hour ago. Anyhow, he's here now. Aside from his conversation with Micky, he's ready to make his presence known. Not realizing the door has already been locked, he pushes on it. expecting it to open. Instead, the force knocks his balance off, throwing him backwards onto the concrete sidewalk. It's all happened so fast that it catches Micky off guard. Responding as quickly as he can, Micky has his arms under Burt's armpits and lifts him back up. Meantime, Burt's crutches are strewn off the curb into the road. Micky's attempt to hold Burt upright is hampered by at least three happenings: he has only one leg, which is a prosthesis; the other foot is missing; and he's drunk as a skunk. Setting him back down, Micky is certain his friend needs his help.

"Burt, you stay where you're at. I'm going for the car. I'm coming back to get you in a couple minutes," says Micky. There's a clear sense of urgency in his voice.

During the few minutes it has taken for Micky to run the two blocks, get in the car, and drive back, a police car has stopped in front of the VA office. It's clear the object of this officer's attention is Burt, who is lying prone on the sidewalk. Micky hopes he can intervene before this officer gets too far into his decision to make an arrest. Taking emergency license with the idea that he can double park long enough to snatch Burt, Micky parks directly behind the patrol car. Practically jumping from the driver's side, he quickly makes his way around the car to the sidewalk. Approaching the two men, half shouting from adrenalin, Micky confronts the policeman. "Sir, I know this man. He's my friend. I'm here to get him off the streets."

With an official demeanor that can easily be interpreted as stoic, the officer rejoins, "This guy's been a nuisance since he showed up here. I'm tired of dealing with him. He's all yours. Just get him out of here. And get that double-parked car out of here before I write you a ticket."

With less than affable approval, Micky gets Burt to his feet, this time along with his crutches. Once they're quasi-stable, Micky half carries Burt to his car.

"Damn good to see you, Micky. I been stuck here since these local asswipes stole my scooter," slurs Burt, still quite inebriated. "If somebody would've pulled that crap in Nam, he'd have had his ass handed to him." Micky has no idea what Burt is talking about, but for the moment he has only one thing on his mind: getting Burt out of here with a minimal amount of conflict. In spite of their different paths, these two have had a lifelong relationship that has looked beyond the other's imperfections. Today is not going to be the exception.

"Are you staying at your grandparents' cabin?" asks Micky, attempting to get some further direction.

Burt looks at him as though this is the stupidest question he could ask, "Hell no. They stole my scooter. Or ain't you noticed? I ain't got no effin' feet. How you 'spect me to get out there—fly?

This is the first moment in which Micky has become aware of Burt's injuries and experienced this kind of belligerent animosity. Now Micky asks, "What the heck am I going to do with you?" The only place Micky is familiar with in Traverse City is the zoo. The decision is quickly made to head there with Burt for long enough to let him sober up and to contemplate his next move. Taking a picnic table close to the water's edge behind the zoo offers them the privacy Micky is seeking.

As soon as they sit down, the zoo's caretaker approaches them. Looking at Burt, the caretaker has a noticeable frown. He says, "I ain't gonna tell you again. I don't want you hangin' 'round here. All you do is stink the place up and scare all the little kids—so move on!"

Burt's expression is one that Micky recalls seeing from their high school days. It's one of hurt—a rejection that is inexplicable and impossible to combat alone. When in high school, Burt had always given his power to Micky because he believed he had none of his own. This is another of those incidents. Burt's eyes slowly turn away. Micky is on his feet, inches from this man's face. In a calm voice and yet remaining forceful, Micky begins, "This man's 'scariness' comes from wounds he received in Vietnam fighting communism. You have the right to say what you just said, but now I'm going to practice my rights and tell you that if you ever harass a wounded veteran again with me present, you'll rue the day!"

The man backs down and immediately apologizes. "I'm sorry. I didn't know. I lost my son there." With his eyes welling with tears of shame, he grasps Burt's hand, adding, "I'm truly sorry." With that said, the man turns and leaves them to themselves.

Burt's whole demeanor has changed once again; it's one of gratitude. "Thanks, Micky. It's nice to know you've still got my back." Two entirely different people are emerging out of this exchange. The realization is that even though this is not Vietnam, they still need to be there for each other in much the same way.

The afternoon has shortly turned to evening. Burt has returned to sobriety and is much easier to converse with. The two friends have spent the last couple hours catching up on each other's lives over the past year. Neither seems to be surprised at the other's experiences. Soon it's time for another decision: where to stay for the night.

"I been stayin' outta the way down by the river, under the pavilion. There's an extra sleepin' bag if you want to join us," offers Burt. Burt briefly gives Micky the scoop on Skeeter and a couple other guys who've camped with him.

Not quite ready for this much outdoors, Micky says, "Thanks for the offer, but I think I'll sleep in the back seat."

Between the warm morning sun coming through the car's window and a few taps on the glass, Micky is awakened. What he meets peering through the window is Burt along with a grinning dentally challenged individual Micky had never seen before. "Hey, Mick, wake up an' piss. The world's on fire!" shouts Burt.

Barely coming to, Micky checks his watch: eight-thirty. It's a new day. The VA office is due to open in a half an hour. Micky looks the situation over for a moment before giving his suggestion, "Hey, Burt, what do you say we hit the VA office first thing this morning? Maybe we can get some of our problems dealt with and move on?"

"Fine with me, Bud. I ain't got nothin' else goin'," says Burt. "You don't mind if Skeeter here goes along, do ya? He ain't got nothin' else better to do. He was a sniper in Korea."

Micky gives this old reprobate a quick once-over, trying to see a hint of his war days, but he can't. All he can see is a broken-down, wine-soaked bum. *On the other hand, if Burt can see a pony in all this man's horse shit, I'm willing to let him tag along; it appears he's looking beyond this man's imperfections the way I should be.*

The appointments with the VA go better than expected. Micky is now able to receive treatment at the closest VA hospital to wherever his residence may be. Burt has finished all the paperwork he needs to have his other prosthesis fitted. Even Skeeter signed up for benefits he never knew he had coming. *The next step after this is to let these two seasoned veterans of the Traverse City streets lead me to where they always go for a free meal.* Happy to accompany them not only for the meal but for the insight into the underbelly of the community, Micky is soon led into the basement of a neighborhood church. The aroma of some kind of stew is overpowering. The tables are set up in long rows overlaid with strips of rolled paper serving as table covers. Each side is occupied by at least fifteen people. Most of them are content to eat quietly, staying to themselves. It almost appears they are eating as if it's just one more of life's cruel treatments that they're forced to deal with.

Most people never observe this aspect of the population unless they come face to face with one of these "down-and-outers" while they're panhandling. Even then, it's often easier to give a few coins rather than become involved with a plight that appears to be out of their reach.

Micky is certain he can't leave Burt here, but he also realizes he has family obligations that can't be ignored. He needs to phone Carolyn and keep her abreast of his doings. After the meal, Micky uses the phone booth outside the building to make his call.

"Hello, Carolyn. Just calling to let you know I got things going with the VA. They're doing the paperwork and are going to send me all that's needed to get my treatment at the VA in Saginaw. We'll have to wait and see how it actually plays out in the real world. I also have found Burt, so I plan on spending a couple days with him before I come home."

Knowing of the close bond Micky and Burt shared in school, Carolyn replies, "Thanks for calling, Micky. Go ahead and do what you need to do. Izzy and I are looking forward to seeing you soon."

With this piece of life in place, Micky's attention is back to Burt and Skeeter. The attention Micky is assigning toward the needs of others has been put in place by people like Chaplain Gohrke and AA's Joe Billings. Thanks to Vietnam, he's discovered his own bottom. He's in touch with his own strengths and weaknesses, and now he's prepared to introduce a life-changing feature into the lives of these fellow vets. All of this harks back to that perceived higher calling at his high school commencement exercise that mystically called him to enter into some type of ministry. Little did he realize it would be to minister to a bunch of broken-down, displaced veterans with little to no fanfare.

After piling back into the Bonneville, Micky asks Burt and Skeeter, "How many of you guys hanging out here on the streets are vets?"

Surprised at the question, Burt says, "Most of us."

Micky follows up with, "How many you guys got alcohol and drug problems?"

Skeeter is the first to speak up, laughingly saying, "The only time I got problems with alcohol or drugs is when I ain't got any."

Burt is a little more pensive. "You know me, Micky. This isn't what I planned for my life. It just snuck up on me. When I lost everything I trusted back there in Nam, I found myself lost when I came back to the real world. Skeeter here is the only guy I've gotten to know well enough where I could trust him. Up 'til then, I been all alone."

Since Micky returned from the war, he's also been experiencing uneasiness. There's been something missing that he is rediscovering with this unlikely duo. It's reconnecting with others who understand what it's like to live one's life in mortal danger and survive. And because it had been obligatory to be there in these otherwise unhealthy conditions, it evolved into a tight community of trust—all for the sake of survival. The process of adjusting to the "real world" without re-establishing this community of trust and survival is proving to have an adverse effect on many of the returnees. Micky is listening with new ears. This idea of re-establishing community among these veterans means it's necessary for each of them to begin to talk with one another and realize they don't have to wing it alone. This awareness is paramount in Micky's plan.

After further discussions with Burt and Skeeter, Micky convinces them to join him in arranging to meet with the church's pastor. This results in spending the rest of the day discussing a format with Burt, Skeeter, and the pastor of the church. Burt is not surprised by Micky's organizational skills, which he had already possessed in high school. What he is more than surprised with is the profound insight Micky has gained into the deteriorated mental, physical, and spiritual condition of the returning vet. Micky explains to the pastor that he doesn't want to compete with the church and its dogma. "I realize the absence of God may be the primary problem with most of us coming back. After what we experienced in Vietnam, many of us have taken a position that we don't believe in God. That may be a good thing, because we probably didn't have a very good concept of God to begin with. We soon found it failed us; what we thought about God didn't sustain us for more than a minute when men were being killed all around us and we thought we were next. My thought is, *that* God has to be abandoned, and a healthier view has to be established. Before that can be done, I believe we need to prepare the soil for any kind of acceptance of this notion. In my mind, this begins with these surviving veterans making a simple reconnection with those who have had similar experiences without doing it in a bar—some place that has a potential to offer more spirituality in alleviating some of their concerns. I believe the setting could be in a church—maybe in the basement. If it's a good enough place to feed their bodies with a meal, we could also use the space to begin feeding a healthier spirit and let God take it from there."

This pastor is listening. His own thoughts are carrying him back to the days after his return from WWII, which he spent lost in alcohol and near insanity. "I was trapped in my own horrific memories," is the way he puts it. His way out had been a "Divine intervention," as he explains it. "They used to call it shell-shock. But much like the prodigal son, I had to have my own pig trough experience before I could come to my senses. I don't believe that anyone can adequately sell another person into accepting the Lord like it's a great car they need to drive, but I do believe that the Lord can show up at the right time using somebody else's hands, feet, and shared experiences." Pausing for a moment to collect his thoughts, the pastor adds, "I don't believe the evil in this world can be met sensibly without God—it would never make sense to me to try it alone. I believe you're on to something good here. Even if it only helps one person, I'm willing to give you a go at it."

The next day at the noon meal, Micky takes the floor. Tapping on a glass, he manages to get the attention of the room. "Any of you guys vets?"

The room is suddenly quiet. One hand goes up. Every head in the room turns to look at this one person. Acknowledging him, Micky continues, "I'm a vet, and I need to talk with somebody that's been there. Will you talk to me?"

Suddenly feeling he's being put on the spot, the man lowers his hand and retreats back into himself.

From out of the other side of the room, another voice speaks up. "I been to Nam. What do ya wanna talk about?" the room remains quiet.

Micky quickly puts some words together. "I want to talk about how it scared the shit out of me and how I haven't been able to sleep or find anybody in my family who knows what I'm talking about."

This admittance sends a shock wave through the entire room. It's as if this kind of admission had been buried so deep and held as a secret by so many for so long that it's lost its normal right of belonging in the human experience.

The man looks at Micky with a blank expression that displays so much. It's like Micky has just opened a Pandora's box of taboo emotions. Suddenly, another man shouts out, "Hell, man, I'm still scared. I ain't never got over it."

Seeing an opportunity arising out of this motley crew, Micky decides to take it to the next level. Referring back to the man who has admitted his fright, Micky continues, "The two of us would sure appreciate it if a few of you guys would stick around for a while and talk to us. It sure would help out." This might be considered a form of trickery—sometimes referred to as a "double Irish reverse"—but it usually is effective in bringing out the best in someone to be of assistance. It's as if it's a place where God prefers to remain anonymous while He makes some straight lines using crooked pencils.

Micky's ploy proves to be a success. More than half of the vets stick around after the meal, drinking coffee and discussing some of their war stories.

A man who just refers to himself as "Sarge" says, "I ain't never told anybody about this, and I don't know exactly why I'm tellin' it now, but you guys are the closest I've felt to some kind of unit since I left Nam. I just wanna say I feel so damn guilty about survivin'. It's like I feel like I must've done somethin' wrong to have made it out of that hell-hole while a lot of other guys didn't. I can't get that damn thought out of my mind."

Another man speaks up: "I would get so mad at God that I'd shoot my rifle in the air at Him for not doing something about all the crap that was going on all around me."

Another, with tears in his eyes, tells how scared he was when they went into a village and how he knows he shot people who probably were just as scared of him as he was of them. "Somewhere I lost my civilized self, and I haven't found it again—maybe I never will," is all he can say for the moment.

A woman nicknamed "Wagon Anne" who stays mostly to herself and drags a wagon around town with all her belongings shouts from the back of the room, "I been in that hell. I was a nurse who cut off limbs and peeled burnt skin from every inch of human bodies. I saw every kind of pain one human can inflict on another. I'm so sad. I hate life."

These men and women have spent too much time living on the streets. In cases like these, homelessness has more to do with faulty social connectedness than a lack of shelter, or even an inability to make a living. They wall off reality with the hopes of making life safe and predictable. The catharsis Micky has hoped would begin is growing in some of these vets. He trusts the direction he's taking and realizes that to have any comprehensive success, he must have a program in place that involves imagination plus innovation and be ready to assist wherever he's needed.

Several men remain silent for reasons only they know, but Micky can see the benefit this kind of reunion can provide—providing it's done with no alcohol or drugs present. This is barely a baby step toward meaningful recovery for these self-exiled castaways. Some hidden shame and guilt have been exposed to the light of forgiveness, which is often expressed by only a nod or a gentle touch from another who shares the same painful loneliness. It's giving hope that this lost connection is wanted and needed. The few minutes this group has spent in open and honest dialogue with each other because of a shared experience is beginning to send fears back where they belong. Miraculously, a small sense of community is developing where none had existed an hour ago.

Micky spends the next week with these men, doing the same thing every day at noon. The vet support meeting is still in the same place at the same time but is beginning to include vets who are living a semblance of normalcy and are happy to find a common meeting ground with other vets. Burt is sticking with the support group, and Skeeter is off the streets and into a facility. With Micky serving as a power of attraction, both Burt and Skeeter have also attended a few AA meetings. Both find this nonthreatening and of use. This is all at a pace that is patient and doesn't give ultimatums. After all, they didn't begin drinking overnight, and chances are good that they won't get sober overnight, either.

Along with Carolyn's support, Micky has arranged to move his small family to Northern Michigan and begin a life here. Until they can get on their feet, Burt is graciously providing lodging at the cabin as long as it's needed. Meanwhile, Micky has found work in the post office as a mail sorter and is prepared to move into town. Carolyn has discovered the man she married is not the man who came home—rather, he's a much more mature, sensitive, humble man who is willing to anonymously do God's work and satisfied to move back into the shadows and let it grow.

EPILOGUE

Thrown against the gates of hell, America's youth are rewired to fight a war that wasn't expected to be won. In many cases, the returning Vietnam veteran found life difficult because many in the media gave readers the impression that it was the soldiers who make war rather than the government. The fallout of this notion resulted in many soldiers bearing the burden of an unpopular war. They became war casualties rather than respected and appreciated veterans. Whether out of frustration or a lack of mercy, the result remains the same: the shame and guilt of an unpopular war were left with the veterans to helplessly agonize through alone. Hopefully, as a nation, we have begun to practice more mercy and cease shooting our wounded.